THE SECONDARY TARGET

Diane Lynn

Paradise Valley, Arizona

Published by: Canta Bello Publishing Company
8465 N. Canta Bello
Paradise Valley, AZ 85253
www.cantabellopublishing.com

Editor: John Nelson
Book design and production: Janice St. Marie

Revised Edition

Printed in the United States of America

Publisher's Cataloging-in-Publication Data

Names: Lynn, Diane, 1944-
Title: The secondary target / Diane Lynn.
Description: [Revised edition]. | Paradise Valley, Arizona : Canta Bello Publishing, [2016]
Identifiers: ISBN: 978-0-9970595-0-2 | 978-0-9970595-1-9 (ebook) | LCCN: 2015958310
Subjects: LCSH: Divorce--United States--Fiction. | Woman lawyers-United States--Fiction. | Lawyers--United States--Fiction. | Victims of violent crimes--United States--Fiction. | Abusive men--United States--Fiction. | GSAFD: Romantic suspense fiction. | LCGFT: Romance fiction. | Detective and mystery fiction. | Medical fiction. | Thrillers (Fiction)
Classification: LCC: PS3612.Y5463 S43 2016 | DDC: 813/.6--dc23

1 3 5 7 9 10 8 6 4 2

To my beloved parents,
who were always there for me,
nurtured and loved me,
and created a home filled with comfort,
security, and happiness,
which enabled me to thrive

Acknowledgments

Writing this book has been one of the most incredible experiences of my life. Two years ago I set out on this journey to turn a lifelong dream into a reality. It was quite an undertaking for me as a first-time author, but I've learned along the way that no task is unattainable when you work hard enough to achieve it.

I first would like to thank my editor, John Nelson, who helped me over a period of nine months with advice, ideas, and constructive criticism. I learned so much from him and deeply respect his talents.

I would also like to thank my brother, Bob Friedman, a publisher and writer who supported my mission and gave me his best advice. I appreciate all his input and help with the editing process.

I am grateful as well to my family and friends who never stopped being enthusiastic about the book. One special friend, Tina, kept urging me to carve out some time each day to do nothing but write. I heeded her advice.

And last but never least, I want to thank my husband, Steven, for letting me put in all the time I needed to write and for continually encouraging me to keep at it. It was his unwavering support and confidence that enabled me to finish this book.

Chapter

One

Exiting the cab at the corner of 50th and Lexington, Beth Scott prepped herself for another stressful day at the office. It was such a beautiful spring morning that she wanted to walk the remaining four blocks to her law offices on Park Avenue. She loved New York in the spring, with its beautiful tree-lined streets where flowers blossomed and permeated the air with a rosy aroma. As she walked along, she passed Bloom's Flower Shop and saw the clerk set out a lovely arrangement of lilies, and on the next block was Studio 501 with its window display of exotic handbags. Yes, spring meant shopping, and she loved seeing the exciting new fashions displayed in the stores. She was ready for the weekend and eager to refresh her wardrobe with some newer designer clothing. At the next window, she stopped to examine her reflection: a black Christian Dior suit and black and tan Chanel shoes. Her black Chanel shoulder bag and Louis Vuitton briefcase completed her outfit. She felt confident being well-dressed and took pride in keeping up with the latest fashions.

As she approached her office building, she took a deep breath and slowly let it out. Feeling energized, she stepped inside ready to fight for her clients.

"Good morning, Maria. How was your weekend?"

"It was great. Thanks for asking," said Maria, as she handed Beth her morning coffee. "Here's the list of your appointments— looks like a full day. You have two messages from Justen Bennett and one call from Lisa Paul."

As Beth sat at her desk, she took a moment to settle into her surroundings, which always helped her start her day with a sense of accomplishment. She first looked outside her window from the ninth floor, with its spectacular view of the city, and then eyed her diplomas on the wall with her peripheral vision. She had worked her tail off to get that law school diploma from Yale, but every minute had been worth it. At the young age of thirty-one, she had achieved her dream as a successful divorce attorney in a prestigious New York City firm—the sky was the limit.

As Beth reviewed her appointments for the day, she noticed that she had two new clients, which always took up most of her day. So she would return her calls first and do some housekeeping before her new clients arrived.

"Hi, Lisa. This is Beth," she said into her office phone.

"Hey, girl. What's up?"

"Well, yesterday I drafted the property settlement request. You're getting the uptown apartment. I'll send it over for your review."

"Boy, he's not going to be happy about that," Lisa said, a catch in her voice.

"Well, he should've thought of that when he started cheating on you."

"Yeah. I'm just glad he's no longer living here. I told you about him slapping me around."

"Lisa, that won't ever happen again. You deserve better and shouldn't stay with an abusive man you can't trust. You're my best friend. I'll be with you every step of the way. I know it won't be easy, but you have a wonderful support system. Just take one day at a time and let your heart be the judge."

"Thanks, Beth. You've been such a good friend. I don't know what I'd do without you."

"Well, you don't have to worry about that, do you?"

Lisa paused for a moment, shifting gears. "Talk about following your heart, how are things with you and Michael? Are you still taking a break from him?"

"You know, I really care for him, but I'm not sure about moving forward at this point. I need more time. He's a great guy who has it all, so I wonder what's wrong with me."

"How long since your last . . . date?" Lisa asked.

"It's been almost three months, and I do miss him. But I'm still not ready."

"You'll figure it out. No need to rush things."

"You know, I tell myself that my career doesn't allow time for my personal life, but if I really cared enough I'd make time, right?"

"You always end up making good choices. Solving problems is what you do best, whether it's your clients' or your own."

"Got another call, Lisa. Will catch you later. Hang in!"

"Hello. This is Beth Scott."

"Look, Ms. high-priced divorce lawyer, I'm warning you to stay away from my wife and stop giving her ideas about how to take me to the cleaners. Do you hear what I'm sayin', lady?"

"Who is this, please?"

"This is Susan Spencer's husband, Mark. I know she met with you about getting a divorce, 'cause I pay the bills and saw your fee on the credit card. Look, bitch, back off! There will be no divorce or you'll both regret it. Stop talking to her! She's my wife, and it's going to stay that way. Have I made myself clear?"

"I'm sorry, sir, but I don't respond to threats very well. Just so you know, this conversation is being recorded. If you want me to stop representing her, then you'll have to speak to her, and she'll have to be the one to terminate our agreement since she's my client, not you. I would recommend that you hire your own counsel, and that's all I can say to you at this point. Good-bye, Mr. Spencer."

Beth felt uneasy as she hung up the phone. She had had angry husbands call her before, but no matter how many times she received this type of threatening call, it was still disturbing. She felt her stomach turning inside out. She walked anxiously around her office a few times. She was fearful of this man and could tell from his voice that he was filled with rage. She was frightened for her client Susan since, in her experience, mean-spirited husbands only led to trouble.

She called Susan and told her about the conversation with her husband. Beth suggested that if she intended to proceed with the divorce it would be best for Susan to move out of the family home and into an upscale women's shelter. Beth could make the arrangements for her when she was ready.

Susan agreed that it was a good plan and the only solution for her if she wanted to end her marriage and remain in one piece. She would let Beth know when she had everything organized and was ready to move forward.

Beth stepped over to her mini-refrigerator and took out a bottle of water, then stood at the window for a moment—her way of cleansing contentious conversations, especially with another one coming.

"Justen, this is Beth returning your call."

"Yes, Beth. Thanks for getting back to me. How are you?"

"I'm fine, Justen, but why are you calling me? I hope it's not about us, because I've already told you that there is no future for us and you really need to move on."

"Beth, I would just like to give it one more try. I'm nuts about you, and I can give you a wonderful life. I'll do whatever it takes. Please give me another chance."

"I'm sorry I don't feel the same way. I wish I did. You're an amazing person. Please don't make this any harder for me than it is. I would love to be your friend, but that's all I can ever be."

There was a long pause at the other end of the line. Beth held her breath, waiting for a positive response. "Well, thanks for speaking with me, at least. But you know me—I will never give up on us. Take care, and I know we're destined to meet again." Justen hung up before Beth could reply.

This was looking like a tough day. She had been threatened by a client's husband and broken a friend's heart, and it was only nine thirty in the morning. Her mind was racing with thoughts of what might be in store for her for the remainder of the day.

Her intercom buzzed. "Beth, your new client, Mrs. Murphy, is here. Should I send her in?"

"Just give me five minutes."

Beth needed a little distraction. She looked at her iPhone to check her texts. There was a short note from her friend Victoria confirming their dinner tonight. She quickly texted her back and told her she would pick up the takeout on her way home and Victoria could bring over the vino. She set the time for seven thirty.

Victoria had been a friend of Beth's for about three years. They had met through a mutual friend and bonded. Beth liked her but found it strange that she never discussed men. What single straight girl in New York didn't talk about men? Beth would always talk to her about her relationships, but Victoria had nothing of her own to say on the subject. Beth, assuming her friend had been deeply hurt and was still in recovery, refused to probe. Victoria was slightly overweight and shy, so maybe she feared rejection. Whatever her reasons were, Beth felt empathy for her and always tried to remain a positive influence. She hoped that one day Victoria would open up about her feelings, and until then Beth would just be there for her as a good friend.

Beth looked down at her text.

Beth, 7:30 is great. Look forward to seeing you. I'll get some great wine. We deserve it. xo Vic

Beth pressed her intercom. "Maria, show Mrs. Murphy in."

A moment later, a very attractive slim woman in her mid-fifties entered the office. She was dressed in a navy blue silk sheath and appeared to have class. She kept pushing her dark brown shoulder-length hair off her face—a nervous habit—and tilted her head downward, hopeful that Beth wouldn't notice her face. Her demeanor was that of shame.

As she sat behind her desk, Beth looked closely at the woman and noticed she had a black eye and both cheeks were swollen and bruised. Beth's heart went out to her. The first thought that entered her mind was how she couldn't wait to make that son of a bitch pay.

"Nice to meet you, Mrs. Murphy. I'm Beth Scott."

"I've heard so many good things about you, and I'm so hoping you'll be able to help me. I apologize for my appearance, for I know how frightful I must look."

"Did your husband do this to you?"

Mrs. Murphy, shook her head in the affirmative. "Ms. Scott, I've been living like this for many years now, and I just have to move on. Can you please help me? I don't know what to do or where to go to get away from him. I'm so scared." She started trembling and began to cry.

Beth handed her some tissues and said, "It's going to be okay, Mrs. Murphy. You have taken the first step by coming into my office today. We'll get through this together. Do you understand?"

"Whatever you say, I will do." Mrs. Murphy buried her face in the tissues.

Beth spent over two hours with Mrs. Murphy, getting as many details as possible about her abusive marriage. She told her to make another appointment for next week, which would give her time to do her due diligence concerning the woman's husband. And at their next appointment, she would advise her about the women's shelter and discuss ways to exit from her home to the shelter.

When Mrs. Murphy left her office, Beth felt emotionally drained but at the same time eager to begin working on her case.

Her client was in dire need of her help, and she intended to give it to her starting at eight tomorrow morning.

The long day was coming to a close. Beth had just concluded with her second new client and was packing her briefcase when her cell chimed.

"Hi, gorgeous. It's Michael. How are you?"

"I'm fine. It's been a long day but a good one, and I was just leaving the office. What's up?"

"I was wondering if I could see you this week. I miss you, Beth. It's been almost three months, and I thought I would've heard from you by now."

"Well, it's springtime, when all the battered wives finally come out to smell the roses."

"Tell me about it. Since the weather has changed, the police have been out on the streets arresting the scumbags I defend, and I'm busier than hell."

"You're so funny, Michael, and you always make me laugh."

"Try me and let me make you laugh through an entire dinner."

"I know you could," Beth said, smiling to herself.

"I have been tempted to come to your office so many times, but I wanted to respect your privacy. I thought we'd at least run into each other on the elevator since we work for the same firm."

"Michael, I'm sorry, but I've been dealing with so much stress at work. I talk to my girlfriends, and you need to talk to your friends. Give me a few more weeks and let me think about it some more. I adore you, Michael, and I hope you know that. My feelings have not changed for you. That isn't the issue. I just need to figure out how deep my feelings go."

"Okay, Beth. I understand. Tell you what—if you're heading home, let's walk a few blocks and then catch a cab, and I'll drop you off."

"Okay. I have plans, but I do need to walk off this day."

"Meet you out front in ten."

They enjoyed a nice walk and easy conversation. Michael did make Beth laugh, which was just what she needed to change her mood. She had almost forgotten how attracted she'd been to him and was glad to find their connection still alive and well. They then picked up a cab outside the Waldorf Astoria, and Michael dropped her off at the Italian restaurant near her apartment. She was pleased that he didn't try to kiss her good night, because she may not have been able to resist.

She picked up the takeout order, carried it home, and, leaving the door unlocked for Victoria, set the bag on the table and hurried to the bedroom to change since it was nearly seven thirty. As she put on her favorite lounging clothes, she thought about how much she loved her little place, especially her pale blue and gray bedroom, which was so inviting to come back to at the end of a long day.

Suddenly there was a knock at the door. "It's unlocked, Victoria. I'll be right out. I'm just getting on my sweats," she called out.

Chapter

Two

"Dr. Burton, Dr. Brandon Burton. Emergency room—stat!" As these words resonated throughout the hospital, the chief surgical resident sprinted down the narrow corridors of NYP/Weill Cornell Medical Center. Everybody cleared a path for the barreling six-foot-tall, brown-eyed, and strikingly handsome doctor.

"What've we got?" Burton asked, bounding into the trauma area.

"A thirty-one-year-old Caucasian female with stab wounds to the chest, blunt force trauma to the head, and multiple contusions and lacerations all over the upper body," bellowed the first-year resident in attendance. "She's unconscious with shallow respirations, so I'm going to intubate her now."

Burton examined the patient and quickly assessed what needed to be done. "Get me a chest tube, and let's get two IV lines up ASAP—one for the blood and the other for Lactated Ringers," he said to the ER staff. "Order four units of blood, and

I want X rays of the head, chest, abdomen, and pelvis—stat. We need to move fast, before she bleeds out. What's her BP?"

"Seventy over fifty and dropping," replied the ER nurse.

"Pulse?"

"Sixty and thready."

The chief inserted the chest tube, and blood immediately started draining from the chest cavity.

"We need to get her to the OR right away. I'm certain there's internal bleeding from the lung, which the X rays will confirm."

"Dr. Jennings," he said to the other surgical resident in attendance, "go out to the waiting room and find her family. Get a consent form signed and fill them in on her condition. Direct them to the OR waiting room, and tell them we'll keep them updated on her condition. I'll meet you in the OR."

"I'm on it, chief." Once in the waiting room, he called out, "Mr. and Mrs. Scott."

An attractive well-dressed couple in their early sixties quickly stood up and dashed toward him. "Yes. We're the Scotts—Miriam and Joseph. How's our daughter? We've been nervous wrecks waiting out here. Is she going to be okay?" said Miriam Scott. Her green eyes were red and teary; and Joseph Scott, a man of medium height with salt-and-pepper hair, had his arm around her, lending her emotional support.

"My name is Dr. Jennings. Your daughter is in critical condition and on her way to the operating room. She has suffered multiple stab wounds and trauma to the head, and has lost a lot of blood. Dr. Burton, our chief surgical resident, will be performing the surgery, and I'll be assisting. He'll come out to speak with you when he's finished. At that point we will be better able to assess the extent of the trauma."

"Is there a chance she might die, doctor?" Miriam asked.

"We're hopeful we can pull her through this. She's young and strong. Let's stay positive. I must leave for the OR now. The waiting room is on the fourth floor."

Before going, Dr. Jennings turned to the uniformed police officer and briefly gave him information for his report.

10

Awaiting the outcome of the surgery that would hopefully save their only child's life would be the Scotts' most trying hours ever. Tears streamed down Miriam's face as feelings of fear and helplessness took over. She looked up at her husband, sobbing, and said, "What could have happened to her? What if we lose her, Joe? It all seems so surreal. Oh God, please help us." Immediately, Miriam and Joseph began to pray.

By the time Dr. Jennings had scrubbed and entered the OR suite, the surgical team was busy prepping the patient and Dr. Burton had taken a quick look at her. Hundreds of accidents, heart attacks, and trauma cases found their way into the ER every day, but he was unusually disturbed about this one. He wondered who would do something so heinous to a woman, and why. Her wounds fit the typical profile of victim stabbings, shootings, and beatings that usually ended up at NYU Hospital, not here on the Upper East Side. His curiosity had gotten the best of him, and he vowed to find answers, but at the moment his thoughts were focused on saving his patient's life.

"Scalpel," Dr. Burton said to the OR tech, holding out his palm. He made his incision at the entry point of the knife, and did a physical examination of the chest wound. He then clamped the bleeders and began repairing the lung. He was hopeful that the damaged organs would be repairable, thus sparing their removal. His examination showed that the knife had penetrated the left lung just inches from the left ventricle of the heart. If the heart had been hit, she might never have survived the attack. *This is one lucky lady!* he said to himself.

"I think I'll be able to do this repair without removing the lung," Dr. Burton said to his surgical team. "She's much too young to have to live with only one lung for the rest of her life. Let's keep infusing blood until we can get her hematocrit up to a respectable level to compensate for the vast blood loss. The last thing we need is for her to go into shock. How are her vitals?"

"Stable," responded the anesthesiologist.

"Great!" said Dr. Burton. "Everything here is going well. Let's keep her stable for another hour, when I should be done. Just keep infusing the blood. I want her to have at least three pints during the surgery."

Over a period of two hours, Dr. Burton made the necessary repairs to the lung, which abated the bleeding. "I think she's going to be okay, but she'll have to be monitored closely, and hopefully there won't be any unforeseen complications. Thanks for a job well done," he said, addressing his surgical team. His patient would now be prepared for transfer to the recovery room, where she would remain for the next forty-eight hours. "Here comes the hardest part," he added. "Talking to her parents."

As Dr. Burton walked into the waiting area, Joseph and Miriam Scott stood up, their eyes flashing with anxiety. He knew immediately that they were his patient's parents. "Hi, I'm Dr. Brandon Burton, and I just finished operating on your daughter."

"Please tell us that she's all right," pleaded Miriam, reaching for his arm for support.

"I have good news. Beth's injuries went no farther than the lung, and no other organs were damaged. We were able to stop the bleeding and save the lung. The placement of the knife was inches from her heart, so we really got lucky there! She lost a lot of blood, which we replaced during the surgery, and we'll keep the infusions going to get the volume back up to normal levels. There was extensive bruised tissue surrounding the lung, but that will heal in time. She'll be in the recovery room for forty-eight hours and then the surgical ICU for seventy-two hours. Your daughter came through everything like a trooper. She must be very strong-willed. We hope there won't be any complications, but one never knows with this type of trauma. One of the nurses will call you from the recovery room when your daughter is stable, at which point you can go in and see her for a short visit, but she'll be unresponsive."

Miriam bust into tears. "Thank you, doctor. We're so grateful for all you've done for our Beth," she said.

Joseph embraced his wife and held her while releasing an intense sigh of relief knowing that his baby girl had survived. He would deal with whatever lay ahead, but at least she was *alive!*

"I'll be checking in on her on a regular basis, and she'll receive the best care possible," Dr. Burton assured them. "We want her stabilized before we start asking questions, and I'd like you to just be with her and offer your love and support until she can tell us what happened tonight. But it will take a while before she's responsive." Then, unable to contain his curiosity about the incident, he added, "Do you know how this happened?"

"We're in shock and don't have a clue about it. Beth lives alone, and her friend Victoria, who had come for dinner, found her on her bed unconscious, with blood everywhere. She immediately called 911 and then phoned us; we came right over to the emergency room. That's all we know. Victoria should be coming over shortly, and you are welcome to speak to her," said Miriam.

"Can you tell me something about your daughter—her occupation, a little about her life?" asked Dr. Burton.

Miriam said, with great affection: "She's brilliant, talented, and beautiful—on the inside as well as out. She's a divorce attorney here in the city, spends most of her time working, and is extremely dedicated to her profession. She has been seeing a young man off and on, but doesn't have a lot of time for a social life. We wish we could see her more often, but during the week her schedule is impossible."

"Thank you," said Dr. Burton. "It's very helpful to me to know something about the backgrounds of my patients. It adds a human element to the equation. Could you please call her firm and let them know that she'll be out of work for at least four weeks during her recovery."

"Yes, doctor. I'll make the call," said Joseph.

"Also, Beth is going to need some assistance with her recovery after she leaves the hospital. Do you both live here in the city?"

"Yes, doctor, we relocated from Baltimore a year ago to be near her. She's our only child, and we wanted to be closer now

13

that we're retired. We'll take care of her for however long she needs us."

"That's great! Beth is very fortunate to have parents like you."

"No, Dr. Burton, we're the lucky ones."

"I'm sure the police will be questioning you about what happened, and hopefully they'll keep me in the loop as well. We'll need to know if her life is still in danger; and if it is, we'll make provisions for her safety while she's in the hospital," said Dr. Burton.

Miriam could not help but notice the compassion and concern flowing from Dr. Burton's warm brown eyes. He was also strikingly handsome, with his dark brown hair and olive skin. She had long ago determined that a person's eyes reveal their true identity—and whether they are happy, sad, insecure, frightened, lonely, loving and warm, or cold and calculating. Ever since, she had often sought to learn about people through their eye communication. And she wanted to learn more about this man who had saved her daughter's life.

"Thank you so much, doctor, for getting her through the surgery. We're forever grateful," she said.

"You're most welcome," Dr. Burton replied, taking note of how becoming Mrs. Scott was, with her slim figure, short blonde hair, and green eyes. Mr. Scott, a handsome older gentleman, was unusually fit and well-built for his age. He thought that Beth, coming from such good genes, had to be a very attractive woman beneath all the trauma she had endured to both her body and her bruised and distorted face.

A moment later, a man in his late thirties, about six feet tall and smartly dressed in a brown tweed blazer and brown slacks, stopped at the information desk, introduced himself as Detective Stevens, and asked if he could meet with the family of Beth Scott. He donned a stylish black hat, which he removed while speaking with the receptionist.

The woman behind the desk pointed to Miriam and Joseph. "Yes, sir. They're over there, talking to Dr. Burton."

The detective, bearing a serious professional demeanor, thanked her and walked to the corner of the lounge, eager to begin his questioning. He was polished and used to dealing with real estate moguls, businesspeople, dignitaries, and other professionals who resided in his East Side precinct. Most of his cases consisted of white-collar crime, some of which turn to violence as well.

"Hi, I'm Detective Walter Stevens with the nineteenth precinct, and I've been assigned to your daughter's case. So sorry that we have to meet under these circumstances," Stevens said, as he took out a pen and note pad from his inside jacket pocket. "First, how is your daughter doing?"

Mr. and Mrs. Scott told the detective that she would be in the recovery room for forty-eight hours.

Dr. Burton then said he would have to excuse himself and get back to his patients, but he wanted to know if Beth was going to have security for her protection while in the hospital, due to the nature of the crime.

"Good question, doc, and I'm glad you're security conscious. I've put in the request, and there will be an officer arriving momentarily. I'll follow up if he's not here in thirty minutes."

"Thanks, detective. That makes all of us feel much better," said Burton. "I'll say good-bye to you, Detective Stevens. Mr. and Mrs. Scott, I'll surely see you later."

The detective then turned to face the Scotts, saying, "Shall we have a seat?" As they sank comfortably into plastic chairs, he added, "This shouldn't take too long. I appreciate your speaking with me under the circumstances."

Mr. Scott responded, "No problem, detective. Whatever we can do to help."

"Do you know if your daughter had any enemies?"

"No, sir, none that we know of," said Joseph Scott.

"When was the last time you spoke to her, and did she seem upset about anything going on in her life at the time?"

"I spoke to her a few days ago." Miriam paused, then added, "I think it was late afternoon on Wednesday, and she sounded happy. If something had been bothering her, she would've shared it with me. We've always been very open with each other."

"What's your daughter's occupation?"

"She's a divorce attorney on Park Avenue. And if I might add, she's a Yale graduate. Just plain brilliant!"

The detective looked up from his note pad and smiled at Mrs. Scott. "Very impressive," he remarked and kept probing. "Do you or your husband know if she was dealing with any clients who caused her to feel threatened? After all, people can get very nasty in a divorce and blame their attorney...or their partner's attorney. Did she ever discuss anything like this with you?"

"No, detective. She rarely got specific about her cases and would only tell us about clients she felt sorry for and how she intended to make things right for them. She is her clients' strongest advocate."

"Can you tell me if Beth has a boyfriend?"

"She was seeing a nice young man until about three months ago. He's also an attorney at her firm. She told me she needed some time away from him for a while. They still care very much for each other, and who knows how it'll end up."

"Did she share with you why she chose to take a . . . pause? Was he mistreating her or putting pressure on her? Anything you can tell me along those lines?" asked the detective.

"No, nothing like that. He was always very kind to her. He cares very deeply for her, but Beth doesn't know how deep her feelings go and needed more time to figure things out."

"What kind of law does he practice?"

"He's a criminal defense attorney," said Mr. Scott. "And a damn good one, too."

"I'm sure he is, sir. But how do you know how good he is?" asked the detective, rather slyly.

"Because Beth told us how he would get questionable clients off all the time by giving them a proper defense."

"What do you mean by questionable clients?"

"You know, really bad guys. Tough guys. People who do terrible things," said Mr. Scott.

"Beth used to always say that Michael had the hardest job in the firm," said Mrs. Scott.

"And why do you think she said that?" Director Stevens asked.

"Because it was stressful being responsible for someone's incarceration or freedom."

"I imagine if he's always fighting to keep his clients out of prison, then that alone would be stressful." Stevens paused for a moment. "Mrs. Scott, can you tell me about the young woman who found your daughter tonight and her relationship with Beth?"

"Sure, detective, but I see her coming this way, so you can ask her yourself."

Detective Stevens turned, saw a young woman approaching who appeared anxious and disheveled, and recognized her from the crime scene earlier this evening.

Victoria went straight over to Miriam and hugged her, saying, "I can't believe such a thing could happen. I don't know anyone who would want to hurt Beth—not in my wildest dreams. How's she doing? Victoria gently released her firm grasp and wiped the tears from her face.

"Don't cry, sweetheart," Miriam said. "She's going to be fine. She just came out of surgery, and we're giving this nice detective some details about Beth's life. Detective Stevens, this is Victoria David, a close friend of Beth's, who found her this evening."

"We've already met—at the crime scene," said Stevens. "I hope you're feeling better, Ms. David, and can talk with me now."

"Yes, detective. Sorry if I was a basket case earlier, but seeing Beth like that unraveled me."

"I understand. It happens."

"Thanks for letting that patrolman drive me home. I'm feeling much better now."

"Good. So are you ready to answer a few questions?"

"Yes, sir, anything to help find the person who did this to Beth. What would you like to know?"

Stevens stared at Victoria for a moment before responding. "Tell me about the moments leading up to the time you found her, as best as you can remember."

"Well, Beth and I had plans to spend the evening together—eat some takeout and just chill and catch up. I haven't seen her in a while, and she wanted to talk about her situation with Michael. I picked up a bottle of wine and went over to her apartment. I knocked, and there was no answer, so I tried the door and it was open. I walked in, calling out her name, and immediately knew something was desperately wrong. The apartment was in disarray: lamps were knocked over, chairs were overturned, papers were everywhere, and all the pieces decorating her cocktail table were on the floor. I then rushed into her bedroom and found her on the bed— blood everywhere. When I went over to her, I could tell she was still breathing but unconscious. I called 911 right away and waited for the ambulance to arrive. In a few minutes the apartment was filled with police and paramedics. I told them exactly what I'm telling you as that's all I know."

"Victoria, does Beth always leave the door unlocked for you when you visit her?"

"Not necessarily, sir. On some occasions, the door is locked and I have to wait for her to let me in. Other times she just leaves it open."

"Did you tell anyone that you were going to Beth's after work?"

"I might have mentioned it to one of my coworkers, but I can't be sure."

"You mean you don't remember?" Stevens asked rather pointedly.

"Not really."

"Is there anything you remember about the crime scene worth noting?"

"I just remember that she was naked and I covered her up with the sheet. Was she raped, detective?"

"I don't know. Usually the medical staff treats life-threatening wounds first. Later tonight a rape kit exam will be done. What time did you last speak to her, and can you tell me about your conversation?"

"Actually, we didn't talk today, we texted each other...about eleven in the morning. Last week we talked about how much we needed to catch up on things, especially her break with Michael. She told me she was very confused and needed to talk to me about some issues with their relationship."

"So you don't know if she was making any stops before going home to meet you?"

"Well, her text said she'd pick up some takeout on the way home and be there by seven thirty."

Detective Stevens digested this piece of information. "Victoria, how long have you known Beth?"

"We've been friends for about three years now. She's a wonderful person, detective; all she ever wants to do is to help people. She is one of the kindest people I've ever met. It just makes no sense."

"Have you ever argued with Beth over anything?"

"No, sir. Never. Sometimes, I've gotten upset with her because I felt she wasn't giving our friendship enough of her time. But I understand that she has a much busier social life than me. I could never catch up to her in that arena. Beth and I both work a lot, but it seems she spends more time with other friends."

"Are you saying that she didn't give you as much time as her other friends?"

"Well, I guess you could look at it that way, but she dates much more than I do."

"Don't you date, Victoria?" asked Stevens.

"Not very much."

"And why is that?" Stevens could easily answer his own question with his visual of her being overweight, her hair unstyled, and her features resembling those of a bird, with her long neck and small beady eyes.

"I do a lot of things by myself, and I spend time with my single friends." Victoria was starting to get restless with the questioning.

"Would you consider Beth your closest friend?"

"Most definitely." Victoria was now outright annoyed with the detective's questions. She asked herself, *Is he trying to rule me out as a suspect? What's this all about? Why is he questioning me about my personal life?* She was agitated and wanted to go home.

As if reading her thoughts, Stevens switched the line of questioning. "Can you give me the names of other friends Beth sees on a regular basis?"

"Yes. Lisa Paul is a very close friend, someone she went to college with and who's also an attorney. Beth confides in her, so she might be able to tell you more. Would you like her number?"

"Yes, that would be helpful. Thanks."

"No problem, detective," Victoria said, somewhat relieved and avoiding his gaze.

Mrs. Scott then added, "Sir, Lisa and Beth were roommates in college and law school. She's Beth's closest friend and like a sister to her. You probably need to speak to her to get more information on the people in Beth's life."

"I'll take your advice and pay her a visit. Do you happen to have her office address?"

"Certainly. I have it right here on my iPhone."

"Can you also give me the name and number of the young attorney Beth had been seeing—the one she's taking a break from at the moment?"

Mrs. Scott pulled up the number of the law firm on her iPhone and gave it to him.

"Well, detective," said Victoria. "I think I'm going to head home now. If there is anything else you need from me, please don't hesitate to call." She handed him her business card.

"Thank you, Victoria. You've been most helpful, and I'll get back to you in a few days. You'll still be around, won't you? No business trips on the horizon?"

"I'll be here, detective. Please find whoever did this to Beth," she said as she headed toward the elevators, all the while exhaling deeply.

Detective Stevens noted to himself that she was a person of interest in this case. He now wished he had detained her at the apartment and questioned her there, minutes after the crime. If she were the perp, she might have confessed. His captain was going to ream him over this rookie mistake.

In his mind, some things didn't add up. How perfect was the timing of Victoria's arrival at Beth's apartment immediately after the attack? How is it that she didn't walk in during the assault? Why was the door left open, which wasn't always the case when Victoria visited? And why did he sense an uneasiness about her—not once making eye contact with him the entire time he was questioning her. Was her unraveling at the apartment an act to get out of there? With so many unanswered questions, he needed to dig deeper into Victoria David's life in order to rule her out as a suspect.

A uniformed policeman stepped into the waiting room and talked to the receptionist. After nodding to Detective Stevens, he took a position outside the OR.

"Okay!" said Stevens to the Scotts. "Looks like my replacement is here. I think I'll return to the crime scene to see if they've discovered anything new. I'll be back tomorrow to see if I can talk to Beth, who hopefully will fill in some blanks. In the meantime, here's my card, and if you think of something that you feel would be important to the case, please give me a call. It's probably going to be a very long night for you, so get some rest when you can. I'll see you tomorrow."

"Thank you, detective," said Miriam Scott.

Moments after Stevens left, Dr. Burton came out of the recovery room to give the family an update. "I wanted to tell you that we had to put Beth into an induced coma until we can stabilize her. We'll continue to monitor her in the recovery room to make sure there's no more internal bleeding and her vital signs remain stable, then we'll gradually wake her up. This would be a good time to go home and get some rest for the night. Please give the receptionist your phone numbers on the way out, and we'll call you if anything changes."

"Thanks so much, doctor, but would it be possible for us to see her briefly before we leave?" asked Miriam.

"Sure. Follow me, and I'll take you back. But let me warn you about all the tubes she's attached to and the many bruises on her face. It looks like she put up quite a fight. She won't look like herself, so please don't be frightened."

"We understand, and we'll do the best we can under the circumstances," Miriam assured him.

Nervous about seeing their daughter in this condition, the Scotts held on to each other as the young doctor led them through the wide electric double doors into the recovery room, a large space with about fifteen cubicles circling a round nurses station in the center. Nurses and doctors were moving from one cubicle to another administering treatment. Some were typing on laptops at the desk. Every bed was occupied, and each cubicle was equipped with a variety of machines. When they discovered Beth lying comatose in her cubicle, with tubes coming out of every orifice of her body and a breathing machine making strange noises as it mechanically pumped air into her lungs, their knees buckled. She had a large chest tube draining blood from her lung, intravenous lines in both arms, a catheter draining urine from her bladder, and a drainage tube transporting excess blood from the entry wound. They had only seen this type of spectacle on TV, and now they were watching their only child fight for her life.

Miriam and Joseph leaned over and held her left hand. "Beth, baby," Miriam said, trying to maintain her composure. "Mom and Dad are here with you. Don't be frightened. You're in the hospital receiving wonderful care."

Miriam then commented to her husband, "I read that a person in a coma can hear the sounds around them and process the information deep in their subconscious."

She turned back to Beth and continued, caressing her daughter's forehead. "Dad and I love you very much, and we know you're going to get through this. You're a fighter, and we want you to fight. Do you hear me? *Please fight!* Remember when you were learning to ride a bike and kept falling off? You were so determined to ride that bike that you just got right back on and tried again and again until you did it. You never gave up. You're not a quitter; you are a *fighter*. We know you can do this, and we'll be beside you every step of the way."

Miriam and Joseph held Beth's hand for fifteen minutes until the nurse suggested that they go home and rest.

"Thank you for taking care of our daughter. Please call us if there is any change in her status," said Miriam.

"Of course we will," the nurse replied. "Don't worry. We'll take good care of her. See you in the morning."

As Miriam and Joseph left the cubicle, tears started to pour down their cheeks. Their emotions, contained for hours, had finally gotten the best of them.

Chapter

Three

Detective Stevens returned to the crime scene a half hour after leaving the hospital. The apartment was still in disarray, and the crime lab team was busy processing the scene, bagging evidence, taking samples for DNA, and dusting for prints. As the detective walked through the apartment again, he began thinking of Victoria David. If she were the perp, would she have planned the assault, or was it the result of an argument or hurt feelings? If the latter, she would have grabbed something sharp, but no letter openers or other sharp items were in sight. Maybe it was a knife they used to cut cheese or slice meat with, he conjectured. "Be sure to check for a hidden weapon or a knife missing from a kitchen set," he told one of the crime scene lab techs. If Victoria was involved in this crime, then she certainly would have had time to get rid of the knife before the paramedics and police had arrived at the scene.

If instead the perp was an assailant who left the scene—a theory Detective Stevens had entertained before speaking with Ms. David—he would've taken the knife with him. So at first

Detective Stevens had had the patrolmen check all the trashcans and dumpsters in the area. Now he asked for all the knives to be brought to the lab to be tested.

Then he looked at his earlier notes. "Hey, guys, what about the door?"

"No forced entry but lots of prints on the outside doorknob. Good luck separating them out," replied one of the lab techs.

"So how's it going otherwise?"

"We got everything in the living room and bedroom. The bloody linens and clothing have already been bagged."

"Be sure to catch the kitchen as well. She had a…friend over."

"Who might not be such a good friend?" another tech asked snidely.

He nodded in agreement then spent over an hour going through drawers, closets, and papers looking for anything that could give him a clue. He tried to open Beth's laptop, but it was password protected. He found some letters from an ex-boyfriend named Justen Bennett and some notes from Michael Hudson, the attorney who had dated her until three months ago. He would take the laptop with him to the precinct so one of the computer techs could access the information. Hopefully, he would be able to retrieve additional information that would be helpful to the case.

"Well, guys, I'm done here, so I'll see you back at the precinct. Thanks for being so thorough."

"Always. We should be wrapping up shortly as well, and we'll get all these samples to the crime lab ASAP," said a third tech.

When Stevens arrived at the precinct, it was after midnight and almost everybody had left, including the captain. He'd catch up with him in the morning. He handed the laptop to one of the "probies" there for the night shift and headed home for a good night's sleep. He had been transferred to the SVC (serious and violent crimes) unit six months ago, and found it to be a lot more wearing than white-collar crime.

As soon as Detective Stevens returned to the station in the morning, he ran into Captain Parker, already on his third cup of coffee. "Hi, Walter, I was looking for you. Got an update on the Scott case." He walked the captain over to his desk.

"Well, no breakthroughs yet," Stevens continued, "but I found some letters at the crime scene that were written to Beth from a man named Justen Bennett. I want to follow up on this lead. This particular one was written two months ago, and their relationship ended more than two years ago. Here, read it, captain. Very interesting. I would say this warrants checking out, wouldn't you agree?"

The captain read as follows:

I haven't been able to think about anyone but you, and I'm not coping very well. I know we can make this work if you only would give me another chance. I've been so distraught, and you're always in my thoughts. Please call me and let's talk. I have to have you. *I know we can make a life together.* Call me, please! I need to talk to you!

Always,
Justen

"Yeah," the captain said with a snort, "that would put him at the top of my list. Go check him out."

Walter Stevens and his partner, Rob Matthews, left the precinct around noon, headed over to the Upper West Side, and located Justen Bennett's apartment building. The two detectives, after being let in by the doorman, approached the concierge behind the desk in the upscale lobby.

"Hi, I'm Detective Walter Stevens, and this is my partner, Robert Matthews. We're here to see Justen Bennett. Could you please check if he's in?"

"Yes, I believe he is. I'll ring his apartment. May I tell him what this is about?"

"It's a personal matter."

"Mr. Bennett, I have two detectives here in the lobby who would like to speak with you. Is it okay to send them up?" There was a pause. Then the concierge announced, "Sure, will do. Yes, detectives, go on up, he's in apartment 29-C. The elevator is over there on your left. I'll program it to stop on twenty-nine. Turn to your left when you get off, and his apartment will be directly in front of you."

Soft elevator music played on the ride up. The detectives were impressed by this elegant skyscraper with its mahogany elevator trimmed in gold around the ceiling and walls.

"Wow, it looks like this woman Beth let a rich one get away. You can't get any fancier than this," Matthews said.

As they approached Justen Bennett's door, it opened slowly, and there stood a well-built, distinguished-looking Caucasian man standing about five foot ten with black hair and hazel eyes. He was wearing Tommy Bahama slacks, a T-shirt, and was barefoot.

"Hello, gentlemen. I'm Justen Bennett. How can I help you?"

"Mr. Bennett. Sorry to disturb you. I'm Detective Stevens, and this is my partner, Robert Matthews. May we come in and have a word with you?"

"Sure, please come in," said Justen Bennett as he motioned them inside.

The palatial apartment had glass windows looking out on Central Park and south to spectacular city views—the most breathtaking the detectives had ever seen. White couches with colorful decorative pillows were arranged on a large white area rug atop dark hardwood flooring, with stunning artwork all around. No expense had been spared in designing this room.

"Wow, some place you have here, Mr. Bennett. How long have you lived in this apartment?" asked Stevens.

"Well, thank you, detective. I love it here and am now enjoying my fifth year."

"Do you live alone?"

"Yes, I do. But might I ask the nature of your visit? I know you didn't come here to check out my apartment. What's going on, detective?"

"We're here to ask you some questions about Beth Scott. Do you know her?"

"Yes, of course I know her. We used to go out, but not anymore. It's been about two years since we stopped seeing each other. Why are you asking?"

"Miss Scott was attacked in her apartment last night, and she's in critical condition in the hospital. Someone tried to kill her, and we've been assigned to investigate the case. Can you tell us the last time you saw her, and where you were last night?"

"Yes, of course. It's been almost a year, I think."

"And last night?"

"Oh, I was here all night. You can check with the concierge," he said rather nervously as he put his hands in his pants pockets. "Please tell me, is she all right?"

"Yes, or so it appears now." Bennett sighed in relief. "We understand that you've been quite upset about the breakup. Is that true?"

"Well, yes. I was very fond of her, but it didn't work out so I moved on."

"We found some letters in Beth's apartment from you, and this particular one was dated just thirty days ago. Can you explain this lover's plea?" Stevens asked, as he handed the letter to Bennett.

He quickly scanned the opening, then gave the letter back to the detective and told him that he was well aware of what he had written. "Yes, I think about her often, but I would never hurt her! I care for her too much."

"Sir, words like, 'I have to have you' and 'We can make a life together' don't sound like you've moved on at all but that you are one very desperate and distraught individual. Would you not agree, Mr. Bennett? Two years is a long time to hold on to a lost love."

"I just wanted to let her know how I still feel about her. She wouldn't return my calls, which really pissed me off."

"Mr. Bennett, this is only one of many letters of a similar nature. It could be characterized as stalking her."

Bennett shook his head. "I wouldn't call it stalking—not by any means. I was just trying to get her attention. You know, overstated for effect."

"And did you ever get any response from Miss Scott?"

"Yes, she called me to tell me that it was over and I had to move on. But I was hopeful that we could start over and try again. I can give her everything, detective. I'm a man of some means."

"And when did she call you back, Mr. Bennett?"

"Yesterday morning."

Detective Matthews spoke up. "Mr. Bennett, could I get a drink of water?" He impatiently motioned toward the kitchen.

"Sure," Bennett responded. "No problem."

While Matthews disappeared into the kitchen, Stevens continued the questioning. "Well, it looks to me like she didn't care about your money, sir. What's the Beatles song, 'Can't Buy Me Love'? Which seems to be the case here, Mr. Bennett. But I suppose that men like you don't take rejection very well. Am I correct?"

"Look, detective, I can have any woman I want, and Beth is the first who's given me a difficult time. But I know she'll eventually come around, and I'm willing to wait."

Stevens asked, "Do you know why the two of you didn't work out?"

"I guess I came on too strong because I really fell hard. She told me that I was too possessive and controlling."

"We understand how badly this must have made you feel. Maybe even angry? Do you get angry often, Mr. Bennett, when things don't go your way?"

"Sometimes. So what? Who doesn't when things go south?"

"Let me ask you point blank, Mr. Bennett: Did you put Beth in the hospital?"

"Hell, no, detective. And I resent the accusation. Really, sir."

"Do you have anyone who can attest to the fact that you were home last night?"

"As I said, you can check with the concierge downstairs. He was here all night and would've seen me go if I had left the building."

"Okay, Mr. Bennett, we'll do just that. But in the meantime, we would like you to stay around town for a while. We'll probably be contacting you for further questioning," Stevens said as Matthews rejoined him from the kitchen.

"Why? I've told you everything, so what's the point?" Bennett said, with a quiver of anxiety in his voice. "Am I a suspect?"

"Until we solve this case, everyone in Beth's life is a person of interest."

"Fine, whatever, but you're wasting your time, detective." Mr. Bennett walked to the door to show the detectives out.

"We'll be the judge of that, Mr. Bennett. Good-bye," said Stevens as they left.

"Oh, detective," Justen called down the hall. "When you talk to Beth, please give her my best."

"I'm sure that will cheer her right up, Mr. Bennett," said Stevens.

As they rode down in the elevator, Stevens turned to his partner. "What was that about with the water?"

Detective Matthews pulled out his cell phone. "Got pictures of all the kitchen knives."

Stevens laughed. "Hopefully we can get a match and a warrant."

Detective Stevens and his partner questioned the concierge at the desk. He confirmed what Mr. Bennett had said—that he was home all evening and he would've seen him if he had left the building.

Matthews cocked his head and asked, "Is there a garage in this building, sir?"

"Yes, detective."

"Is it possible that Mr. Bennett could have left the building from the garage and you wouldn't have seen him exit?"

"Yes, it's possible, but I have cameras right here at my desk, and I would've seen him unless some of the cameras weren't working."

The concierge was going to leave it at that, but Stevens said, "Call security and ask if any of the garage cameras were down last night."

After a brief conversation with the chief of security, the concierge told the detectives that two of the cameras were broken and parts were on order.

"Sir, gather up the tapes from last evening from the garage and call me when they're available. I'll also need a report from your security chief stating how long these cameras have been down."

"Oh my, this is serious, isn't it?" the concierge said, hoping he wouldn't lose his job over it.

"Thanks, and what did you say your name was?"

"Phillip Harvey, sir."

"Thanks, Phillip. I'll look forward to your call," Stevens said as he handed him his business card.

Back at the precinct, Joe Weatherly greeted Stevens and Matthews, saying, "I checked out the names you gave me, and everyone had an alibi. But I was unable to reach the lawyer Ms. Scott just broke up with." He looked at his notes. "Michael Hudson. He's been in meetings all day."

"Okay, Joe, no problem. I had planned to go over to his office, anyway," said Stevens. Turning to his partner, he added, "I'm going to stop by the hospital to see how Beth's doing. Look over the forensics, and show the lab guys your knife photos. If anything comes up, you know where to find me."

Detective Stevens found the Scotts in the ICU waiting room. They looked weary, as if they hadn't slept in weeks.

"Mr. and Mrs. Scott, how are you today? Did you get some rest last night?"

"Not much, detective, but thanks for asking. She's still in an induced coma, and the doctors say she'll most likely be like this for days. Her vital signs are stable, though, and so far so good," said Mrs. Scott.

"Well, I would say that's good news," Stevens replied. "Status quo is okay at this point. Do you mind if I ask you a few more questions?"

"Not at all. What do you need to know?"

"I questioned Justen Bennett earlier this morning and just wanted to know if you could tell me something about him. Did you know that he'd been sending Beth stalking-type letters, and wanted to start seeing her again? We found these letters in her apartment. In fact, I happen to have one with me that I would like you to read."

The detective took the same letter he had shown Bennett out of his pocket and handed it to Miriam.

After reading it, she looked shocked. "She never said anything to me about these letters. I guess she didn't want to worry us. Oh, dear, do you think he did this?"

"We don't know, but he's definitely a person of interest in this case. How well do you know Justen?"

"We only saw him three or four times, when we would meet them for dinner. He seemed awfully nice and is quite successful, detective. He was really into Beth and wanted things to progress, but for some reason Beth was reluctant. She did not tell us why, but she ended it and commented that he didn't handle it very well. I don't think she wanted to deal with the pressure he was putting on her. She was too busy with work, and he couldn't deal with the demands of her career."

"Anything else I should know about Justen that would have caused him to hurt Beth?"

"Just that when she broke up with him, he called and wanted us to talk to her. He was very upset, sounded angry, and was desperate to get her back. We told him that we don't get involved in Beth's personal matters."

"And what did he say to that?"

"He was unhappy with our answer, and we never heard from him again. I told Beth about the phone call, and she said that he was not for her, much too possessive and controlling, and sometimes he scared her. That's when she decided not to see him again."

"Can you tell me what you think she meant when she said he scared her?"

"Just that he was so possessive, which made her very uneasy, like when someone is always in your face," said Mrs. Scott.

"Do you know anything about his occupation?"

"Yes, Beth told us that he's a sports agent and represents professional athletes. I think some of his clients play for the Knicks."

"Thanks. Every little bit helps us piece this puzzle together. I'll keep you posted on the investigation. Take care, and I'll see you soon. You have my card, so please call me when Beth wakes up."

"We certainly will, detective. We really appreciate your diligence." Mr. Scott said.

After saying good-bye to the Scotts, Stevens returned to the station.

"The perp must have worn gloves and paper shoes. We have nothing definitive from the lab," said Matthews as Stevens took a seat at his desk across from him. "We have DNA from her boyfriend, Michael, which is to be expected, and they also found Victoria David's DNA all over the place, and on the bedpost, which she could've touched when she found Beth. We went back to checking trashcans and dumpsters near the crime scene, where the perp might have disposed of incriminating evidence. That's about it for now, Walter. How'd the hospital visit go, and did you get over to Hudson's office?"

"I was able to get more info on Justen Bennett from the Scotts. It seems that he's a sports agent and represents some big names in the NBA. I need you to ask around about Bennett's character—see if he has a temper and how he handles his clients. His line of work can be very confrontational, and he'd need to be rather bullheaded settling contract disputes."

Matthews added, "Having a type A controlling personality would be par for the course."

"I called Michael Hudson's office, and his secretary told me he would not be available until later this afternoon. I'd like to review the report from the crime lab and then go see him. But first I need another cup of coffee."

"I'll get it for you," said Matthews. "And then I'll work on Justen Bennett's contacts. You know, some of his old clients might've gone into . . . other lines of work."

"Yeah, busting kneecaps instead of chops. Good idea. I'll check in with you later," said Stevens as he grabbed his jacket to head for Michael Hudson's office.

Detective Stevens arrived at Cavanaugh, Lewis and Strong around 3:45 p.m. and stopped at the front desk to ask for Michael Hudson. The receptionist directed him to the elevator and told him to get off at the seventh floor, where he would be shown the way to Hudson's office.

Hudson's secretary buzzed him over the intercom. "Excuse me, sir. There is a Detective Walter Stevens here to see you. May I show him in?"

"Yes, please do," replied Hudson.

Stevens walked into a magnificently appointed legal office overlooking spectacular views of Park Avenue. There were two large shelves filled with law books. The furniture was dark mahogany, set around a conference table in front of the expansive window to take advantage of the view. Mr. Hudson's desk was on the opposite side of the room facing the conference table. On the west side of the room was a small sofa with two chairs across from it. In Stevens's opinion, this office smelled of success. What was it with Beth that attracted these high-powered men?

"Mr. Hudson, I am Detective Walter Stevens, and I'd like to ask you a few questions, if I may."

"Sure, detective. Come in. Who's been a bad boy now?"

"Excuse me?" Stevens said as he took a seat opposite Hudson at his desk.

"I'm a defense lawyer, and I represent bad guys. I assume this is about one of my clients."

"No, something more personal. I'm investigating a case concerning Beth Scott, and I need to ask you some questions."

"Beth! What kind of questions?" he asked in alarm. "What's

this about? Is she okay?"

"Oh, I'm terribly sorry. I thought you had been informed. Well, sir, yesterday evening someone tried to murder Beth. Stabbed her in the chest. She was beaten up pretty badly and has multiple contusions and a concussion."

"Oh my God," he said, his hand to his forehead.

"She's still in the recovery room, after having surgery at NYP/Weill Cornell Medical Center. I'm here doing a routine follow-up with her friends and associates. Do you mind answering some questions?"

"Who could've done such a terrible thing to Beth?" Michael asked, visibly upset.

"That's what I'm trying to figure out. When was the last time you had any contact with her?"

"Actually, I called her yesterday morning and left a message. I wanted to ask her out. She called me back in the afternoon and agreed to let me walk her part of the way home after work. So we walked and talked a bit and then took a taxi the rest of the way. I dropped her off at the corner of her apartment around seven o'clock. She said she was going to the restaurant across the street to pick up her dinner order."

"How is it that you knew the time? Did you look at your watch?"

"I remember glancing at it."

"Can you tell me what you talked about, Michael?"

"Just how she was still on the fence regarding our situation and needed more time." He paused. "We'd been dating for a year, detective, and were taking some time off."

"And were you all right with that?"

"Actually, detective, I'm getting a little tired of it all."

"What do you mean, sir?"

"I've just about had enough of her indecisiveness. When we were together, it was great, and I cared for her very much. But then she decided she needed some time apart so she could figure things out. I was upset with her, and I won't deny it. But I had nothing to do with this! That's for damn sure!"

"Do you remember the name of the cab company?"

"I believe it was Blue Diamond. Why are you asking?"

Bypassing Michael's question for now, Stevens asked, "And where did you go after you dropped Beth off?"

"Home."

"And how far was that, Mr. Hudson?"

"About six blocks."

"Does your building have a doorman?"

"No."

"So can anyone verify that you went straight home after Beth was dropped off?"

"Yes, the taxi driver," said Michael. "Why don't you check with the company? They'd have a full report of every fare that evening. But then you already knew that, right?"

"Yes, Mr. Hudson," Stevens said. But in the detective's mind, that proved nothing. He could've exited the taxi and grabbed another one to Beth's apartment in time to attack her before Victoria arrived.

As if he were reading the detective's mind, Hudson added, "I went inside, poured a glass of Châteauneuf-du-Pape, turned on my computer, and checked my stock portfolio online. My computer will have a log-on and -off time."

Stevens stared at him for a moment.

"Detective, I'm a defense attorney, but now I would really like to go see Beth, so are we almost done here?"

Stevens raised a finger, indicating he needed a minute more. "Well, given your practice, do you know of any cases Beth was working on that might have involved a client who could be a suspect?"

"As a matter of fact, she told me last night about one who was pretty bad. She was representing the wife, and the husband was acting like a complete asshole. He would call her and tell her that his wife was being irrational and that Beth had encouraged the divorce. He would say pretty nasty things to Beth, but she just ignored it. He didn't want the divorce and was trying everything he could to prevent it."

"Can you give us his name?"

"She normally doesn't mention the client's name when she's working on a case, but this was different."

"How so?"

"They were friends—we'd dined out when we were together. She is representing Lisa Paul in the divorce, and it has put her under a lot of stress. Lisa is divorcing her husband, Brian, because Beth discovered that he was cheating on her. I'll get my secretary to give you his full name and address, but I need to get to the hospital."

"I appreciate that," Stevens said. "Just one more question, Mr. Hudson. Would you have any reason at all to want to harm Beth?"

"Of course not! I love the woman, despite her being stubborn and bullheaded. Why would I ever want to hurt her?"

"Sorry, sir. Just doing my job. I have to ask everyone that question. You understand that better than most. There has to be that missing piece somewhere, and I'll find it. Trust me, I'll find it," Stevens said.

"Well, detective. Anything I can do—I mean *anything*—just call on me. I want to get the bastard as much as you do."

As they walked out, Detective Stevens made a mental note to check with his computer forensics guy to see if log-on and -off data could be altered.

Chapter

Four

"Can you tell me what floor Beth Scott is on?" Michael asked at the information desk in the lobby of NYP/Weill Cornell Medical Center.

The young lady behind the desk couldn't help but stare at this handsome guy. Then she looked at her computer screen and said, "Her family is in the waiting area on the fourth floor," and pointed him in the direction of the elevators. "Turn to your left as you exit the elevator, and there you'll see the waiting room."

"Thanks," Michael replied, disturbed by how simple it was to locate a patient's whereabouts.

In the waiting area outside the recovery room he recognized Beth's parents, whom he had met many times when he and Beth had been together. Their faces were lined with worry and he felt uncomfortable seeing them under these dire circumstances.

"Mr. and Mrs. Scott, I came as soon as Detective Stevens told me what happened. How's she doing? Is she going to be all right?"

"Oh, Michael, how nice of you to come," Miriam Scott replied in a weak voice. She appeared distraught, with her blouse hanging loose outside her skirt and her hair uncombed. Michael could see how the long hours of waiting had taken their toll on her. "Let's put it this way: we have a lot of praying to do. She's in an induced coma, but the surgery did stop the internal bleeding. Only time will tell."

"Do you mind if I wait here with you for a while?"

"Of course not. You're more than welcome to stay, but she's not allowed any visitors besides us."

"I understand. I'll just sit here with you for a bit and keep you company. I won't stay long."

"Thank you, Michael. That's very kind of you."

Michael took a seat next to Miriam. "It'll help me as much as you."

She reached over and squeezed his hand. They chatted about mundane subjects, which at least helped to pass the time.

Thirty minutes later Dr. Burton arrived and asked how they were holding up.

"We're hanging in there, doctor, but how's our girl?" asked Miriam.

"Well, everything is about the same: we see no signs of improvement but no signs of weakening either. We're keeping her in this coma for as long as it takes to stop her brain from swelling any further. She was hit pretty hard in the back of the head and has a great deal of inflammation. The chest tubes seem to be draining less and less blood as time passes, which is good. Her brain scans look normal, so we know she did not sustain any irreversible damage. I truly feel that she is going to pull through this. She appears to be very strong. Please continue to speak to her in a soft tone and give her encouragement, as you've been doing. Family support plays a huge role in a patient's recovery."

Michael jumped in. "Doctor, I'm Michael Hudson—a good friend of Beth's. I was wondering if I could see her."

"Usually I only allow family of coma patients inside. Might I ask the nature of your relationship to Beth?" Burton asked.

"We've been dating off and on for about a year, and I'm a colleague at work."

"Thank you. I just need to know all the people who're going to be involved in Beth's recovery."

"Please consider me one of them." Shaking his head, he added, "I just saw her last night. What a difference twenty-four hours can make. Unbelievable! Do you know when she'll regain consciousness, and if she'll remember what happened and who did this to her?"

Dr. Burton knitted his brow. Not a typical concerned-friend question.

Michael explained, as he observed the doctor's skepticism, "I'm a defense lawyer. Comes with the territory."

"Can't say at this point. Some trauma patients remember everything, others never recall what happened to them. We'll just have to play the waiting game."

"I see," Michael said.

Dr. Burton heard his name being paged. "I have to run. It was nice meeting you, Michael. Let's hope for a good day tomorrow. Good afternoon, Mr. and Mrs. Scott."

Michael stayed at the hospital for another hour, long enough to support Beth's parents as they anxiously awaited their next visit with her. He tried to cheer them up but they preferred little conversation. While he remained focused on Beth, his thoughts brought him back to how they first became acquainted in the gym at work.

When she had walked through the swinging doors, there had been an instant connection as he looked up while lifting weights and their eyes met. She was one of the most beautiful women he'd ever seen—and she was standing right in front of him! She had a gorgeous figure and a radiant face; her long blonde hair fell softly down her back, and her green eyes sparkled. He remembered dropping his weights and introducing himself. They chatted for a short time while working out, and discovered that they were employed by the same law firm. She had an effervescent personality so alluring that he knew he wanted to see her again, and the feeling was mutual. She agreed to meet him at Charlie's Place after work that same evening. He remembered receiving her text message, which read: *Hi, I'm packing up my briefcase and on my way. See you at eight. Gym Girl.*

Their first meeting went extremely well. He felt drawn to her the moment she strolled into the bar dressed in a chic designer suit and carrying her Louis Vuitton briefcase, exemplifying the quintessential New York professional woman. They talked for four hours, eager to learn everything they could about each other. She spoke with passion and joy about each topic they discussed, bringing a sparkle to her eyes. It turned out that they came from similar educational backgrounds—she from Yale, and he from Harvard. More importantly, Michael found her mesmerizing.

Soon after, they began a relationship, but it had to be clandestine. The firm had a policy that discouraged office fraternization, something that often occurred among the attorneys, causing the higher-ups to turn a blind eye.

Michael's thoughts drifted back to the first time they made love, a few months after they met. He had taken things slowly because he respected Beth and wanted her to have his complete trust before becoming intimate. They went to the theater and then dinner, eventually ending up at Beth's apartment. She invited him up for a nightcap, and he eagerly accepted. They had had a wonderful evening, and since the mutual attraction that had been there from the beginning was now uncontainable, they made love. It was more than magical for him. He had never felt more satisfied, and he hoped it was as pleasant for her. He remembered her saying, "You make me feel so beautiful, and I feel such comfort in your arms."

As time went on, their sex life remained enormously pleasurable for both of them. He enjoyed exploring her body and learning about her sexual pleasures. He never wanted to rush her and was intent on giving her the time she needed to reach her maximum pleasure point. He took care to please her in every way he could rather than focus only on his own needs and desires.

Michael had made love with his share of women, but with Beth it was different. She was like no other woman he had ever dated. She was self-assured, thoughtful, and endearing. She never complained; no matter how tough her cases were, she faced them head-on and always with composure. Michael felt he had much to learn from this woman of valor. Just being in her presence could make him a better person.

This is why he was giving Beth time to decide about their relationship. He didn't want to lose her, but he didn't want anyone else to have her either. And while he knew in his heart that she loved him, it had been three months and he was getting a little discouraged. Whenever he thought she was stringing him along he experienced feelings of resentment.

Lost in reverie, Michael suddenly heard Dr. Burton speak. "Mr. and Mrs. Scott, you can go in now to see Beth for about ten minutes. She had more swelling in her brain due to excess blood buildup, so we had to drain it with a shunt, but she came through the procedure just fine, and her vitals look good. We'll keep the shunt in for a couple days to make sure the excess blood is evacuated."

"We're eager to see her," said Miriam. Turning to Michael, she added, "Will you be here when we come out?"

Michael stood up. "It's after six, so I need to finish up some things at the office, but I'll keep in touch. Here's my card. Please call me if there's anything I can do. I'd like to stay informed."

"We'll be happy to, Michael. Thanks for coming."

As Beth's parents walked through the automatic doors of the recovery room, he tried to imagine what Beth was enduring on the other side of the wall, and he was left feeling repressed, helpless, and somewhat vacant. He thought that if they were still together this tragedy might never have happened.

Matthews had been going through their suspect list, but no one seemed to have a motive at this point except Justen Bennett, who was looking more like a nut case than a perp. His alibi checked out, and there was no DNA at the scene. As for Victoria David, despite her hurt feelings it was unlikely she would have repeatedly stabbed her friend. Earlier, Detective Stevens had told him what he'd learned about Lisa Paul's husband, Brian: he was not a happy camper about his wife divorcing him, despite his own infidelity, and was a total jerk to Lisa and to Beth. Matthews was happy to add Brian Paul to their meager list.

Stevens was still not completely convinced of Michael Hudson's innocence. Beth had put him on the back burner, which he wasn't liking at all. He was nervous when questioned, as guilty people often are; besides, he was the last friend to see her before she was attacked, and he had had time to get back to her place before Victoria arrived. Moreover, his computer log-on alibi was flimsy at best. Stevens wondered if Michael and Beth had argued before he dropped her off, which could have pushed him over the edge. He did admit that he was getting tired of being played by Beth and was frustrated by her indecision concerning their relationship. Stevens made a note to interview his cab driver.

First, however, he wanted to get a feeling for the anger level of Beth's clients and their spouses. Divorce cases were known to provide a trigger for violent men. "Hey, let's pay Dr. Paul a visit," he said to Matthews.

"Okay, I'm ready. Cheating husbands make great suspects."

Since Brian Paul was an orthodontist, Detective Stevens thought it would be best to question him after office hours. So, at six o'clock, after calling first, Stevens and Matthews visited the doctor's office in Chelsea.

"Who shall I say is here?" the receptionist asked.

"Detective Walter Stevens and my partner, Detective Matthews."

"He's just finishing up with his last patient, so please have a seat. It shouldn't be too much longer."

"Thank you, Wendi," Stevens said reading her name tag. He couldn't help but notice that she was very beautiful and had a well-endowed figure. That, combined with her long, curly auburn hair and large brown eyes with fake eyelashes, made him wonder if she was the "other woman" in the divorce case, even though she looked somewhat tawdry. He could understand how hard it would be to work with someone so voluptuous and always keep things on a professional level.

"Detectives, may I get you anything to drink?" asked Wendi.

"Water would be great, thank you," said Stevens.

"And, anything for you, detective?" she asked, leaning over and exposing some of her assets to Matthews.

"No thanks. I'm fine . . . for now," he laughed. Stevens gave him a look.

About ten minutes later, Brian Paul came out to the waiting room and introduced himself. "How can I help you, detectives?"

"Can we go back to your office, Dr. Paul? I think it best not to speak out here," he said.

"Absolutely. Please follow me."

The detectives walked down the hall to Brian's private office and closed the door. The room was modest but professional, with many diplomas on the walls and books in the bookcases. There were a few photos of him and an attractive woman, who appeared to be his wife, Lisa, along with a photo of him with an elderly couple, who were probably his parents. Brian Paul was wearing a long white lab coat with "Dr. Paul, DDS" embroidered on the pocket. His starched blue shirt and blue paisley tie were visible under his coat. He was an attractive man, with a ruddy complexion and brown hair. He still had his magnifiers on his forehead, which he removed after he sat down at his desk, facing the detectives.

"How can I help you, gentlemen?"

"Dr. Paul, we're here to ask you a few questions. It shouldn't take long."

"What's this about? One of my patients?"

"No, a more personal matter. Do you know Beth Scott?"

"Yes, she's my wife's divorce attorney. Why do you ask?"

"Well, sir, two days ago she was brutally attacked and almost lost her life. She's in the recovery room at NYP/Weill Cornell Medical Center. Someone beat her up so badly that she needed extensive surgery. We're interviewing everyone who knows Beth— friends, clients, and their spouses. Hopefully someone will have some information to help us find her attacker."

"I'm sorry to hear that. How is she?" Paul asked.

"Her condition is very guarded at the moment. We understand that you're going through a messy divorce, and you've said some pretty nasty things to Beth concerning it. Would you like to explain yourself?"

"Detective, everyone who goes through a divorce knows the stress that it puts on those involved. Sure, I've said some terrible things, but it's not uncommon considering the loose accusations that are flying around. But why would I hurt Beth? Just because she's representing my wife? I don't think so, detectives."

"Did you ever hit your wife, Dr. Paul?" Detective Matthews asked.

"No."

"What if we ask your wife—will her answer be the same?"

"What are you getting at, sir? No, I don't beat up women. One night we had a terrible fight, and I pushed Lisa against the wall. But that was it! Nothing more. I've never laid a hand on her."

"So, Dr. Paul, it sounds to me like you have somewhat of a temper. Is that correct?" Stevens asked.

"Everyone gets angry when provoked, but I know how to control my temper."

"Do you consider throwing someone against the wall controlling your temper?"

"It only happened once."

"Can you tell us where you were two nights ago?"

"Yes, I was home alone."

"Can anyone corroborate that?"

"I don't have a doorman in my building, so I can't...'corroborate that,'" he said cuttingly. "Am I a suspect, detective?"

"Let's just say for now, a person of interest."

"That's the most ridiculous thing I've ever heard. I'm not a violent person. I get lawyers to resolve my disputes."

"You know, sir, sometimes people do crazy things in the midst of a nasty divorce, especially in the heat of anger. We know that Beth discovered you were cheating on your wife and really messed it up for you. Wouldn't you say that pissed you off a bit? After all, you had a good thing going until she discovered your little secret. The best of both worlds: a fine wife to come home to in the evenings, and a lover and playmate during the day when you could steal some time alone."

"Wait a minute! I did not attack Beth. Yes, I was angry with her, and that bitch had no right putting a P.I. on me. I thought she was my friend for so many years, and she sure fooled me, detective. But I know how to control my emotions, and I don't go around stabbing people."

The detective told Dr. Paul that maybe if her friend Beth were out of the picture, Lisa would listen to reason and not go through with the divorce. This way Dr. Paul could keep things just the way they were. What man wouldn't want that? To have your cake and eat it too! But Beth found out about his affair and assumed this was not the first time he had cheated on her best friend. It's what she did for a living, and she knew the scenario much too well. There was never just one!

"So tell me, Dr. Paul, did you speak to anyone that night who could confirm that you were home?"

"No. I got home late, had a bite to eat with a glass of wine, watched some TV, and went to bed."

"Okay, sir, then we'll need to search your office and your home. Either you give me permission or I'll have to get a search warrant. Your choice. What'll it be?"

"You have no right to search my home and office. I've done nothing wrong."

"I'm afraid I have no choice. You're a definite person of interest in this case: you have a motive and no alibi. The judge won't even blink at my request for a warrant. If you're innocent, then you have nothing to worry about."

"When do you want to do this search?"

"Well, we need to call in our forensic team, but in the meantime I'd like to have a look around your office—with your permission, of course."

"Go ahead. Do whatever you need to do," Dr. Paul acquiesced. "I have nothing to hide."

"Thank you, sir." Stevens now turned to his partner. "Rob, call the office for a sweep here and at his apartment."

"Sure thing," Matthews said, taking out his cell phone and walking out to the reception area.

"By the way, this is a nice picture. Are these your parents?" Stevens asked.

"Yes, and unfortunately they're both deceased."

"Sorry to hear that," Stevens said, as he took his handkerchief from his pocket to blow his nose.

"Is this a picture of you and your wife, Dr. Paul?"

"Yes, that was taken a few years after we were married, before she turned into a bitch." Quite the looker, Stevens thought to himself.

Detective Matthews returned to the office and announced, "A forensic team is heading out to the doctor's apartment, and another is coming here."

He and Stevens were eager to see what they would discover, for Dr. Paul had not only a motive and no alibi, but a history of spousal abuse and a demeanor that, in their opinion, was a little too cool and detached. All these factors usually added up to something!

The next morning Detective Stevens was eager to get to the office and follow up on the results of the search of Dr. Paul's home and office. He had instructed the dentist not to leave town during the investigation.

"Hey, Walter, we have the rape kit back on Beth Scott," said the captain. "The son-of-a-bitch must have used a condom—

there was no semen or vaginal trauma found that would indicate rape."

"I figured as much; this perp is pretty damn smart. I think he watched too many crime shows and learned how to cover his tracks, or he was a professional. But I think we have a prime suspect."

"Who?" the captain asked.

"Well, yesterday when Matthews and I questioned Dr. Paul and told him what had happened to Beth, I never mentioned that she was stabbed. I said that she was attacked and hurt pretty badly. Later on when I was questioning him, he said, 'Of course I was angry with Beth . . . and emotions go all over the place during a divorce . . . but don't I go around stabbing people.' I never used the word *stabbing*, so where did that come from? It hasn't been on the news yet, and he would've had no other way of knowing that she was stabbed."

After Stevens shared the latest developments in the case with him, the captain said, "I think you need to bring the orthodontist to the station for some serious interrogation."

Stevens thought for a moment then said, "You know what, maybe we should talk with this wife first. He did mention an incident of spousal abuse."

"Yeah, give us some history to pound him with," Matthews added.

The captain nodded. "Make it a one-two punch: talk with her this morning, round him up this afternoon."

"And book him this evening," Matthews added.

The captain smiled. He was right to have put these two young guys together: Mr. Soft Touch and Mr. Hammer, he liked to call them. He expected great things from them.

Chapter

Five

Beth was making steady progress when Dr. Burton felt that it was time to slowly bring her out of the induced coma. The blood drainage from her lung and brain had tapered down to a level where the tubes could be removed. Afterward, any excess blood would probably be minimal and absorbed into her body. Dr. Burton administered a drug into her IV that would counteract those that had induced the coma and cause her to slowly regain consciousness. Up to eight hours would be needed for the drugs to take effect and return her to a conscious state. It had been four days since the attack, and now she was a survivor.

Once she was awake, he would monitor her for at least twenty-four hours before taking her off the respirator and having her breathe independently. Whenever she began fighting the breathing tube, he would know she was ready to be extubated.

He had spoken to the Scotts and advised them of his plans to awaken Beth. They were thrilled, although worried about her brain function as there was currently no way of knowing if the head trauma had caused permanent damage. Would her speech be affected, or her memory and cognitive ability? They knew they had good cause for concern.

Six hours had passed since the drug was administered, and Beth was slowly starting to stir. Dr. Burton kept a close watch on her and checked in once an hour, anticipating her waking up sooner than later as she was determined and strong. At one point, he held her hand and said, "Beth, if you can hear me, please squeeze my hand. I'm Dr. Burton, and you're in the NYP/Weill Cornell Medical Center intensive care unit. You have had surgery, and you're going to be just fine. You have a breathing tube down your throat, so that's why you are unable to speak. Can you hear me?"

After a few moments, he felt a gentle squeeze on the middle of his palm. She opened her eyes and stared up at him. "Does this breathing tube bother you?" Again, he felt another gentle squeeze on his hand. "Okay Beth, it won't be in there much longer, but first let's see how well you do once you're fully awake. If you remain stable with good vital signs for the next six hours, then I'll consider removing it. Is that a deal?" Beth motioned to him with the slightest nod of her head, which he took as a yes.

Eager to share Beth's progress with her parents, Dr. Burton stepped into the waiting room and told them: "Beth is waking up out of her coma and responded to questions by squeezing my hand. I told her where she is, and that she had undergone surgery, but that's all. I didn't mention what happened to her. I explained to her that she has a breathing tube and hopefully within the next six hours I'd be removing it."

"Oh, my dear God. That's just great! Can we see her?" asked Miriam.

"Absolutely, I'll take you back."

When Joseph and Miriam got to Beth's bedside, her eyes were open. They held her hands and leaned in to kiss her. As she stared up at them, a tear fell onto her cheek. She knew exactly who they were. She then put her hand on her breathing tube and attempted to pull at it.

Miriam called for Dr. Burton, who stepped over. He could see that Beth was pulling on the tube and thrashing her head from side to side, wanting it out *now*. He asked the Scotts to step out for a moment while he removed the tube. Afterward Beth started choking, but he assured her that was a normal response during and after its removal. Dr. Burton then put a nasal cannula in her nose to feed her oxygen. After a minute or two, she settled down and was breathing normally. Dr. Burton was more than pleased with her progress, but at the first sign that her breathing had become labored, he would have to reinsert the tube. He motioned Beth's parents back to the cubicle.

"How are you feeling, sweetheart?" Miriam asked as she leaned close in to her daughter's face.

Much to their surprise, Beth answered, "Okay," in a very weak, hoarse voice. Her throat would be uncomfortable for a few days due to irritation from the tube. Beth then asked in a raspy whisper, "Where am I, Mom? Why?"

"Beth, honey, let's talk about that tomorrow. I don't think you should be speaking now. You need to give your throat a rest."

"Was I in an accident?" she asked in the slightest whisper.

"No, sweetheart, you weren't." At that moment, Miriam looked up at Dr. Burton, unsure of how to respond without upsetting her.

"Beth," said Dr. Burton, "I would prefer if you didn't use your voice for a day or so. You need to let your throat heal. You've had that tube in it for four days now, and it's been very traumatized. As for the circumstances of your…injuries, that has to wait as well. In a few more days, all of your questions will get answered. Okay?"

"Okay," Beth answered, so softly that she could barely be heard. Then she turned her head to the side and closed her eyes.

"Beth, honey, get some rest. Dad and I are going downstairs for a cup of coffee. We'll be back shortly. We love you," said Miriam.

En route to the cafeteria, Miriam and Joseph spotted Michael in the hallway. "Hi. How's she doing? Any change?" he asked.

Joseph touched Michael's arm and reported, "She's awake, and the doctor removed the breathing tube. Isn't that wonderful? Most importantly, she's responsive and knows who we are."

"Are you serious? That's the best news I've heard all week. Does she remember anything?"

"We don't know yet. She wasn't told what happened to her and is not allowed to speak, or she'd have a million questions. So Dr. Burton wants to give her another day or two to let her throat heal a little."

Michael nodded in agreement. "Probably best if I wait to see her as well."

"I agree, Michael," said Miriam.

"But I'll still stop by every day until then."

"That's fine, Michael. And hopefully it'll only be another day or so."

The next day Dr. Burton told Beth that he would probably be moving her out of the ICU the following day and into a private room on the post-op unit. She was tolerating breathing on her own with no problem, and her vital signs were good. There were no signs of bleeding anywhere; her incisions were also healing well and showed no signs of infection. She was on her way to a complete recovery.

"Beth, you're doing great," said Dr. Burton. "And I'm so proud of your fast progress. You are quite the fighter."

In a very soft, quiet voice, Beth responded, "Thanks, Doc, but I can't be out of commission for long. I have clients who need me, so I'll do whatever it takes to get out of here fast. First, I need to know what happened to me. Can you please tell me?"

"Hey, let's slow down a bit. Is your throat still irritated when you speak?"

"It's so much better. Still slightly sore, but nothing I can't handle. Now will you answer the question? Someone is going to have to talk to me eventually, right?"

Dr. Burton replied, "Yes, Beth. You need to know. You were attacked in your apartment while you were waiting for your friend Victoria to visit. Do you remember anything at all about that night?"

"Everything is very fuzzy, and I don't remember much. I remember certain things, but I thought it was a dream."

"Do you have any idea who could've done this to you?"

Beth put her hand over the area where her surgery had been performed and asked, "What's this?" Then she gently touched all around her swollen and distorted face. "According to what I feel on my face, I suppose that I don't look my best," Beth said, adding humor to the situation. "So what does the other person look like?"

Dr. Burton replied, "That's your surgical incision. You were stabbed in your lung, but we were able to repair the damage and spare its removal. You had a lot of bruised tissue and head trauma from being hit in the back of your head. You're a very lucky young woman, Beth. It might take a few weeks, or even a few months, but your memory will come back. Usually people remember something that triggers the brain into recalling more of the incident. Don't tax yourself now with trying to recall anything—you'll only get frustrated. Let it happen naturally. I know this is difficult, but please be patient and know that as your physician I'll be with you every step of the way."

"Thanks so much, doctor. I appreciate everything you've done for me. I don't know how I can ever repay you."

"Getting well is the best payment any doctor can ask for, or at least for me it is."

Beth smiled. She really liked this doctor. He seemed so genuine and not all business.

Back at the precinct, Detective Stevens put a call in to Lisa Paul to schedule an interview. "May I please speak to Mrs. Paul? This is Detective Stevens calling from the NYPD."

"Please hold, and I'll connect you," said the receptionist.

"This is Lisa Paul, how can I help you?"

"Hi, Mrs. Paul, this is Detective Stevens, and I'm working the Beth Scott case. Do you have time to see me today? I need to ask you some questions."

"Oh yes, of course. It's horrible what happened to her. I've talked with Miriam and have stopped by the hospital, and she seems to be doing better."

"Yes, that's what we hear."

"Is one o'clock good for you, detective?"

"That works great. I'll see you soon. Thanks, Mrs. Paul." Stevens was eager to hear what Mrs. Paul had to say about her husband. If she admitted that he abused her, it would strengthen the case against Dr. Paul.

Promptly at one o'clock, Detective Stevens was sitting across from Lisa at her desk. "You have a beautiful office, Mrs. Paul." Not only was he checking out her office, but he also took note of how attractive she was—tall and thin, with big blue eyes, long light brown highlighted hair, and high cheekbones on her porcelain face. Her husband must be crazy, he thought. Why would anyone cheat on this woman?

"Thanks, detective. I spend a lot of time here, so it needs to be comfortable. Now, how can I help you with Beth's case?"

"I understand that you and Beth are best friends and that she was representing you in your divorce. I need to ask you some questions about your husband."

"Not for long, but whatever you need, detective.

"Okay, so when you were living with Dr. Paul, did he ever get physical with you?"

"Do you mean did he ever hit me?"

"Yes, or push you down, or smack you around?" Stevens asked.

"Yes, he did a few times. I kept questioning him about why he was out late so many nights and suspected that he was cheating on me. So I confronted him one night; he got very angry and pushed me, and I fell to the floor. I tried to call the police, but he grabbed the phone out of my hand and hung up. I never filed a report."

"How many times would you say that he got violent with you?"

"Maybe three times. Another time he actually knocked me to the ground, and once he slapped me across the face."

"Did he get angry often?"

"Not during the first years of our marriage, but toward the end when he was cheating on me and I was getting fed up with it and questioning him, he did. After finding out that he was having an affair with his assistant, I told him to move out."

"How did that go?" Stevens asked.

"Well, I'm a lawyer and I took care of it," Lisa said, steely-eyed.

"Did he ever threaten to harm you or Beth during these divorce proceedings?"

"He said some pretty nasty things, but I think it was all in the heat of the moment, and I really don't think he meant it. Would he act on it? I'm not sure. But since he started drinking more, he has been...erratic."

"Thank you for being so forthright, Mrs. Paul."

"I gather from your questioning that Brian is a suspect?"

"We're checking every angle that we can. He certainly had motive. Beth was the one who discovered his cheating and told you about it. And he did get rough with you when you questioned him about his infidelity."

"Well, I hate to think that Brian could do something this... heinous."

"Mrs. Paul, or may I call you Lisa?"

"Sure, I prefer that. I plan to take my maiden name back after the divorce."

"Lisa, can you think of anyone who would want to hurt Beth? Even going back to your college and law school days, did she have any enemies, or was there anyone you knew who disliked her?"

Lisa responded rather emphatically. "Detective, there is not one person on this planet who doesn't like Beth Scott. They just don't exist. So I'm afraid I can't be very helpful. But of course,

I don't know much about her clients' situations. You might want to explore that somewhat."

"We'll definitely question her secretary about a possible suspect. Well, I certainly appreciate your taking the time out to speak to me. You've been most helpful. Have a good afternoon, Lisa," he said, gazing into her eyes.

Detective Stevens returned to the precinct and told Rob Matthews about the spousal abuse Lisa had endured. This meant that Dr. Paul lied, for he said he never hit his wife.

"Yep, all the signs. We need to pick him up, bring him in, and sweat him out," Matthews said.

"I agree. This guy could've done it," Stevens replied. "And you should see his wife. What a looker!"

Matthews added, "I'll tell the captain we're on our way."

Moments later, the two detectives were in Dr. Paul's office asking to see him.

"He's with a patient. I'll let him know you're here, detectives. Please have a seat. It won't be too much longer," said Wendi.

As the detectives sat down, they noticed three women with children waiting to be seen. Dr. Paul wasn't going to be happy about why he and Matthews were here, he thought, wondering if this situation would set him off. They waited about fifteen minutes before Dr. Paul appeared.

"What's up now, detectives?"

Stevens didn't want to make a scene in front of the children, so he asked Dr. Paul if they could go back to his office. In a huff, Dr. Paul turned around and led them down the hall.

"Dr. Paul, we're going to need you to come down to the precinct with us. We have more questions for you."

"Are you shitting me, detectives? I can't just walk out of my practice; I've got a full schedule this afternoon—that's good money down the drain because you're on some wild goose chase. I'm not going anywhere. So just get the fuck out of my office, now!"

"Sir, we have probable cause, given your history of spousal abuse, your threats to Ms. Scott, and your lack of an alibi. We're asking you to come with us quietly, but if we have to we'll handcuff you and drag you with us. The choice is yours," Matthews said.

"Spousal abuse. Did you talk to Lisa?" Dr. Paul asked, but Stevens didn't answer him. "That bitch," said Dr. Paul.

Dr. Paul took a deep breath. He couldn't let people see him being forcibly detained. "Okay. Give me a minute." He pressed the intercom on his desk. "Wendi, you have to cancel the rest of today's appointments. I've got to help these detectives with a case. So close everything down when I leave, and take a half day."

Dr. Paul took off his white lab coat, donned his sports jacket, and led the detectives out into the hall. "Let's go this way. I don't want to walk through the waiting room." They turned right and exited by a back door into the hallway. They took the elevator down to the lobby and went outside to the detectives' unmarked police car.

At the precinct, the detectives led Brian Paul into the interrogation room. The captain was alerted and stood behind the two-way glass to view the interrogation.

"Have a seat, sir. Would you like a cup of coffee or a cold drink?" Stevens asked.

"No, thanks. Let's just get this over with."

"Very well," Stevens said as he and Detective Matthews sat down across from him.

"You guys have nothing and are trying to pin this on me, right?" Dr. Paul asked in exasperation. Neither of the detectives responded. "This is a fucking joke! I'm a professional with a long-standing and successful practice, and you think I'd jeopardize that because my wife's lawyer is a fucking bitch. You have it all wrong. I'm not your guy, detectives."

"We just need to clear a few things up, and the sooner you cooperate, the sooner you can leave. So just settle down and don't make this any more difficult than it is," Stevens told him.

The detectives spent the next two hours asking Dr. Paul questions about his divorce, his affair, his relationship with Beth, and his movements on the night of the attack, since he claimed to be home and nobody could verify that. However, the search of his home and office had not turned up anything incriminating, so they would have to force a confession.

When Stevens asked him how he knew that Beth was stabbed, he replied, "A good guess, I suppose. When you told me what happened and that she was in surgery, I figured it had to be a gunshot or stabbing. I'm a doctor and a good listener, detective, and I've seen my share of police shows."

"You're a dentist, not a surgeon," Matthews added.

"You told me that she was beaten up pretty badly, and if someone is going to shoot somebody they wouldn't waste time beating them up first. So I figured that she was stabbed. That's just being logical, detective."

Stevens responded, "And you didn't think to tell us that you've hit your wife several times and not just pushed her once, as you told us?"

There was silence for a minute before Dr. Paul retorted. "Well, I wouldn't say that I hit her, but I did push her down once. Only once."

"And why did you push her down?"

"We had a fight, and I lost my temper. She made me really angry, and I guess I just lost it."

"So, it's a fact that you have been known to get violent with your wife," Matthews said.

"I'd say overly aggressive, detective."

Stevens rolled his eyes. "What was the fight about?"

"She accused me of having an affair."

"And were you?" Matthews asked.

"Yes, but it meant nothing. It was just all about sex and nothing more. I told her she was the only one I loved and that would never change."

"So, you think it's okay to have an extramarital affair if it's only about sex with no emotional involvement?"

Silence again.

"Sir, I asked you a question," said Matthews.

"I suppose not," Dr. Paul responded, lowering his head.

"How many times did you smack your wife around during the course of your marriage?" asked Matthews.

"I resent the insinuations that I'm a wife beater, detective."

Detective Stevens replied, "Well, isn't that what you are, Dr. Paul?"

"No, absolutely not! I didn't make a habit of hitting my wife. As I already told you, it only happened once."

"That's not what we heard, Dr. Paul," Stevens said.

"What do you mean?"

"Well, I questioned your wife, and she stated that you knocked her down several times and even slapped her once. Do you have any response to those accusations?"

"I think she overstated the facts to try to make her point. It was only once."

"You expect us to believe your story over your wife's? After all, she's the one divorcing you, Dr. Paul."

The captain opened the door, and asked Stevens and Matthews if he could have a quick word with them.

"We'll be right back, Dr. Paul. This will only take a minute. Sit tight." The detectives joined the captain behind the two-way glass.

"What's up, captain?" Stevens asked.

"Well, guys, the hospital just called, and guess who's awake and talking?"

The detectives smiled at the captain, and Stevens said with a sigh of relief, "Thank God. We finally have a witness."

Matthews and Stevens returned to the interrogation room. Dr. Paul was sitting at the table with his hands over his cheeks and a forlorn look on his face.

"How angry were you with Beth for discovering your affair with your assistant?"

"Look, I love my wife, and this affair meant nothing to me. I was going to end it anyway. I knew my wife was getting suspicious.

I was going to come clean with Lisa, but then everything blew up when she had me followed. I know I could have patched it all up with her, but I wasn't given a chance when Beth stepped in and began handling the situation for Lisa. Then things started to get nasty, and Lisa asked me to move out. I think she wanted it over long before I had the affair, but I didn't."

"Well, sir, you have a funny way of showing your wife that you love her. You know adultery is grounds for divorce."

"And so is spousal abuse," Matthews added.

"Look, detective, my wife works long hours, and a man gets lonely. She was more interested in her career than in me, and I knew it. But I still didn't want a divorce. Beth just really fucked it up for us by encouraging the divorce, leaving no time to seek out options to help save our marriage. And yes, I *am* upset and angry with her! But no way did I do this to Beth. I'd never hurt her."

"Well, Dr. Paul, you have access to surgical instruments, as you've pointed out, as well as gloves and paper shoe covers, which we believe were all used in this crime. From what you told us, it sounds like you had every reason to want to make Beth pay for what she did to you. So you know what I think? That temper of yours once again got the best of you, and you took it all out on Beth. Am I getting warm, doc?"

There was no response from Dr. Paul. The interrogation continued for another thirty minutes, making it a total of two and a half hours, and Dr. Paul was sticking to his story.

Finally, Dr. Paul lashed out. "I am *not* answering any more questions, so either arrest me or release me. I've had enough of this bullshit." He stood up and started to walk toward the door.

Stevens instructed him not to leave town and that he would be calling on him again.

Dr. Brian Paul continued walking straight out the door, never looking back.

They had no hard evidence to legally hold Dr. Paul and had no choice but to release him. But the question still remained: how did Dr. Paul know that Beth had been stabbed? Stevens did not believe his story that he had figured it out for himself. It was just the kind of inadvertent slip that perps make in the heat of the moment and the reason to pressure them during interrogations. However, now that Beth was awake, he was hopeful she would soon remember something about her attacker that would help them with an identification. Next stop: the hospital.

Chapter Six

$\mathcal{D}$etective Stevens approached the woman at the reception desk in the ICU waiting room and flashed his badge. "Hi. Could you page Dr. Brandon Burton and tell him Detective Stevens is here to see him?" He looked around but didn't see Beth's parents, so he took a seat and pulled out his iPhone to check his messages.

Ten minutes later, Dr. Burton entered the waiting area.

"Doc, how's it going? We received a call that Beth is awake. Do you think I could speak to her?"

"I don't see why not, detective, but only for a few minutes. And let me warn you, her memory of the incident is blocked out—only brief flashes. Also, she speaks in a whisper due to the hoarseness in her throat from the breathing tube. So please don't ask too many questions. It's painful for her to answer, and I don't want her to become agitated."

"Thanks, doc. I won't be long."

Detective Stevens was directed to Beth's bed. She was resting peacefully, with only the IV running and the oxygen cannula in her nose. Her nurse told him that she was being transferred out of ICU in the morning and was making wonderful progress. Nonetheless, he was taken aback by how bruised and battered she looked.

"How are you, Beth? I'm Detective Walter Stevens, and I've been assigned to your case."

She squinted at him. "Okay," she said, pausing a moment. Then she added, "I've had better days."

"May I ask you a few questions?"

"Sure," she said in a whisper.

"Can you tell me anything at all about the night you were attacked?"

Beth put her head down, closed her eyes, and rubbed her temples. She began speaking very slowly as if straining to get every word out, almost in a daze. "All I remember...I was waiting for my friend Victoria to come over." She paused again and said, "This is so hard!" She continued, "Then I heard the door open... walked out into the living room, and then it all went blank. Sorry!"

Stevens nodded. This means the assault happened immediately, with no preliminary baiting like a revenge-minded jilted lover or friend would do. Interesting, he thought, whoever did this was likely on a mission.

"Don't worry, Beth. The doctor says that your memory will slowly return, and when it does you'll hopefully be able to identify your assailant."

"So you think it's somebody I know."

"Since it wasn't a robbery, that's our best guess." Stevens paused. "We think Dr. Brian Paul could be a suspect. He was pretty disturbed that you put a private detective on him and seems to be quite hostile about it. He said you really messed things up for him and his wife. Do you remember if you spoke to him recently about the divorce?"

Beth hesitated before responding. "He called me about two weeks ago to ask if I could talk Lisa out of going through with the divorce. I said no." She thought for a moment. "Brian wouldn't do anything like this. He's mostly all talk."

Stevens was about to dispute that observation but thought better of it. He told Beth he would check on her in a few days and started to leave when he barely heard her say, "Wait." Stevens turned around and stepped back to her bedside.

"What is it, Beth?"

"I just got a flashback." She paused to think a moment. "It was a big guy . . . who attacked me. I know Justen was stalking me, but this guy was even bigger."

"Yes, we've talked with Justen, but for now I see Dr. Burton coming over to kick me out. So I'll have to go. Take it easy and get well, Beth."

While the detective turned to leave, he put his hands in his pockets, thanked Dr. Burton for letting him speak to Beth, and stepped out as the automatic double doors opened. In the waiting room, he saw Beth's parents and Michael Hudson walking in. They exchanged greetings, then Hudson pulled him aside.

"Detective, did Beth remember anything?" Michael asked.

Stevens shook his head but wondered why this was the first thing he would say, given Beth's condition. "Not much, other than the perp was a big guy." Stevens looked Michael up and down. He was a big guy. "But she did remember that Justen Bennett wouldn't leave her alone? Did Beth ever complain to you about this guy stalking her?"

"She told me about Justen wanting to see her again and that she was getting strange phone messages and letters from him. I told her to call the police, but she said she was just going to ignore him." Michael was silent for a moment and then spoke rather quickly. "There is something else, detective. About six months ago, she met Justen for drinks to make certain he understood that she wasn't going to see him anymore. It was at a sports bar, and some big-time sports celebrities said hello, but a few rough-looking ex-athletes who looked like real lowlifes were also there. It made me wonder."

Stevens nodded. "Counselor, we're both thinking along the same lines. I definitely need to check out these ex-athletes." Stevens said his good-byes and walked out as if on a mission to follow up on these new leads.

Michael sat down in the ICU waiting room where he'd been hopeful of seeing Beth for days now. She was on his mind day and night, but he remained vigilant. He turned to the Scotts.

"What's the latest word?"

"She's being transferred to the post-op floor tomorrow if her chest X rays are good."

"Do you think I can see her anytime soon?"

"Why don't you tell the nurse you're a good friend? I think she'll let you see Beth since she's so much better. But her voice is weak and she has difficulty speaking, so please bear that in mind."

"Thank you. I'll make it short."

Michael was escorted to Beth's cubicle and given a ten-minute period of visitation. He quickly surveyed the room, collecting his thoughts before approaching her bed. He didn't want to upset her, for he knew their relationship was tenuous at best since when he last saw her she had made it clear that she was not ready to resume. When Michael reached her bedside, her eyes were closed, so he waited for her to open them. He took her hand, and she looked up.

"Michael, hi," she whispered.

"How are you, gorgeous?"

"Not very gorgeous now."

Michael shook his head. "Beth, I'm so sorry for what happened to you. I wish I could've prevented this."

"Not your fault. Nothing you could've done, Michael."

"The doctor says you're going to be fine. I've been coming over every evening, hanging out with your mom and dad. They've been such troopers through this whole ordeal. You're very lucky to have them. I can't stay long, but I wanted to tell you that I'm here for you if you should need anything."

"Thanks."

Almost as an afterthought, he added, "Boy, do I want to nail this motherfucker for what he did to you. So all you remember is that he was a big guy?"

Beth closed her eyes and tried to remember more. Michael saw her strained expression. "It's all right, Beth. It'll come back to you. Just rest and get better."

She smiled and squeezed his hand.

"I see the nurse giving me looks that it's time to go. I'll be back tomorrow."

"Good-bye, Michael," she said, closing her eyes and turning her head to the side, as if she was ready to fall asleep.

The next morning Dr. Burton examined Beth to make sure she was well enough to be moved out of the ICU later that day. He sat on the edge of her bed and used his stethoscope to listen to her heart and lungs. "Take a deep breath. Let it out. Again. Again. Now cough." He removed the chest piece. "It all sounds good in there. I'm going to order another X ray, and if it checks out then we'll move you down to the post-op floor. I think you're doing great."

Beth was thrilled, and for the first time since she had awakened she was smiling broadly. "That's so encouraging. I'm on my way back!"

"I'm very pleased with your progress. Beth. You're a strong resolute woman, and it shows in your quick recovery. Very admirable."

"You're so sweet, Dr. Burton, and you've taken great care of me—I'm eternally grateful. May I call you Brandon?"

"Of course, please do! Dr. Burton is much too formal after what we've been through together."

"Thank you, Brandon, and when I get home I promise to cook you a wonderful dinner to show my appreciation."

"Hey, look at you, not even out of the ICU and you're already cooking me dinner. Well, I accept. It would be my greatest pleasure to see you back in the thick of things, doing what you love best."

Brandon turned to leave Beth's bedside, but not before giving her a big smile. Residents were warned about getting too close to their patients, but in this case it was already too late.

No sooner did Brandon walk out than Lisa Paul came in, noticed the doctor, and quickly she did a double take. "Beth, I've been worried about you," she said, stepping over and taking her hand. "I came by when you were still in the coma and sat with your parents. They've been updating me daily on your progress. It's so good to see you awake. I need you, girlfriend, so hurry up and get out of here."

"Believe me, Lisa. I can't wait to go home. I hate hospitals!"

Lisa looked over her shoulder. "Well, if that was your doctor, I think I might trade places with you."

"Yes, and he's single. Can you believe it?"

Lisa put her hands over her heart. "I think I need some chest X rays myself."

Beth laughed so hard it hurt. "Lisa, you always make me laugh."

Lisa saw her strained expression. "Okay, but let's keep it low key for now." She paused. "So when do you get out of here?"

"Not soon enough. I feel like I've deserted my clients."

"Everybody understands, especially me," Lisa said, squeezing her hand.

"So Brian is okay with our settlement offer on the apartment?"

Lisa replied, "Let's not get into that now. Okay, girlfriend?"

Beth nodded. "If I'm discharged next week, as soon as I get home I'll get busy on your case."

"I know you're worried about it, Beth. But you need to give yourself time to heal. Do you hear me? It can wait another week. Not to worry," Lisa said.

"Yes, I guess I'll just lay back and play footsy with Brandon."

Lisa narrowed her eyes. "Well, don't overexert yourself." She let go of Beth's hand. "I have to go—my ten minutes are up. I'll be back tomorrow. Have a good night's sleep, and listen to the nurses...and the doctors."

At the station, Detectives Stevens and Matthews were rehashing the bare facts of Beth's case. They had no DNA other than

Michael's, which was no surprise since he was the last man to have a relationship with Beth. The medical examiner confirmed that the weapon was more a shank than a kitchen knife, as if the perp hadn't planned to kill her. Either way, the weapon still had not been found. There was no forced entry, and after extensive questioning of the neighbors no one had seen anybody come out or go in around the time of the crime other than Victoria. But it had been Detective Stevens's experience that these Upper East Side people weren't terribly concerned about their neighbors. Stevens now looked across the desk at Matthews. "The one solid lead that we have is Beth's flashback that the perp was a large man. Dr. Paul and Michael Hudson are big guys."

Matthews added, "But Justen Bennett isn't."

"Unless, he used one of his cronies. What did you find out from the background check on Bennett?"

"I spoke with some of his ex-clients, and they weren't so happy with him, to say the least. We need to go to the gym in Washington Heights where a few of them work out, and see what they have to say. Wanna take a ride over there?"

"Yeah, but be sure that you're packing."

They drove north on FDR Drive to Harlem River Drive and got off at 155th Street, the border between Harlem and Washington Heights. They pulled up in front of the West Side Gym on 163rd Street. Stevens had heard it called a "a tough gym for tough boys," but as they walked in they realized they wouldn't call any of the guys here "boys."

Matthews pulled out a list of names and stepped up to the front desk. He flashed his badge; the girl didn't blink an eye. "Ms. Castro, any of these guys here today?"

She looked it over. "Yeah, Pedro and Alonso are working the free weights over there." She pointed to two very big guys lifting what looked like four hundred pounds.

"Thank you, miss."

The detectives walked into the weight room, their badges flopped over their breast pockets. They stood back and allowed the men to finish their sets.

When the two guys stood up, it was apparent that they were both six foot eight or so, and nearly as broad. They glared at the preppie white guys. "Wanna try your hand?" one of them asked.

"Don't think so. We're Detectives Stevens and Matthews of the NYPD, and we understand that Justen Bennett used to be your agent. Is that correct?"

"Yeah," they both answered. One of them moved up to Detective Stevens. "I'm Alonso Carter, and why are you asking?"

"We're investigating a case that Mr. Bennett might be involved in, and we need some background on him."

"Like what?"

"Can you tell us a little bit about Justen's temperament? Like, would you say that he has a calm nature, or is he more volatile?"

"Definitely more volatile. There is nothing calm about that guy," said Alonso.

"How do you mean, sir?"

"Well, let's put it this way. If we didn't do what he wanted, which wasn't always in my best interest, then he would really lose it. He'd yell at me, threaten to tear up my contract, tell me I was finished and nobody else would pick me up."

Pedro added, "The little white guy acted like I knew nothin' and he was 'the man.' You know what I'm saying?"

Matthews replied, "I think I do. A control freak who, when he doesn't get his way, gets really mean."

"Yeah," Alonso said. "He acted like we were his property and he could do whatever he wanted with us."

"Was he that way in his personal life as well?" Stevens asked. The two of them exchanged looks. "I mean, do you think he was capable of . . . hiring somebody to beat up an old girlfriend?"

"Maybe. And yeah, the little fucker wouldn't do it himself. He'd hire it out. Wouldn't want to mess up his thousand-dollar shoes," Alonso said.

"This is what we're trying to find out. So let me ask you guys, did he ever contact you, or anybody you know, about helping him...settle a score?"

They both shook their heads. "We still got game and are trying to get back. But some of the has-beens might consider it," Pedro added. "Bennett's smart. He wouldn't use locals; out-of-state guys only."

"Well, I think you've given us the lowdown on Justen Bennett, and for that we thank you. It was nice meeting you, and we enjoyed watching you play; hope you get back in. But seems like the rules are really hampering tough play anymore."

"Yeah, tell me. Enforcers like us could clean clock back in the good old days." Alonso turned to Pedro. "Maybe we should be taking ballet lessons."

They both had a good laugh.

"Guys, if you could ask around...Know what I mean? We'd make it worth your while."

"Sure thing, detective," said Pedro. Stevens handed them cards.

As the detectives were leaving, Alonso yelled, "Hope you get your guy. I'm sure it would make some brothers really happy in prison to see new bait."

Chapter

Seven

Four days had passed since Beth was moved into her private room on the surgical floor. She was recovering well, walking down the hall each day, and sitting up in a chair to read. There were no complications from her surgery, and she was becoming stronger every day. But she still had no memory of what happened to her on that awful night. It was all a blur, and each time she prodded her memory she would become more frustrated when it failed her.

Beth enjoyed seeing Michael on his now-daily visits, but realized that she was not ready to think about her future with or without him at this point. She also started feeling closer to Dr. Burton, but not in a doctor-patient way—it was becoming personal. She was a good judge of character and could tell he was really a decent guy. He had a professional demeanor yet showed real concern for his patients and their families. He was always kind and genuine. This impressed her and made her want to get to know him better. She doubted that he would ever be interested in her in any way except as his patient; but he did accept her dinner invitation, which she took as a sign of personal interest. It was always the highlight of her day when he came into her room and she could be flirtatious and have a little fun with him.

Beth felt as if she'd been given a new lease on life, and therefore she wanted to enjoy all that it had to offer. She wanted to get married and eventually have a family, though she wasn't completely sure about Michael being *the one*. They had a wonderful time together and an insatiable sexual appetite for each other. She had never experienced such a sexual high with any other man, yet she was perplexed. How did she know that their sexual attraction wasn't overshadowing everything else that was so relevant to making a long-term relationship work? She also respected Michael and knew he would make a wonderful husband and a good father. He was thoughtful, caring, and altruistic—very good qualities in a man. But she still had her doubts. *Why this hesitation to move forward?* This question troubled her greatly. Beth wanted to keep things just as they were, but she knew Michael was getting antsy and was pushing her for a commitment. And there was now another stumbling block: her sudden and unexpected interest in Brandon. How could she even be thinking about anyone else if she had deep feelings for Michael? The more she thought about it the more it baffled her.

While she was lost in thought, Dr. Burton sauntered into the room. "Well, how's my favorite patient doing today?"

Surprised, Beth looked up and said, "I'm great! But I want to know when can I go home."

Brandon sat down on the edge of her bed. "Maybe in a few days. I'd like to repeat some of the blood work and do another round of X rays, and then I think you'll be good to go."

"Brandon, I think I'm ready now. I need to get back to work. My clients must think I've abandoned them."

"Beth, you shouldn't be going back to work for at least two more weeks. You had a pretty bad concussion, and it'll take time to feel like yourself again. You must be patient. You think you're ready, but you're really not. Trust me. Also, the surgical incision must heal from the inside out, and you must continue with the wound care to prevent infection. You need plenty of rest to give your body time to heal. I must say, it took quite a bit of work in there," as he pointed to her surgical site, "to mend the damage to your lung. I know you've been doing breathing treatments with the inhalation therapist, and you're making steady progress, but these treatments need to continue for at least another week for your lung capacity to return to normal. And we'll give you the equipment to continue these treatments at home."

"Okay, Brandon, I get it. I guess I thought if I was released from the hospital, I could go back to work. I understand what you've said to me, and it makes sense. I'll do it, for I desperately want to get well. But would you have any objection to my secretary coming to the hospital to fill me in on my cases? I promise I'll only spend an hour with her. I just need to instruct her on what needs to be done for the week."

"I'm okay with that, as long as it's no more than an hour. But if you start to tire, then tell her to come back tomorrow."

"I will." Beth paused, her face now etched with concern. "So when do you think I'll remember what happened to me that night?" she asked. "There's something I don't understand. If I can remember everything else about my life before the attack, why can't I remember that night?"

The young doctor took Beth's hand and said: "Because you were severely traumatized, and you subconsciously blocked it out of your mind: the emotional trauma coupled with the concussion resulted in your memory loss of the attack. We call this dissociative amnesia, which means it was caused by a traumatic event. This type of amnesia is never permanent, and your memory can return rather quickly. So I don't want you to worry about this anymore. Let nature take its course."

"I want to tell the police so they can arrest this maniac. I don't feel safe with him still out there, and I'm fearful that he might try again."

"It'll come, just don't push yourself too hard. It's like when you want to remember something and you can't, and you shift your focus and then later it comes to you." Beth nodded. "Something will happen that'll trigger your memory. It could be a voice you recognize that you heard that night, or someone's body build resembling your assailant's. It'll happen. Trust me," said Dr. Burton. "Also, when you return to your apartment, memories may slowly start to surface as you reorient yourself to the scene where it all happened."

"Okay, I trust you and I'll let nature takes its course," she said and smiled, thinking that applied to her feelings as well. "Thanks for being so patient with me, Brandon. It must be difficult to deal with a type A personality like me."

He returned her smile. "Yes, you're a real handful."

That could be suggestive, she thought.

More seriously, he added, "Don't worry, Beth. Everything will work out. But I've gotta run; I'm due in surgery."

As he left, Beth's eyes fixed on how nicely his blue scrubs hugged his adorable butt. She was still smelling his cologne, and was desperately yearning to snuggle her face in the fold of his neck. Now that she was more alert, there was much more to observe of this handsome young doctor. There was definitely an attraction on her part. But how could he be attracted to her the way she looked?

Knowing that she could not go back to work for another two weeks, Beth's concerns about her job and her clients became more worrisome. She needed to talk to her best friend, Lisa, and assure her that she could work on her case while she was at home recuperating. She was also handling three other divorces and started to hyperventilate realizing how much time had lapsed without any attention given to them. Beth needed to talk to her assistant and get an update on each one of them. She called Maria and asked her to bring their files to the hospital. Maria politely resisted her request, concerned about her boss's recovery, but Beth told her that she had her doctor's approval.

Maria arrived about an hour later. On entering the hospital room, she was a little taken aback by Beth's appearance, with her face still swollen and bruised and looking like she had been in a street fight. The woman always looked so immaculate, she thought, with her hair long and flowing, dressed to the nines, and her makeup always perfect. She couldn't believe Beth's resilience—to be in this condition and all that was on her mind were her clients. She was the most dedicated lawyer Maria had ever worked for.

"Hi, Beth. How are you doing?" Maria asked.

"I'm slowly on the mend, and I really appreciate your coming over here, Maria. I know how much you hate hospitals. First of all, let me apologize for my appearance; I must look awful to you, but, believe me, this is an improvement." Her assistant nodded in amazement.

"Do you have all the files?"

"Yes, I do, and I can fill you in on everything that's been going on since you've been out. But please don't apologize for your appearance. I'm so happy you're getting better."

Beth and her assistant reviewed work-related matters for over an hour before she began to tire. At this point she realized that Dr. Burton was right—she wasn't ready to go back to work full-time yet. She was unable to process all the updates in the files and had to go over them several times to get everything clear; nor could she make her usual leaps in logic. Tired and ready to stop, Beth told Maria to update her clients and let them know when she'd be back at work. She also gave her instructions on what needed to be done that week.

After Maria left, Beth's frustration almost got the best of her, particularly with regard to letting Lisa down at such a pivotal point in her case. She had been ready to negotiate her settlement when everything came to a screeching halt. Lisa's divorce was one of Beth's more difficult cases since she was personally involved and cared deeply for both parties despite Brian's recent bad behavior. They had been friends for years and had shared many meaningful times together, but now it was all tumbling down. Distressed by these feelings, she drifted off to sleep.

When Beth awoke, her mom and dad were sitting in her room. "Hi, sweetheart. How are you feeling?" her mom asked.

"I'm good. Thanks for coming. The doctor says I might be able to go home in a few days if my chest X ray and blood work are okay. Isn't that great news?"

"Yes, it is. And Dad and I would like you to stay with us until you are on your feet again. That way we can take care of you and you won't have to bother with day-to-day things." Her mother paused. "Besides, we don't want you staying alone in that apartment until the police catch this guy."

"Oh, Mom, that's very kind of both of you, but it won't be necessary. The police will be patrolling the neighborhood more and checking in on me. And I have to be close to the office so my secretary can bring over my work. I'll be fine, Mom. Don't worry."

"Then let me come stay with you for a few days, just to get you settled in. I'll make sure you have good nourishing meals, and I'll help you with your wound care and breathing treatments. Would that be all right?"

"Okay, Mom, that'll be fine, and it's very much appreciated."

"It would certainly make your dad and me feel so much better if you weren't alone." Miriam went on to tell Beth that she had already cleaned up Beth's apartment, put everything back in order, had the locks changed on the door, and added a new deadbolt above the original one.

After his visit to the Westside Gym, Detective Stevens had felt justified in getting a warrant for Justen Bennett's phone records and client list for the last five years. He wanted to see if Bennett had hired one of them to do his dirty work. The captain had agreed and processed the warrant.

Now sitting across the desk from his partner, Stevens said, "Rob, I think this is a good lead. Maybe just being served at his office and knowing we're snooping in all the right places will make him crack."

"Well, I don't think it'll take much to muss his hair, embarrassing him like this," said Matthews. "In fact I might enjoy ruffling his feathers a bit. He's such a prick!"

Stevens nodded. Neither of them liked the guy, but they had to keep it professional.

Two hours later, Stevens and Matthews, warrant in hand, were at Justen Bennett's high-rise office announcing their arrival to the receptionist.

"Please have a seat, and I'll let him know you're here," she replied.

Stevens thanked her and took a seat in the waiting area. He was impressed by the wood paneling and polished hardwood floors, although he'd expected nothing less. Bennett enjoyed the finer things in life, and it showed in his office as well as his apartment. Pictures of famous athletes, all personally signed, covered the walls. To the left were the executive agents' offices, and to the right was a long room sectioned off with cubicles and junior agents plying their trade.

Bennett stepped into the waiting area and said, "Nice to see you guys again. Catch your man yet?"

"Well, that's why we're here," Matthews replied, handing him the warrant.

Bennett, taken aback, opened the document and read it. "You've got to be kidding me. You think I'm a suspect?"

"Well, a person of interest," said Matthews.

The office activity around them had come to a halt, and everyone was looking their way. Bennett said, "Detectives, let's discuss this 'misunderstanding' in my office."

"Okay," Stevens said, "but you might want to get your secretary on it now."

Bennett shook off his suggestion and escorted them back to his office, where he offered them seats with a spectacular view of the city and asked if they would like anything to drink. "So what's this all about?" he asked, scrutinizing the document in his hand.

"It's a warrant for your client list and your cell and office phone records."

"May I ask why?"

"We need to see if any of your contacts were involved in Beth's attack."

"Now why would one of my ex-clients want to hurt Beth?"

"Because you paid them."

"What! Have you lost your mind, detective? My ex-clients are all well-off and wouldn't need to be paid to beat up somebody. They're sportscasters, speakers, and coaches. They're not violent men, detectives; they're all famous athletes."

"Well, we talked with a few at the Westside Gym who weren't fans of yours. They said one of these ex-clients, who's not so famous anymore, might do this job for you, especially if you paid them well."

"Look, not everybody makes the grade, and I have let go of my share of low earners, so you're going to find a few bad apples. But you're way off base here, detectives."

"Well, Mr. Bennett, we'll be the judge of how off base we are. So please have one of your staff get us what we came for."

"Wait a minute! You really think I had one of my clients do this to Beth?"

"Something like that, yeah."

"No way, detectives. I was upset that she dumped me. But I already told you that I would never hurt her. I loved the woman. Why don't you believe me?"

"Because of two words—*motive* and *means*—even if your alibi holds up."

Justen Bennett collapsed in his chair. The detectives looked at each other. The guy was playing it for all it was worth. He pushed the button on his intercom and asked his secretary to come in. He now looked up at them more hurt than outraged.

"You guys. Got nobody else for it, so go pick on the rich guy."

"Look, Mr. Bennett, from what we hear, you fell pretty hard for Beth, and you're a man who doesn't take no for an answer.

So there's a reasonable assumption to look more closely at your activities."

"Well, there's nothing here. You're just wasting your time while Beth's real attacker is free and getting out of the hospital." They stared at him. "I called; I'm concerned about her."

Somebody knocked lightly on the door. "Come in," Bennett said. A strikingly beautiful young woman stepped into the office. "Sally, please get these gentlemen the information they want and then show them to the door."

Stevens and Matthews waited in the reception area for thirty minutes while Bennett's secretary gathered the material. Finally, she came out and handed them a thumb drive. "That's the list you requested. The phone records will take another day."

"Thank you, Sally." Steven paused. "Do you mind if I ask you a question?"

"Not at all."

"Do you like working for Mr. Bennett?"

"Yes, of course. He's a real…gentleman, and you wouldn't believe my last Christmas bonus."

It's all about the money, Stevens thought. The detectives hurried back to the precinct and reviewed the information they were given on Justen Bennett's client list. There were about seventy-five names. They were waiting for the cell phone records from two companies, since Bennett changed carriers about two years ago. If they could find calls from any of the men on the list after they left Bennett's company, they might be able to connect the dots.

"Hey, Walter, look what I just found. This guy has a record for armed robbery and dealing drugs. He's out on bail and his name is Franco Barrera. Justen represented him when he played for the Knicks four years ago. He didn't finish out his contract 'cause he was caught dealing and they let him go. I wonder if Bennett felt Barrera owed him big time," said Matthews.

"Good work, Rob. Hopefully the cell records will connect them—or him—with someone else. This looks very promising. Maybe we caught a break."

Chapter Eight

It had been a week since Beth was discharged from the hospital. Her mom's stay turned out to be a blessing: she did the shopping and laundry, cooked nutritious meals, oversaw the breathing treatments, changed the wound dressings, and was there for anything else Beth needed. Beth was grateful for her mother's assistance and was now ready for her to return home. Miriam agreed, but only if her daughter promised to check in with her every day to let her know she was okay.

Beth kissed her mom good-bye and double-locked the door. Afterward, she looked around her apartment and felt a little frightened. The hospital psychologist had prepared her for this eventuality. It was a normal part of the healing process. But she was determined to keep her mind occupied so her fears wouldn't consume her. She wanted to resume a full life again, and refused to live with trepidation. That first morning by herself, Beth walked through the apartment over and over again, staring at everything and trying to relive that night, hoping that she'd remember something...anything! But nothing jumped out at her.

The phone rang, and the caller ID indicated that it was Michael.

"Hey, Michael. What's up?"

"Just checking in. Is your mom still with you?"

"As a matter of fact, she left today. Mom was a great help, but I need to get some sort of normalcy back in my life by being alone again, though I guess I'm still feeling slightly edgy right now. You know, not as completely relaxed at home as I used to be."

"I totally understand, Beth. Would it be okay if I came over after work?"

"Sure, I would love to see you, and can you pick up a bottle of wine? I'm dying for some good vino; it's been so long, and maybe it'll take the edge off, somewhat."

"You got it. I'll be over at five thirty with your favorite Kim Crawford Sauvignon Blanc. Do you need anything else?"

"No thanks. Mom has taken care of just about everything. I'll see you soon."

Beth was relieved that Michael was coming over, and she wanted to look presentable for him. So for the first time since she'd been home, she fixed her hair, put on some makeup, and, looking in the bathroom mirror, felt good about her appearance once again. The swelling and bruising on her face was much better, and she could practically cover it with makeup. She did not want anyone to remember her battered face.

Michael arrived with Beth's favorite wine and also brought over a selection of fine cheeses. "It's good to see you back home, Beth," he said, giving her a big hug.

"You have no idea how good it feels to be out of that hospital and on my way to complete recovery. I couldn't be happier."

Michael opened the wine while Beth prepared a cheese-and-cracker tray. At one point he looked over at her. "How do you feel about staying alone? Would you like me to sleep on the couch for a couple nights?"

"You're so sweet, Michael, but I have to do this on my own— learn to live my life again, just as before, and try not to think about what happened. I will not live my life in fear. The psychologist said that this would be the most difficult part of my recovery—overcoming my fear of this guy returning to hurt me again." She paused, then shook her head. "But since I can't remember what happened I don't know who to be afraid of."

Michael reached over and took her hand. "Beth, you're such a strong person, and if anyone can do this, it's you. The police are still watching your apartment, so that should help you feel more secure. And I noticed that your door is double-bolted. You mustn't worry."

Michael poured two glasses of wine, then he and Beth sat side by side on the sofa.

"Michael, I'm so grateful for your continued emotional support. It means a lot to me."

"You know my feelings for you, and that's never going to change."

"I appreciate that, and you know, too, that I care about you very much. But let's not go there tonight. I hope you understand."

"Sure. We have lots of time for that." He raised his wine glass, and Beth followed. "Cheers," Michael said as they clinked glasses. "Let's try some of this cheese."

"Would love some," Beth said.

"There was this great cheese shop right next door to the wine shop. The owner saw my bottle of Sauvignon Blanc and said this aged French Charouce would go great with it." Michael spread some of the creamy cheese on a cracker and put it up to Beth's mouth. "How's this?"

Beth closed her eyes to savor the taste. "Yum. It's great. I love the nutty, slightly salty flavor."

The evening went by quickly as they chatted, watched the French film *Amour* on Showtime, and drank their wine slowly until the bottle was empty. Beth was feeling much more relaxed and mellowed out.

"Beth, are you sure you don't want me to spend the night? I can sleep here on the couch and make you breakfast in the morning before I leave to get dressed for work."

"I guess it would be okay, Michael. You're so thoughtful. But you know it's only prolonging the inevitable."

"I know, Beth, and you'll be alone plenty of nights. But not tonight."

"The linens are in the hall closet. Thank you, Michael."

Beth woke up the next morning to the smell of freshly brewed coffee. Before she could get out of bed, Michael walked in with breakfast on a tray.

"Oh my God, this is great. I haven't even brushed my teeth yet. You're very prompt, Michael. It smells wonderful, and I'm starving. Haven't had much of an appetite lately."

"Please enjoy, Beth. Is there anything else I can do before I leave for work?"

Beth looked up at Michael in awe. She couldn't believe how solicitous he had been with her. He was truly a good guy, and she was lucky to have him in her life.

"Michael, you are the best, and thanks so much for everything. I'm so glad that you stayed over. Have a great day at the office. I wish I were going with you. I really miss it."

"You'll be back soon, Beth, and it'll all be there waiting for you when you return. Call me if you need anything."

While Beth ate her breakfast, she kept thinking about Michael. It was the small things that showed how much he cared about her: coming over her first night alone, bringing that wonderful bottle of wine, and fixing breakfast for her. He couldn't have been more attentive!

Even in her condition, she remained strongly attracted to him and could not help but remember the wonderful sex the two of them always had together. He was so good in bed. She flash-backed to when he surprised her on her last birthday. Michael had taken her to dinner at the Plaza Hotel and gotten a room for the night. He loved to be spontaneous and surprise her with evening venues other than a quiet dinner or a show.

When they had walked into the suite on the twenty-ninth floor, Beth couldn't believe her eyes. The entire back wall was glass, with views of the city and Central Park that were spectacular. It was one of the most impressive sites she had ever seen of New York, with magical twinkling lights shining off in the distance. The city lights glistened, and the night sky was crystal clear. This view brought excitement but also tranquility to her mood.

"Oh, Michael, this is just so beautiful. I feel as if I'm dreaming."

Michael had wanted the evening to reflect his strong feelings for Beth. "I'm so glad you like it. I thought it would be a nice way to spend your birthday."

"I'm over the moon, really," she remembered telling him.

The room was beautifully furnished. In the center was a beige, sectional, cushy sofa with colorful pillows positioned in a semi-circle facing the expansive windows, which were framed by stately draperies with large valences. The U-shaped mahogany bar was stocked with all kinds of liquor. Soft classical music was playing throughout the suite, which was partially absorbed into the plush beige carpeting that felt like silk beneath her bare feet. The bedroom, which had the same view of the city as the sitting room, had a huge canopy bed with the finest linens in gold and beige. The bathroom was palatial, with double sinks, a huge jetted tub for two, shower, toilet, and bidet. The faucets were gold, and the counters, shower, and floor were all done in white marble. Never before had she spent a night in such opulence.

Michael popped open a bottle of Krug's Brut Vintage champagne and poured them glasses, which they sipped as they sank into the soft comfortable couch and stared at the view. It was mesmerizing, and neither of them felt it necessary to speak a word, for fear that this special moment would vanish. When the music changed to a Johann Strauss waltz, Michael stood up and motioned for Beth's hand.

"May I have this dance, madam?"

Beth took Michael's hand as he gently pulled her off the sofa, and they began to dance to the slow waltz. After a few spins, he tasted her lips softly, and then nuzzled his face into her neck, breathing in the scent of her perfume that was exciting him by the minute.

"You smell so wonderful. What're you wearing?"

"Essence, by Cartier."

"I'll have to remember that."

He pushed her hair back away from her face as he began kissing her forehead and cheeks until he found her lips parted. He positioned his lips near hers, barely touching, as he stared into her warm green eyes.

His moves were slow and sensuous, with an undulating motion as he held her tight. Beth followed his lead, while moving her torso and hips against him with the same slow, languid pace until there was no space between their bodies. She could feel his broad masculine chest pushing into her breasts. He began kissing her passionately, and she felt his long tongue at the back of her throat. Her arms were wrapped tightly around his neck. She felt his erection getting harder with each movement of her hips. He unzipped her dress and gracefully let it fall to the carpet as her body fluidly slid from side to side against his. She unbuttoned his shirt while he unfastened her bra and let it fall off her shoulders. He kissed her shoulders and said, "You are so, so beautiful." She felt his warm rock-solid body pressing against her breasts and could feel her nipples harden. He then reached his hand down her side, slipping his fingers through her thong and sliding it down her legs, leaving her naked to his touch. Soon, they were both stripped of their clothing and still dancing, but hardly moving in front of the beautiful luminous skyline of New York.

Michael then picked Beth up and carried her into the bedroom, pulled back the white down comforter, and gently placed her on the silk sheets. She felt like a princess whose knight, with his unsheathed manhood, had arrived. Her heart was beating faster and her breathing became heavier. Oh my God, how I want him, she thought. But his pace was very slow and controlled. He started kissing her face, working his way down to her neck, shoulders, and breasts. He kissed her breasts so gently, caressing each one as if it were a delicate breakable object.

"I adore you," he said.

Beth was so caught up in the moment that she couldn't speak.

He caressed her abdomen, putting his tongue into her belly button, while his other hand was gliding down her inner thigh. By now she was ready for him to take her, and she didn't know how much longer she could wait. She grasped him and held on firmly while his fingers found their wet destination. Her breathing became heavier by the second. She was panting and moaning, "Oh, oh, oh," so softly. He then lifted up her hips with his hands, and gently moved her to the edge of the bed. He knelt on the floor, his face between her thighs. He kissed her inner thighs, moving his tongue along until it reached the soft folds of flesh he wanted to caress. Within a few seconds, every nerve ending in Beth's body was convulsing as she continued building up to the culmination she'd been longing for all evening. She was ready now to succumb, feeling ecstasy from the gentle yet erotic movements of his tongue.

"Michael, you make me feel so damn good. I…Oh my God! *Oh my!"*

Shortly after her release, Michael moved her back up the bed, then gently lay on top of her, holding her buttocks in his hands while entering her, thrusting back and forth with a rocking motion, hopeful she would climax again. He had unfeasible control and held back his excitement until they were both ready to explode. As he filled her, he felt her lower body tense. All of her senses were heightened with each thrust. She felt beads of perspiration on her forehead as she tensed into a state of rigidity. It felt as if she had crossed over a threshold into a new erotic dimension. Their bodies were in sync and prepared to receive the ultimate reward to satiate their strong desires and passions. They released themselves simultaneously. Beth had never experienced pleasure of such magnitude as she had that night.

After their lovemaking was over, she and Michael took a relaxing bath while finishing the bottle of champagne. They dried each other with the warm plush towels that came off the heated towel rack next to the tub. Before they drifted off to sleep, Michael wrapped his arms around Beth, making her feel warmer and safer than ever before.

"Michael, this evening has been more than wonderful, and your tenderness is endearing. We're so good together, and I'll remember this night always."

"Beth, you make me so happy, and I never want this night to end. I knew from the day we met that we'd have something very special together. Happy birthday, babe."

"I can hardly believe that it's been only six months since we met. It feels like we've been together forever."

Beth remembered everything about that night as if it happened yesterday. After Michael's visit last night, she wanted to resume their relationship. There was no way she could let this amazing, empathetic man slip through her fingers. She decided that she would give him another chance, for he had shown his devotion to her in many different ways. And she really needed his support to get her through this nightmare she was living.

Beth's reverie was interrupted by the chime of her cell phone.

"Good morning, this is Beth."

"Hi, Beth. This is Walter Stevens. How's it going being back home?"

"Detective," she said sitting up. "I can't tell you how great it is to sleep in my own bed. So what's up? Any new leads?"

"Well, we've been checking out Justen Bennett's ex-clients. We have a theory that maybe he paid one of them to beat you up. As I said, it's just a theory. Some of these guys are pretty tough customers, so it's possible for the right amount of money one of them would have done Bennett a favor."

"Well, I can't imagine Justen doing that, and nobody I met with him seemed the type, detective."

"As I said, we're just chasing down leads. But I wanted you to know we're determined to get this guy."

Beth sighed deeply. "That's really good to know. I appreciate the update. I'm hoping my memory will return soon, and when it does, you'll be the first to know."

"Well, anything will be helpful. Just keep that in mind."

Detective Stevens hung up the phone and looked across his desk at Matthews. They had followed up on one of Bennett's guys who had served time after his career ended and was now out on bail. A few months ago, according to Bennett's phone records, there were calls exchanged between the two men. They questioned Bennett, and of course he said they were friendly chats about what was happening in his life at the present. The ex-con told them that he wasn't even in town the night of the attack, and his alibi checked out. Stevens and Matthews had their men still checking on other ex-clients who could have done this job for Bennett, but so far they hadn't turned up any real suspects. They were frustrated, to say the least.

"Hey, Rob," Stevens said. "You know, Beth's boyfriend of sorts defends a lot of bad guys. I wonder if one of Hudson's ex-clients might've wanted to get back at him by beating up his girlfriend."

"Get back at him for what, Walter?"

"Maybe losing their case, or getting a longer sentence than expected. They always blame their lawyers, not themselves."

"Well, it would definitely be a walk in the park for some of these guys."

"Okay, so let's pay Mr. Hudson a visit," Stevens added.

They stood up. "Great. Time to get my ears popped again," Matthews said. "Think any of these guys would ever get a ground-floor office?"

Stevens laughed. Rob was really fun to work with and made the job more enjoyable. They worked well together, and if they could nail this perp, it would certainly be a stepping stone to their next promotion to lieutenant.

Chapter
Nine

Detective Stevens called ahead to Michael Hudson's office as they drove downtown. His secretary checked, and said Michael would shuffle his schedule to fit them in. When they arrived at Michael's seventh-floor office, the receptionist greeted them and, after about five minutes, showed them into the counselor's office.

"Detective Stevens," Michael said and shook his hand. Then he reached for Matthews's, saying, "I don't believe we've met."

"I'm Robert Matthews, Stevens's partner. Nice to meet you, sir."

Michael showed them the two chairs opposite his desk. "Please, gentlemen, have a seat. Can I get you anything to drink?"

"No thanks, we're good," Stevens said.

"So what's this about, detective?"

"Well, after exploring other options, it dawned on us that you deal with a lot of tough guys. And it led us to think that one of your past clients could've been...very unhappy if you lost their case. And it doesn't seem unreasonable to think that, if so, they might want to show their malcontent by getting back at you in some way."

"Like beating up your girlfriend," Matthews added.

"But, detectives, if I lost my client's case he'd be in jail. So how does one attack Beth from prison unless…"

"The prisoner hired criminal friends on the outside, which is never a problem. Can you think of anyone angry enough with you that he could've done this to Beth?" Stevens asked.

Michael thought for a moment. "Now that you mentioned it, yes." Michael buzzed his secretary. "Meredith, can you bring me the files on Giachetti and Assanti?"

"Right away."

"Frank Giachetti was found guilty for a chain of bank robberies. I lost the case and the appeal, and he was pretty pissed off at me. But the evidence was stacked against him, and he had no chance of beating this. I did the best I could, but sometimes the best isn't enough. And to make things worse, the money was never recovered, which was around three million."

"Assanti went down for dealing drugs, and the D.A.'s case was pretty solid. They'd been watching him for years, and eventually he was picked up in a sting operation. He got ten years."

"You said they were 'pissed off,' but did they express it to you in any way?" Matthews asked.

Michael nodded. "I do remember receiving some letters from Giachetti threatening me, but nothing came of it."

"Was he just blowing off steam or was he serious?"

"Well, he's particularly mean-spirited—shot a guard in the leg at one holdup because he mouthed off. But I'm used to it."

Meredith entered and handed Michael the two files.

"Thank you, Meredith. Okay, let's see what we've got here. First, though, please call the prison and get the disposition of these two men."

Stevens looked puzzled. "You think they were paroled?"

"No. But bad behavior can limit privileges, like visitation rights."

"Good idea," Stevens said.

Michael went through the first file and handed Stevens a letter Giachetti had written. It was long and rambling, listing his complaints, but ended with: "One day soon, you'll get yours, Mr. Big Shot Lawyer. You'll pay dearly for letting me rot in this hell hole. Your final hours will come."

Stevens handed the letter to his partner, telling Michael, "I can't believe you chose to ignore this."

"As I said, detective, it comes with the territory; I've received letters like this before, and so far nobody's acted on their threats. It's just a way of venting their anger."

"Michael, this guy could be a prime suspect. We need to interrogate him right away."

Michael's buzzer went off. "Michael, Assanti died six months ago of a heart attack. Giachetti is still serving out his sentence, and according to the warden he's a model prisoner," said Meredith.

When Michael returned to perusing Giachetti's file, he came across a notation about the Mob. "Detective, it looks as if ole Frank here had a connection to the Mob," he said to Stevens.

Matthews looked up from the letter. "Would've been easy enough to hire one of those guys to do a job, especially with his stash."

Michael nodded and started to take this visit more seriously. "Jesus, I hope I didn't cause this."

"Counselor, you're not responsible for their actions." He nodded. "But I think Rob and I will pay Mr. Giachetti a visit. Can I get a copy of that letter?"

"Sure, right away. And I'll have Meredith call Sing Sing Correctional Facility and set it up."

"You've been a great help, Michael," Stevens said, as the two detectives made their way to the door.

Michael remained pensive for a moment, then looked up and replied, "Good luck, gentlemen. Let me know how you make out."

While Sing Sing penitentiary was only thirty-five miles north of the city, it took well over an hour to drive there in the afternoon traffic. Detectives Stevens and Matthews were impatient to talk with Giachetti. This was by far the best lead in a case in which nothing else had panned out.

On the way, Stevens called the D.A.'s office to discuss a possible deal if the suspect admitted to his involvement in the crime. He was serving a fifteen-year term, but if he gave up the person whom he hired to beat up Beth, the D.A. would agree to take three years off his sentence, though still no parole. He would also have to reveal where the money was hidden. The detectives were hopeful that he would accept the offer. Of course, that's if he was guilty, but Stevens had the feeling he was their guy.

When they got to the prison, one of the guards led them to Warden Stewart's office. His secretary, who looked like she could have been an ex-con herself, buzzed him.

"Warden, Detectives Stevens and Matthews from the NYPD are here to see you."

"Please show them in, Mable." She worked her way out of the chair, stepped over to the office door, and opened it as if it were a monumental task. She didn't wait to close it, so Matthews did.

"Warden, you got Michael Hudson's call about Frank Giachetti?"

"Yes, and I got him moved to an interrogation room for you, but what's this about?"

"We're investigating a case where a young woman was brutally attacked and left to die. His lawyer was the woman's boyfriend, and Giachetti had written the counselor a threatening letter saying that he would pay one day for him ending up in prison."

"So you think he hired somebody on the outside?" Stevens nodded his head. "Well, he's really been a model prisoner, and we haven't had any problems with him at all. So far his incarceration has been unremarkable. Of course, the tougher the guy the less poaching from others."

"Yeah, we hear he's got Mob connections, which probably helps." The warden nodded in agreement. "Can you provide us with his visitor's list for the past year?"

"Sure, I'll get right on it, and I'll have Oscar, my head guard, take you to 'The Box.'"

Detective Matthews snickered, "I bet yours is tighter than ours."

The Warden responded, "Yeah, our guys are generally a lot tougher."

"Thanks, Warden," Stevens said.

Oscar, despite his wimpy name, was a brick wall of a guy. He was about two hundred and fifty pounds, bald, and mean-looking. Someone you wouldn't want to piss off. He walked them past a series of administrative offices into the prison proper, where "The Box" was one of the first rooms. He unlocked it. "I'll wait out here and keep an eye on our friend."

Stevens asked, "I know he's supposed to be a model prisoner, but what's the scuttlebutt on him?"

Oscar smirked. "Well, when they behave this well, you know they're up to something."

The detectives stepped into the interrogation room, where their prisoner was waiting. The room was about ten by twelve, no windows, and had a rectangular table with four chairs around it. There was a large round lamp with one bulb hanging from the ceiling over the table. Other than the water cooler in the corner of the room, there was nothing else occupying space—it was all very generic and cold. Giachetti was sitting at the table in an orange jumpsuit, shackles on his wrists and ankles. He appeared to be a very muscular six foot four, with dark black hair and a black moustache.

"What the fuck took you guys so long?" he asked.

The detectives sat down. "What, you late for your afternoon manicure?" Matthews spit out.

"Ha ha. Funny guy." He turned to Stevens. "So what's this about?"

"Frank, my name is Detective Stevens, and this is my partner, Detective Matthews."

"So?"

"Well, do you remember your lawyer, Michael Hudson?"

"Of course I remember the fucker. What about him?"

Stevens took several letters from his briefcase and put them on the table. "Do these letters look familiar to you?"

He glanced at them. "Yeah."

"We want to know why you wrote these threatening letters to your attorney."

"Because I was pissed off at the asshole. He totally fucked me over and sold me down the river."

"Mr. Giachetti—or may I call you Frank?"

"Sure, call me whatever the fuck you want."

"Frank, Michael Hudson defended you to the best of his ability, but it was up to the jury, and they found you guilty. So why are you blaming Hudson?"

"Because, as I told you, he fucked up the case."

"Okay, let's move on. Do you know a Beth Scott, who happens to be a friend of Mr. Hudson's?"

"No. Never heard of her," he said. Both detectives watched his facial expression for any giveaways that he was lying.

"I think you've heard of her, Frank. In fact, I think you had her beaten up so bad that she landed up in the hospital and almost died. After all, isn't this exactly what you said in your letter? *'You will pay, Mr. Big Shot Lawyer.'* So you hurt a good friend of Mr. Hudson's really bad. Isn't that what happened, Frank?"

"Are you fuckin' nuts? No, I didn't have anyone beaten up. I just wanted to scare him with the letters and let off some steam. And besides, how can I harm anyone when I'm locked up in this hole?"

"Well, Frank, I'm sure there's lots of people on the outside who owe you favors, especially with you having three mil stashed away."

"I never robbed those banks, and I don't have shit stowed away."

"Yeah, well, you're just full of it, aren't you," Matthews sneered.

Giachetti stared at him, then turned to Stevens. "Now I might pay two bits to get this guy beaten up."

"So, we've established your modus operandi," Matthews added.

Giachetti laughed.

"Come on, Frank," Stevens said interrupting this exchange. "People like you can get anything they want done outside…for a price."

"How am I supposed to know who that asshole hangs out with?"

"Ever hear of a P.I.?"

"So you're sayin' that I hired a P.I., had Hudson followed to see who he was hangin' with, and then decided who I was going to beat the shit out of. Is that right?"

"Yeah, that's exactly what I'm saying. And, I'm also saying that if you cooperate and give us the name of the person you hired, the D.A. is willing to cut some time off your sentence."

Giachetti shook his head. "You want me to confess to a crime I didn't commit, for what?"

"Three years," said Stevens.

"Ha, ha, ha. What a joke! Some fuckin' deal! I don't think so, detective. Did you two smoke a joint before you came here?"

"Also, you need to tell us where you stashed the bank's money."

Giachetti was really laughing now. "Oh, please stop. This is so funny it's hurting me."

Stevens opened his briefcase and slid pictures of Beth's battered face across the table to him. "I don't find this amusing, Frank." He glanced at the pictures and pushed them back at the detective.

"If you're proven guilty of threatening someone's life and attempted murder, then we can add another fifteen years on to your sentence. Let's see, you're about thirty-five now, and you could be out of here by the time you're forty-seven and still have a full life ahead of you. But if you don't cooperate you'll be over sixty when you get out, and that's assuming you've survived this place. So be smart, Frank. Take the deal!"

"Go pound sand up your ass, detective. I ain't taking no deal for somethin' I didn't do."

"Okay, Frank, I'll give you a couple days to think about it, and I'll be back."

"Don't waste your time. I got nothin' else to say."

Detective Stevens then motioned to Oscar to take the prisoner away, and as Frank was shuffling in his shackles toward the door, he turned around to Detective Stevens and said, "Give my best to the counselor."

After the prisoner was taken back, Warden Stewart came into the interrogation room. "Here's the list you wanted, Detective Stevens. I believe it's all there from the last two years. Hope it's helpful."

"Thanks, warden. We appreciate your cooperation. If you could instruct your guards to keep an eye on him and report any suspicious behavior, that would be a great help. We suspect that he'll make another attempt at Beth, or even Michael Hudson this time."

"I'll definitely put him on the 'eyes-on' list for now."

The first half of the drive back to the precinct was quiet. Finally, Matthews spoke up, "He's one tough son of a bitch." Stevens nodded his head. "But we've got to keep pounding him 'cause he's our man. I can feel it in my bones."

"Yeah, the smug bastard did it. I have no doubt about it, but now we've got to prove it."

"Well, we need to go over that visitor's list with a fine-tooth comb," Matthews added.

At the precinct, Stevens called Michael Hudson to fill him in on what had happened at the prison. "Michael, we visited Giachetti at the prison this afternoon, and he's still harboring quite a bit of hostility toward you. I don't trust the bastard as far as I can throw him, and I personally think he did it and that he's not done yet. I just want you to be very cognizant of your surroundings at all times. Always check to see if you're being followed."

"Thanks for the heads-up, detective. But what about Beth?"

"I'll contact her, and since she's already been attacked, I think I can get renewed surveillance."

"That's good. Do you think I need protection until you can make your case?"

"Michael, the department can't provide it, and I hope you understand. But if you want to hire someone I certainly wouldn't discourage it. It's always better to be safe."

"Thanks, and I'll give it some thought, detective."

Stevens hung up the phone and glanced across the desk at Matthews. His partner looked up.

"Hey, Walt, there's a guy on Giachetti's visitor's list who has been back four times in the last four months. This looks promising. I mean, he's never had more than three different visitors in an entire year. The guy's name is Angelo Giovanni. Smells Mob to me. Definitely not Polish."

Stevens looked around the room to make sure nobody had heard his partner and might report racial profiling. "Let's run this guy's profile and see what we come up with."

Stevens stood up from his desk and approached one of the newer office grunts. "Jonathan, I need everything there is to know about an Angelo Giovanni—as fast as the speed of sound."

"Got anything else, like a Social Security number or an address?"

Stevens rolled his eyes. "Hey, Jonathan," Matthews yelled, "he eats anchovies on his pizza. You should be able to follow that trail."

Stevens shook his head. He needed to have a talk with his partner.

Chapter

Ten

*B*eth had been home for almost two weeks and was working a little each day on her divorce cases. She and Lisa met several times to finalize the agreement before Beth sent it to Brian's attorney. The judge had finally set a trial date, but hopefully they would settle the case before it went to court. The last thing Lisa wanted was to drag this contentious divorce into the public eye. Lisa knew that Brian was hiding assets and had much more to bring to the table. However, she didn't want to draw this out by digging any deeper and was more concerned about being awarded their apartment. She couldn't afford to replace it with her share of a sale. Beth was ready to negotiate the agreement and get it signed by Brian.

"Morgan, Brown and Lewis," the receptionist answered.

"May I please speak to Jake Gibson? It's Beth Scott calling."

"Please hold."

"Hello, Beth, how are you?"

"I'm fine, Jake. Look, I'd like to set up a meeting with you and your client to discuss the settlement agreement I sent over.

Now that we have a court date, we need to start negotiations; my client doesn't want this going to trial, and I assume yours is in agreement. Does next Wednesday at two o'clock work for you?"

"I'll call my client and get back to you, but I can tell you he's not entirely happy with this proposal."

"Hence the need for negotiation," Beth said.

Gibson chuckled. "That's what I like about you Beth—right to the point."

"Thanks, Jake. I look forward to hearing from you soon."

As soon as she clicked off, her cell phone rang. The caller ID was blocked.

"Hello," she said tentatively.

"Beth, this is Dr. Burton. How are you doing?"

"Oh, hi," she said, caught off guard. "I'm fine. Just catching up on my caseload." Her heart started to beat rapidly hearing his voice.

"Well, I'd like to stop by and check on your progress. When would be convenient for you?"

"I'm here 24–7, so anytime is fine. I assure you I'm not going back to the office until I get the okay from you."

"Good. That's what I want to hear. So would tomorrow early evening be good for you?"

"Absolutely. Just come over between five and six o'clock—I'll order some takeout."

"Terrific," he said. "Are you still doing your breathing exercises?"

"Diligently, and it's getting better every day."

"Good. I'll see you tomorrow around six, and if anything changes, I'll let you know."

Beth was glad to hear from Dr. Burton; she was still harboring a schoolgirl crush on him that had started in the hospital, one that she thought would probably evaporate over time like the others had. While she was unable to cook and had mentioned takeout, it would be top of the line. This was the least she could do to show her appreciation for everything he had done for her.

The next night, when the doorbell rang, Beth scooted into the bathroom and took a quick peek at herself in the mirror, fluffed her hair, and then went to the door. She looked through the peep-hole, as Detective Stevens had insisted, and opened the door to greet Brandon. He had flowers in one hand, a bottle of wine under his arm, and his medical bag in the other hand. Beth relished the shocked look on Brandon's face. The last time he had seen her she had been battered and bruised, and certainly not pretty.

"For my favorite patient," he said, handing her the flowers and wine. "Wow, you look terrific!"

As he stepped past her into the apartment, he took a closer look at her face. "You've healed wonderfully, and . . ." He hesitated before adding, "You are really beautiful, Beth!"

Beth blushed slightly as she closed the door and followed Brandon into the apartment. She had curled her hair and applied soft makeup to her face, with a little blush to give her some color so the pallor wouldn't sneak through.

"Thanks so much. It's very thoughtful of you. I love red roses and white wine," she said, as she smelled the roses. "Lovely. They smell delicious." She took out a vase from the kitchen cabinet, filled it halfway with water, placed the roses in it, and set it on the dining room table.

"Dinner's warming up. I hope you like surf and turf. Figured you'd be hungry after a long day."

"Well, you thought right," Brandon said. "What a nice surprise. I'm starved, but had figured on Chinese or something. First I want to examine your chest and listen to your heart."

"You say the nicest things, doctor," Beth said with a smile. It was now Brandon's turn to blush.

"Okay," he replied self-consciously. He took her arm and escorted her over to the sofa. He removed a stethoscope from his bag while Beth unbuttoned her blouse. As Brandon was examining her, she could not help but observe how attractive he looked in his brown slacks and yellow button-down shirt underneath his camel-colored Polo sweater. She could smell a hint of a cologne but couldn't identify the scent. This was the first time she had seen him out of scrubs and in regular clothes. She was glad she had put on makeup, given that he was so close to her during the examination.

After they enjoyed a nice dinner together and a few glasses of wine, the conversation flowed much easier. Brandon wasn't on call, and was able to drink. Afterward, they cleaned up the kitchen together, corked the wine bottle and put it in the refrigerator, and moved back to the couch in the living room.

"So tell me, Brandon, I'm curious. Why did you choose to become a surgeon? It's such a stressful profession, with so many life-and-death calls every day. Do you like all the drama that comes with the job?"

"Well, I don't know about the drama, but my dad's a surgeon in Boston, and ever since I was a little boy I've heard him talking about both the challenges and rewards of heart surgery, of all the lives he's saved, and I just got hooked on surgery as a profession."

Beth listened and suddenly realized, "Is Dr. Mark Burton your dad?"

"Yes," said Brandon with a coy smile.

"I've heard of him. I've seen him on TV and perused his books at the bookstore. He's quite world renowned."

"Yeah, I'm very proud to be his son and carry on the tradition."

"So, you're from Boston, right?"

"Yes. I went to Harvard undergrad before going to Columbia for med school. I wanted to go out of town to establish my own identity and have a chance to make my own way without treading behind on my dad's coattails. New York has its own elite circle, and that did it for me."

"That's why I came here after Yale," Beth added.

"My mom is also a physician," Brandon said. She specializes in pediatrics. My parents met in med school at Washington University in St. Louis, and decided to do their respective residencies in Boston. I'm an only child, which was a good thing. My parents hardly had enough time to raise me with their busy work schedules. So I had a nanny who prepared my lunches and took me to grade school, but at the time I didn't mind. This was normal in our social class. I would see my parents in the evening for dinner, and when they couldn't make it they'd get home just in time to say good night. I got used to it and never expected anything more."

"It sounds to me like you missed your parents a lot while you were growing up."

"Yes, I did, but I knew they loved me even though they weren't always there. As I got older, I understood the scope of their demanding careers, and I had the utmost respect for both of them. But it was lonely, and I missed out on a lot of nurturing that most kids get, which I didn't realize until I was an adult. I had to be self-sufficient at a very early age. And I guess that explains why relationships have always been difficult for me; I didn't have the best role models. In fact, I can't even say that my parents have a happy marriage—they're both married to their careers even before each other."

Beth was very impressed by Brandon's willingness to be truthful and forthcoming about his parents and his upbringing, but it was easy for her to see that he still had issues with them. This would've concerned her if they were anything more than friends, which was probably why he could talk to her effortlessly—there were no expectations, just a free and candid exchange of histories and ideas. She enjoyed his company and was happy she could be a sounding board for him. Sometimes it's much easier to open up to friends than lovers. It was obvious to her that he felt comfortable talking about his personal life, and she was certainly eager to listen.

"So now tell me a little about you. I think I've said enough about me for one evening."

"Well, I think you learned a lot about me from my parents. You know that I'm a divorce attorney, I live alone, and I got attacked. That's about it! Oh, and I'm in a holding pattern in my relationship with Michael Hudson, whom I believe you've met."

Brandon laughed. "Your life can't be summed up in two brief sentences. There has to be much more to the beautiful Beth. Tell me how you ended up in New York; your parents told me you're from Baltimore. And how do you like to spend your free time?"

"Okay, you win," Beth said, putting her hands up. "I went to Yale for college and law school. I've always had this tremendous drive to succeed in whatever I did and was a real workhorse. I wasn't that social, and missed out on many college activities in order to study. I graduated cum laude in my law school class, which gave me an edge in procuring offers from top firms in New York, and that's how I ended up here. I always wanted to live in the big city since I love the excitement and the energy that I get from city life. It offers everything and lacks nothing." She paused. "Well, except being unsafe, I guess, but life's a risk anywhere you go. And there's no other city like it in the world, in my opinion."

Brandon smiled and said, "I agree; there's certainly nothing lacking in this city, which brings me to my next question. What do you like to do in your free time?"

"I love to go to theater, ballet, and museums, and take long walks in Central Park, where there's always something going on, like a concert or art exhibit. And what about you when you're off? How do you like to spend your time?"

"Actually, I love to take walks in the park as well. I enjoy being outside as much as I can, since I'm inside under fluorescent lighting most of the time. After being in the hospital for seventy-two-hour stretches, I crave being out in fresh air." Beth nodded in agreement. "You know, I'll need to recheck you next week, and I could meet you in the park instead of your apartment. It would be nice for both of us to get some fresh air while I pull out my stethoscope and listen. Sound good?"

"Well, I hope you don't expect me to open my blouse," Beth said with a smirk.

"No, your wounds are healing nicely. In fact, fresh air is what the doctor orders for healing wounds."

"Well, if it's doctor's orders."

It was almost ten o'clock when Brandon stood up, followed by Beth. "It's getting late, and I think I need to be going. Thanks so much for dinner and the good conversation. I really enjoyed the evening, Beth. You're doing great, and I think you're well on your way to a complete recovery. I'll call you next week to schedule our 'checkup in the park.' But if you have any problems before then, please let me know. Get as much rest as you can, and continue with your breathing treatments. Then we'll talk about you going back to work."

"I'm glad you were able to stay for dinner. I loved getting to know you better. Thanks again for the flowers and wine."

Beth showed Brandon to the door and gave him a smile as he stepped over to the elevator. She closed the door, double-locked it, and started to get ready for bed. Having a man in the apartment naturally triggered her recall of the night of the attack, but she couldn't remember a single detail. After she changed into her pajamas and slipped into bed, she stared all around her bedroom, with light spilling in from a streetlamp, as she lay in bed waiting to fall asleep. Still no recall of anything! *Maybe tomorrow will trigger something new*, she told herself before drifting off to sleep.

The next morning, Beth was in the kitchen getting her first cup of coffee when Detective Stevens called.

"Good morning, Beth. How are you today? Hope I didn't wake you."

"No, I've been up. What is it, detective?"

"First, I'd like to ask if you've remembered anything since you've been home."

"I would've called you if I did. So no, sorry, I haven't."

"Just checking, Beth, but I'd like to ask you some questions about your friend Victoria David, the woman who found you that night."

"Sure, what would you like to know?"

Diane Lynn

"Well, how long have you known Victoria? And tell me how you two met."

"I've known her for about three years. We met through a mutual friend at the firm. She's an investment banker, single, and works long hours like I do, so we have a lot in common. We became good friends, and we see each other about once every two or three weeks when our schedules permit."

"How well would you say you know her, and do you feel like you can trust her?"

"Well, I'd say that we're good friends, and, yes, I feel like I can trust her. But I don't know much about her background, and she's never confided in me about things going on in her life. I'd say it's more of a social friendship. Why are you asking? You don't think she had anything to do with this, do you?"

"I just need to consider every option here, and make sure all bases are covered. I never take anything for granted, and every person who's come in contact with you must be thoroughly investigated. That's all I'm saying. Can you tell me if she dates a lot, or has a boyfriend now?"

"No, there's no one in her life. She doesn't date a lot and hasn't been in a serious relationship since I've known her. She has a weight problem and is self-conscious about it, which might be a factor."

"Isn't investment banking pretty much male-dominated?"

"I'd say seventy percent men. But there are a lot more women in business and in new start-ups opening the doors for women in this field. Why do you ask?"

"Hear me out," Stevens said. "Has she ever made comments to you about how pretty you are, or showed you any signs of jealousy?"

"Oh, I see where you're going with this, and you're way off base, detective. Victoria! No way, sorry. No way!"

"Now, Beth, just remember, I'm only exploring possibilities and just trying to get a beat on anyone who could have a motive or reason, even unconscious, to cause you harm or let it happen. She's not a suspect, only a person of interest at this point."

"Well, she's said to me many times that I'm the luckiest girl in the world, and I have everything that any girl could want. She would tell me that I was beautiful, successful, never had a weight problem, and could have any man I wanted. But I took it as a compliment, and thought she was happy for me. It never crossed my mind that she was envious of me or ever wanted any harm to come to me. She's my *friend*, detective."

"Well, Beth, this is what we're trying to figure out. Some women can be very malicious and do pretty cruel things out of subconscious resentment. That's why we always look to the victim's friends first. Most victims know their assailants. I, personally, don't think Victoria was involved, but I still have to clear her as a person of interest before I move on. That's all."

"I understand, detective. You're just doing your job."

"Beth, I also want to inform you that we did interrogate one of Michael Hudson's ex-clients who's serving time for a string of bank robberies. He's got ties to the Mafia and was openly angry with Michael for losing the case and the appeal. Subsequently, while in prison, he wrote Michael some threatening letters stating that he was going to make him pay for his incarceration."

"Oh my, that doesn't sound good."

No, it doesn't, and he's probably our number-one suspect. Now we've suggested that Michael hire protection until we can investigate further. After interviewing this guy, we also decided to extend your surveillance."

"You think he did it?" Beth asked.

"Well, we feel pretty sure that he was involved in some way, like possibly hiring someone on the outside to carry out the attack. They might've even tapped your cell or home phone, and I'll be sending one of our guys over to check on that tomorrow. So you see, this is the reason for the questions about Victoria. How did he find out that she was coming over that night at seven thirty, and slip in to attack you just before she arrived? We've always been suspicious that you were attacked so close to her arrival. It would all make sense if your phone was tapped and the perp knew the time Victoria was coming over. Or if Victoria was their informant."

"So you're saying that this person set up Victoria?" Beth asked with a catch in her voice.

"Yes, that's one possibility." Steven paused, then added, "Or she told him for a price."

"No way, detective. Never happened."

"Don't want to upset you, Beth, but again, we have to check out all possibilities."

Beth was silent for a moment, thinking this over. "Detective, are you trying to tell me that I'm still in imminent danger?"

"I don't know, Beth. If this guy in prison hired somebody, and they know we're going after them, he might try again, sooner than later."

"Should I hire someone, detective?"

"No, I don't think that's necessary. We're going to be more hands-on this time, put someone on the ground outside your apartment and another detail following you to and from work."

Beth sighed. "That's a relief."

"I'll call you tomorrow and let you know what time one of my men will be over to check your phones."

"So, will the department continue with the surveillance till you arrest him?"

"I'm hoping as much, but I'll inform you if that changes, so you can line up your own people."

"Okay. Thanks, detective. I was just starting to feel relaxed in my own home again, and now I have to watch every move I make. This is a *nightmare*. When will it end?"

"I hope soon, Beth. We're tracking down all the guy's known associates. So it's just a matter of time."

"Thanks, detective. I'll talk to you tomorrow."

"Good-bye, Beth. Keep your chin up. We've got 'em in our sights."

After she clicked off her phone, Beth took a minute to think about the conversation. She had been looking forward to getting out and returning to a normal life. But everything had just drastically changed. She'd have to be constantly looking over her shoulder wherever she went now. This was no way to live. She had to do something, force herself to remember something—*anything*—that could help the police catch this animal. She decided that tonight, around the time the attack occurred, she would bring herself back to that night and hopefully her memory wouldn't fail her.

Chapter Eleven

*M*ichael had been sitting at his desk just staring into space. He had had a restless night, and so he'd come in early but couldn't focus on his work. His mind was on Beth. He picked up the phone and called her.

"Good morning, Beth. Sleep well?"

"Oh, Michael, I'm so glad you called. I remembered something last night, and I was just going to call Detective Stevens."

"Well, that's good news. I hope the memory wasn't too painful." He paused. "Do you want to talk about it?"

"Okay. In the hospital, I had a flashback that it was big guy who attacked me, but then my mind went blank. Last night I saw him more clearly. He was stocky and wearing a black hoodie. When I stepped into the living room and saw him, I tried to run, but he grabbed my arm and pulled me around. I was so scared; I just knew he was going to rape and kill me. I tried to scream, but he put his hand over my mouth, and then everything went blank." Beth paused to catch her breath. "Michael, it felt like I was reliving it all over again. The whole thing is just freaking me out. I was doing so well, and now I'm scared out of my mind."

"Beth, what you're experiencing is perfectly normal, and you have every right to be scared about what happened, but remember now you have protection, day and night, until he's caught. The detective said it's a two-man team—one guarding your apartment and the other following you wherever you go. So please don't be frightened. They're optimistic that they'll catch this guy sooner than later."

"Michael, Detective Stevens said it might be one of your ex-clients, someone who sent you threatening letters. Why didn't you tell someone in your firm or call the police? You never even mentioned a word to me."

"I get threats all the time and have never taken them seriously. I figured the guy was just venting his anger and he'd eventually cool off. But I was wrong about this one; and if this guy hired someone to beat you up, then I blame myself for all of it. Beth, I'm so sorry! I don't know what else to say. Because I was foolish, your safety was compromised. I'll never forgive myself, and I hope that you'll be able to forgive me. Again, I'm sorry for just sloughing it off."

"Michael, it's not your fault. These are the types of clients that you defend. This is your job."

"Well, this has made me think long and hard about being a little more selective about whom I represent."

"Are you going to get surveillance as well, Michael? After all, you're in danger too."

"The police won't be providing it, but I've given it some thought, and I'll probably hire someone."

"Michael, I'm worried about you."

"Okay, that settles it. I'll hire someone. I don't want you to worry."

Beth took a deep breath. "You know, sometimes I end up with clients' spouses who get just as pissed off as your clients, and for a while the police thought the culprit might've been Brian Paul. So this cuts both ways."

"I know. I think lawyers are becoming an endangered species." Beth chuckled. "Well, I'm glad I can still make you laugh."

"You always do it for me in every way, Michael."

"So how about I come over tonight, keep you company."

"That would be great. I figured tonight would be difficult for me, but not now."

"Text me when you're ready, and I'll pick up something for dinner."

"You're a sweetheart. But please hire someone for yourself until this is over."

"I'll make the call as soon as we hang up. Thanks for pushing me on this, Beth."

That night Michael was especially cognizant of the people around him as he walked to Beth's apartment, even looking over his shoulder once or twice to see if he was being followed. The bodyguard he hired wouldn't be starting until the morning. He had never been fearful of anything, but Giachetti was one tough bastard, and if he had hired someone it did give Michael pause. He was one tough bastard, and he wouldn't put this past him. Michael picked up sushi on the way, and as he approached Beth's building he saw a man standing out front and assumed he was a cop.

"I'm Michael Hudson, and I'm going up to see Beth Scott," he said and shook hands with the guy.

"Michael, may I see some ID? Nothing personal. I'm sure you understand."

"No problem, officer." Michael reached for his wallet and flipped it open to his driver's license.

"Okay, you're fine. I have you on my visitor's list, so now that we've met I won't have to stop you again."

"No problem. And your name?"

"Charlie Larson."

"Thanks, Charlie. Keep up the good work."

Michael took the elevator to Beth's apartment and knocked.

"Who is it?" she asked, checking the peephole.

"It's me, babe." The door opened. "Got some good sushi for ya. Hungry?"

"You bet. I'm always ready for sushi." She gave Michael a big hug, then took the bag and set it on the kitchen table.

"I have to tell you that your guy downstairs is top notch. He asked me for ID. He's even got a list of names to check off. You can relax; you're in good hands."

"Really? That's a relief." She gazed into his eyes. "You're always looking out for me, aren't you?"

"Well, it's certainly easy on the eyes, my dear."

Beth smiled.

They ate the sushi, and, as always, Beth had to show Michael how to properly hold his chopsticks. "See, put your index finger on top of the stick."

He could do better, but he liked the instruction, her hands touching his. After dinner, while cleaning the dessert plates, Michael couldn't resist giving her a peck on the cheek. She turned her head to meet his lips and kissed him passionately. She needed Michael close to her tonight, his arms wrapped around her and feeling him inside her. While this desire for intimacy was driven by fear, she also seemed to be falling in love with him again.

For his part, Michael was taken aback by Beth's aggression and figured she was turning to him for security and comfort. He had been hesitant about being too forward since he didn't know how she was feeling toward him and he did not want to compromise her strength. Still, he instinctively took her into his arms and kissed her with unbridled passion. He remembered how he loved to kiss her and feel her soft curvaceous body beneath him. Now they both were getting aroused. "Are you sure you're up to this?" he asked in a whisper.

Beth said, her warm breath caressing his face, "I want you, Michael, now more than ever."

Michael continued kissing her while lifting her onto the kitchen counter. It had been so long since they had made love, and he wanted to take it slow, but their mutual arousal was building, and he knew neither could wait. Michael slid his hand underneath her dress, his fingers finding her thong and then her wet folds, all the while kissing her ear and whispering, "You're the most beautiful and sexy woman alive." He buried his face inside the opening in her blouse, moving toward her breasts, while Beth unhooked her bra and exposed her swollen nipples to his lips. His fingers now slid her thong down her legs to her ankles, while her fingers undid his pants and released his erection. Michael was kissing her breasts, her neck, and then his tongue explored her mouth, while his hands, enjoying her soft and smooth skin, traveled around her back and down her sleek body.

"Michael, I never realized how much I missed your touch. I had almost forgotten the incredible feeling it is to desire you. It's been so long. I want you, so much."

"Babe, I've never wanted anybody like I want you right now."

"Then take me," she whispered in his ear, her panting breath driving him mad.

Michael gently entered her and pulsated inside her, moving his hips back and forth, while holding her small rounded buttocks in his firm hands. Only a few seconds passed before he reached a pinnacle and was left breathless. Beth jerked her head back as her body became rigid. Then her breathing became heavier and her sighs deeper, her orgasm imminent. There was a brief pause, and then the gates broke and they exploded into each other, their bodies shaking with wave after wave of released pleasure. It felt as if they'd never missed a beat, and while it had only been three months, the psychological time was much longer. But now both timelines had come together in this moment.

"Michael, I'm glad you're here. You can't imagine how much I needed you, wanted you. With all that's going on, I feel like you anchor me, that I'm whole when I'm with you."

"Beth, I want to protect you as best as I can. I'll be with you as much as you need me now. Please lean on me, and we'll see this through together."

Michael lifted Beth off the counter and set her down. As they made their way to the bedroom, she said, "Michael, I know I'll sleep better tonight with you beside me."

"Me too, Beth." Michael took her hand as they stepped into the bedroom.

Later that night, with the moonlight shining through the window and creating the perfect romantic setting, Michael and Beth made love once again. They couldn't get enough of each other, and both felt that the lapse of time and the trauma that had ensued had only brought them closer together.

They slept deeply, and in the early morning hours Michael went back to his apartment to shower and dress for work. The dawn's light crept into the room as Beth awoke, turning onto her side to where Michael had slept. She felt his absence but knew he was somehow still there. She then spotted a note on her bedside table.

Beth, thank you for a wonderful evening, and an even more wonderful night. I miss you already. I'll call you later this afternoon. I adore you. You were amazing last night! Have a wonderful day.

Love,
Michael

Beth held the note close to her heart and placed her other hand on his pillow. She knew their relationship was picking up just where they had left it more than three months ago.

Beth was looking forward to today, for Brandon was coming over to give her a final checkup and hopefully tell her she could return to work on a part-time basis. She rolled out of bed, had toast with her coffee, checked her email, showered, and dressed. She was hoping Brandon would come early enough for her to spend a few hours at the office that afternoon.

The phone rang, and it was Brandon. He told her he'd be there around four o'clock and they would take a walk in the park together, as previously planned. The fresh air would do them both a world of good.

So it would be a home-office day, but at least she could run some errands in the morning. She greeted Charlie, the police officer, at the front door of the building, and they walked together for about thirty minutes. Then she stopped at the little corner market and picked up a few items before returning home.

When they arrived, there was another officer out front. "Beth, this is Aaron Collard. We switch off, someone's always here to watch the building while one of us watches you," said Charlie.

Beth shook Aaron's hand. He was younger than Charlie, but well-built and appeared capable.

"Guys, I'm going out again this afternoon around four with my doctor. I assume one of you will be going with me?"

"That'll be me, ma'am," Aaron said.

"Thanks so much, guys. I'm grateful for your protection."

Charlie took her up in the elevator. Beth opened the door to her apartment, and he stepped inside first to made sure it was safe for her to enter. After he left, Beth double-locked the door. She almost felt like a prisoner in her own home, but this was to be her life until the police made an arrest. Every time the phone rang, Beth prayed it would be Detective Stevens calling to tell her they had apprehended the man who had attacked her.

She went to her desk and started to work on her caseload. The top file in the stack was Lisa's divorce. Beth was looking forward to meeting with Brian's attorney next week, and hopefully they would iron out any disputes about the proposed settlement and finally put this case to bed. But she had not yet received confirmation about the time and date of the meeting.

She wanted her best friend to get the apartment, which is what Lisa really wanted, letting Brian have whatever else he claimed. After two hours, Beth began to tire, so she had a little lunch and took a nap. By the time she woke up, she was rested and refreshed for Brandon's visit and hoped he'd clear her to return to work.

When Brandon approached Beth's building that afternoon, he was greeted out front by a plainclothes police officer, who inquired, "May I ask who you're visiting?"

"Beth Scott. I'm her doctor." The officer checked his visitor's list.

"May I please see some ID?"

"Sure, no problem." Brandon showed him his hospital ID.

"Thanks, doc. I'm sure you know that Miss Scott has twenty-four-hour surveillance."

"No, I didn't, but I can understand."

"There'll be another officer following you and Miss Scott to the park."

"Oh, that's great. Is it okay if I go up now?"

"Go on up. You've been cleared from this point forward."

Brandon knocked on the door and waited a moment until Beth checked the peephole.

She opened the door. "Hi, Brandon. Thanks for coming."

"I was just put through the whole identification process with your surveillance before I could see you. What's up?"

"Let's take our walk, and I'll fill you in."

"Are you ready?" Brandon asked. Beth nodded, saying, "All set."

"By the way, you look terrific. I can see that you are rested and perky."

"I feel great, Brandon, and I'm eager to get back to work. This will be my second walk of the day. It's a beautiful afternoon for it."

"Shall we?" Brandon said and opened the door for Beth.

As they walked to the park, with Collard following fifty yards to the rear, Beth updated Brandon on her case—how Detective Stevens had felt he'd identified the man in prison who had hired someone to beat her up and that he may still be after both her and Michael. This was the reason for the surveillance.

"Well, I'm glad they're making progress, but it's alarming that someone might still try to hurt you again."

Beth squeezed the doctor's arm. "I've got twenty-four–seven coverage, outside and inside." Beth mentioned this so Brandon would know about her renewed relationship with Michael.

"What do you mean by inside?"

"Well, Michael and I have renewed our relationship, and he's staying with me at night."

Brandon nodded and said, "Oh, that's great, Beth. I'm happy for you. And I feel much better that you're not alone."

"I do, too."

It was a beautiful summer day in Central Park, with rolling green hills and the trees stretching their full branches across the park lawn. They walked over to the gazebo and took a seat on one of the benches. There was a warm breeze coming off the lake, and the sun was shining brightly, without a cloud in the sky. They watched the ducks move quickly from one end of the lake to the other as if carried by the breeze. They sat in silence for a few minutes, enjoying the picturesque view from the gazebo.

"Beth, I'll check you physically in a minute, but emotionally are you ready to return to work with all its stress?"

"Most definitely. I like to meet things head on, and I'm not going to let this threat slow me down. Besides, my clients have been so patient, and I do need to get them squared away."

Brandon nodded. He liked her gumption. "Okay, may I listen to your chest and heart?" he asked, taking the stethoscope from his bag.

"Certainly."

Brandon moved the chest piece to different areas of Beth's chest, heart, and back, asking her to breathe in and out at times. Then he took her pulse. "Well, Beth, everything sounds great— regular heartbeat, deep breathing, regular pulse. I think you're doing fine, and I'll give you an 'all-clear.'" She beamed. "Are you having any problems at all?"

"No, nothing. I just tire easily, and I know I can't go back for an eight-hour day. I know my limitations, honestly."

"So, why don't you start back half days and gradually progress as you acquire more stamina. Make sense?"

"Absolutely." Beth felt relieved that she could go back to the office. "Brandon, I can assure you that I've come too far to be foolish. I will not overexert myself."

"I know, Beth, but remember half days means just that. You come home and rest, not continue working."

Beth smiled and squinched her face. "Yes, doctor."

"I think we should be getting back now. I don't want to tire you out—you have a big day tomorrow."

Brandon walked Beth back to her apartment, and felt a bit of a letdown. He was hoping their friendship would develop into something deeper. But with Michael back in her life, he'd have to settle for her friendship. He had never had a friend like Beth, with whom he felt comfortable talking about anything. He could never open up to anyone as he had to Beth. Brandon knew he had something special with her, and he was prepared to settle for whatever was available to him. Being Beth's friend enriched his life, and he was grateful that he could at least be a part of it.

Chapter

Twelve

*A*ngelo Giovanni, who had visited Frank Giachetti in prison four times in the last four months, worked on the construction of Brooklyn's Atlantic Yards B2 Residential Tower. As Stevens and Matthews were approaching the construction site, they could hardly believe the massive structure being erected there. There had to be thousands of workers on the job, along with cranes and other massive machinery, to build one of the world's tallest modular towers.

"Wow," Matthews, said. "I bet we'll find half of the wops in Brooklyn here on this site."

"Dammit, Rob, watch your mouth. This is not the place, if there is any, for inappropriate ethnic remarks. Understand? They've got every nationality in New York working here. The NYPD doesn't need that kind of press."

"I get it, Walt. Do you think I'd talk like this in front of them? I'm not that stupid."

"Well, you made a comment in front of some of the boys yesterday, and all you need is one to get his back up and you're squaring off with the captain, whose wife's Italian. You get my drift?"

"Yeah, I hear whatcha saying. Not to worry."

Angelo Giovanni was the first name on the list of people they planned to interrogate. He was a crane operator on the project, and, hopefully, he was on the job today. They found the job-site office and knocked on the door of a large trailer with a company logo displayed on its side. A tall man, large in stature, wearing a construction hard hat, boots, and an orange lime-striped safety vest, answered the door.

"What can I do for you, gentlemen?"

The detectives flashed their badges. "We're Detectives Stevens and Matthews of the NYPD. Can we speak with you for a minute?"

"Sure, come right in. I'm Dirk Higgins, the construction supervisor." They stepped inside the double-wide trailer and briefly looked around; it was more like a modern office than the work shed they expected to find.

"Nice place," Stevens added.

"Yeah, home away from home. Lots of meetings with architects, subcontractors, and knuckleheads," he said with a smirk, "which is probably who you're looking for."

"Could be," Stevens said. "Does Angelo Giovanni work here?"

"Yeah, he works the heavy cranes. Hope he's not in trouble."

"Just need to ask him a few questions," Stevens said.

"Okay," Higgins picked up his cell phone, glanced at a chart on the wall, and punched in a number. "Angelo, need to see you ASAP. You up or down?" He listened for a moment. "Okay. Five minutes."

Higgins turned to the detectives. "Guess you're going to need some privacy." Stevens nodded his head. The supervisor waved a woman over. "Betty, put our guys here in office 2 and take Giovanni back when he arrives."

"Thanks, Dirk," said Stevens.

"I've got to check on something. Be back in ten," Higgins replied.

Stevens and Matthews were sitting at a table when Betty showed Giovanni inside. The man wore a hard hat, gloves, and a safety vest. He was about six feet tall, had long black hair tied back in a ponytail, olive skin, and was very large and muscular. The detectives exchanged wary looks; he was big enough to be Beth's attacker.

"Hi, Angelo. I'm Detective Stevens, and this is my partner, Detective Matthews. Have a seat."

Angelo sat down and took off his gloves. "Detectives? Did I do something wrong?"

"That's what we're here to find out, Angelo," Stevens said. "Do you know a Frank Giachetti?"

"Yeah, we worked together on a construction job couple years ago . . . before the guy got sent up for bank robbery. Why do you ask?"

"We have your name down as visiting Frank four times in the last four months. Would you like to tell us the nature of those visits? For some reason, we don't think it was talking about ole times."

"It was a personal matter, and I can't talk about it."

"Well, this is an attempted-murder investigation, and if you don't want to land up in the cell next to your friend, then I suggest that you tell us what you know. Giachetti hired somebody to do some dirty work for him, and we think it's you," Matthews added.

"No, I didn't do any 'dirty work' for anybody," he said as he moved to the other side of the chair. "You see the size of this site out there? I've got my hands full just keeping up with my job."

"Have you been short of money lately, Angelo?" Stevens asked. "Tell us a little bit about your financial situation. Or do you want us to do some digging ourselves. We have the resources to find out where you spent your last dollar, what places you frequent, where you shop, and how much money you have in the bank. Even your gambling chits."

This last remark seemed to hit a raw nerve. "I've got nothing to say."

Matthews's temper flared as he moved closer to Angelo's face. "Well, Angelo, I have plenty to say about a woman who was attacked, beaten up badly, and left to die by a big guy about your size."

"I don't know what the fuck you're talking about," Angelo spit out, sweat forming on his forehead, his eyes darting back and forth.

"Does this woman look familiar to you?" Matthews asked as he showed Angelo a picture of Beth all battered and bruised.

"No way. I had no part of that!"

"You want to tell us why you went to see Frank, or do you want us to put you in a lineup?"

"Okay, okay, I went to see him to ask for a loan. I knew they never found the money from the bank robberies, and with him being in prison I figured he won't need it for another ten years, and I'd have plenty of time to pay it all back."

"What did you need the money for?"

"I'd rather not say. You know, bills to pay. Shit like that."

"Come on, Angelo, you expect us to believe this bullshit? Crane operators get paid well. I mean, who'd go to a convicted felon to borrow money to pay bills? What did you need the money for?" Stevens said with an edge to his voice, losing patience with the man.

"Why does it matter what I needed the money for?"

"We'll be the judge of that, not you!"

"Well, I won't squeal on anybody, and I won't use names. I had to pay back a gambling debt."

"Or you would've had a few limbs broken?" Matthews asked.

"Something like that, yeah."

"We don't care about the gambling ring you're a part of. That's not why we're here, and you don't have to tell us anything about it. We want to know what happened when you went to ask Frank for the money."

"Nothing happened. What do you mean?"

"Well, we know these kinds of guys don't dole out money out of the kindness of their hearts. So what did he ask you to do for him in return?" Stevens picked up the photo, putting it in front of Anthony's face and said, "Did he ask you to do this?"

"No, no! He just wanted me to deliver some messages, that's all."

"What kinds of messages: couple whacks to the head, a knife to the chest?" Matthews asked. "You'd be the perfect guy to put a woman in the hospital for him."

"Hell, no, that's not my style. I don't do shit like that, detective."

"Okay, then what *did* you do for him?"

"I delivered sealed envelopes to a postal box and took others back to him. Like a mailman. That's it! I didn't hurt nobody. You've got the wrong guy."

"Okay, Angelo, I'll try and strike a deal for you with the D.A. if you tell us what was in those envelopes."

"You're wasting your time. I have no idea what was in those envelopes, or who they were meant for. I never saw the person who picked them up from the box."

"Okay, if you want to play it that way I think you'd better come down to the station with us to discuss this matter further," Stevens said.

"Are you arresting me, detective?"

"No, I'm not placing you under arrest, but you do need to come with us." The detectives and Giovanni stood up and walked out of the office to find Dirk taking a cigarette break in the front.

"Dirk, we'll be taking Angelo down to the precinct. We need his assistance on this case we're working on."

"No problem, go right ahead. Angelo, I've got you covered here. Don't worry."

"Thanks, Dirk. I'll be back before the end of the day."

"Let's go, Angelo," Detective Matthews said, grabbing his arm to lead him out of the trailer.

It rained the entire way back to the station, and Giovanni remained silent. They took him into the interrogation room and offered him a cup of coffee or glass of water. He declined both.

Detective Stevens walked around the room with his arms crossed and his thumb holding up his flat chin, appearing to be deep in thought.

"So let's see now. Angelo, you're saying that you visited a convict for four months just to deliver messages from him to someone you never met—someone whose number you didn't have in case you were late or something?" Giovanni nodded. "You're insulting my intelligence, buddy, if you expect me to believe this story. I ask you again: What was the nature of your visits to this man over a four-month span?"

"I did what I was told, that's all. He said he'd give me five hundred dollars for each delivery to the postal box and five for the delivery back to him. I agreed, since I wasn't doing nothin' wrong, just being a delivery man. He said no harm would come to me, and I really needed the money to pay off my gambling debt. I had no idea what was in the envelopes, and I didn't ask. I was told the date and time that I had to be at that postal box to deposit the letters, and the box was open every time I arrived. I guess the guy who was picking up the letters was somewhere nearby, but I never saw him. I never waited around, and was told to leave the area as soon as I put the letters in the box. In total, I made six deliveries and collected three thousand dollars from Giachetti, which was also left for me in the postal box. I guess the guy picking up the letters had the key, hid outside when I arrived, and then locked the box back up after I took off. That's the whole truth, detective, and all I know. I swear."

"If we put you in the witness protection program, and you help us put this man away, then you'll be free and not have to fear for your life."

Angelo responded, "How can I help you when I don't even know who the man is, and never saw him? I couldn't identify him if my life depended on it. I never spoke with him or met him. And he knows that I couldn't ID him, so why would he come after me? Thanks for the offer, detective, but definitely not necessary. I don't want to live the rest of my life hiding from a guy I could never identify." He paused and then asked, "Do I need a lawyer?"

"I don't know yet. Maybe, because you were an accessory to a crime," Stevens told him.

"Where did he phone you when he wanted to make contact?" Matthews asked.

"He'd call me at home, and "private" would come up on the caller ID, so I could never call him back. He would leave a message with the date and time each delivery was to take place, and I would do exactly what he asked. Every delivery I made to Frank in prison was basically a drop-off. There was no conversation because it would've been recorded."

"Do you know, Angelo, that if you're withholding information in an attempted-murder investigation you can be prosecuted? Am I clear?"

"Yes, sir, I'm clear on that. I've told you everything I know. All I did was deliver messages from a guy in prison to a postal box and back. You can't arrest me for that."

"Angelo, you were helping a convicted felon, with a history of violence, and a jury would be hard-pressed to believe that you didn't know this was for criminal activity, even if you didn't know the specifics."

"Detective, you can check with the prison guards. They intercepted every letter before giving them to Giachetti."

"How can you prove that those letters weren't opened and resealed so you could read them."

"Go check with the guards—they're the ones who review every letter before it goes to the prisoners and those he passes to a visitor. They'll tell you if they were opened before they got into their hands."

"We'll do just that. You can go now, but stay in town for further questioning. You're not off the hook yet, Angelo, you hear?"

"Yes, sir, I ain't going anywhere. Good-bye, detectives. Thanks for a thrilling afternoon. Later."

After Giovanni left the station, Detective Stevens called the warden to request copies of any letters Frank Giachetti had written that were picked up by his runner, Angelo, to be delivered to some mystery man who could have attacked Beth. The warden told him that he'd check the man's prison file, see what he could come up with, and call him back later that day.

All letters written by the prisoners were read before being mailed out, and all letters received by the prison for the inmates were checked before being released to them. The warden called Stevens back and told him that he had Giachetti's letters from the past four months and that he would fax them over to his office, but he warned the detective that while they appear normal, they were suspicious. Thinking back, he didn't remember signing off on these letters before they were placed in Giachetti's file. So whoever gave the okay to the guard to give them to the prisoner, it wasn't him. But they had still followed protocol and had photocopied each letter that had apparently bypassed his approval and had put them directly into the prisoner's file, the originals going to Giachetti. Now the warden would have to do some digging and discover who the prisoner had bribed to both receive and send these letters without his knowledge.

The detective thanked him for faxing over the letters. "I'll take a look at them, see what we're dealing with here, then get back to you."

"Okay, detective. I appreciate it. And if you find there's some code being used, I'd like to be informed about this inmate and his 'outside' activities so I can act accordingly. And I'll let you know who the mole is after I do some investigating."

Detective Stevens hung up the phone and began perusing the content of the letters. The letters seemed normal, what you'd expect from a hardened criminal: complaints about everything from the food to the warden. But there was a lot of repetition and unusual language usage, and he suspected that some type of cryptic message was hidden within the text that only a code specialist could break. The detective asked the captain who he could call to unscramble coded text. The captain gave him the name of a specialist in deciphering cryptic code language who used to work for the National Security Agency. The detective called the code specialist but got his voicemail. He left a message and hoped the man would call back soon. These letters could contain an order to strike out at Beth again, or Michael Hudson.

After three hours had passed, the detective placed the call again, and this time the man answered. "This is James Ross."

"Hello, Mr. Ross, this is Detective Walter Stevens at the NYPD's nineteenth precinct, and I'm working on a case where I could use your help. I understand that you're 'the man' when it comes to unscrambling cryptic code."

"Yep, that's my background. What do you have?"

"Some letters written by an inmate, and I'm certain they're connected to a case we're working on. They appear to be nothing unusual as written, but they don't feel right, if you know what I mean, and I'm wondering if there's a hidden message disguised within the text."

Ross laughed. "So he didn't use an Ovaltine disk from the 1930s?"

Stevens laughed. "You mean one of those kids' spy rings?"

"Yeah. A simple substitution cipher. This sounds a lot more sophisticated and interests me. Go ahead and fax them over, and I'll take a crack at them."

"Thanks, James."

Stevens figured it would take a few hours for this expert, but he would wait. These letters might reveal the guilt of Giachetti and his accomplice.

Stevens picked out a file on another ongoing investigation and got busy. Two hours later James Ross called back.

"Hi, detective. I figured it out, and I'll fax the messages back to you right away. I've seen this code before, but it wouldn't be obvious to anyone who's not familiar with ciphers. He used the second letter of every word to create a shorthand message, kind of like the language you see in text messages. But you were right, the messages are instructions to do harm."

"I knew it!" Stevens almost shouted. "James, I can't thank you enough, and I really commend you on your work."

"Tell me when you nail the bastard."

"You got it."

Detective Stevens hastily walked over to the fax machine and waited for the translated letters to come through. He picked up the first one, which read:

Need make life messy for law Hudson. Follow to find out friend. Do magic her. After first, do next. Friend hurt bad. Lites out lawyer. 100 Gs. In? Frank

"Hey, Rob, look at this," Stevens said as he handed the letter across the desk. "Just got it back from the code guy."

Matthews read the letter and said, "Holy crap, Walter! Michael Hudson is in imminent danger."

"No shit, Sherlock," Stevens said as he picked up the phone to warn Michael Hudson, who was sufficiently alarmed to double his bodyguard protection. Then they informed the captain, and he added additional protection on Beth Scott's detail.

The detectives had to get up to the prison to interrogate Frank Giachetti immediately. On the drive, Stevens called the warden and clued him in on the hidden messages. For him this now became a criminal investigation of his own personnel, since these letters were an indication of a serious crime in the making. Hopefully, Stevens and Matthews could get a confession out of Giachetti by showing him the messages, and could get him to call off the hit man who was targeting Hudson. They also figured that this outside guy was a professional, and did this type of work for a living. He knew how to cover his tracks and would be sure to leave nothing that would implicate him in the crime. This is why no evidence was found at

Beth's crime scene, and why Beth was not raped and nothing was taken from her apartment. This crime was an assault, and limited to bodily harm carried out by a professional paid by Frank Giachetti.

Chapter

Thirteen

What do you want? Who are you? I'm waiting for my friend Victoria, and she'll be here any minute. No, no! Please don't hurt me.

Beth woke up trembling and sat straight up in bed after experiencing a series of horrid flashbacks from the night of her attack. She was sweaty and shaking from fear, trying to orient herself back to her surroundings. *Oh my God, I must've remembered something from that night,* she told herself. Paralyzed by fear, she remembered a knock at the door and telling Victoria that the door was open. She had been in the bedroom changing her clothes from work and had heard the door open, expecting Victoria, but instead there stood a tall, stocky man wearing a hooded sweatshirt, black gloves, and sunglasses. She now had a visual of her attacker. She turned to look at the clock radio. It was seven thirty in the morning.

She reached for the cell phone on her nightstand and called Detective Stevens.

"Nineteenth precinct. Officer Tully speaking."

"Hi, this is Beth Scott calling. I need to speak to Detective Stevens, please."

"Yes, ma'am. Please hold, and I'll get him for you."

A moment later, Stevens's reassuring voice came on the line. "Hi, Beth. This is Walter. How are you?"

"Detective, I remembered something about that night when I woke up this morning. I'm still shaking."

"Beth, I'll be right over. Just sit tight."

"Okay, I won't go anywhere."

Beth hung up, quickly showered and dressed, and was ready to leave for the office when Detective Stevens arrived. He knocked on the door as she was sipping her coffee. Once again she checked the peephole before opening the door.

"Please come in," she said, her face expressing concern. "Can I pour you a cup?"

"I'm good. I've had my three cups already." Beth nodded, and they both sat down at the kitchen table. Stevens pulled out a notepad from his inside jacket pocket. "Just go ahead and tell me what happened."

Beth repeated what she recalled from her flashback that morning and described her assailant to the detective. He then began asking questions to prod her memory.

"Did he say anything before you blacked out, or do you remember anything that jumps out at you about his person: tattoos, scars, moles?"

"The hoodie covered his arms and most of his face, so I didn't see his skin. I just remember asking him who he was, and him grabbing me and knocking me around. I tried to defend myself, but he was too strong."

"Okay, I'd now like to do a reenactment of the attack. Sometimes it helps people remember things. Do you mind giving it a try?" Stevens asked, then paused. "Are you up for it?"

"If it'll help," she said, her voice shaky.

"Do you have a sweatshirt with a hood?"

"Yes, but it'll be too small for you." Beth stepped back into her bedroom.

She returned with a black hooded sweatshirt and gave it to the detective. He opened the front door and went out into the hallway. "I'll close the door, put on the sweatshirt and glasses. When I knock, I want you to be standing where you were that night, and respond exactly how you remember, okay?"

Beth nodded then walked back to the bedroom and waited for the detective's prompt. She heard him knock on the door and yelled out, "Victoria, the door's open. I'll be right out."

Stevens opened the door and trudged into the apartment as Beth stepped out of the bedroom. The sight of him made her freeze as the terrifying memories surfaced. *It's him*, she said to herself. *Oh my God! What do you want? Who are you? I'm waiting for my friend Victoria. She'll be here any minute.*

The detective grabbed Beth and simulated an attack, nearly hitting her, then holding his hand over her mouth. She struggled to get away. He held her closer, almost hurting her. Then Beth remembered him saying in a very low deep voice, *Don't fight me, bitch.*

She managed to pull away and then suddenly remembered picking up a heavy glass vase and hitting him in the face with it causing him to bleed. This made him very angry and he balled up his fist saying, *How's your boyfriend, bitch?* Then he hit her, and she blacked out.

Stevens pulled off the hoodie and looked back her. Beth shook her head clear. "I can't believe that I *just* remembered that. Wow. That's awesome!"

"Well done, Beth. I'm sorry if I got a little too rough with you."

"No apologies needed, detective. It worked."

"Can you show me the glass vase that you used?"

Beth looked around the living room, but it wasn't on the side table where she always had it displayed. "It's not here," she said, knitting her brow. "How could I not notice that it was missing?"

"You're suffering from traumatic amnesia, and sometimes that's very selective, according to Dr. Burton."

"Okay, but let me check a few more places. Maybe, my mom cleaned off the blood and put it away without saying anything." Beth checked all the closets, and it wasn't there. "Well, I guess it's not here."

"I'll check the office. They might've taken it to the lab to test for blood or prints."

Beth thought of something. "So if he made reference to my boyfriend, doesn't this confirm that it was Michael's client in jail?"

"I think that connection is pretty clear now." Detective Stevens stepped over to the door. "You've been a trooper, Beth, and I'm so proud of you. Are you going to be all right?"

"Actually I'm more relieved than shaken."

"You're a strong woman, Beth." Stevens opened the door, then turned back to her. "I'll get back to you about the vase, whether we have it or not."

"Good-bye, detective, and please know how much I respect your work."

"Coming from you, Beth, that's a real compliment." Stevens walked out and closed the door behind him.

Beth tried to compose herself before leaving for work. It was a traumatic start of her day, and she didn't want to bring this negative energy to the workplace. She grabbed her briefcase and purse and headed out the door. Her bodyguard was waiting at the front entrance.

"Good morning, Miss Scott. I'll be escorting you this morning," Aaron said as he stepped over to open the car door.

Beth was still slightly shaky and unsettled. "Aaron, could we walk to work this morning?"

"I think it best that I drive you."

"Aaron, I just had a traumatic recall of . . . that night, and I need to walk it off. Please, just today. I think it'll help calm me down somewhat."

"Okay, I understand. But I'll have to call it in," he said. Beth nodded.

After the call, they started walking, and to distract herself Beth asked Aaron about himself and shared a little of her own background. It was a pleasant walk, which took her mind off of the morning's events and put her in a better mood.

When Beth arrived at her office, she was greeted by Maria. "It's so good to see you back, Beth. We've all missed you," Maria said, giving her a hug.

"Thank you. It's great to be back," Beth replied, looking around. "I never realized how much I missed this place."

Maria looked over at her escort. "Oh, Maria, meet Aaron Collard. He'll be with me wherever I go and sitting outside of my office today."

"Mr. Collard, so nice to meet you. If you need anything, please let me know."

"Sure thing. Hope I won't be in the way."

Aaron took a seat outside while Maria and Beth went into her office to go over the day's schedule.

"So what do we have going on, Maria? Fill me in."

"The first item is to call Brian Paul's attorney, who has not gotten back to us on this Wednesday's settlement meeting. There's only one week left before the court date, so you need to get on him."

"I can't imagine why Jake hasn't called. Please get him on the phone. I need to light a fire under his ass." Maria nodded. "Do that, and then we'll talk about my other cases."

Maria walked back to her desk and made the call. Thirty seconds later, she buzzed Beth to pick up on line four. It was Brian's attorney, Jake Gibson.

"Good morning, Jake. We still good for Wednesday?"

"Yes, I have it down for three o'clock."

"Why didn't you get back to me?" Beth asked.

"Back and forth with the client. Didn't get him on the same page until yesterday."

"Okay, we'll be there on time, and make sure your client's ready to settle because I won't file an extension, and we will be prepared to go to court on Friday."

"I think he gets that," Jake said. "See you then."

Beth buzzed the intercom for Maria to come back into her office. She hastily walked over to Beth's desk and took a seat across from her. She always brought in her note pad.

"I need an update on Susan Spencer and Caroline Murphy. The last time I saw Caroline, I could tell, by the bruises on her face, that she'd been beaten up. And I'd spoken to Susan about going into a shelter, which she was prepared to do. You told me in the hospital that you had called them both to say I'd be out of the office for a while." Beth paused and wrinkled her brow. "But to be honest, Maria, I don't remember your telling me if you heard back from either of them."

"Yes, I did tell you. When I called them, they both said they would wait for you to come back to work before making any changes in their situations. I told Susan that if she couldn't wait for you I would help get her into a shelter, and that's the last conversation I had with her."

"Okay, then, let's get Susan on the phone, and I'll see what's going on. After I speak to her, call Caroline."

Maria went back to her desk to place the call.

"Beth, I've got Susan Spencer on line one."

"Susan, this is Beth Scott, and I wanted to let you know that I'm back at work. How are you doing?"

"It's been rough, Beth, the abuse has continued and just doesn't let up. I need to leave him as soon as possible!"

"I'm so sorry. I feel like I've deserted you," Beth said with emotion in her voice.

"Oh no. Don't feel that way. What happened to you was far worse than anything I've gone through."

"Well, I'll fix this. Don't you worry. How soon can you come in?"

"Tomorrow. You name the time, and I'll be there."

"Let me check my schedule. I'm only working half days." Maria had updated appointments on her computer that morning. "I have ten o'clock available, if that works for you."

"I'll be there at ten sharp. Thanks, Beth. Have a good day."

Beth was relieved that she hadn't gone to another attorney during her absence. Susan needed to be placed in a shelter, and Beth was the best at selecting them and sorting out the details.

She buzzed Maria. "Please get me Caroline Murphy on the phone, and put Susan Spencer on the schedule for ten tomorrow morning."

"Right away."

As she grabbed a bottle of water out of the fridge, Maria buzzed her phone, "Caroline is on line two."

Beth stepped back to her desk and took her seat. "Caroline, this is Beth Scott calling. I believe the last time we spoke was the day before I went into the hospital. I'm back now. How's your situation?" There was a pause. "Is this not a good time to talk?"

"I think you have the wrong number. Good-bye." And suddenly there was a dial tone on the line.

Beth was at first taken aback by Caroline's rude response, but then she realized that her husband must have been in the room. At least Caroline knew she was back in the office and prepared to go forward with her case. Beth figured Caroline would call back as soon as she was alone.

Beth now had Maria pull out the remaining case files, and she went through and made notations on each of them. After the last one, she glanced at her watch and noticed it was two fifteen. She had promised Brandon only half days for the first week, and she had already exceeded her time limit for today. She buzzed Maria and told her she'd be leaving for the day and if anything came up she could be reached at home. As she was packing her briefcase, her boss, Jeff Greene, stopped by and stood in her doorway. He was the managing partner, and the fine lines on his face showed premature aging due to the stress of the job. His hair was all gray; for a man of only fifty-five he appeared much older. Beth had always liked his cordial, to-the-point attitude about matters.

"Hi, Beth, may I come in for a minute?"

"Absolutely, Jeff."

"Welcome back. I can't tell you how good it is to see you at your desk again. How're you feeling? You look great."

"Thanks. I'm doing well, and couldn't wait to be back where I belong."

"Beth, I want to tell you how sorry I am for what happened to you. And I speak for the entire firm. Michael Hudson informed me that the police have a suspect, one of his ex-clients, but I'm sure you know that. I only wish Michael would have informed me or someone in the firm about this nut job. I can tell you that policies are going to change here as a result of this incident. We can't have our attorneys be put in harm's way." He paused for a moment before continuing. "Your time off will not count against your sick leave or vacation time, and we'll cover any insurance overlays. Is there anything I can do for you?"

"Jeff, that's really considerate of you. I can't think of anything else at the moment."

"I know you and Michael have twenty-four-hour protection, and I'm grateful for that. But if you want to work from home until they apprehend this guy, please feel free to do so. I don't want to put you in any more danger. Am I clear, Beth?"

"Thanks, Jeff, but I need to come into the office. I've been going crazy at home, and I can work much better from here. As you see, Aaron is with me at work, and Charlie is guarding my apartment. So I'm in good hands, and I feel completely safe."

"Okay, whatever you prefer." He stood up. "This firm values you as a person as well as a top-notch attorney."

"Thanks so much, Jeff. You don't know how much I appreciate your kind words. I think you know this firm is my life."

"Yes, I do, Beth. You're one of our most dedicated young lawyers." Jeff gave her a big hug and added, "Stay vigilant, and always remember we've got your back."

Beth walked out of the office behind Jeff Greene and told Maria that she was calling it a day. It was a very busy first day back and she felt fatigued. She turned to Aaron, smiled, and said, "I'm ready to go home, Aaron. And I think we should take a taxi."

"Yes, ma'am. That's a good idea." Then he turned around and, with a smile and a wink, said to Beth's assistant, "See you tomorrow, Maria." Collard was enjoying this auspicious assignment due to a crush he had on Maria.

At the precinct that afternoon, Detective Stevens went down to the evidence room to look for the crystal vase Beth had used to strike her attacker. It was not logged in for evidence. Stevens checked the lab, but it wasn't there either. The vase was never taken out of the apartment, unless the perp took it when he left, which was highly unlikely. It was large and heavy, and if he were on the run, he wouldn't want to be carrying it around. So what happened to that vase?

"Beth, hi. This is Walter Stevens," he said when she picked up the phone. "The vase isn't here, so could you have one last look just to be sure?"

"Okay, but as you know, my apartment isn't very big, and there are only so many places to look, detective." Beth searched everywhere, but to no avail.

Stevens thanked her and hung up the phone. If the attacker took it out of the apartment, he most likely disposed of it nearby. Unfortunately, it was too late to check the neighborhood trashcans.

"Hey, Rob," Stevens said looking across the desk at his partner. "Since the perp was cut by the vase when Beth struck him, he probably needed stitches. Let's check the local emergency rooms to see if he came in for treatment that night or the next morning."

"Okay, I'll call New York Presbyterian over on 168th, which is closer to where some tough guy like this might live," said Rob.

"I'll go in the opposite direction—Bellevue on 26th—and I'll also check NYU on First Avenue," said Stevens.

Stevens looked up the number of Bellevue. The operator transferred him to the emergency department.

"Emergency room, Marsha Allen speaking."

"Ms. Allen, this is Detective Stevens from the NYPD. Who would I need to speak with about patients treated in your ER on a particular date? Do you have some sort of admitting log, and is your ER monitored with cameras?"

"Yes, we have both, detective. Let me transfer you to the person in charge of monitoring."

A moment later another voice came on the line. "This is Dave Wong. How can I help?"

"Mr. Wong this is Detective Stevens from the NYPD, and I need your help."

"Certainly, what can I do for you?"

Stevens gave him the time and date of the attack and described what the perp was wearing. "Could you check your video files and see if anyone matching this description was treated around that time or the next morning?"

"Sure, detective, but I'll need some time. Let me call you back."

"Please." Stevens gave him the number.

Two hours had passed, in which Stevens had made inquiries to several other hospitals, when he picked up one of the incoming calls.

"Detective Stevens, nineteenth precinct."

"Detective, Dave Wong here. I think I found who you're looking for. Come over and take a look at this video. He certainly fits the description you gave me."

"Be right over. Shouldn't take long. And thanks for getting back to me so quickly."

Stevens put the phone down and looked over at his partner. "Today's our lucky day, Rob. Bellevue might've caught our perp on tape, a guy who fits the description and arrived thirty minutes after Beth's attack. We need to get down there right away."

Walter and Rob grabbed their jackets and hastily walked out the door. Finally they had caught a break. Hopefully, they would now be able to ID their perp. Stevens turned on the sirens of their unmarked police car, and they managed to maneuver through forty blocks of late-afternoon traffic to arrive at Bellevue in approximately thirty-five minutes.

At the reception desk, Matthews flashed his badge and announced, "We're here to speak to Dave Wong."

"One minute, please." The clerk, who had introduced herself as Anita Parker, looked down at her computer screen and retrieved Wong's number.

"Is this Dave Wong?" she asked, pausing for his response. "I have two detectives here who would like to speak to you. Can you meet them at the reception desk? Okay, great. Thanks." She hung up the phone and looked at the detectives. "He's on his way."

They waited a few minutes before a young, geeky-looking Asian male with a buzz cut and black rimmed glasses approached the desk. "Hey, guys. I'm Dave," he said as he extended his arm to shake their hands—a very informal kind of guy. "Let's head on back to the computer room, and I'll show you what I found."

"We're with you, Dave. Lead the way."

The small room had a bank of six monitors on the wall, each fixed on a different area of the emergency room. Dave took a seat at the desk and turned on monitor one, which displayed the main hallway leading to the treatment area. He showed the detectives the tape from the night in question, stopping the tape when a man fitting the description of the suspect appeared. "Is this your man?" Dave asked.

The detectives moved closer to the monitor. "Jesus, Walter. This guy looks like he could be our perp," Matthews said. "Can you play this clip in slow motion?"

"Absolutely."

Walter and Rob watched the tape in slow motion as the suspect walked into a treatment room. "Well, he's tall, large, and muscular, with a hoodie and dark glasses—the whole nine yards," said Rob. "He's holding a towel to soak up blood from his left cheek. Son of a bitch! He *has* to be our guy, Walt."

Then Dave pointed to monitor two, which covered the cubicle, where they saw the suspect lie down on the treatment table. They watched as the nurse, her back partially to the camera, removed the towel from his face, washed the wound, and assisted the doctor in suturing the laceration. Unfortunately, the detectives were unable to view his face because the view was blocked by both the nurse and the doctor. When they stepped back, the suspect turned his head away from the camera, pulled the hoodie over his face, put on his sunglasses, then got off the treatment table. Viewing monitor one, they could see the suspect approach the desk and pay for his treatment in cash before leaving the ER.

"Dave, where would we find this patient's name and address?"

"You can get that from the front desk. They have an admitting form that every patient must fill out."

"We're going to need a copy of these tapes."

"Sure thing," Dave answered. "I can email you the file. Give me the address. It might take me an hour or·so."

"We'd really appreciate it." Stevens handed Dave his card. "Thanks for all your help." The detective and Matthews walked out of the office and back to the admitting desk.

"Hi, Ms. Parker. Seems I need your assistance once again. May I please see your patients' admitting log for this date and time?" Stevens asked, handing her a sheet of paper with the information. "I assume the patient is required to fill out a form with his name and address, correct?"

"Yes, sir. And also on the form is the reason for the visit."

"That's just what we need."

It didn't take long for the clerk to identify their suspect by his injury from among those seeking help that night. She pulled up his admission form and printed out a copy for the detectives. They did a quick rundown on the name and address and determined that they were fake, but "cut on cheek" was given for the reason he came in. Since he had paid in cash, there was no credit card info for a back trace. They thanked Ms. Parker and headed back to their office. As soon as he received the video file, Stevens would turn it over to their computer experts to see if they could capture or construct an image of the man's face that was in the shadow cast by his hoodie. The detectives had seen this done on another case, and it was good enough to create an image for facial recognition.

Next, Stevens had to figure out if Giachetti had been linked to any hit men in the Mob before he went to prison. He was determined to find out who they were and if someone in that group fit the description of the man on the tape. But without a picture of any sort it would be difficult. Everything was riding on what his highly skilled computer team could come up with.

While diligently working away and buried in mug books of criminals with Mob associations, Detective Stevens received a call. "This is Detective Stevens, can I help you?"

"Hi, detective, this is Victoria David—Beth's friend who found her that night."

"Yes, Victoria. What can I do for you?"

"Well, I've been trying to remember something more that could be helpful. Believe me, I went over it a million times."

"And?"

"When I turned the corner two blocks from Beth's apartment, I saw a black SUV speeding away. I didn't give it much thought; it wasn't as if they were in front of her building. But the more I thought about it, they could've been, since I saw the car from a distance and my perspective could've been off. I mean, I got there shortly after she was attacked, and I now wonder if that SUV could've been the getaway car."

"Did you happen to get the license plate number?" Stevens asked hurriedly, trying to stay calm.

"No, I'm sorry. It was too far for me to read it, but my boss has an Escalade, and the back end of that car looked just like it, even from a distance."

"You've been a big help, Victoria. Wish I had heard this earlier, but thanks for calling."

"Oh, you're welcome, detective. Sorry about that."

"Rob, that was Victoria David calling to say that a black SUV sped away from the scene of the crime." Matthews shook his head in disbelief. "Can you believe she just remembered this now? I think amnesia must be contagious." Stevens paused and more deliberately added, "That would explain what happened to the knife and the vase, and how the perp got to Bellevue so quickly."

"And disposed of the evidence in some public trashcan half-way there," said Matthews. "If only we'd had a heads-up that night. Son of a fucking bitch."

Chapter

Fourteen

ichael's bodyguard, Henry Stone, followed twenty feet behind him on the way to Michael's apartment, which was in an upscale elevator building without a doorman. As they approached it, Stone came forward. They rode up in the elevator together. Stone was substituting for Michael's regular bodyguard and wanted to make a good impression.

"Michael, wait in the hall until I check everything out," Stone said. He opened the door and walked around the small one-bedroom, masculine-looking bachelor pad decorated in shades of brown and black. There was a black leather couch and a brown-and-black tweed fabric chair with an ottoman. Nice digs, Henry thought to himself. The large flat-screen TV on the wall opposite the couch was perfect for viewing sporting events. The small galley kitchen had been remodeled with white wood cabinetry, granite counters, and stainless steel appliances. As he walked into the bedroom, which had a queen-size bed with one night stand, he looked in the closet and under the bed. He then opened the door to the bathroom, which had only one sink and a small stall shower, but was richly appointed with stone finishes and brass hardware. After he made sure all the windows were locked, he let Michael enter.

"Everything is secure, sir. I'll be posted outside the front of the building. Here's my cell number if you should need me for anything."

"Thanks, Henry. If you get thirsty, please come up for a soda." Michael closed the door and put down his briefcase just in time to answer the phone.

"Hi, Michael. This is Detective Stevens. How are you?"

"I'm great. What's up?"

"Beth tells me that you're leaving for Boston on a business trip, and I want to encourage you to bring a bodyguard with you."

"I'm sure I'll be fine since I'll be going out of state. And hopefully, when I return you'll have caught your man."

"Michael, these are Mob guys. They travel too."

Michael paused to reconsider his position. "I think I'll be fine, detective, and I really feel good about getting out of town. It'll be nice to have a few days where I don't have to worry about someone coming after me. But thanks for your vigilance."

"Well, I disagree, but have a safe flight, and good luck in Boston."

The next morning Michael went to the office early to prepare for his business trip. He was traveling to Boston to interview a potential witness for one of his high-profile murder cases. If the deposition went well, the man's testimony could be crucial in winning the case for his client. He called Beth before getting buried in preparation.

"Hi, babe, good morning. How're you feeling?"

"I'm fine, Michael. I miss you. Are you coming over tonight after work? I can throw something together, and, with a bottle of wine, we'll be good."

"Sorry, Beth. As you know, I'm going to Boston tomorrow, and I have lots of preparation still to get done. Probably be up till midnight."

"What a bummer, Michael. I'll miss you. What's that old saying? Absence makes the heart grow fonder."

"For sure. I tell you what. If a miracle should happen and I get done even by ten o'clock, I'll swing by for a nightcap."

"Ooh, that sounds naughty."

"I wish." Michael paused. "I'll let you know either way."

Beth spent the evening preparing and eating a good dinner, slowly enjoying her wine, and catching up on some reading. At one point, she glanced at her wall clock: it was nine thirty. It didn't feel like Michael would make it over for his "nightcap." Ten minutes later he rang her.

"Hi," she said. "I already know. You're not coming. I understand."

"So sorry, Beth. Like I said, I'll be up till midnight. This prep is a real bitch!"

"Just call tomorrow night after you get settled in your hotel," Beth said, trying not to sound too disappointed.

"Will do. And pace yourself at work. There's always another day. I don't want you too tired when I return, if you get my drift."

"I hear you," she said half laughing.

"I've got plans for us. A little getaway surprise, and that's all I'm going to say."

"Oh, now you've got me wondering. Gonna keep me guessing, huh?"

"It wouldn't be a surprise if I told you."

"Well, have a safe flight, and I can't wait till you get back."

"Me, too. I'll call you from the hotel and let you know how the deposition went. I'll be back late Saturday, so let's plan on spending Sunday together."

"Sounds great. And then will you tell me about the surprise?"

"Absolutely. Love you, babe."

"Me, too. Ciao, good lookin'."

So far, Detective Stevens's search for Giachetti's Mob connections hadn't panned out; it was further stymied when the computer experts couldn't extrapolate a credible image from the hospital footage of their perp. They needed a fresh approach. He looked across the desk at his partner. "Rob, we need to expand our search parameters to anybody who had contact with Giachetti before he went to prison. In addition to Mob members, we should check out all his past jobs and interview people who worked with him. Somebody knows something, and we just need to find them."

"Okay, Walter, let's get right on it." Matthews paused, running his hand through his hair. "I know it'd be crazy for Giachetti to order a hit now with us on his case, but he's one vindictive bastard, and I wouldn't put anything past him."

After many hours of digging, Matthews discovered that a few years back Giachetti had worked for a construction company in the Bronx that had been hired by the city to repair roads and bridges. He was the head foreman for two years and had a twenty-five-man crew. "Walter, I've got something. Grab your jacket. We're going to the Bronx."

Matthews and Stevens pulled up in front of the Waterloo Construction Company, which was located in a warehouse in an industrial part of town. Finding the door locked, they pushed the button on the intercom. A scratchy voice said, "Please identify yourself."

The two exchanged looks, thinking this must be a rough neighborhood. "We're detectives with the NYPD. Can you please buzz us in?"

The door clicked as it unlocked, and the detectives walked into the vestibule where there was a woman sitting at a desk behind a glass partition.

"Hi," said Stevens. "We're Detectives Stevens and Matthews with the Manhattan NYPD, and we're investigating a case. May we ask you some questions?"

"Tell me what this is about, sir, and I'll direct you to the right person," the woman replied.

"We need a rundown on a former employee by the name of Frank Giachetti."

The receptionist stepped around from behind the partition. "Sure, detective, just follow me, and I'll take you to Mr. Bailey."

As the detectives followed her down the hallway, they noticed the building was typical of other construction companies with its sterile white walls and cubicle offices separated by wallboard. There were only four executive offices, and they were led into the one closest to the front, with the nameplate "Operations Director" on the door.

"Excuse me, Mr. Bailey. This is Detective Stevens and Detective Matthews from the NYPD, and they need to speak with you about a former employee."

"Please come in, detectives, and have a seat. Who are we talking about?"

"We're investigating a case concerning an employee of yours from 2006 to 2008 by the name of Frank Giachetti. We need to know everything you can tell us about him, especially who he was close to on and off the job."

"Well, he was a fairly good foreman, and what I mean by that is he could be very tough on his men. Went out in the field with them every day and really made them toe the line. While that was good in some ways, he also made a lot of enemies playing Mr. Tough Guy. But he got his men to work hard, and they would've done anything to get on his good side."

"Mr. Bailey, did you know why Giachetti left your employment, and did he tell you where he was going next?"

"No, he just didn't show up one day, and that was that. Really pissed me off. There were rumors that he went to work for one of the Mob families in the city, but I never knew in what capacity." Bailey shrugged his shoulders. "I never heard from him again, but later I read in the newspaper that he was arrested for a string of bank robberies. I tell you, I was a little surprised. I never expected that from him. It just goes to show, you never know about people."

"Mr. Bailey, would it be possible for me to see the files of employees who reported to Giachetti, and can you point out those he was friendly with?" asked Stevens.

"Sure. Wait one minute, and I'll have my secretary bring in the employees' personnel files, which will have photos, and give you all the contact information we have on them. I know on the weekends they would hang out at one of the local Bronx bars, 'cause he'd always tell me stories on Monday morning." Bailey reached over and punched his intercom. "Marge, look up Frank Giachetti's history and give me the files of everybody who worked with him."

Bailey now turned to the detectives. "So what's this about? Isn't Giachetti still in jail? I read in the paper that he got fifteen years."

"Yeah, he's still in jail, but he was involved in masterminding a crime on the outside: we believe he hired one of his friends to do it and used some of the bank money to pay him off. So we're just checking out every possible accomplice. We think it could be one of the men who worked under him here since this was his last job before he started robbing banks."

"I see, detective. Do you know how much the person got paid by Giachetti to commit this crime?"

"Sorry, can't disclose the amount," Stevens said.

"I understand," responded Mr. Bailey.

His secretary now brought in a stack of files and placed them on the desk. "Thanks, Marge."

"Mr. Bailey, do you mind if I borrow these files briefly? I promise to have them back to you by Friday."

"Okay, detective. Take all the time you need."

"Thanks. You've been very helpful."

The detectives were halfway down the hall when Stevens turned and went back to Mr. Bailey's office. "Sorry to bother you again, but do you know if Giachetti worked a night job, or was this his only gig?"

"Well, he once told me he had to take a job as a night security guard at a bank to make extra money, which didn't make sense given what he made here. Then I read in the paper about the robberies, and one of the banks hit was where he worked."

"Guess he was scoping it out. Thanks again," Stevens said and walked out of the office.

Detective Stevens wondered if one of these workers could be his accomplice in Beth's attack. Giachetti worked with these guys for over two years, and despite being a tough foreman he probably formed a strong bond with some of them. Or did the guy in the hoodie work for one of the Mob families? One of these construction men seemed more likely, for the money offered was equivalent to almost two years' salary on the job. And the Mob paid you for a bank job. You didn't pay the Mob. They took care of their own business.

When the detectives arrived back at their office, they split up the folders. Mr. Bailey had pointed out the men Giachetti was the most friendly with, and they both started with that group first. While combing through the photos, they found ten men who fit the profile of the man in the hospital video. They were mostly tall, large in stature, and very strong-looking, with black hair. Six of the men were still employed by the construction company, but the remaining four had left. They all needed to be interviewed, and the four who had left the company had to be found. Detective Stevens engaged two of his best detectives for the task of locating these four men, and they would start by checking their files for any forwarding addresses since the guys moved around a lot. In the meantime, he would bring in the others for questioning. All he had to do was find the one who had a scar on his left cheek and no alibi for the night of the attack.

Matthews called Mr. Bailey back to ask if any of Giachetti's coworkers had a scar on his left cheek.

"You know what, detective. I couldn't say. They'll all be coming in this afternoon to pick up their paychecks, so if you want to come back you can see for yourself."

"I think we'll do that. What's a good time to catch them?"

"They'll all show up by five. Never miss a payday."

The detectives arrived early and interviewed the six friends of Giachetti, but no one had a scar on his left cheek and all had alibis for the night in question. So the next step would be finding the four men who had left the company. They asked Mr. Bailey

159

for forwarding addresses on Anthony Giordano, Carlos Mercado, Salvator Barboza, and Guiseppi Rossalino.

Bailey swiveled his chair around and opened the bottom drawer of the file cabinet behind him. After a few minutes, he located what he was looking for. "Okay, here are the employment verifications files on these men." He turned and handed the files to Stevens, who took two and gave the others to his partner. They perused the files, asked for copies, and then headed out.

Back at the precinct, Detective Stevens and his task force focused on finding these four men and assigned their caseload to other detectives since, with Michael's life in jeopardy, time was of the essence in this case. Of the four, they were able to quickly locate two: Anthony Giordano and Carlos Mercado.

Les Girls had a huge sign over the entrance and pictures of topless women in neon lights on each side of the entry. The detectives went inside, where they encountered loud music, topless dancers gyrating on the stage, and a roomful of whistling men, all fixated on them.

"Hi, baby, you're cute. Wanna have some fun?" asked one of the dancers, as she leaned over to rub up against Matthews's chest.

The detective smiled at the young lady and flashed his shield. "No thanks, miss. I'm here on official business," he replied, trying not to gawk at her half-naked body. "Can you direct me to the manager?"

"Sure can, but if you change your mind, know that I've always had a thing for cops."

"Thank you, I'll remember that," said the detective, as he wiped his brow and blushed. The two of them followed her to the manager's office.

"Hey, Sam, there's someone here to see you."

"Thanks, Bridget, now get back to work."

"Sir, I'm Detective Stevens with the NYPD and this is my partner, Detective Matthews. We're looking for a Mr. Anthony Giordano. Is he here?"

"What's this about, detective?" asked Sam. "He's not due in until eight tonight—one of my best doormen. Hope he's not in trouble."

"We just need to talk to him," said Stevens. "Can you give me his home address?"

"Okay." The man fingered through the Rolodex on his desk, wrote down the address, and handed it to Stevens.

"We'd appreciate it if you wouldn't mention that we came around. We don't want him making himself scarce before we get back here. You understand?"

"Yeah, I get it," he said angrily. "But don't come around and start harassing my staff in front of customers."

"We're investigating a serious crime," Stevens said, "and we're asking for your cooperation in answering a few questions."

"Okay, but make it quick. I have an establishment to run, and I've wasted enough time with this shit. What do you want to know?"

"We need to know how long Giordano has been employed, as you say, at your establishment."

Before responding, Sam glared at Matthews and said, "Oh, this one's a comedian."

"Just answer the questions," Stevens said.

"He's been here three years. Does his job well."

"Do you know any of his friends, or where he goes on his days off?"

"Nope and don't care—that's his business. As long as he shows up for work and does his job, I've got no beef." Sam pointed to the address slip he had handed Stevens. "I believe this is all you need. Now, this meeting is over, and don't let the tits hit you in the eye on the way out."

Stevens and Matthews walked out of the office without a response. As they passed the stage, they saw the young lady who had approached them now dancing in her birthday suit.

They headed straight over to Giordano's address. It was a tenement building on the Lower East Side, and his apartment was a fifth-floor walk-up. The detectives climbed the stairs and were both out of breath when they reached the fifth floor. "Didn't realize what lousy shape I'm in," said Stevens. They walked down the long hall to Giordano's apartment and knocked on the door.

"Yeah, okay. Who is it?"

"It's the NYPD. Open the door," said Stevens.

After a few moments, the door was cracked open, and the detectives were face-to-face with a man about six feet tall, with dark hair, and weighing about two hundred and fifty pounds. He was a little taller than the man in the hospital video, and he didn't have a scar on his left cheek.

"Are you Anthony Giordano?" inquired Stevens.

"Yes. What's this about?"

"May we come in? We're investigating a crime, and we need to ask you some questions."

"Come in. I got nothing to hide," Giordano said, swinging the door open.

The detectives stepped inside and walked over to the kitchen table and its four chairs. "Shall we?" asked Matthews, pulling out a chair to sit down. He looked around the one-room apartment. The kitchen was at one end, the living area in the middle, and a bed in the far right corner. There was a worn-out sofa with a TV across from it. The entire apartment must have been five hundred square feet at the most, and all of it in need of repair. There were no curtains or blinds on the windows and no rug on the floor. Just bare concrete. What a dump. By the looks of his living quarters, this guy could've really used the money that Giachetti was offering.

"No problem, take a load off," Giordano said.

After they were seated, Matthews got to the point. "Do you know Frank Giachetti?"

"Yeah, we used to work together at a construction company a few years back. Why do you want to know?"

"Well, let's just say that he hired someone to do some dirty work for him, and we need to find that person."

"I haven't spoken to Frank in three years, not since we worked together. He was my crew foreman, and then one day he never showed up, and no one ever saw him again. Isn't he in prison for some bank robberies? I kind of remember hearing about that."

"Do you know a woman by the name of Beth Scott?"

"Nope. Who's she?"

"Someone who was assaulted and left to die by a man hired by Giachetti."

The man nodded. He got the drift of this conversation. "Well, that wouldn't be me, detective. I've never heard of her before. Wish I could help you, but you're looking at the wrong guy. I like women. I don't hurt them; I look after them."

"So, you never got a call from Frank Giachetti asking you for a favor?" Matthews inquired, staring right through him. "You know, if you come clean now, we can cut a deal with the D.A."

"Don't need no deal! Didn't beat up anybody," Giordano spit out excitedly.

Stevens could see that Giordano was unraveling. "Calm down, Anthony. We're just asking." This had the intended effect. "Do you know anybody who was tight with Giachetti on the job who might do this crime?"

"No. We all went out for drinks occasionally, but I don't know who he kept in touch with after he left. It wasn't me, that's for sure."

"Do you mind if we take a look around?"

"Be my guest. There's nothing much here. This ain't the Waldorf, detective."

Matthews and Stevens briefly walked through the apartment but didn't uncover anything useful.

"Well, if you think of anything, please give us a call." Stevens handed him his card.

The detectives ruled out Giordano as a possible perp. He was very believable, and his alibi checked out: he was working at the strip joint the night of the attack, and he didn't have a scar. So now they'd go on to the next suspect, Carlos Mercado.

From the verification file, Mercado had taken a job with Delano Meat Packing, located on the far side of Harlem in a large run-down building.

"Hello, we're with the NYPD," said Detective Matthews, flashing his shield at the man behind the front desk. "We understand that Carlos Mercado works here and would like to speak with him."

He looked at the badge, then stared back at the detectives. "I'll call him. Should only take a few minutes."

"No problem, sir."

About five minutes later, a stocky man with black hair and a black moustache walked down the hallway toward them. "Hello, I'm Carlos Mercado. How can I help?"

"We're Detectives Stevens and Matthews from the NYPD. Nice to meet you. We need to ask you a few questions. Is there someplace we can sit down?"

The man behind the desk pointed across the hall. "Use Bob's office, Carlos," he said.

The three of them stepped into the office, which was set up like a conference room with a small round table. They all took a seat.

"What's this about, detective?" Carlos asked.

"Do you know Frank Giachetti?" asked Stevens.

"Yes, I used to work with him at Waterloo Construction. Why are you asking?"

"Were you very friendly with him?"

"Well, we'd go out for drinks on the weekend. Not every weekend, but once in a while and, on a rare occasion, after work. He was a pretty tough boss, so the guys would try to loosen him up with a few drinks. That's all."

"Do you know Michael Hudson and a young lady by the name of Beth Scott?"

"No. Why do you ask?"

"Have you been in contact with Frank Giachetti since you left the construction job?"

"No, I haven't. I heard he got prison time for some bank robberies. What does this have to do with me?"

"Well, it seems Mr. Giachetti paid someone off to put Miss Scott in the hospital after leaving her for dead. He arranged this from prison, and we need to locate his accomplice. We're looking into all his friends from his previous employment, and that's how we got to you."

"Jesus. That's a kicker, but don't look at me 'cause I had no part in it."

"This person was offered a lot of money for the job. I'm sure someone like you could put one hundred grand to good use, right?"

"Hey, no way. It wasn't me. Yeah, I could use the money, but I didn't do it and wouldn't do anything like that for money." He was scrambling, which was what they wanted. "You know, there is a guy Frank was real friendly with who always showed up for drinks at the bar and most every time sat next to Frank. They were really tight off the job. His name is Sal Barboza, and he was always telling us we worked too hard, like we should find another job that paid better."

Stevens looked at his partner and said, "Barboza is one of the guys on our list. Now, isn't that a coincidence?" Carlos stood up and closed the door, then sat down and lowered his voice. "I think that guy had Mob connections, and it appeared to me that he was looking for recruits."

"So what are you saying? That he came along for drinks to persuade some of the guys to join the Mob?"

"That's exactly what I'm saying, detective."

"That's pretty iffy, if you ask me," Matthews said.

"Well, I overheard him talking about it with Frank one night. Said they were looking for some muscle, and that some of Frank's guys looked tough enough."

"And did either of them approach you about it?"

"Barboza asked me if I was happy with my grunt-work job once. I got his drift and begged off."

"Thanks Carlos, you've been a big help. If you think of anything else, let us know." Stevens handed him his card, and they got up and left. They were eager to locate Barboza and pay him a visit.

Chapter
Fifteen

Salvator Barboza now resided in Boston, working for the DiNunzio Mob family. After he left Waterloo Construction, his cousin Carmen DiNunzio recruited him for their Boston operation. While there, he stayed in touch with Frank Giachetti and agreed to be his guy on the outside for whatever Frank needed. Barboza was not only muscle but also plenty smart. The Mob leaders had taught him well, and he knew how to take someone out and never leave a trace of evidence. He had flown back to New York after Giachetti asked him to take care of the Scott woman, and he knew he had the cops baffled since they were chasing down local suspects. He was pleased that he'd outsmarted the NYPD, all their detectives, and the department's sophisticated lab technology. He was damn good and he knew it. No fucking cops were going to outsmart him.

Barboza had a Mob contact follow Michael's latest case—a high-profile murder—in the newspapers. He then called his secretary and asked for an appointment, and she told him that Michael would be in Boston late Wednesday and all day Thursday and

Friday, but could make it on Monday. He was very charming on the phone and got the secretary to relinquish information that he knew she was not permitted to give out. Barboza gave a phony name and set the appointment, one that he knew neither he nor the attorney would make. He called only five-star hotels in Boston, like The Ritz-Carlton, InterContinental, and the Four Seasons, to find out where Michael was registered. He hit the jackpot on the third call: the Four Seasons. He would head over there today and do his due diligence. He needed to check out the kitchen staff, the bar, and see how the hotel was laid out.

He began planning the hit in his mind: *Will I need a key to go up on the elevator? How close is the bar or the lobby to the reception desk, so I'll be able to spot Hudson walking in? Since he'll be arriving late, he will probably order room service.* He'd wait for the waiter to bring up the order, which he would then intercept; he'd dispatch the guy and change into his clothes. Also, he'd bring along a small suitcase with a gun, paper shoe-covers, and a laundry bag with street clothes, including his large-brimmed baseball cap, to change into. And to catch the room number he'd have to be close behind Hudson when he checked in, so he needed to dress like a businessman.

Barboza got the word from his contact man that Hudson was arriving at eight thirty and would probably get to the hotel by nine. With this in mind, Barboza arrived early and went into the bar, where the lighting was subdued and there were no cameras. The bar was crowded, which was in his favor, allowing him to blend in with the patrons and most likely never be noticed. He had a drink while waiting, but he did not have to wait long before spotting Hudson as he wended his way over to the reception desk. Barboza paid his tab, left the bar, and, lining up behind Michael, pretended to be busy texting on his phone.

"Good evening, sir, and welcome to the Four Seasons. Are you checking in?" asked the rather pretty blonde desk clerk.

"Yes. My name is Michael Hudson," he said as he placed his credit card on the counter.

She quickly checked for his reservation. "Okay, sir. Here it is. I have a lovely suite on the fourteenth floor with a city view, room 1401. I think you'll be pleased. Can I get a bellman to assist you with your bags?"

"That won't be necessary. I'm traveling light. But may I ask what time your restaurant closes?"

"In another hour, sir. We have a full room service dinner menu if you prefer."

"That sounds even better. Thank you."

The desk clerk passed him the electronic room key. "I hope you enjoy your stay, sir."

"Thank you," Michael replied. With his suit bag slung over one shoulder and his briefcase in his other hand, he then headed to the elevator.

Barboza stepped out of line and strolled away from the reception area and out the front door. Aware that Michael would go to his room and order room service rather than coming down to the restaurant, he walked around outside, making himself scarce for about twenty minutes and allowing Michael time to settle into his room and place his dinner order. He then went back inside and took the elevator to the fourteenth floor, used his contact's pass key for the utility closet, and hid there with the gun, its silencer already attached, in his pocket, staying put till the waiter would arrive with the food cart.

Michael, meanwhile, had stepped off the elevator at the fourteenth floor, scanned the room number plaque on the wall, turned left, and headed down the hall. Since it was late, he had decided to make himself comfortable and order a light snack and a glass of cabernet from room service. He would chill out and turn in early. He had a long day ahead of him tomorrow.

The suite had a beautiful sitting room with tastefully appointed furnishings, decorated in browns and dark green. There was a round conference table on one side of the room with a chandelier overhead. On the wall opposite the hunter green sofa there was a fifty-five-inch flat-screen TV. The bedroom had a king-size bed with plush linens and a duvet cover; there was a huge armoire with another flat-screen TV housed inside, and a lounge chair and ottoman next to the bed. The bathroom was opulent, with black granite walls and floors and white marble trimmings, a jetted tub, a separate shower, and double sinks with gold faucets. Beth would love this bathroom, he thought. In the sitting room, Michael closed the green and brown floral drapes, but not before he took a moment to enjoy the view of the brightly lit Boston skyline, with its amazing variety of architecturally distinct skyscrapers. The shimmering city lights made him think of how one day he would like to bring Beth here for a weekend escape. She loved the excitement and energy of cities, and Boston surely offered that. He thought it would be nice to share its ambience with her as it was quieter, with less hustle and bustle than New York. Without the 24–7 background noise of sirens, horns, and street sounds, the people were not as stressed out. Michael had enjoyed it immensely while attending Harvard Law School. Unfortunately, on this trip he would have no time to visit colleagues who had stayed on after graduation. When he returned with Beth, he would introduce her to his law school buddies.

The suite looked inviting to Michael after a long trip, and he was eager to get out of his suit and into the hotel's terry cloth robe. He placed his dinner order and then decided to give Beth a call before it got too late.

"Hi, gorgeous. I'm already settled in my hotel and wanted to check on you before the time got away from me."

"Michael. So glad to hear from you. How was your flight?"

"Uneventful, but it's still been a long day, and I'm anxious about tomorrow's meeting."

"I know things will go well for you. You worry too much. It'll all work out. You'll see."

"I wish I was as optimistic as you, Beth. How do you always remain so positive?"

"I think about all the people who care about me and I about them. It's what got me through my recovery, and when I get down, I think about you, or Mom and Dad, and I'm right back there again."

"Good advice. I think I'll pin your picture inside my suit coat."

"Oh, Michael. You're so funny."

"Well, at least my meeting isn't until late morning, so I'll review my notes tonight and recheck them in the morning."

"Sounds like a plan, honey. Call me afterward and let me know how it went."

"Will do, babe. So tell me, how'd your day go? Are you back to kicking those husbands' asses?"

"You bet. I've set a meeting with Brian's attorney for this week and hopefully I'll get Lisa's settlement signed, sealed, and delivered. We're finally in the home stretch."

"How's Lisa holding up?"

"She just wants it over. She's emotionally drained. I hope you're being careful, Michael. I worry about you with this lunatic still running around. Did your bodyguard come with you?"

"No, Beth, I didn't feel it necessary since I left town. Don't worry, honey. I'll be safe here. The police are looking for the guy in New York."

"Well, if you say so. But it still doesn't hurt to look over your shoulder once in awhile."

They talked another ten minutes and hung up feeling secure and reassured about their relationship being back on track. Beth was starting to get more comfortable with her feelings, and her doubts about their courtship were lessening with each loving contact like tonight's phone call. Even though they were hundreds of miles apart, she felt close to him. Time would tell, but for now she was happy and optimistic about the future.

Michael was enjoying the surroundings of his beautiful suite and thinking about Beth. He thought that when he returned to New York he'd invite her to come back to Boston so she could meet his friends, see the city, and visit his alma mater. He felt confident that their relationship was headed in the right direction. This made him happy and hopeful.

Barboza had cracked open the utility closet door on the fourteenth floor and was watching the hallway. Ten minutes later, the elevator door opened, and when he saw the waiter roll the food trolley off the elevator, he stepped out of the closet and approached him. "Excuse me, but is this order for room 1401?" asked Barboza.

The Hispanic waiter, appearing well starched in his uniform, cheerfully responded, "Yes, sir, is that your room?"

Barboza quickly pulled a rope from behind his back and dragged the waiter by his neck into the nearby utility closet. He acted so fast and with so much force that the waiter was unable to utter a sound. Barboza closed the door and twisted the rope until the waiter fell to the floor. He then put a plastic bag over his head and tied it around his neck to make sure there was no air left for him to gasp. He stripped the waiter of his clothing, removed his own business attire, slipped into the starched uniform, jammed the gun and paper shoe-covers into a deep pocket, and tucked the laundry bag with street clothes, and now his business attire as well, on a shelf under the trolley. After stuffing the body in large black garbage bags, Barboza positioned it at the back of the closet, behind an abundance of cleaning supplies, then exited the closet and locked the door from the inside. He approached the trolley, took the gun out of his pocket, placed it under the dome covering the plate, and proceeded to roll the trolley down the hall to room 1401. His timing was impeccable, for not one guest got off the elevator or walked down the hall with the possibility of identifying him.

He knocked on the door. "Room service," Barboza said. The door was opened with the safety latch since Michael remembered what Beth had said.

Barboza smiled at Hudson's wary face through the crack in the door. Hudson then opened the door and showed the waiter into the sitting room. Barboza wheeled the trolley in, placed it alongside the round conference table, and pulled out a chair for his guest.

Hudson gave him the once-over and thought to himself, What a nice appearance he makes in his starched white uniform. "Thank you," Hudson said. "That'll be fine." He then walked over to the end table, picked up his wallet, removed a ten-dollar bill, and handed the waiter the tip before he sat down.

Barboza said, "Thanks so much, sir. You're most generous. Please sit down and enjoy."

After Hudson sat down, Barboza placed the dome-covered plate on the table, removed the stainless steel cover, and before Hudson could react, picked up the gun, placed it against Hudson's chest, and shot him directly in the heart. His lifeless body slumped over the table, and blood began to gush out of the entry wound in his chest.

Barboza placed two fingers on his mark's carotid artery and waited until his pulse was impalpable, after which Hudson took his last breath. Barboza was wearing the waiter's white gloves and now pulled out the paper shoe-covers and slipped them over his shoes. He next smoothed out the carpet from the door to the table to erase any footprint impressions. He found Michael's cell phone on the table and put it in his pocket, then took out his street clothes from the laundry bag under the trolley. He removed the waiter's now blood-splattered uniform and put on his street clothes. The uniform, shoe covers, gloves, and gun were all put in the laundry bag, along with the business attire. Barboza cracked the door to make sure the hallway was clear, took the bag, and left, sliding the Do Not Disturb sign over the doorknob on his way out. He sprinted down the hall to the Exit door leading to the stairs and hurried down fourteen flights with his baseball cap pulled over his forehead and eyes.

Barboza exited the hotel by the side door, unnoticed. He briskly walked to the nearby subway station and took a train to

South Boston, where there were many homeless people standing around who would never be able to identify him. There he went down a dark alley and found a trashcan, where he dumped the laundry bag and threw a match inside. Several blocks over was a strip mall with a large dumpster in the back, where he discarded the gun and cell phone. Using his phony name, he checked into a fleabag motel and confirmed his flight back to New York for the next day. Tomorrow night he would deliver another letter to the postal box to inform Giachetti that the job was done. He called the letter courier, Angelo Giovanni, and left a message for tomorrow night's pickup. After he collected his final payment, he would return to Boston, and nobody would be the wiser for it.

The next morning housekeeping found Michael Hudson's body. Within fifteen minutes the room was teaming with police, crime scene investigators, and the medical examiner. The police roped off the entire floor until they could collect their evidence and have the body removed to the city morgue. Detective Tyler Simpson was assigned as the lead investigator on the case. He was one of Boston PD's best detectives, with twenty-five years on the job. He wasn't tall or intimidating, but his manner was very direct—a take-charge kind of guy. Simpson had dark brown hair, freshly cut and styled, and a slight beer belly, but was professionally dressed in black trousers, a white open-collar shirt, and a black herringbone blazer. After flashing his badge to one of the cops stationed in the lobby, Simpson was directed up to the crime scene on the fourteenth floor.

As Detective Simpson entered room 1401, he said, "Fill me in, boys," and then approached Michael's lifeless body.

"Looks like one straight to the heart," answered the medical examiner.

"I'm Detective Simpson," he said, putting out his hand. "I didn't get your name."

"Elliott Sydney, the medical examiner," he said to Simpson. "Nice to meet you."

"Are you new in the department? I'm used to working with Angela Shea."

"She retired. I just started last week. Glad to meet you."

"Likewise, Elliott. You transfer in?"

"I was the medical examiner in Springfield. Needed more of a challenge."

"Well, you'll certainly get it here. So what can you tell me so far?"

"He was shot at point-blank range. And, by the size of the wound, it looks like it could've been a thirty-eight." Simpson nodded. "I put the time of death around ten last night.

"Poor fellow didn't know what hit him," said one of the investigators. "Looks like he ordered room service, and the killer was disguised as a waiter, hid the gun somewhere on the food cart, and blasted him right in the heart. His name is Michael Hudson, from the Big Apple. By the looks of the paperwork in his briefcase, he was an attorney who came here to work on a case. We've been unable to find a cell phone. The perp must've taken it."

"Did the perp leave us any calling cards?" Simpson asked.

"No prints on the trolley, even brought paper shoe-covers to smooth out any footprints," the investigator told him.

"So what does that tell us, Eddie?"

"A contract hit by a professional. And I'm not holding my breath for DNA either."

Simpson nodded. "I suspect the gun is long gone as well, but just in case he got spooked by a patrol car or a beat cop, have the uniforms check the dumpsters for the gun."

Eddie headed out as the medical examiner turned to Simpson. "Once we retrieve the bullet from his chest, I can identify its caliber." He paused a second. "From the powder residue on the vic's shirt, I'd say he put the gun right up to his chest."

"What does that tell us, Elliot?" Simpson asked. At this stage in his career, he was also training those coming up.

"It was personal," Elliot said.

"Yeah, somebody settling a score." Simpson took his note pad and pen from his inside jacket pocket and started taking notes. "Marshall," he said addressing another detective, "let's knock on every door on this floor and see if anyone saw the perp go in or out of the room last night." Next, Simpson called out to a uniformed officer, "Robinette, get the manager up here. We need to question every employee who was on duty last night. Let's find out who the waiter was who brought up the dinner. He's crucial in this case. Let's find him now!"

Within ten minutes the manager, Barry Sullivan, came up to the suite and identified himself to Simpson. "What can I do to help?"

"We need to find out who was on duty last night in the kitchen and delivered this room service order," Simpson said. "The time of death was just about the time the food was delivered."

"No problem. I'll pull up the schedule."

"Also, could you please call in your entire kitchen staff, bartenders from the bar, and the people at the reception desk last night. Anybody on duty who might've seen something."

"I'm on it, detective. I'll have everyone come back now and gather in the conference room. It might take a little while, but I'll explain the urgency."

"Thanks, Barry. Also, I'll need your switchboard to check all the calls that came in or out of this room last night, and have an IT person gather the lobby footage from your surveillance cameras."

"Got it."

Detective Simpson searched the room himself and went through the victim's personal belongings while the manager was rounding up the employees on duty last night at the time of the murder. An hour later Simpson walked into the conference room where Barry Sullivan was waiting for the rest of the employees to arrive. There were about ten men and women seated around the table. Simpson walked to the front of the room and addressed the staff.

"Good morning. My name is Detective Tyler Simpson, and I'm investigating a homicide that occurred in room 1401 at approximately ten o'clock last night. Is there anyone here who can tell me who took the food service order up to that room last night?" There was no response.

The manager then said to the detective, "That was Tony Alvarez who was assigned to the fourteenth floor last night. We thought he skipped out afterward because he never came back down and hasn't been answering his cell phone."

Simpson nodded. "Take one of my men and go through every closet and utility room from the thirteenth to the fifteenth floor."

"Oh my. You don't think...?" Sullivan asked tentatively.

"Let's not presume anything yet. Just check." One of the detectives stepped forward and walked off with the manager.

Simpson handed several employees in the first row Michael Hudson's photo, copied and enlarged from the license in his wallet. "Please pass these around and see if any of you remember seeing this man last night—at the reception desk, in the lobby, the bar, or just walking around. One young woman raised her hand. "Yes, detective. I registered him when he checked in. He asked me what time the restaurant closed, and I told him and added that we offered a full room service dinner menu. A very polite and handsome gentleman. Then I saw him walk toward the elevators."

"Did you notice anyone standing near him while he was checking in?" Simpson asked.

"No, sorry, I don't recall. It was pretty busy."

"Anybody else notice anything strange around that time?"

Someone else raised his hand. "I was bartending last night. There was a guy sitting at the end of the bar nursing a drink but really focused on the lobby, and then suddenly he got up, threw money on the bar, and hurried out."

"Are there cameras in the bar?"

"I'm afraid not, but I could give you a description."

"Good. I'll have you sit down with one of my detectives. Don't leave."

Barry Sullivan walked into the room, his face pale as a ghost's. "Detective, we found Tony Alvarez in the fourteenth-floor utility closet. He was strangled to death." Everybody in the room gasped.

"Barry, keep everyone here just for a little while longer. I need to get back upstairs right away."

Simpson took the elevator to the fourteenth floor and followed the officer down the hall, where he showed him Tony Alvarez's body with a plastic bag over his head and wearing a T-shirt and jockey shorts. He was stuffed into two big black garbage bags in the back of the storage closet two doors down from the elevator. The closet was very deep, and all of the mops, buckets, and various cleaning supplies were in front, and the shelving unit was moved to the corner and placed in front of the body.

"What a damn shame," Simpson said, shaking his head. "Poor guy. Only doing his job, but at the wrong place at the wrong time. How unlucky can you get? Now we've got a double homicide. Another day, another body. Our new medical examiner is going to have a busy week. Eddie, get the manager to call the victim's wife and have her come down to ID the body."

"I'll get right on it."

The ligature marks on Tony's neck made it obvious to the detectives that the murderer had grabbed him, placed a rope around his neck, and pulled him into the closet, then strangled him and suffocated him with a plastic bag. Next, he changed into the victim's uniform, put his own clothing into a laundry bag, and carried it out with him.

Simpson took out Michael Hudson's business card from his wallet and called his office. "Michael Hudson's office. This is Meredith speaking."

"Hi, Meredith, this is Detective Simpson from the Boston PD. Are you Michael Hudson's secretary?"

"Yes I am, detective. Are you helping Michael with his case?"

As many times as Simpson had made these types of calls, it never got any easier. He hated giving such bad news over the phone, but in this case he had no choice. "No, ma'am," he said. "I'm afraid not. I'm so sorry, but I have some distressing news. Mr. Hudson was murdered last night in his hotel room at the

Four Seasons." There was no response. "Hello, hello. Meredith, are you there?" Still no response. "Hello, anybody there?"

Detective Simpson kept the connection and two minutes later a man's voice came on the line.

"Hello, who is this, please? What's going on? One of our secretaries just fainted."

"This is Detective Tyler Simpson with the Boston PD. To whom am I speaking?"

"I'm Eric Swanson, a colleague of Michael Hudson's. Can you tell me what's going on?"

"I'm so sorry, Mr. Swanson, but Mr. Hudson was murdered last night in his hotel room at the Four Seasons here in Boston. We're in the process of investigating the crime."

"What? Did you say murdered?"

Simpson took a deep breath before answering. "Yes, sir. I'm afraid I did."

"So that's why Meredith fainted. Oh my Lord, how dreadful!" Simpson could hear Swanson call out in a panic, "Get Jeff Greene down here ASAP. Hurry! Tell him it's urgent!" He now spoke into the phone. "This is unbelievable! It can't be happening."

"Eric, I'll need to speak to Meredith as soon as she regains her composure. Could you please give her the message?"

"Certainly, detective. She's being looked after right now. Poor girl. She and Michael were very close. She's going to take this hard."

"I understand," said Simpson.

Simpson left his number and would wait for Meredith's call. She was the only one at this point who would be able to provide him with Michael's family information, which would be his next call.

In New York the managing partner, Jeff Greene, came down to Michael's office to find Meredith lying on the couch with a wet towel on her head. By now, there were three other attorneys in the office standing around in a state of shock. "Will someone tell me what's happened?" Greene asked.

Eric Swanson, a second-year associate, replied, "Michael Hudson was in Boston for a deposition and was murdered in his hotel room last night shortly after he arrived. Meredith just got the call from the Boston PD and passed out cold. Jeff, what are we going to do?"

"Holy mother of God," Greene replied. "Do we know what happened?"

"No," Swanson said. "The detective wanted to speak with Meredith to get more information, but she fainted."

Jeff sat beside Meredith and said, "I'm so sorry, Meredith. This has to be a huge shock. Please take the rest of the day off and go home. You need some time to let this settle. Do you have someone who can be with you?"

"Yes, I'll call my boyfriend. But first I have to call the detective in Boston back. I don't want to let Michael down."

"Okay, Meredith, call and talk to him, but give yourself a minute to pull it together. It can wait." Greene's mind was churning. "I'll call Detective Stevens and inform him of Michael's death. Meredith, you'll also need to speak to Stevens before you leave."

"Okay, if I can just take a moment," Meredith said with tears rolling down her face as Eric tried to console her.

"Take deep breaths, dear. I'll get you some water."

Ten minutes later, Meredith called Detective Simpson and gave him all of Michael's contact information for his family and briefly said something about the threat to his life. "Jeff Greene will have Detective Stevens from the NYPD call and fill you in on the details about the case. Sorry, but I have to go now," she said, as another wave of uncontrollable sobbing erupted.

"Eric, take Meredith to the employee lounge," Greene said. "I know Detective Stevens will want to question her when he arrives."

"Certainly, sir." Eric then stepped over to Meredith and, holding her arm, helped her out of the chair. Meredith slowly walked out of the office but not before glancing at Michael's family photos on the bookshelf.

Then Greene pulled up the number of the NYPD and punched it in on his cell phone.

Detective Stevens and Matthews were coming back from their interviews with one of Giachetti's former crew members from Waterloo Construction. As they walked into the station, Stevens said, "Well, Rob, I think we're definitely getting close, and it looks like what we heard from Carlos Mercado today is crucial to our case. We need to find this Salvator Barboza. Let's put every available man on it."

A few minutes later one of the other detectives shouted out to Stevens. "Hey, Walt, pick up on line five. There's a Jeff Greene wanting to speak to you."

"Thanks, Harry. Got it."

"Hello, Mr. Greene, Stevens here. How can I help you?"

"Detective, we've never had the pleasure, but I'm the managing partner in Michael Hudson's law firm. We received a call about thirty minutes ago from a Detective Tyler Simpson with the Boston PD releasing some terrible news. Michael Hudson was murdered last night in his hotel room at the Four Seasons around ten o'clock. We're all devastated! It looks as if Giachetti got to him after all. That bastard!"

Stevens was speechless and went silent for a moment. "What can I say, sir? This is such a tragedy! And we were on to the hit man who did it. We had no idea he was in Boston. We've been trying to locate him locally, with no luck. We just ran out of time. Dammit to hell! Can you give me the detective's name in charge of the case in Boston again?"

"Sure. It's Tyler Simpson. He called, and Michael's secretary Meredith gave him a few details of the case.

"Thanks, Mr. Greene, I'll take it from here. This makes me sick. Such a good guy. What a waste."

"One of our best lawyers, detective. He'll be greatly missed. And now I'll go on beating myself up wondering how we could've prevented this. If only we'd known earlier about the threats, maybe Michael would still be alive."

"It is not your fault, so please don't do this to yourself. Everything possible was being done to find this creep. We just ran out of time, but we've got him on our radar now, and both he and Giachetti are going to pay for it."

"Are you going to tell Beth?" Jeff asked.

"She wasn't at the office today?"

"No, she's working from home."

"I'll be right over, Jeff. I need to talk to Meredith. Then afterward, I'll go to Beth's apartment and tell her. I'll call her doctor as well, just in case she might need something to calm her down. I know this is going to be tough on her." Stevens hung up the phone while staring across his desk at Matthews.

"Did I hear what I thought I heard, Walt? Did that bastard get to Hudson?"

"Yep, he was murdered last night in his hotel room in Boston."

"Fucking animal," Matthews said, running his hand through his hair. "Can't fucking believe it!" Matthews stood up and tried to walk off his anger. He slammed his fist on his desk, knocking over the phone and some papers. The other policemen in the room turned to see what the commotion was about, but Matthews wasn't done. He turned around and kicked the metal file cabinet, making a loud clanging sound, which brought the captain out of his office.

"What's going on out here?" yelled Captain Parker.

Stevens stood up to face the captain, with the fingers of one hand to his temple. "Cap, on the Beth Scott case we're too late. Michael Hudson was murdered last night in his hotel room in Boston. We just got the name of a prime suspect this afternoon, and I'm willing to stake my retirement on the fact that he's our guy. It really sucks! We probably were just one day too late. And the thing that really gets me is that I told Michael to take his bodyguard with him. He said that since he was going out of state he'd be fine. I should've insisted, captain. I blame myself. It's *my* fuck-up!"

"Listen, Walter," Parker said, his hand on Stevens's shoulder. "Don't start the blame game. You know how this stuff works. You do your very best, and sometimes it isn't good enough. As detectives, we aren't the Almighty and can't control everything; cases take on legs and run the way they want sometimes, and this is one of those times. A day late is better than not nailing him at all."

"I know, captain, but it's still hard to swallow. And the hardest part is yet to come—breaking the news to Beth. They were together again and planning a future. I need to do that soon. It's gonna be rough. These are the times I hate this job."

"Well, if it's any consolation, I'd rather it come from you than just about anybody else."

Stevens almost teared up. "Thanks, captain. I appreciate that. It helps."

Captain Parker patted him on the back and went into his office. Stevens turned to his partner. "Rob, I'm going to Michael's office to question Meredith. Round up the team, and let's find everything there is to know on Barboza. I want this guy caught yesterday. We need to give the Boston PD a rundown on our case and everything we find about him. He's most likely still in Boston, and we need to get them an ID."

"I'm on it, Walt."

When Detective Stevens walked into Michael Hudson's office, he found his secretary composed and sitting in a chair. She was very professional-looking in a navy blue suit, with her light brown hair pulled back in a bun. Her eyes were red from crying, and her eye makeup was smeared. There were five attorneys in the room talking about Michael and consoling one another when the detective walked in and headed toward Meredith.

"Meredith, I'm so sorry for what happened to Michael. I know this must be a huge shock to you and the firm. But I need you to remember anything that might help us catch this guy. Are you up for that?"

Still visibly shaken, Meredith said, "I'll try my best."

"Do you remember taking any calls recently where you told that person that Michael was going to be in Boston?"

"Yes. Last week a Mark Stone called and asked for an appointment. I gave him Michael's available dates. He then asked why he wouldn't be available on the other two days, and I said that Michael would be in Boston. He was very smooth trying to get information. So now I understand why he asked about those days, so he could follow him. Oh my God, I told the killer where he was going. This is all my fault. He followed Michael to Boston and killed him!" Meredith broke down sobbing once again.

"You had no idea at the time, so please don't blame yourself, Meredith." Stevens took his handkerchief out of his pocket and gave it to her. "Did you happen to get his phone number or contact information?"

"No, he told me he'd call me back to confirm his meeting next week. I asked him how Michael could reach him, and he said he'd prefer to call Michael, and that was the extent of the conversation."

"I'm sure he used a bogus name, but I'll check it out. I'll also need the name and phone number of the detective who called you from Boston."

"Here it is," she said, handing the detective a sheet of paper containing the information. "And do you have the number of Michael's parents?" Steven's asked.

"Yes, I'll get it for you." She walked out to her desk to retrieve the number. "I did call the detective back in Boston and gave him these numbers."

"Thanks a lot, Meredith. Can you think of anything else Michael might have said that would be worth noting?"

She thought for a moment. "No, detective. But if I remember something, I'll call you immediately."

"You've been a big help, Meredith. Take care of yourself."

"I will, detective." Then she turned to Eric and said, "I'm ready to go home now."

"Absolutely, Meredith. Let's get going," Eric replied.

Jeff Greene stood up and announced, "Detective, I would like to go with you over to Beth's apartment and be there for support when you tell her."

"Sure thing. My car is right out in front. You'd better stiffen your upper lip, Jeff. This isn't going to be easy."

"I know, detective. That's why I want to go. I feel some culpability here. I had no idea that secretaries were telling prospective clients the whereabouts of our attorneys. This was a breach of confidentiality. I'll make sure a memo goes out tomorrow."

Next, Stevens phoned Beth. "Hi, this is Detective Stevens calling. How are you?"

"I'm well, detective. Do you have some good news for me?"

"Well actually, I'd like to stop by if that's all right with you."

"Sure, come on over. What's this about?"

"I wanted to update you on the case. I'll tell you everything when I see you."

Stevens and Greene left the office and headed over to Beth's apartment. On the way, Stevens called Dr. Burton to inform him of the situation, and he agreed to come be with Beth when she was told the news.

Traffic wasn't too heavy, and Stevens and Greene pulled in front of Beth's building twenty minutes later. Stevens told the bodyguard about Michael Hudson's murder and asked if Dr. Burton had arrived yet. When Charlie shook his head no, Stevens said, "Send him up as soon as he arrives."

"Will do, detective."

As the two men got off the elevator, Stevens asked, "Are you ready for this?"

Jeff Greene shook his head. "No way. I've never had to do anything like this before. You're taking the lead on this one, and I'm just here to comfort her."

"Not to worry, Jeff. Unfortunately I've done this before, but it never gets any easier."

Stevens knocked on the door. He heard Beth say, "Who is it?"

"Detective Stevens."

Beth checked the peephole and then opened the door. She was surprised to see Jeff Greene standing beside Stevens.

"Jeff, what are you doing here?"

The two men stepped into the apartment. "I asked Detective Stevens if I could come with him." They walked over to the sofa.

"Can we sit down?" asked Stevens.

Beth nodded and took a seat across from him, with Jeff sitting next to her. "What's this about?" she asked, suddenly feeling apprehensive.

"Beth, we're here to tell you what happened to Michael last night." A puzzled look came over Beth's face, and frown lines appeared on her forehead.

"Was he in an accident or something? I just spoke with him last night from his hotel room in Boston." Beth asked.

Stevens continued, "After he checked into his room, he ordered dinner from room service, and the waiter who brought it up was a hit man who shot him in the chest."

Beth turned white and was speechless. Both men were silent. After a few moments, Beth asked, "Is he okay? Did he survive the gunshot? Is he in the hospital?"

Jeff reached over and took Beth's hand firmly. "No, Beth. He's not okay."

"Are you trying to tell me that Michael's dead?"

"Yes, Beth. He was shot directly in the heart at point-blank range. There was nothing anyone could've done. It happened so fast he didn't know what hit him."

Beth began sobbing. Jeff put his arm around her and held her close.

Brandon arrived, saw Beth crying, and sat on the other side of her. "Beth, I'm so terribly sorry."

"Brandon, I just can't believe this. Where was his bodyguard?"

Stevens responded, "He didn't think it was necessary to bring him to Boston. He was sure the perp was here in New York and he'd be safe there." Beth put her hands over her face and continued to sob. "Oh my! This is God-awful. I don't know what I'm going to do."

"Beth, there is nothing for you to do except deal with your grief," Brandon said. "Just put everything else in pause mode and feel your way through this horrific upset. I can give you a sedative but don't want to numb you out." Beth nodded her head through her tears. "You shouldn't be alone, and I would recommend going to your parents' house for a few days. You need to be around people who love you and can be supportive."

Stevens stood up and said he had to get back to the precinct and that they were chasing down a very good lead. "Beth, I'm leaving you in good hands here. I'll let you know more after I speak with the detective who's handling the investigation in Boston."

"Am I going to be next?" Beth asked Stevens, visibly shaken. Brandon took a knitted throw off the back of the sofa and placed it around her shoulders. Beth buried her head in the blanket and kept picturing Michael's face as it was when he had been sitting on her couch. She remembered his soft touch and gentle demeanor. Such a kind soul, she thought to herself. Way too young to leave this world with so much left to accomplish.

"Please don't think like that, Beth. Michael was always the target. They hurt you to hurt him. That's all. And we think we know who it is. We're very close to making an arrest. I'll keep you posted, Beth." Stevens looked at the two men beside her. "Gentlemen, thanks for being here for her. I'll talk to you later." Stevens left the apartment and told Charlie to keep alert, but doubted if they'd come after Beth again. He felt certain that Giachetti's mission had been completed.

Brandon took Beth to her parents' house, and Jeff Greene went back to his office, determined to instigate practices so this would never happen to one of his lawyers again.

Stevens returned to the precinct and took a seat at his desk. "How'd it go, Walt?" asked Mathews.

"About as bad as you would expect. That poor girl has been through so much, and then I had to drop this bomb on her."

Matthews tossed Stevens a file. "This is what we've come up with so far on Barboza."

Stevens quickly read through the two single-spaced pages of background. "Rob, this is great. Your team pulled it together really fast."

Stevens took a deep breath and tried to focus on what he had to do next. "Got to call the Boston detective." Matthews nodded and got back to work.

Stevens picked up his cell phone and punched in the number. "May I please speak to Detective Tyler Simpson? This is Detective Stevens from the NYPD calling on the Michael Hudson case."

"Oh yes, detective, he's been waiting for your call. Hold for a minute."

A moment later, the man picked up the call. "Detective, this is Tyler Simpson. Terrible thing what happened to that young man."

"I know, and we'll work together to nail the bastard. We have a suspect by the name of Salvator Barboza. He used to live in New York but left a year ago to work for the DiNunzio crime family. Are you familiar with them, detective?"

"Sure am, and we've been trying to put them out of business for years."

"So can you give me all the details on the murder?" asked Stevens.

Simpson told Stevens that it was a double homicide. "The killer intercepted the waiter with the food trolley and dragged him into the utility closet, where he strangled him to death. Then he put on the waiter's uniform and disguised himself as one of the staff so he could enter the room. He had placed the gun under the dome on the plate and then, after Michael was seated, removed the dome and blasted him in the chest. Made a quick getaway down the stairs. And that's all we know at this point. We questioned the staff on duty and every guest on the floor, and no one saw anybody. We're checking for prints, but doubt if we'll find anything. It looks like a professional hit, detective, and you know how that goes. Hard to make a case without any evidence, unless there's a witness."

We have a sketch from the bartender, so if I can locate him on the premises I could bring him in for questioning."

Stevens added, "Please keep me informed when the crime unit has completed its investigation."

Simpson said that the gun had not been found in the room. "I'm sure he disposed of it somewhere, but we'll let you know when the crime scene investigation has completed its evidence gathering and if we have any DNA. We'll get a ballistics report on the bullet to identify the weapon. Usually, if it was a Mob hit we can tie the model to the Mob. They always use the same weapons. When it's close range like this one, it's a Beretta PT 92 or a Glock 36. We'll let you know as soon as the medical examiner completes the autopsy. We're very familiar with this Mob family's choice of weapons."

"That would be great, Tyler. Appreciate it. But we wanted to give you a heads-up on our end so you'll understand the whole picture. The guy we suspect is Salvator Barboza, who was hired by a man named Frank Giachetti, serving time here in New York. Hudson represented him when he was caught for bank robberies and lost the case and the appeal. So this job was payback. Giachetti also hired Barboza to beat up Hudson's girlfriend first, who almost ended up dead. We were able to track down Barboza to when he worked a construction job and Giachetti was his boss. Even though he lived in Boston, he flew back here to beat up Hudson's girlfriend and then returned to Boston. We have a feeling that he'll be coming back to New York to make contact one last time with Giachetti and pick up his money for the hit. So I'd have your men check out the airports today and tomorrow. I doubt that he'd go back to where he resides tonight. He'll definitely make himself scarce."

"Yes, you're probably right. I think he'd be holed up in a hotel tonight near the airport," said Simpson.

"One other thing. The girlfriend, also an attorney—a Ms. Beth Scott—can probably identify him in a lineup."

"That's good to know 'cause our case could be all circumstantial at this end if we can't recover any DNA. I'll start doing financials on him as well, but these Mob guys are pretty good at hiding their assets. If you can give me the date of the attack on the girlfriend, I can try to see if he had any large bank deposits around that time—or if he has a safe deposit box, we can get a court order to open it."

"Absolutely, detective. No problem. Let me know if there's anything else you need. Meantime, we'll continue to tie up the last loose ends back here. Good luck."

"You got it, detective. I'll be in touch."

Stevens clicked off his cell phone. He sat back in his chair but got a sick feeling in the pit of his stomach as he thought about Michael. Such an accomplished guy with an amazingly bright future and what looked like a possible happy marriage to the beautiful Ms. Scott—all swept away in a matter of seconds. Sometimes this job really sucks, he thought.

Chapter

Sixteen

*H*aving carried out the hit on Michael Hudson, Barboza was now eager to pick up his final payment. He was settled in his motel room, and he would call Giovanni to schedule a letter pickup for tomorrow night and inform Giachetti that Hudson was dead. He had picked up a pizza on the way to the motel and ate that first, with a couple beers to take the edge off.

Barboza stepped outside to the pay phone and called Giovanni. The answering machine came on. "Leave a message," it said.

"Hey, Giovanni, I need another pickup tomorrow night at nine o'clock. Please don't be late. It's very important that you show." Barboza's flight was scheduled to arrive at six thirty in the evening. He would take the subway to Brooklyn and walk to the post office on Fulton Street, drop off the letter, and make himself inconspicuous until Angelo picked it up. Then he would lock up the box and walk away. He would return the following night to pick up his money and then fly back to Boston.

The next afternoon, as Barboza was getting ready to leave for the airport, his cell phone chimed. He answered. It was his boss.

"Hi, Sal, this is Carmen. You doing any side jobs these days?" Barboza caught his breath. "Reason I ask, is that the Boston PD has put out a BOLO on you. Wanna tell me about it?"

"Jesus," he said, wondering how they connected him so soon. "Yeah, took out a lawyer for an ole friend of mine. Paid a hundred grand, so the 'family' has fifty grand coming their way. I'm en route to New York to pick up the money."

"Was this at the Four Seasons?"

"Yeah. Guess your guy at the BPD filled you in?"

"It's a real mess, Sal. A double homicide. And the NYPD has also connected you to the attack on the guy's girlfriend in New York. You're not going anywhere. You need to make yourself scarce and do a little work on your identity. You know, shave off your moustache, color your hair or shave it off, and don't go back to your place. They've got it staked out. You know the drill, so get to it! Also, the girl in New York says she can identify you. You might have to take care of that situation too, if you know what I mean." He paused. "Jesus, Sal."

"Boss, I don't know how that's possible. I had on a hoodie and black sunglasses. She never saw my face. And it didn't take long to knock her out. It would be impossible for her to ID me with any degree of certainty. That's pure bullshit! There's no way."

"I'm just telling you what I hear. And when you slip up on a personal hit, it's your ass, not the 'family's.' Got it? This had nothing to do with us and we can't be linked to it. You understand? We can't protect you."

"Yes, I understand. I know what I need to do. Thanks, boss. I'll lay low for a while and figure out another way to get our money. I'll be in touch."

"Ditch your cell and get a burner phone, then let us know where you're hiding out."

"Will do," said Barboza. He now had to rethink his plan: he couldn't fly back to New York, so he'd have to figure out another way to contact Giachetti and arrange to get the money. *What a fucking mess! I need to get my shit together. I let the "family" down. I'll have to make sure the bitch in New York can't ID me. I'll figure something out and make it right.*

After Carmen DiNunzio hung up the phone, he turned to his henchman Cosmo, who was sitting on his leather sofa picking his nails with a knife. "Get Gino. I may have some cleanup work for him."

"You takin' the worm out?"

"Cosmo, get your skinny ass out of here and do what I say."

"Sure thing, boss."

Walter Stevens stumbled into the precinct around eight the next morning a little hung over. After yesterday's shock wave, he and Matthews had downed a few beers at Jake's Dilemma, a West Side cop bar, and didn't get out of there until two in the morning. Clutching his coffee cup, he sat at his desk and found a phone message from Giovanni that had been logged in late last night. He returned the call.

"What's up, Angelo? This is Detective Stevens."

"I got another message on my machine last night from Barboza, scheduling a pickup for tonight at nine. What am I supposed to do?"

This woke Stevens up. "Great, Angelo. This guy killed the girl's boyfriend last night in Boston and is coming back to pick up his money. You be there at nine, and we'll have the place staked out so we can nab him. Any questions?"

"Just make sure I'm out of there before you arrest him. You know what the Mob does to rats."

"Not to worry. He won't enter the post office until he sees you leave."

"Any reward money?"

"Angelo, you're lucky we don't lock up your ass as an accessory," Stevens spit out. "Stay there until we can retrieve the recording." He hung up the phone.

Rob Matthews had come in as Stevens was talking. "So Barboza's coming in for a letter exchange?"

"Yeah, looks like it. We need to get a techie to Angelo's house pronto to erase the message from his machine."

Matthews called tech support and gave them Giovanni's address and the work order.

"Rob," Stevens said, looking at him across his desk. "We have a full day on our plate so far. We need to pay Giachetti another visit and force a confession from him. And we need to arrange a stakeout of the post office in Brooklyn for this evening."

"It's on Fulton, and there's a deli right across the street where we can catch a bite to eat while we're waiting." Stevens looked surprised. "Those Brooklyn girls are really something."

"Well, let's just hope you don't get recognized."

They went into Captain Parker's office and told him about a possible stakeout and the trip to Sing Sing. He agreed to both and said he'd get his second-in-command, Lieutenant Daniels, to set up the stakeout while they head to the prison.

As they left the office, Stevens said, "Yeah, let's get some payback for Michael and Beth."

The two detectives arrived at the prison around eleven o'clock and were led by one of the guards into the interrogation room to wait for Giachetti. They were prepared to offer him a deal if he would identify Barboza as his accomplice for Michael's murder and Beth's attack. Two guards led Giachetti into the room in shackles, and he shuffled to the chair across from them.

As the prisoner sat down, Stevens told him. "Frank, I believe you know my partner, Detective Matthews. We're here to inform you that Michael Hudson was murdered in his hotel room in Boston last night, and we have a suspect who's linked to you. We're in the process of locating Salvator Barboza. You worked with him at Waterloo Construction, remember? And we know he's the guy you hired to kill Michael Hudson and assault Beth Scott. Are we getting warm, Frank?" He paused hoping to get a reaction from Giachetti, but the prisoner was blank-faced, cold as stone.

"Look, Frank, murder for hire is a federal capital crime and can get you a death sentence, so unless you want a date with the needle, confess and opt for a plea bargain. We know that Barboza is your outside man."

"Sure, I knew Sal Barboza from my construction days. But that doesn't mean I had anything to do with him afterward. I haven't seen or heard from that guy in years. So, detectives, if this is all you got, I think you need to get off my case 'cause I got nothin' more to say."

"Don't play dumb with us, Frank. We know you set the whole thing up with Barboza, using Angelo Giovanni as your messenger."

"Prove it."

"We have all your letters that were written in a cryptic code, which we had translated, where you gave instructions to have Michael Hudson followed and then told Barboza to beat up someone close to him. We also saw in the letters your plan to murder Michael Hudson. And Giovanni said you paid him three thousand dollars to deliver the letters back and forth from you to the postal box in Brooklyn. And now we have a voice message from Barboza last night on Giovanni's phone scheduling another pickup tonight, which we assume will be the letter informing you that Hudson is dead and Barboza wants his money. Beth Scott can identify him. So unless you want to switch cells to death row, you need to cooperate with us. You may be able to swing a deal if you give up Barboza as the hit man. The more cooperative you are, the easier it'll be on you."

Stevens leaned forward and continued. "One final thing, Frank—now that we have you for Michael Hudson's murder, you'll need to tell us where the money is hidden that you stole in the bank heists if you want a deal with the federal prosecutors."

"You clowns are really amusing. You think you're so smart. Well, just let me tell you that if you think you're gonna find Barboza, you're both bigger idiots than I ever figured. From what I hear, ole Sal has a good job with the DiNunzio family in Boston. And do you think they'd ever let one of their boys get caught where he could leak information? Don't think so. Sal will end up buried in Belle Isle Marsh first. So good luck with that, detectives, and without Barboza you've got a big fat zero."

"Look, Frank, the DA has talked with the US Attorney's Office and they're prepared to take the death penalty off the table if you confess and give up the money and your go-between. I need you to do that *now*, Frank," said Stevens.

"Detectives, I think we're done here. When you find Barboza, dead or alive, let me know. Guard, get me the fuck out of here. I've had enough of these jerks."

After Giachetti was hauled away, the detectives went to see if Warden Stewart had discovered the prison mole who was facilitating the letter exchange. When they arrived at his office, his secretary, a new girl, buzzed the warden and then showed them into his office.

"Nice to see you again, warden," said Stevens. "I don't know if you've heard, but Michael Hudson was killed in his hotel room last night in Boston."

Stewart shook his head. "Son of a bitch, and the fucker pulled it off from here." He stood up to walk off his anger. "Doesn't set a very good example for the other prisoners."

"No, it doesn't, sir. Speaking of which, have you come up with anything on Giachetti's mole yet?"

"Yes, I did. It was my secretary who took the bribe and collected a nice piece of change for passing the letters through to Giachetti. Last time I hire an ex-con for anything around here. She's being held on bribery charges by the locals, but now it looks like they might add 'accessory to murder.'"

"Well, we may need her to testify, so keep her under wraps," Stevens said. The warden nodded his head. "Want to fill you in on our interview with Giachetti. He's still holding out and won't confess. We're sure Sal Barboza is his accomplice, and we need to find him. What we don't need is him calling out to Carmen DiNunzio. Can you restrict his phone privileges?"

"Sure, but unless I throw him into isolation he'll get somebody else here to pass the message."

"And you can't do that?"

"Sorry, detective. The rules work both ways. But I'll have my guards keep their eyes and ears open."

"Thanks, warden. We appreciate anything you can do. Have a great day."

Stevens and Matthews arrived back at the precinct extremely weary and disappointed. Without Giachetti's confession, they would have to capture Barboza and sweat it out of him.

Stevens called Detective Tyler Simpson in Boston to pass along Giachetti's threat that Carmen DiNunzio would take out Barboza before they could nab him for the crime. Simpson agreed and said they had his place staked out and were chasing down all known associates. They next checked with Lieutenant Daniels, who had set up the stakeout of the Fulton Street post office in Brooklyn.

"Are you sure your guy is going to show?" he asked Stevens.

"Just getting ready to check airline reservations. But he's owed a healthy piece of change and will want to collect it fast. I'll let you know what we turn up."

Matthews found out that Barboza was booked on a flight back to New York tonight but had canceled it this afternoon. "Shit, Walter. Barboza is still in Boston. He canceled his flight."

"No, maybe not," Stevens said. "He could've used a fake name and double-booked. You know all of these guys have phony IDs and credit cards for when they need them. We should still do the stakeout and see if he shows up. The cancellation could be to throw us off. He knows we're on to him."

"Yeah, sounds feasible to me. I think we're right to go ahead with the stakeout, but let's tell Daniels." The lieutenant agreed and they moved forward.

At eight o'clock Stevens and Matthews took a booth at the front window of the Cambridge Deli, across the street from the post office. Their backup was in place, with some plainclothes officers on the inside and others outside waiting in a designated Yellow Cab area. At nine o'clock Angelo Giovanni showed up and went inside to open the postal box. It was locked. He waited about ten minutes and then left. He did what he had always been instructed to do by Barboza: "If no one shows after ten minutes, leave." Daniels kept his team in place for another hour and then made the decision to pull them off. Stevens and Matthews stayed longer, but Barboza was a no-show. If he planned on coming tomorrow, then he would most likely call Giovanni later with instructions and they could set it up again.

The next morning, Stevens placed another call to Detective Simpson in Boston. "Hi, detective. This is Walter Stevens calling. Barboza booked a flight to New York last night to pick up his money but canceled. We staked out the post office thinking he might've booked another flight under an alias, but he never showed. I think his Mob guys heard about the BOLO and clued him in."

"Yeah, I agree, detective," Simpson replied. "Looks like he's gonna hide out here for a while until things cool down a bit. I just hope we can get to him before DiNunzio, if Giachetti's right. I ran his photo by the employees who were on duty the night of the murder. The bartender said that he got a pretty good look at him. We should have the ballistics report back in a few days, and that will confirm the type of weapon used. I'll get back to you, Walter, as soon as I have something. As I said, we've staked out his apartment, but if he's in hiding he won't be back."

"I agree. So we need to dig into his past and see where he'd hole up," Stevens said.

"I figured as much, and we asked the neighbors up here, but he pretty much kept to himself, and nobody knew him very well."

"Thanks, Tyler. I think with us working both ends we'll be able to nail him quickly. Good luck."

The detectives and their team were making this case their top priority. They continued to search for any information on Barboza that they could find. They discovered that he had a cousin with the same last name who lived in the city. After locating his place—a ramshackle walk-up apartment building in Washington Heights—Stevens and Matthews climbed the three flights of stairs and knocked on the door.

"Mr. Barboza, this is NYPD. Please open the door."

The door was cracked open slowly, and a large, stout man with dark hair, brown eyes, and a ruddy complexion stood in front of them. He had the kind of skin that one gets from too much alcohol. They could see the resemblance to his cousin, Sal. After they flashed their badges, Barboza asked, "What's this about, detectives?"

"May we come in, Mr. Barboza?"

"Sure," he said and opened the door wider for them to step inside. "Please have a seat," he said, pointing to a round beat-up kitchen table that looked like it would fall apart if anyone leaned on it.

"Sorry, we didn't get your first name, sir."

"It's Ray. Just call me Ray."

"Ray, is Salvator Barboza a relative of yours?"

"Yes, he's my cousin on my father's side. Why are you asking?"

"We're investigating a few crimes that we think Sal was involved in, and we need your help."

"What type of crimes?" Barboza asked with a puzzled look.

"Pretty serious," Matthews responded. "Like murder serious."

"No way, detectives. I can't believe Sal would be involved in murder. He's really a good guy with a big heart. I think there must be some mistake."

"No, there's no mistake. We have proof, and we need to track him down. When was the last time you saw him, and have you been in contact with him since?"

"About three months ago. He came in for business and only stayed two days."

"What kind of business?" Stevens asked.

"I don't discuss his business with him," Barboza said. "I have no idea what he does."

Stevens turned to Matthews and said, "Three months ago fits into the timeline for when the Scott girl was attacked." He turned back to Barboza. "So, Ray, you said he only stayed two days but never mentioned what he was doing here? Now think really hard, Ray, because if you know something and are not telling us, then you are an accessory to the crime. *Capisce?*"

"Well, he was supposed to stay two days, but it really was only one night. He called me on the second night and said he had a situation and was going back to Boston. That was the last time I spoke to him."

"Okay, now we're getting somewhere," said Stevens. "He didn't come back here, Ray, because he was in the emergency room getting his face stitched up. He attacked a woman, and she fought back and hit him with a glass vase, putting a gash in his cheek."

"Oh my God! Why would he do that, detective?"

"For a lot of money, Ray. It seems as if your cousin is a strong arm for the Mafia."

"Please don't tell him that I told you anything. He's been very good to me and helped me out when I lost my job. I feel terrible that I might be getting him into trouble. I don't want to be responsible for causing him any harm. That wouldn't be right."

"It also wouldn't be right not to cooperate on a murder investigation."

Ray shook his head in dismay. "Who did he murder, detective?"

"Sorry, Ray, I can't discuss the details of the case with you. The murder occurred in Boston. But we think he's going to come back here to collect his money from the guy who hired him. So we need your cooperation. If you hear from him, please call us," Stevens said and put his card on the worn-out table, causing it to shake a bit. "You're asking me to rat out my cousin, detective. That doesn't make me feel very good."

"Can't help that, Ray. Your feelings are the last thing I need to worry about," said Stevens. "I've got a job to do—I must apprehend a dangerous criminal. And if you don't help us, we can charge you with aiding and abetting. I hope you understand that, Ray, or you'll share a cell with your cousin. So what's it gonna be?"

"Like you said. You leave me no choice. I'll do whatever you ask." Ray lowered his head and shook it back and forth, saying, "I can't believe this is happening. What a fucking mess. Why would Sal do such a thing? I just don't get it!"

"Ray, do you have a picture of your cousin?" asked Matthews.

"Sure. I'll get it." Ray removed some photographs from a drawer in a corner table. Matthews, meanwhile, eyed the apartment and quickly surmised that it would definitely be a candidate for a bulldozer. The whole place was dilapidated.

"Here, this is one with the two of us," said Ray, handing a photograph to the detective.

Stevens looked at the image and compared it to the one he had in his pocket of Sal in the emergency room. "Quite a resemblance," he said, showing the picture to Ray. "So tell me, is that the same man, Ray?"

"I believe so, detective. It looks like him."

"Okay, Ray. So this is what's going to happen now. We need you to call us right away if you hear anything from Sal. We know he'll be back, but we don't know when. He's gone into hiding in Boston. He's got the Boston PD, the NYPD, and probably the Mob family he works for all looking for him. Do you have any idea where he might be? You might be saving his life."

"How's that, detective?"

"Most likely the Mob family he works for has a hit out on him so there'll be no ties to them. We need to find him before he gets killed. Does he have any family or close friends in Boston where he'd go?"

"We have an eighty-year-old aunt who lives alone in Dorchester. Her name is Rosie Addeo, and I spoke to her just last month. Quite a pistol, that one! Curses like a sailor. I'll get the number and address for you."

"Thanks, Ray. That'll be a big help. Anybody else you can think of?"

"Aunt Rosie is the only family we have. She never had kids, and Sal was her favorite. He always took care of her. If it were me, that's where I'd hide out. And maybe he'd think the same way since the last name is different and he'd be harder to track. But I would definitely start there." Ray disappeared into the kitchen, where he pulled out his address book and wrote the number and address on the back of a grocery receipt. "Here you go," he said, handing it to Stevens.

"Thanks, Ray. You've been a great help."

"Would you let me know if you find him? And you're not gonna mention my name, right?"

"No, not now. But if the case goes to trial, you could be called to testify. Hopefully, it won't get that far and you won't have to worry about it. Let's just take one step at a time. We'll be in touch," Stevens said. "Oh, we'll be tapping your aunt's phone, so if you call and warn him, it's prison time for sure."

"I wouldn't do that. I'm staying clear of the whole thing."

"Good." Stevens nodded to Matthews, scooted with him out the door and down the stairs, then added, "Rob, let's tap his phone as well. He's very close to Sal, and blood is thicker than water."

Back at the precinct, Stevens told his partner, "I need to call Simpson and let him know what we just learned from Ray. Get the taps set up while I talk to him."

"Right away. What if I put a police car outside to show him we mean business?"

"Great idea. Just a twelve-hour stakeout and he'll get the message." Stevens picked up the phone and called Detective Simpson.

"Boston PD, Hailey speaking."

"Officer Hailey, I'd like to speak to Tyler Simpson. It's Detective Stevens from the NYPD."

"Hi, Walter, whatcha got?"

"I think we've got a closer. Spoke to Barboza's cousin today, and he gave me the name, address, and phone number of his

Aunt Rosie, who lives in Dorchester. He said they've been tight for many years and Sal might be hiding out with her. You need to check it out."

"Great, Walter. Thanks. I'll get right on it. But I've got some news as well. The word on the street is that Barboza is a dead man. Looks like one way or the other the bastard's going down."

"But if we get to him first, we take down Giachetti as well, and that's the big fish."

"I got it," Simpson said.

Chapter

Seventeen

*B*eth and Brandon stepped out of the taxi in front of a beautiful brownstone apartment on 86th and Park. Brandon carried her overnight bag. Beth had called her mother on the ride over to let her know she was coming, without telling her what had happened to Michael. She didn't want to discuss it on the phone.

"What a beautiful neighborhood," Brandon said. "I love tree-lined streets in the city, where you can see the seasons change right outside your window. Wonderful location. How long have they lived here?" Brandon was tryng to distract Beth with small talk.

"About two years, and they love it," Beth said as Brandon stopped to look around.

"You'll be coming up with me, won't you?"

"Of course. I'll tell them about Michael."

Beth reached over and squeezed his hand. "Thanks, Brandon. That's really nice of you."

As they approached the doorman, Beth said, "Hello, Louie, this is my friend Dr. Burton. How are you?"

"Good afternoon, madam," he said with an English accent. Turning to Brandon, he added, "Sir, nice to meet you." Louie held the door open for them.

Inside, the gentleman behind the reception desk stood up from his chair. "How are you, Miss Scott? Good to see you again."

"And you, too, James. This is Dr. Burton. We're here to see my parents."

"Hello, sir. Pleasure. I'll program the elevator for you. Go right on up."

"Thank you."

The elevator automatically stopped at the fourteenth floor, where Beth and Brandon stepped out. The hallway was nicely laid out, with a beautiful carpet in beige and browns revealing circular and rectangular designs in the weave. There were small crystal light fixtures spaced equally down both sides of the corridor.

Beth knocked on her parents' door. "Mom, it's Beth."

The door opened, and her mom embraced her. "What a surprise. I'm so happy you dropped by, sweetheart." She noticed the strained look in Beth's eyes but didn't say anything. "Brandon, welcome. It's good to see you again."

"Likewise, Miriam," he replied.

Joseph hugged his daughter and shook Brandon's hand. "How are you, doctor? To what do we owe this visit?" Joseph noticed his bag. "You're spending the night, doc?" he said jokingly. "Please come in and have a seat. Can I get either of you something to drink?"

Brandon replied, "No thank you, sir." He and Beth sat on the sofa; her parents sat on chairs across from them. "There is something rather distressing that I need to tell you both," Brandon added.

Beth started to tear up, and her mom said, bewildered, "Oh no, is there a medical complication?"

Brandon replied, "I thought it best that I come over with Beth to tell you. Michael was murdered last night in his hotel room in Boston."

Miriam gasped. "Oh my God." She dashed over to sit beside her daughter on the sofa.

Brandon continued. "The police from the NYPD and Boston PD are working on the case, and they assure us that Beth is not in danger."

Joseph leaned forward in his chair. "Beth? Why would Beth be in danger?"

Beth took a Kleenex from the box on the side table then spoke up. "I didn't want to alarm you, but it seems I was attacked as payback from a felon because Michael, who had represented him, lost his case."

"What a shock! I can't believe this. He was such a wonderful man," Miriam said, her voice trembling.

Joseph turned to Brandon. "Where are the police on this?"

"They were days away from arresting the guy and are now tracking him down in Boston."

Her father stood up, as did Brandon. Joseph sat on the other side of Beth and wrapped his arms around her. "I'm so sorry, baby. I can't imagine the pain you're feeling now. Have a good cry. You'll feel better if you let it all out. And you can stay with us as long as you need to."

"Thanks, Dad."

Brandon stood "I need to go. Beth, if you like, I can accompany you to the funeral."

"Brandon, that's nice of you. But I'll have everybody at the office for support."

Joseph said, "Is it safe for her to travel?"

"I can't answer that. I'm sorry. If the police thought it was unsafe, then you would be informed of it, so I wouldn't really worry."

Joseph wasn't satisfied with that answer, but Miriam interceded, saying, "Brandon, thank you for bringing Beth over. That was kind of you."

"Miriam, Beth, if there's anything I can do, just call me. I know what a shock this is, and I want to help."

"Good-bye, Brandon, and thanks again," Beth said, tears still rolling down her cheeks.

Brandon let himself out of the apartment.

Beth had a sleepless night, dreading the morning, when she would have to call Michael's parents in Madison, Wisconsin. Morning arrived much too fast for her. She placed the call to Mrs. Hudson, planning to extend her sympathies and get the details about Michael's funeral. As the phone was ringing, she had no idea what to say to a mother who had just lost a son in the prime of his life. Beth could only imagine her grief.

Mrs. Hudson answered, and Beth said, "Hello, Mrs. Hudson, this is Beth Scott. I wanted to call and tell you how sorry I am for your loss. I can't imagine what you're going through, losing such an amazing son. I'm so, so sorry! And I want you to know that I loved him very much."

"Oh, Beth. Thank you for your sweet words. Yes, it's been…well, horrendous. I haven't slept a wink since we received the news," Mrs. Hudson said in a low soft voice, barely audible. "We're just trying to understand how this could happen." Mrs. Hudson began to weep as she added, "Beth, he loved you, too. He spoke about you often and was planning to bring you home to meet us. We were all so excited and had such high hopes for the two of you."

"As did I," Beth said. "He talked about his family a lot. He loved you all so much. Can you give me any information yet about the funeral? I plan to attend."

"Michael's dad's in Boston now getting the body released and brought back home. The funeral will be this Sunday at the Hillcrest Presbyterian Church."

"I know a lot of us from the firm are coming, including the partners."

"How nice of them," Mrs. Hudson said. "I'll look forward to finally meeting you, Beth. I wish it were under happier circumstances." She paused, choking up again. "It's just so hard to imagine our lives without Michael."

"I understand," said Beth. "It'll be hard for everyone who knew him. He was a big part of all of our lives. Please take care, and I'll see you on Sunday."

"Thanks so much for calling, Beth. I really appreciate your making the trip. Good-bye."

Ironically, Sunday was the night she and Michael were to have dinner together after his return from Boston. Now, instead of dinner and a night on the town, she'd be attending his funeral. She knew she had to go, for there was no other choice. She was dreading it, afraid she wouldn't hold up. Beth would call Meredith to book her flight along with the other attorneys from the firm. It would be much better to travel with friends who'd all be experiencing grief.

When she phoned, Meredith explained, "Jeff Greene booked a private jet at the firm's expense. He didn't want us having to deal with other passengers."

"Wow. That's great. I dreaded being around strangers and crying and having to explain myself."

"We're flying out Saturday afternoon at three. Jeff's also booked us into a hotel in Madison. I'll let you know when I get the particulars. And, Beth, I'm so terribly sorry for your loss."

Attending Michael's funeral would probably be the hardest thing she'd ever done. Elderly people who had lived their lives are supposed to die, not young men like Michael. He was accomplished in everything he'd set out to do in the world. He had a wonderful, exciting, and challenging life awaiting him, and now it was suddenly over.

There were six attorneys, two partners, and three secretaries going out on the Saturday afternoon flight due to arrive in Madison that evening. The service was scheduled for eleven o'clock the next morning. The senior partner and one other associate, a close friend of Michael's, would be speaking at the service.

They all arrived at the church early, allowing time to speak to the family before the service. Beth went up to Michael's parents, gave them each a hug, and was unable to contain her tears. She could see his parents' resemblance to Michael. His mother was of medium height with short brown hair, styled in a bob, and radiant skin. Her figure was perfect, and she carried herself with style and grace. Her large brown eyes were tearful, but held warmth and affection when she spoke to Beth. "I'm so glad you're here, Beth. You're as beautiful as Michael described," Mrs. Hudson said as she handed Beth a tissue to wipe away her tears. "I know how hard this is for you, as well. Would you please sit with us in the front row? I think Michael would like that."

Beth shed more tears and nodded. "Thank you. I'd be honored, and I so want to meet everyone Michael was close to, so I can put faces to the people who meant so much to him."

Beth then went over to Michael's dad and hugged him. "I'm so sorry," Beth said. Those were the only words she could utter at that moment. He was very handsome and looked so much like Michael with his deep-set blue eyes and light brown hair, graying at the temples.

His dad responded, "Beth, you're everything and more that Michael told us about you. It's easy to see why he fell in love with you. I'm so pleased you came. It means a lot to our family, and I want to thank you."

"Mr. Hudson, I adored your son. We were planning our future together, and I can now see what I'll be missing in not being a part of this family, which saddens me deeply."

"Beth, we'll always consider you a member of our family, for that's what Michael would've wanted. Please remember that we'll always be here for you, and we want you to stay in touch and visit us on occasion."

Beth was so touched that she began to cry. Mr. Hudson put his arm around her. "Don't you cry, pretty lady. Remember the good things about Michael, and that'll carry you throughout your life."

The service began promptly at eleven. There were many speakers, and each one spoke highly of Michael. His friends from high school, college, and law school all described him as a true friend and a wonderful colleague. Everyone loved and admired him not only for his many achievements but for the kindness he always showed to others.

The ride to the cemetery, on a winding road lined with large trees of different varieties, was somber. Beth stared out the window at the light rain trickling down the car windows. The wind, stirring in circles, lifted the leaves into the air. In all, it was a dismal day, which was very appropriate for the burial.

Beth's colleagues in the car were silent during the entire drive. As the car approached the gravesite, she watched the pallbearers remove the casket from the long black limousine and place it over the burial site. At this point, Beth froze and couldn't move out of the car. "Beth," said one of the other attorneys, "are you coming?" Beth just stared at the casket, picturing Michael inside and didn't respond. "Beth, it's time," he added more urgently, extending his hand to help her out of the car. A few moments passed before Beth took her colleague's hand and stepped out of the limousine.

"Thank you," she said. "I'm sorry. This part is so terribly hard. I don't know if I can watch."

"I'll be right beside you, Beth. Hang on to me. You'll be fine."

The service was short, and Beth turned away when they lowered the coffin into the ground. When she heard the squeaking noise from the mechanism that lowered the coffin deeper into the earth, she began to weep at the thought of leaving Michael there all alone. She walked back to the limo holding her colleague's arm. As the car slowly drove away from the burial site, Beth turned for one last look, only to see an empty space where Michael had been placed in his final resting spot. It seemed cold and heartless to leave him in the ground covered by six feet of dirt. She wanted to sit there with him for at least a little while longer. She was filled with feelings of despair and helplessness as they drove back to the Hudson family home.

By now the rains and wind had intensified. Again no one spoke, yet the silence was comforting. There was nothing anybody could say to make the dire situation any better. Beth was consumed with thoughts about Michael. And she assumed her coworkers were lost in their own memories of him, as well.

When they arrived at the family home, the street was already lined with cars, so they parked a short distance away and used umbrellas. As Beth stepped into the house, she found Michael's mom and dad sitting on the sofa, with friends and family offering their condolences. Feeling a special bond with Michael's family, she waited for an opening then approached them and took Mrs. Hudson's hand. "It was a lovely service, and so reflective of Michael's nature and personality. You have much to be proud of, hearing how Michael touched the lives of so many people. You'll have their remembrances to carry with you for the rest of your life."

Michael's dad, a distinguished-looking man who seemed to share his son's caring nature, stood up and said, "Beth, Michael seemed very happy to have you in his life. I want to thank you for giving my son so much joy in the last years of his life. It means a lot to me to know that he was in a good place when he passed. That gives me peace." Mr. Hudson put his arms around Beth and hugged her affectionately. She could not help but tear up, feeling his intense pain.

The Hudsons reminded her of her own family, so warm and loving. She wanted to keep them in her life, for they were truly caring people who would always remind her of Michael. It was difficult to say good-bye, for she knew of the unimaginable grief that she was leaving behind for his parents to endure.

The next day in Boston, Detective Simpson, based on the update he had received from Detective Stevens, informed his team of Barboza's hideout in Dorchester. "We'll need the SWAT team on this one. I don't think the bastard is just going to walk out the front door without a fight. I hope I'm wrong, but I'd rather be safe than sorry. Charlie, inform the boys of the detail and that we're leaving here in thirty minutes."

"I'm on it, boss," said Charlie.

Barboza had been on the phone most of the day trying to set up the hit on Beth. Knowing that she could ID him left him no choice but to take her out. The "family" wouldn't be happy with this situation and wouldn't want any connection to him on another off-the-books hit. He told them he'd clean up the mess but couldn't ask them for help, especially now that he had to lay low. He called one of his strong-arm friends in New York who was not connected to the Mob, and asked for his help.

"Hey, Mickey, this is Sal Barboza calling. How the hell are you?"

"I'm okay. What's up, Sal? Where've you been the last two years? Haven't seen ya around."

"I relocated to Boston. Better opportunity. You still doing jobs for hire?"

"What'd you have in mind?"

"Make someone disappear. Pays ten Gs. Interested?"

"Not for ten Gs, Sal. Prices have gone up. It's rough out there. Not too many guys left doing this type of work that don't have Mob backup. Big risk on your own."

"Well, what's the going rate?"

"Twenty-five."

"Wow, you ain't kiddin' things have gone up. That's a little steep for me. Are you negotiable?"

"Sorry, Sal. Like I said, too risky."

"Hold on a minute, I hear someone calling me." He put the receiver down and stepped into the hallway.

"Sal, got some lunch ready. Pasta Fazul—your favorite. Come, before it gets cold."

"Okay, Aunt Rosie, I'll be there shortly. Just on the phone. Smells great." Then he spoke into the receiver, saying, "Mickey, I'll give it some thought and let you know. I'm a little tight for cash right now. I'll see if I can come up with it and get back to you."

"Whatever, Sal. That's my price."

Barboza tried to figure out how he was going to get the money. If only he could collect on what was owed him for the hit on Hudson, he'd have the money to pay the "family" their half and the money to take out the girl. It suddenly came to him: he'd call his cousin Ray in New York and have him do the pickup from the postal box. But first he'd enjoy his lunch. He sat down at the kitchen table before a steaming bowl of soup set out with crackers and iced tea. While eating, he looked around feeling comfortable in this forty-year-old home where everything had remained the same as when he was a kid.

"Aunt Rosie, this is delicious, as always. You're the best."

"I'm so glad you like it, Sal. You know how much I love to cook for you."

The next moment, there was a knock at the door. "Open up, Boston PD."

Sal jumped up from the table. "Aunt Rosie, go into your bedroom and lock the door. I'll take care of this. Hurry, *go!*"

"Is everything all right, Sal?"

"Don't worry, just go into the bedroom. Now!"

Rosie shuffled out of the kitchen and hurried up the stairs to her second-floor bedroom. Sal went into the guest room to retrieve his revolver and then stepped over to the front door. He waited. "Open the door, Sal. We know you're in there. We've got the place surrounded. You don't want to put your aunt in harm's way, so just come out with your hands up and no one will get hurt!"

"Don't shoot," Barboza said, laying his gun on the floor as he slowly opened the door and put his hands up. The police picked the gun up and frisked him. It was the same caliber weapon, a 45, that was used to murder Michael. "No problem," Barboza said. "I'll go peacefully and be out in twenty-four hours."

As the SWAT commander cuffed him, he yelled toward the stairs, "Aunt Rosie, I need to straighten out a little misunderstanding. I'll be in touch." They led him out the door as a uniformed officer read him his Miranda rights.

When they arrived at police headquarters, Barboza was led into an interrogation room and pushed down into a chair. Detective Simpson took a seat across from him. "You've been a busy boy, Sal."

"What's this about?"

"I think you know why you're here. If you used this weapon," Simpson said, holding up Barboza's gun, "the ballistics report on the gun used to murder Michael Hudson will tie you into it. Even if you dumped the gun used in the murder, we can place you at the scene and find a DNA match. Nobody's that clean on a double homicide. But you have some wiggle room here, because we want Giachetti, too. Tell us if he hired you to murder Hudson, and the feds will take that into consideration."

"The feds?"

"Murder for hire is a federal capital offense, Sal, which carries the death penalty."

"I want a lawyer. I'm not talking to you anymore without one."

Simpson replied, "The word on the street is that there's a hit out on you, Sal. Your bosses are just waiting to spring you so they can put you six feet under, at which point you won't be able to give them up for a lesser plea. So do you really want out?"

Another detective poked his head in the door and said, "Simpson, need you for a minute."

Simpson followed him out of the room. "What's up?"

"One of the Mob lawyers is here. He wants to sit in on the interrogation and try to spring him."

"Yeah, right on time. I was just telling the perp what's going down with them."

Simpson stepped back into the interrogation room and took his seat. "Well, Sal, it looks like I was right. Your employer sent a lawyer over. Shall I have him come in, or would you prefer to breathe a little longer and get your own lawyer or a public defender?"

Barboza considered his options. He knew that Carmen DiNunzio liked to cut his losses, and what the detective said made sense. At least he had a fighting chance staying locked up. He stared at Simpson and remained silent.

"I asked you a question, Sal."

"Yeah. I heard ya. I can't afford a lawyer, so send in one of your state flunkies, but no newbie."

"Don't worry. If you're indicted and claim to be indigent, the feds will assign a defense attorney familiar with capital crimes."

Barboza sunk his face into his hands. He knew he was really up against some major shit now.

Chapter Eighteen

A week after the funeral, Beth was still consumed with thoughts of Michael and found it difficult to concentrate on her work—or anything else, for that matter. She had had high hopes of becoming a couple with him, then getting married and having children together. She kept recalling visions of the good times they shared, his soft, gentle touches, his kind words and laughter. Getting back to the gym might help me achieve some normalcy, she thought, but she wouldn't go to the one in their building since her memories of first meeting Michael there were still raw. With Michael's death following so quickly on the heels of her own attack and long recovery, her life had been filled with sadness and despair. She must move on, she told herself.

Beth soon decided to turn her misfortunes around and have a more positive outlook on life, ridding her soul of the sadness and despair. She'd start by concentrating on everything that was good in her life. In the hope that catching up with Brandon would lift her spirits, she gave him a call. "Hi, Brandon. I'm back from the funeral and wondering if you'd like to meet for a drink after work."

"I'm glad you called, Beth. Of course, I'd love to see you. How about if I pick you up at seven thirty, and then we can decide where to go for dinner. Would that be all right?"

"Perfect. I look forward to seeing you, Brandon."

"Me, too, Beth. And again, I'm so terribly sorry for your loss."

Brandon arrived promptly at seven thirty and gave Beth a quick hug. "It's so good to see you. Despite everything that's happened, you look wonderful," he said, though he could see sadness in her eyes, and her incredible spark for life was merely a flicker.

"Thanks, but I wish I felt wonderful. This has hit me hard, and I'm trying to deal with it, but it's...touch and go. I really need to be around people. I could always talk to you, Brandon, and I certainly could use a friend's support now."

"Beth, I'm happy you called; I do want to be here for you. Whatever I can do to help you feel better, just tell me. It's going to take some time, and you can't rush your feelings—from pain to anger, and even to feeling sorry for yourself. Your heart has been severed, so to speak, and just like after surgery, it needs time to heal."

"I feel better already. Thanks for your wonderful advice." Beth took his arm as they walked to the elevator. "Now, let's go get some dinner. I feel like sushi. Is that all right with you?"

"Perfect," Brandon said. "I know a wonderful place."

The next day Beth put in her first full day of work at the office since the funeral. Concentrating on the demands of her practice kept her thoughts off of Michael. She was doing what she loved, and realized how much her clients needed her help. Lisa's settlement hearing had been rescheduled for this Friday, and she was eager to finalize it. Beth buzzed Maria and asked her to get attorney Jake Gibson on the phone.

"Hi, Jake. Sorry about the reschedule on the Paul case, but it couldn't be helped."

"Beth, I'm so sorry about what happened to your colleague. What a tragedy! I saw the article in the paper. Such a brilliant attorney and so highly regarded in his field of practice."

"Thank you, Jake. We're all taking it pretty hard."

"Hope they get the bastard soon and hang him high."

"They have a suspect in custody."

"That's great," he said, then paused. "So, do you have anything new on the settlement, or are we still negotiating on what you last sent over?"

"Everything remains the same. Lisa won't budge on getting the apartment but is more flexible on support."

"Well, I'd like to finish this up, so I'll press Brian on it, and I'll have him there this time."

"I appreciate that, Jake. See you then."

Beth hung up the phone and called Lisa. "Hi, Lisa, this is Beth."

"Beth, how are you? I'm so terribly sorry for your loss. I didn't want to call, knowing you'd need some alone time after the funeral," Lisa told her.

"I appreciate that, Lisa, and I truly needed the breather. But I'm back to work now and ready to finally put your divorce to bed. Just checking to see if you're set for Friday's settlement meeting."

"Yes, I certainly am, and I can't wait."

"Have you spoken to Brian?"

"No, I refuse to take his calls; all he does is ask for my forgiveness and for me to come back to him. Beth, my trust in him is broken. Although I still have feelings for him, I know there can no longer be a marriage."

"I agree with you, Lisa. It just wouldn't work anymore, and it's best to make a clean break."

"Listen, do you want to meet for dinner tonight? I haven't seen you in so long, and I really miss you, girl."

"Okay, I'd love it. But not too late. I've had a really long day."

"Me, too. Let's eat at that little Indian restaurant around the corner from your office at seven. And I'll make sure you're home by nine."

"Deal. See you soon."

A moment later, her friend Victoria called to ask about Michael's funeral and let her know the detectives had made an arrest.

"I'm afraid they're going to ask me to fly up there and pick him out of a lineup," said Beth.

"Try not to think about it now. Maybe they won't."

"Well, it's what *I* would do," Beth added, then decided to drop the subject. "So what's new with you, girlfriend?" She asked.

"Not much, same ole thing. Work, work, and more work. Everyone has a better social life than me, that's for sure."

"You really need to start going out and meeting people, Victoria, and have some fun."

"And with whom do you suggest I do that?"

"Have you ever considered a dating service?"

"No, I've never tried one, and I guess I'd have no objection. Is there one you'd recommend?"

"Well, I've heard good things about Mingle with Singles. It's expensive, but they actually do their homework, background checks and all, and find men who are suited for you. What do you have to lose? I think it works much better than those online dating sites. It should be worth a try, don't you think?"

"I'd be willing to check it out. Thanks for the tip."

"You're most welcome. Would you like to meet me for lunch tomorrow?"

"That would be great. Can't wait to catch up. I'll put it on my calendar. Just shoot me a text when you come up with a time and place."

"Great. Thanks. Talk to you tomorrow. Have a great day."

"You too, Victoria. Bye."

Beth worked on her case files the rest of the day. Several of Michael's friends who had gone to the funeral with her stopped by to ask how she was doing. A few also discussed a memo that had been sent around by the senior partner regarding threats from clients. It would now be mandated for any attorney who received a threat of any kind to inform one of the managing partners immediately. Nobody had had any idea that Michael was being threatened by his client. Beth wondered if things would have turned out differently had he told one of the partners about it.

"It is hard to believe that Michael wouldn't ask for help with these threats," said Jack Manor, one of Michael's defense colleagues. "I received threats last year, and I informed Jeff Greene, who informed the police, and they handled it."

"How?" Beth asked.

"I don't know what they did, but I never heard from the guy again. It's the type of thing that can't be ignored, especially when you're dealing with criminals."

Jeff Greene stepped into Beth's office and said, "So it seems the two of you got the memo?"

"Yes, Jeff, and we're very happy about it. Great idea!"

"If Michael would've only informed us about these letters, we could've worked through it together and maybe he'd still be alive. But the point is that no one in this firm should have to go through such a thing on their own. The police should've been called in to investigate. I feel this firm bears some responsibility for his death, and for you getting attacked."

"Oh, no way is the firm responsible for either," Beth said adamantly. "This was about dealing with a hardened criminal who wouldn't be happy with anything less than an acquittal, which was impossible given the evidence against him."

"Okay, but this type of behavior toward our firm on the part of any client will not be tolerated, thus the memo. This went too far. It sickens me that we had to lose such a competent, brilliant attorney—and a wonderful human being."

"I know, and I think everyone shares your feelings," Beth added. Jack nodded in agreement and stepped out of the office.

"How are you coping, Beth?" Jeff asked, sitting across from her. "You've really been through the mill. First, your attack and now Michael's death. You're to be admired for your strength and courage. We're all here for you, Beth, to help in any way we can. So don't forget that."

"I appreciate it, Jeff, but I need to stay busy now. My clients need me, and I've fallen behind on my schedule. I won't let them down. My work is what keeps me moving ahead with my life."

"I really respect you, Beth. You're quite remarkable, and a damn good attorney. But any time you find thoughts of Michael impinging on you, please take the rest of the day off and go home to deal with it. Don't ignore how you feel. We're totally supportive of you while you're healing from the grief."

"Jeff, you're so kind and understanding, and I'm fortunate to be with this firm. Thank you."

Jeff Greene, having been brought up to date on the investigation by Detective Stevens, went through Michael's files and familiarized himself with the Giachetti case. It was a difficult case to win; the evidence was stacked against Giachetti. Michael noted that he was probably guilty but it didn't matter since his job was to give his client the best defense possible. The jury had found him guilty, but Michael had been able to get him a lesser sentence as it had been his first conviction. He could've been sentenced to twenty years, but he got only fifteen and would be up for parole after eight. No other attorney could've done a better job for this client. But, for whatever reason, Giachetti felt that Michael hadn't represented him adequately.

When Greene finished reviewing the case, he called Detective Stevens. "Hi, detective, this is Jeff Greene from Beth's law firm. Just wanted to tell you that I've reviewed the court transcript line by line and Michael couldn't have provided a better defense. Giachetti had no right to question Michael's handling of his case, and I'll testify as an expert witness to that. This was wrongheaded thinking and malicious intent, and I hope he gets the needle for it."

"Appreciate it, Jeff. I'm in close communication with the Boston PD, and we're working together. While Barboza killed

Michael in Boston and will be tried in federal court there, Giachetti will be tried here, and I'll let the district attorney know about your testimony," said Stevens.

"Thanks, detective. Everyone is eager to get justice for Michael Hudson and his family and friends. Let's nail them both."

About two weeks after Beth returned from Michael's funeral, she got a call from Detective Stevens. "Hi, Beth. This is Detective Stevens. How are you?"

"I'm doing fine, and trying to get on with my life. What's going on, detective?"

"Well, Beth, as you know, they have your assailant in custody in Boston and also have quite a lot of evidence to prosecute him for Michael's murder."

"Yes. And I've waited a long time to be able to sleep at night."

"The Boston PD wanted me to ask you if you'd be willing to travel to Boston and try to ID him in a lineup. If you could, then with your testimony the D.A. would have a tie-in with Michael's murder. He wouldn't be able to see you, so no worries there. Does this sound like something you'd be willing to do?" Stevens could sense that Beth was uncomfortable with his request, as she hesitated before responding.

"I know how much my testimony would mean to the case. And I do want to do it. I only hope that I'll be able to go through with it when I get there."

"We would appreciate it, Beth. I know it won't be easy, but it could help get him the death sentence."

"Okay, detective. I need a little more time. I'll get back to you."

"Beth, if you need a week or two to get used to the idea, then that'll be no problem. I don't want to rush this and cause you to have a setback. You're doing so well. So take the time you need and call me back if you think you'd be up to making the trip. We know this could prove to be very traumatic for you, and we want you to be well prepared if and when you decide to go."

"Thank you, detective. I appreciate your sensitivity. I'll speak to my family and get back in touch."

On Friday, Beth had another productive day at work. She and Lisa had their meeting with Brian Paul's attorney and signed the settlement agreement. Lisa and Brian, unable to even look at each other, let their respective attorneys do all the talking. Beth got everything Lisa wanted. Lisa did not ask for spousal maintenance, but the apartment would be hers, free and clear. Brian signed the agreement and wasted no time leaving the meeting. Lisa, ecstatic that she could now move on with her life, decided this victory called for a celebration. So she and Beth honored the occasion by going to a trendy restaurant in Soho, where they had a festive dinner with a bottle of fine champagne.

During dinner, Brandon called, and Beth promised to call him back when she got home. She was missing him and had a lot to tell him in regard to the case. He didn't even know that her attacker and Michael's murderer was in custody.

Beth arrived home about nine thirty, changed into her PJs, and returned Brandon's call.

"Sorry, Beth. I've been so busy at the hospital that I'm not keeping up with my friends. One of my interns transferred to another program, and I'm very short-staffed. I'm supposed to get some relief soon. I miss you, and I want to catch up. Have you been doing well?"

"Yes, Brandon, I'm fine. I have so much to tell you that I don't know where to start."

"Tell me everything, and how about starting right now."

"Well, since we last met, they arrested Michael's murderer and the Boston PD called and wants me to go there for a lineup to see if he's the same guy who attacked me. I just closed Lisa's case, so I could fit it into my schedule. But I'm a little hesitant and don't know if I'm up to it. I could use a change of scenery, but I'm afraid seeing him again will cause me to relive it all and set me back."

"Beth, as your doctor, I'm advising you to take as much time as you need before you decide. You have to feel strong enough emotionally to see this man again. This is a big deal, and I don't want you to have a setback." Brandon paused before adding. "I could also use a break, so how would you like some company if you go? As you know, I'm from Boston, and I'd love to show you around. I also think it's best that you don't take this on by yourself. I'd like to be there for support."

"Brandon, how sweet of you to offer. I accept. You're a sweetheart and always have my best interest at heart. How can I resist? I'd love you to come along. Emotionally, I think I would welcome someone with me. And who could be better than my doctor?"

"I hoped you'd say yes. I'll make all the arrangements, and I know the perfect place to stay. It's a small but quaint and elegant hotel, and I'm sure you'll love it. It reminds me of you. Classy! Just take your time in deciding when you're ready, and I'll handle the rest."

"Sounds wonderful, Brandon. How can I thank you enough? Let me toss this around for a while, then I'll let you know. I need a little more time, but I also want to get it over with. I'll let you know when I think I'm ready."

"No problem, Beth. Take all the time you need. That guy isn't going anywhere."

"Thanks, Brandon, sounds like a plan. Good night."

Chapter

Nineteen

*T*hree weeks later Beth finally felt confident about making the trip to Boston. She called Brandon to get a date that worked for him and then phoned Detective Stevens.

"NYPD, Benson speaking."

"Hi, this is Beth Scott calling. May I please speak to Detective Stevens?"

"Sure, hold one minute and I'll get him for you."

"Hi, Beth. This is Walter. How are you?"

"Oh, I'm doing much better, thanks. It's a lot to deal with."

"I understand. You know, I was just planning to give you a call. Boston PD is getting antsy for you to come do the lineup."

"Well, that's the reason for my call. I'm ready to get this done. Dr. Burton will be accompanying me for moral support, and we can both get away next Friday. If you can set it up for us to come in the early afternoon, that would be great. We'll be taking the ten o'clock flight out that morning and should be arriving around ten forty. We could be at police headquarters by twelve thirty as long as there are no unforeseen delays. I prefer to do this sooner in the day than later."

"Sounds like a good plan, Beth. I'll call Detective Simpson and let him know, and then I'll get back to you to confirm."

"Thanks for your help, detective."

"Thank you, Beth. I know you'll be much happier to have this behind you."

"You've got that right. Have a great day."

Since Michael's death, she and Brandon had been seeing each other on his nights off. At first he was there as a friend for emotional support, but then they really started enjoying each other's company, and she noticed her feelings for him were growing stronger. Beth was feeling more like her old self again, and Brandon was positively the reason. She had something to look forward to at the end of her day, whether it was his call or meeting him for dinner. She was finally in a good place in her life once again, and the dark cloud that had been hovering over her had finally lifted. After this trip, she could put this whole nightmare behind her.

The plane was on time when Beth and Brandon landed at Logan Airport. They picked up their luggage and took a taxi to their hotel, where Brandon checked them in.

"Here's your key, madam," Brandon said, handing her the room key. "My room is right next door."

"Thank you, Brandon. What a quaint hotel. I love this lobby, with its beautiful antique furniture. It has a royal European ambience," she said, looking up at the gold-leaf chandeliers. "And I love the oriental rugs that give it a feeling of coziness and charm."

The hotel was privately owned and one of a kind. There were only thirty-five rooms and six floors. Brandon had booked two suites on the top floor, hoping to make this a very special weekend for Beth. She had suffered so much hardship in the last three months, and Brandon wanted her to start enjoying life again without trepidation. This weekend would be about closure and turning her life around.

The elevator stopped at the sixth floor, and Beth and Brandon stepped off. The bellman was right behind with their luggage and led them to Beth's room first. He opened the door and motioned to her to enter the warm, inviting sitting room, which took her breath away. The furnishings were all antiques in dark rich woods with fabrics of cream and gold, plus touches of bronze. Beth felt as if she were in a small palace. The bedroom had a wooden four-poster canopy bed with gorgeous Frette linens, also in creams and golds, and lots of fluffy pillows in the same shades of bronze that were in the living room. The bathroom had double sinks and a jetted tub and shower, both large enough for two. The white marble floor and the towel racks were both heated. Oh, such indulgence, Beth thought. It was an elegant, charming suite that made her feel like royalty. She had never before been surrounded by such opulence.

"Oh my! Brandon, this is just so beautiful. I love everything about it." She gave him a kiss on the cheek and said, "Thank you."

"I'm so happy you like it. I knew this would be the perfect place for your first getaway and to raise your spirits."

Brandon tipped the bellman, saying, "You can drop my bags in the room next door. Thank you."

"How can I thank you for all of this? I'm blown away by your generosity."

Beth started to unpack and get organized. Even though she was becoming a little apprehensive about the lineup, she felt comfort knowing that Brandon would be with her. She realized how special this man was, constantly showing her how much he cared and always putting her needs first. Maybe this relationship could really become something, she thought to herself, but it was much too early yet to make any predictions. She would take one day at a time.

"Beth, we need to leave. Let's get this over with and start our vacation." Brandon put his arms around her and gave her a hug. Beth admired how he took charge. She made decisions every hour of every working day, and on her days off it was nice to let somebody else take the reins.

"I'm nervous but ready," Beth said, as she gazed into Brandon's big, beautiful brown eyes, which reflected both his strength of character and great empathy.

"You'll be just fine, and I don't want you to worry for one minute. No pressure. Just identify him or not. They already have him for Michael's murder. And I'll be right beside you." They left the hotel, grabbed a taxi, and headed over to police headquarters.

At the front desk, Beth identified herself to the officer in charge. "I'm Beth Scott, and Detective Simpson is expecting me."

"Nice to meet you, Beth, I'm Officer Brady. I'll call Detective Simpson right away. Have a seat over there."

A few minutes later a distinguished looking man about six feet tall with wavy black hair came up to them. "Hi, you must be Beth. I'm Detective Tyler Simpson. So nice to meet you. And thanks for coming."

"Hi, detective. This is my friend Dr. Brandon Burton."

"Nice to meet you, sir," Simpson said, as he shook Brandon's hand. "Are you the doctor who saved Beth's life after the attack?"

"Well, I had . . ."

"He's a wonderful doctor, detective, and a good friend," Beth added.

"Well, thanks so much for being here for her."

"You know, this is a little scary for me, and I just hope I can get through it and not let you down, detective."

"Don't you worry, Beth. You're going to do just great," said Simpson. "The lineup is being set up now, so it'll be just a few minutes. Beth, I know this will be difficult for you, but I want you to remain calm and take all the time you need when you look at these men—none of whom will be able to see you. If you can remember anything your attacker said to you before he knocked you out, we can get him to repeat it. Or if you can recall anything about his appearance, such as a tattoo, a scar, or some other mark on his body, that would be helpful."

"I do remember him saying something like, 'How's your boyfriend, bitch?'"

"Okay, we'll get each of them to repeat that phrase, and maybe it'll trigger your memory if the voice sounds familiar. Are you ready?"

"Not really, but let's do it." Beth took Brandon's hand as her stomach turned to knots. She had no idea how she was going to react when she saw these men.

Brandon put his other hand on Beth's back and asked, "Are you all right?" She nodded as they followed the detective into a small room with a large glass picture window. On the other side of it, the five suspects filed into the narrow room and stood at their marks. Each one had a number around his neck, and they were all wearing black hooded sweatshirts and black sunglasses. Beth stared very intensely at each one of them. Because of the assailant's hood and dark glasses, she had never really gotten a good look at his face. She had seen only a small bit of his hair from under the hood and remembered that it was jet black. But she did recall that he was tall and stocky and that his voice was gruff. The detective asked number one to step forward and had him repeat, "How's your boyfriend, bitch?"

Beth stared pensively at him and concentrated for a long moment before she shook her head and said, "No, that's not him. His voice is too soft."

The detective had each of the other four men do exactly the same as the first. All the while Beth remained extremely introspective.

"Can you have number three step up and say it again?"

"Certainly, Beth." Simpson switched on the intercom. "Number three, please step forward and repeat the same phrase."

Beth listened carefully, closed her eyes, and tried to bring herself back to that fateful night. She nodded, certain that this gruff voice was the one she'd heard that night. She opened her eyes and looked at the man again: he was definitely built like her assailant—tall, large, and muscular. He also had a scar on his right cheek from where she'd hit him with the glass vase.

"Yes, I think that's him. I'm almost certain."

"Beth, I want to tell you that you've just identified Mr. Salvator Barboza, the man we have in custody for murdering Michael Hudson and now for attacking you. Great job. And we're so grateful to you for being strong enough to stand up and identify your attacker. Not everyone can do that. Now, he'll also be tried for your attempted murder in New York and, hopefully, will get a federal death sentence if convicted. Case closed! Thank you so much, Beth," Simpson said as he led Beth and Brandon out of the lineup area and back to the conference room.

Beth hugged Brandon and breathed a huge sigh of relief that she hadn't panicked and her memory hadn't failed her.

"Can we go now?" she asked Simpson.

"I'll need you to sign some paperwork verifying your ID of him. It'll only take a minute. Please have a seat for a moment. Can I offer you a cup of coffee or water?"

"No, thank you. We're going out to celebrate over a nice lunch," Brandon said.

"And a few drinks," Beth added, as everyone laughed.

"Be right back," Detective Simpson said.

After about ten minutes, the detective brought in the forms for Beth to sign, and they were ready to leave.

"There you go, detective. You don't know how happy I am that this is over."

"Believe me, I *do* understand; I feel the same way. This is a tough criminal who's being taken off the streets and will no longer be hurting anyone."

"Thank you. And good-bye, detective." Beth and Brandon walked out of the precinct rather hastily and never looked back.

"Now that that's behind us, let me show you Boston. We have two days in front of us, so let's just have some fun," said Brandon.

"Where are we going, Dr. Burton?"

"Well, first we're going to have lunch at one of my favorite French restaurants, La Voile. I think you'll really like it."

They sat outside under a red umbrella and sipped white wine. Then they had vichyssoise for their soup. For her main course Beth ordered the lobster roll, and Brandon the Dover sole.

"Are you enjoying your lobster?" he asked.

"It's really fresh and yummy. You were right—this place is great. I mean the street setting is right out of Paris, and the food is a culinary delight." She took another bite of the lobster after swallowing her last sip of wine.

"I knew you would like it. Another glass of wine?"

"Only if you'll join me."

"Of course."

After spending two hours at lunch, they went to the Museum of Fine Arts. They both enjoyed art, even though their individual tastes differed. Beth liked contemporary and abstract art, while Brandon preferred Impressionism. They enjoyed viewing both and discussing the interpretations of many of the abstract pieces. Exploring the captivating world of art was something neither of them had much time to do in New York, so it was a real treat to do so in Boston. Next they went to the Institute of Contemporary Arts, much to Beth's delight.

It was six o'clock when they arrived back at the hotel to relax a bit before dinner. Beth invited Brandon into the living room of the suite. "Please have a seat," she said as she opened the draperies and took in the beautiful city of Boston spread out before them. Since it was summer, daylight lingered until around nine. "Wow, what a view. Absolutely, gorgeous," she said staring out the window.

"Yes, that's part of the hotel's charm—the great views."

"Thank you for a wonderful day, Brandon. I enjoyed the museums, and I'm still tasting the delicious lunch."

"Isn't this just the greatest city? I'm so glad you like it."

"It truly is. And thank you again for arranging everything."

"My pleasure, Beth. I'm enjoying it as much as you. I really don't get back here enough." Beth sat down across from him. "I made dinner reservations at nine; I knew we'd have a late lunch. Is that okay?"

"I prefer that, Brandon. It gives me time to take a bath and relax. It's been a rather full day."

"Absolutely. I think I'll go back to my room and maybe even take a power nap."

"Brandon, you're welcome to stay and chat for a little while."

"You must be tired, and may even need some…process time. The police lineup was an emotional thing for you," he said, heading for the door.

"Always thinking of me," Beth said and kissed him on the cheek. "I like that in a man."

He smiled. "I'll be back at eight thirty. The concierge said it's about a twenty-minute taxi ride to the restaurant."

"Okay, I'll be ready. See you soon."

Beth felt very relaxed and decided to indulge in a hot bubble bath. While soaking in the tub, she cogitated on how happy she was that the lineup was over and she had done what she needed to do. Looking directly at her assailant was a real shock, and she had a moment of irrational fear, thinking he could just jump through the glass and attack her again. She was glad to be holding on to Brandon's arm, using his body to somehow shield her. Lunch and the museum tours were a tonic to her jagged nerves. He must've known as much; Brandon truly thought of everything. He is such a genuine, caring person, she thought. The more time she spent with him, the more Beth admired his character. She wanted to get to know him better. As with all things, time would be the revealing factor. They had only been seeing each other on a platonic basis for a little over two months now following their doctor-patient relationship. Her mind drifted off, imagining other scenarios, like what life would be like with Brandon as her love interest rather than Michael. She realized that she was smiling when she entertained these possibilities.

Promptly at eight thirty there was a knock at the door. Beth wanted to look special tonight for she had a lot to celebrate: the man who attacked her and killed Michael was behind bars for good. She could now start living normally and enjoying a social life without having to always glance over her shoulder. Beth looked very chic in her short tight black dress, its plunging neckline showing just enough cleavage to still be regarded in good taste. Wearing her high-heel Louboutins, she felt like a million bucks. She scooted into the bathroom and quickly fluffed her hair before opening the door.

"Wow! You look amazing." Brandon stood at the door staring at her. This was the first time he had ever seen her dressed up. She looked so beautiful that he couldn't take his eyes off of her. He even noticed that she had styled her hair differently.

"Well, thank you, sir," Beth said. "You don't look so bad yourself," she added, checking out his gray slacks, black blazer, and white shirt with a monogrammed cuff. Oh, does he look sharp! So handsome, she thought.

Then Branden said, "Shall we?" And, taking Beth's hand, he led her downstairs to the waiting taxi.

The taxi pulled up in front of the Meritage Restaurant situated in the Boston Harbor Hotel. When Brandon gave the maître d' his name, they were led to a table overlooking the waterfront. He pulled the chair out for Beth to sit down.

"Madam, for you."

"Thank you, sir," Beth replied.

The restaurant was packed, and theirs was the only open waterfront table. "How did you get this table?" Beth asked.

Brandon smiled. "Had my dad's secretary call in the reservation. Even with two weeks' notice, I couldn't get a Friday night reservation here."

They had a delectable dinner and, while the harbor view was alluring, hardly ever took their eyes off each other the entire time. They discussed politics, families, careers, and life in general. Brandon was particularly interested in her careerist views, having seen that too much emphasis in this area had wrecked his parents' marriage, and in telling her that he planned to remain in New York to set up practice when he finished his residency next summer. Beth was pleased, and had wondered if he would go back to Boston to be with his family.

Two hours had passed, though it felt like two minutes so relaxed were they, and happy being with each other. Beth felt like she had a new lease on life, and Brandon was part of the reason. He was mostly responsible for pulling her out of her blue funk. She could never thank him enough. When they got back to the hotel, Beth invited Brandon inside.

"Are you sure you're not too tired?" Brandon asked.

"No, please come in. The night's young."

Outside the window, the city sparkled and seemed alive. "Brandon, I'm in love with Boston, and I would very much like to come back."

"Well, Beth, I think that can be arranged. It's so beautiful in the fall, with the changing of the leaves. We'll have to plan another trip, that's all."

"Okay, you've got a deal."

Beth had let Brandon sit on the couch first and then took a seat beside him. She smiled at him, and he put his arm around her and asked, "Beth, may I kiss you?"

"Yes, I'd like that."

Brandon kissed her passionately and, after a long lingering moment, pulled away. He didn't want to rush it.

Beth said, "That was very nice, Brandon. Let's try it again." She now pulled his head close and kissed him again with equal passion. After they broke their clinch, Beth told him, "Brandon, I'll never forget what you did for me today. I couldn't have gotten through that lineup without you."

"I'm glad I could be there for you."

They continued to kiss for about fifteen minutes when Brandon stood up. "I think I'd better be going, Beth. It's getting late, and you need a good night's sleep."

"Would you like a nightcap before you go?"

"That would be nice." Brandon approached the bar area, where he spotted a bottle of fine tawny port. "Do you like port?"

"Yes, very much."

He opened it and poured two glasses. "To your new start on life," Brandon said clinking his glass to Beth's.

"Very good," said Beth after sipping her port. "I like it."

"Beth, I just wanted to tell you how much I've enjoyed being with you today. I feel like I've gotten to know you better, and I like what I see—very much. I hope you'll allow me to see more of you when we get back to New York."

"Of course, Brandon. You've given me hope that there *is* life after loss, that people can move on after tragedy."

"Thank you, Beth. So tomorrow I was thinking we'll have breakfast in the hotel, and then maybe we could walk around and let me show you some of the sites. The old homes and churches are quite fascinating, and then we could have lunch at a great local bar and grill, take a stroll through the park, and then it'll be time to leave for the airport. So we'll check out after breakfast, and the concierge will hold our luggage for us."

"Sounds great. I love colonial architecture. That would be a real treat. Can't wait."

Beth walked Brandon to the door, and once again, he took her into his arms and kissed her good night. After closing the door, she realized how physically attracted to him she was, and how much she desired him. It was much too early in their relationship to allow for sex since she did not want to rush such an important part of their courtship. She deeply missed intimacy in her life, but now, thanks to Brandon, she knew in her heart that she would have it once again.

Chapter
Twenty

Three weeks had passed since Beth's return from Boston, and she was charging ahead at work. Her relationship with Brandon was progressing rather quickly into more of a courtship. They spoke at least once a day and tried to meet for dinner twice a week, depending on their schedules. Thinking back, she recalled that she had started to develop feelings for Brandon when she was in the hospital but never allowed herself to explore them since after being discharged she had reconnected with Michael. Beth was elated that her friendship with Brandon was moving to the next level, for she knew that what they had together was built on mutual respect and trust. She hoped to follow her heart, start building a new life, and put the past behind her. She realized after losing Michael that life is fragile, and she wanted to live every day as if it were her last.

Her secretary buzzed her on the intercom. "Brandon is on line one."

"Thanks, Maria."

"Hi, handsome. What's up?"

"How's your day faring? How about if I meet you at Vianetto at seven?"

"Sounds great. How'd you know I'm in the mood for Italian tonight?."

"Because I can read your mind."

"Well, okay. If that's the case, what am I thinking right now?"

"That you can't wait to see me?"

"Oh, Brandon, you *are* a mind reader. It's been four days, and I do miss you."

"I miss you, too. See you at seven. Ciao, baby!"

After dinner, they went up to Beth's apartment. As she opened the door, Brandon said, "Beth, I have to be back at the hospital by ten. I'm on call tonight. So that gives us an hour."

Beth hardly heard him as she scurried around her apartment, still checking out the place after all this time. Coming out of the bedroom after a quick look, she told Brandon, "I don't know when I'll be able to stop doing this."

"Beth, you're safe now. It's over. Please don't live this way anymore."

"I'm trying, Brandon. I'm *really* trying. I'll get there—you'll see."

"I hope so," Brandon said, leaning over and giving her a kiss. "You've always known how much I care for you, haven't you?"

"Sort of," she said shyly. "It was confusing in the hospital—less so now."

"Well, Beth, let's not overthink things, just be ourselves, and eventually it'll become clear how we really feel about each other.

"Brandon, that's the first time either of us has broached the subject. I respect your frankness; I much prefer being open and honest with each other, and I like your idea of letting things fall into place naturally."

The next morning, Beth awoke refreshed, having had her best sleep in months. As she was getting ready for the office, she kept thinking about last night with Brandon. She felt as if their friendship had now become a romance, and she was thrilled with the prospect of what the future would hold for the two of them.

By midmorning she had interviewed two new clients, both with good reasons for wanting to end their marriages—not spousal abuse, like most of her other clients, but infidelity. Beth worked on her new files the rest of the day, lining up private investigators so her clients could obtain proof that their husbands were cheating on them. Armed with concrete evidence, she could proceed with divorce filings.

Friday rolled around quickly, and Beth was ready for a little R and R. Brandon called her early in the morning and told her to pack a small suitcase and that he'd pick her up around five. She had no idea where they were going, but she was packed and waiting for him when he arrived.

"Hi, sweetie. Ready to go?"

"You bet. So you're not going to tell me where we're headed?"

"Nope. Gonna keep you guessing. You'll never figure it out, so don't bother to try."

About two hours later, they were in rural Connecticut, meaning this it wasn't a trip to the beach, as she had speculated. After a long drive down a winding road, Brandon pulled up in front of an adorable cottage with a thatched roof and rustic brick exterior. There were many large, mature trees on the property, and the leaves were just starting to turn orange and crimson. Beth could see the lake from the driveway and her chin dropped. "What's this place, Brandon? It's so beautiful here."

"I bought it when I moved to the city four years ago, hoping that I'd use it as a retreat from the hospital. But, unfortunately, I haven't been able to enjoy it very much. I thought you'd like it here, and I wanted to bring you up for a weekend. So what do you think?"

"I think it's marvelous. I'm in love. It's the most charming cabin in the countryside that I've ever seen. I can't wait to see the inside."

Brandon carried their bags to the front door, opened it, and gestured for Beth to step inside. Once inside, she explored every room. "Brandon, this is so charming. I love the big stone fireplace in the living room and the bedroom. Did you pick out the furnishings?"

"No. Believe it or not, I was lucky and bought it furnished. It even came with a fully equipped kitchen and linen closet. Now follow me—I want to show you the best part." Brandon took Beth's hand and led her out the kitchen door and down to the picturesque lake. There was a sailboat docked at the pier. The view of the house, lake, and sailboat looked like a Monet painting.

"It came with the boat, too?"

"Sure did. Don't you just love it? Come, take my hand and I'll walk you inside." Beth followed Brandon as she stepped off the pier and onto the deck of the boat. It had a small galley kitchen inside and a sitting area. A few steps down led to a small bedroom and shower.

"Brandon, how come you never told me about this incredible property?"

"There was no reason to. Now I feel as if I want to share it with you, and it would be a nice place to visit on weekends instead of hanging around the city. So do you like boating?"

"Yes, it's always been one of my favorite things to do, but I never have the opportunity anymore."

"It'll be getting dark soon, so we'll sail out first thing in the morning."

"Oh, I'm excited, Brandon. Sounds like a lot of fun. We can make sandwiches and bring some wine."

"That's the plan," said Brandon." They sat on the sofa in the main cabin. Brandon opened a bottle of wine that had been chilling in the wine cooler and poured Beth a glass. He toasted, "To us." They sipped the wine, relaxing and chilling out after a long week at work. "Beth, I'm so happy to be here with you, sharing all of this. On its own it's great, but if there's no one to share it with what's the point?"

"I've always dreamed of having a rural home for weekend retreats. And then you bring me up here. Amazing! It's like our minds are always thinking on the same wavelength. After talking a bit and finishing the bottle of wine, they walked back up the path into the main house. It was dusk, and there was a chill in the air, so Brandon lit a fire in the living room. "Beth, I'm going to cook you dinner. I have a housekeeper who shops for me and fills the fridge so when I get here there's no need to run off to the grocery store. I know how you like to take baths and relax, so please feel free to while I get dinner started."

"Great idea. Are you sure I can't help you? You know that you're spoiling me, terribly."

"No, I insist." He carried her bag to the master bedroom. "Here we are. This is your room. I hope you'll be comfortable here. I replaced all of the mattresses in the house so they'd be new and fresh."

"Thank you, Brandon." He thought of everything, she told herself. She observed how romantic the room was with its fireplace opposite the bed. The tub was very large and had candles placed around the ledge.

"Enjoy, your bath," Brandon said then walked back to the living room. This was the first time Beth had seen Brandon's domestic side. She had always liked men who could cook. Just a few minutes later, Brandon knocked at her door and said, "Forgot to give you this," handing her a glass of her favorite wine.

Beth unpacked while running the bathwater and adding some bubble bath salts. She lit the candles before stepping into the tub. She then put her hair up into a ponytail, and placed her head on the rubber pillow at the back of the tub. This is relaxation personified, she thought. After the drive through the country, the wine, and now a hot bubble bath, what more could she ask for? Life was good in this moment: Brandon was treating her like a princess, and she was loving every minute of it. But as the bath salts soothed her strained muscles, a wellspring of deeper feelings arose. She wondered if it was a little too soon after Michael's death to start enjoying herself and with another man. *I*s there an appropriate waiting period? she asked herself. Or is that determined by how I feel? Checking in with herself, she felt she deserved to move on with her life free of guilt. With that, she dismissed the thought from her mind and just enjoyed the bath.

About fifteen minutes later there was a knock at the door. "Everything okay?"

"Yes, it's just divine in here. I'm so relaxed that I don't think I'm ever coming out."

"Well, if that's the case then I'll have to come in. Do you mind if I join you?"

At first, Beth was slightly taken back. She didn't expect this approach, or at least not so soon. She quickly got in touch with her feelings and realized it was something she did indeed want to do. Beth had known that they'd probably have sex this weekend, but she thought it would be tonight. She quickly resolved in her mind that, yes, it's okay, and the spontaneity of it all only added excitement to the moment.

"Sure, Brandon, come join me. I'd like that very much."

He stepped into the bathroom wearing a robe and stared at her lying peacefully in the tub. "You look so beautiful," he said, watching the bubbles swish up against her neck. Actually she looked downright angelic. He disrobed and walked over to the tub.

Beth couldn't speak. Brandon's body was perfect, even more than she'd imagined—great muscle tone, a broad chest, and well-defined pecs. His abs were flat, and his six-pack was prominent. His manhood was large and partially erect—the personification of masculinity. Brandon slipped down into the tub facing her, placing his legs on the outside of hers, which were partially stretched out. Her perfectly shaped plump breasts were just above the waterline, her nipples covered by the bubbles. She appeared to him to be floating among the clouds as the bubbles surrounded her. It all felt surreal to Brandon, as if she were posing for a Renoir masterpiece. But this was real, and he wanted to savor the moment forever.

"Brandon, you've been wonderful to me, going back to my first day as your patient. I've never been treated as well by anyone else. I can see now what a special person you are, and I've grown to care about you deeply."

"Beth, I know what we feel for each other now extends much further than a friendship, which established a wonderful foundation for this deeper bond. I want to be in a committed relationship with you. Nothing would make me happier."

"And I want to be with you, Brandon." She leaned closer to him and kissed him on the lips. He had a stunning face, with his huge brown eyes, high cheek bones, and olive skin. He always appeared as if he had captured the best part of the sun. His nose was perfectly proportioned to his face, and his chin looked like it had been chiseled by the hands of a sculptor. He had dimples on each side of his mouth that were deeply defined with each smile. He was truly one of the most handsome men she had ever met. To her he was like Adonis, the god of beauty and desire in classical mythology, loved by Aphrodite, the goddess of love. He had it all, and now she was certain that she wanted it all.

He cupped her face in his hands and kissed her passionately, slipping his tongue into her mouth. He stared into her green eyes in admiration of her beauty. His erection became more engorged as it lengthened, and his arousal was now certain. Beth, acutely aware of his stimulation, enveloped him in her hand, and began stroking him gently.

In turn, his fingers found their way to their desired destination, arousing her as he gently massaged her erogenous spot.

Beth's breathing became heavier and she said, "Oh, Brandon, can you even fathom how much I want you now?"

"Yes, Beth. I've been waiting for this moment even longer than you."

He now pulled her on top of him and she gently guided him into her as the water swished back and forth around them. Their breathing grew increasingly heavy, and beads of perspiration appeared on Brandon's forehead. Beth moved her body in a slow rocking motion in sync with the movement of the water as he caressed her breasts. Her nipples hardened in response to the soft gentle flicks of his tongue. He now kissed her ears, flicking his tongue in and out before kissing his way back down to her face and neck and back to her breasts—tenderly, lovingly. He gently tugged on her nipples with his lips, just enough to create an erotic sensation without inflicting discomfort. Beth moaned softly as her heightened arousal increased her rocking. She sighed deeply, expressing her pleasure. Brandon was holding back, waiting for the right time to release. She felt his index finger in just the right spot, caressing her, which was immeasurably exciting, moving her into another dimension of pleasure. While Brandon was now thrusting faster, pulsating back and forth inside her, Beth climaxed with such intensity that her whole body went into spasms. Brandon couldn't hold back any longer, and released himself into her while whispering, "I adore you, Beth, and am falling in love with you."

Neither of them moved while their breathing calmed and their rapid heartbeats slowed. They just stared into each other's eyes with great feelings of contentment. Beth could feel Brandon's erection inside her, so she remained still. She sensed that he was content to be in this moment, their bodies blending, for a while longer before retreating.

Beth finally said, "I can hardly believe this coming together is happening, Brandon. It feels so good, so right, that I can finally express my feelings for you."

"Beth, I've been taken with you since you were my patient in the hospital. You have no idea how hard it's been watching you from afar, knowing I could be your friend and nothing more. Of course, I was happy to have your friendship and would have never let it go."

"Brandon, I understood how you felt, and I was conflicted, knowing that I belonged with Michael while at the same time sensing this strong pull toward you. I kept telling myself that things have a way of working out and, with patience, all would eventually become clear. After Michael died and my feelings for you rushed forward, I felt guilty for having them. But now I know this was meant to be, and I've come to accept it."

"I understand, Beth, but I also know that the past is the past and the present is now. We'll get through this together, for it'll be about *us* from now on, and not just you or me. Let's focus on giving each other the happiness we both deserve."

"Oh, Brandon, I do love you. It feels so right being with you and you make everything perfect. My mom always told me that there's a reason for everything that happens in a person's life journey. Now I know she was right: I had to go through that hell for it led me to you. Life works in strange ways, but who are we to question it?"

Brandon and Beth got out of the tub, and while she dressed, he went to his room and slipped into jeans and a pullover sweater. She met him in the living room, where he had a fire burning. "Sit here and enjoy the fire while I put dinner on the table," he told her.

"No, I want to help you," Beth said, following him into the kitchen. "We're a team now, and that means we do everything together. That's the way I want it."

"Okay, if you insist," Brandon said and handed her the warm bread just out of the oven. "Put this on the table, and I'll bring out the salads."

Beth smelled a delicious dinner cooking in the oven. "When did you have time to learn to cook?" she asked Brandon.

"I've always loved to cook and took a few classes while I was in college. I find it most enjoyable. But I don't like cleaning up afterward."

"Don't worry, I'm happy to clean up. What're we having, chef?"

"I made roasted lamb with my own special seasonings and sauce. Hope you like it."

Dinner was fabulous, as was their lovemaking that evening on the rug in front of the cozy fire. But it was sailing out with Brandon on the lake the next morning, dropping anchor, eating a picnic lunch, and then lying back in his arms watching the clouds race overhead that was the real highlight of this weekend for Beth.

The drive back to the city came much too soon. She could have stayed forever with Brandon in that charming cottage by the lake.

That weekend was a turning point in their relationship, for now they had a bright future to plan together. Beth had much to tell her parents since they had no idea that she and Brandon's bond had transcended their doctor-patient friendship. Tomorrow would be a new beginning. There was finally a shining light at the end of the dark tunnel in which Beth had been barely surviving for such a long time.

Chapter Twenty-One

*B*arboza had been sitting in his cell for two days waiting for a meeting with the public defender when two guards stepped up, unlocked the cell door, and entered. One of the guards said, "Turn around. Your lawyer is waiting for you." The guards cuffed and shackled him, then led him out of the cell, down a hall, through a corridor, and into the interrogation room. Barboza shuffled over to a chair across the table from a middle-aged man with dark hair graying at the temples and large brown-rimmed glasses, who was wearing a three-piece suit with a starched shirt and matching tie. Barboza thought to himself that this guy couldn't get any more stereotypical-looking for an attorney.

"Hello, Mr. Barboza. My name is Barry Mitchell. I'm from the public defender's office, and I've been assigned to your case," he said as he stretched his arm out to shake his client's hand.

Barboza was not happy about using a public defender and spit back, "Yeah, so what took you so long to finally get your ass over here?"

"Well, with anything involving the state system there's a lot of paperwork that has to be jumbled around. Also, I had to familiarize myself with the facts of your case so I could give you some recommendations."

"You telling me now that you know what you're doing?"

"Well, I'd hope so. I've been doing this for twenty-some-odd years and have won my share of cases. I think you have bigger things to consider than my credentials, so let's move on, shall we?"

"Whatcha offering?" Barboza asked.

Mitchell opened the file and began reading through it. "I see where the prosecutor has a pretty solid case against you. They have one of your guns, which is the same caliber gun used to murder Michael Hudson."

"That proves nothing. Lots of people carry a 45. What else?"

"The bartender at the Four Seasons met you at the bar the night of the murder."

"Also proves nothing. I was meeting a friend for a drink. That's all."

"The girl in New York whom you put in the hospital picked you out of a lineup."

"Fuck that! Also nothing. We were wearing black hoods and sunglasses, and you can't see shit through that."

Mitchell responded, "She recognized your voice, which is very distinctive, Sal."

"That won't hold up in court, and it's not enough for a conviction, and I think you know that already," Barbosa said. "Got any DNA?"

"No."

"Didn't think so," said Barboza with a sneer.

"The federal prosecutors don't think they need it. The police have established a connection between you and Giachetti: letters spelling out what he hired you to do. They even have you on tape calling the runner Giovanni, instructing him when to be at the postal box for the letter pickups. Also, they have proof of you flying to New York the day before Ms. Scott's attack and returning to Boston the next day."

"I went down to visit my cousin," Barbosa insisted.

"They also tracked down your airline reservations to fly back to New York on the day after Hudson's murder. And they have the tape of the phone call you placed to Giovanni, instructing him to make another letter delivery, which was probably your request for your payday for the murder."

Barboza smiled. "Have you heard that tape?"

Mitchell shook his head. "My bet is that there's no mention of any murder, just instructions for a letter pickup." Mitchell sat back in his chair. "Okay, it's all circumstantial evidence against you, Sal. But it's a shitload and, in my estimation, enough to convict you, especially if Giachetti fingers you." He paused to let this sink into his client's thick skull. "And, as your lawyer, I think your best bet is to confess that Giachetti hired you. Cut a deal before he does. Murder for hire is a federal offense, and the federal prosecutors will be seeking the death penalty on this. If you cooperate, I can work a plea for you, possibly avoiding the needle, in exchange for life in prison without parole. Let me take this to them now because Giachetti is being offered the same deal to give you up. If he takes it first, you're screwed and are sold down the river, my friend. So what's it going to be, Sal?"

"First of all, you're *not* my friend. You're some lawyer who couldn't make it on the outside. You walk in here, and the first thing out of your mouth is for me to confess. Trying to take the easy way out? What's your plan for my defense? I want to hear what else you've got to offer because so far I ain't buyin' it, you hear? I believe you're a *defense* lawyer, or did I hear you wrong? Aren't you supposed to *defend* me? What the fuck is going on here, Mitchell?"

"Look, Sal, from what I've got here in this file, you don't have much of a defense. I could play the circumstantial-evidence card, but this is a double homicide, and Boston juries, with all the syndicate crime here, have been known to convict in such cases. I don't think you want this to go to trial, for surely you *will* get the death penalty. I'm here to save your life. This is the only choice you have, in my opinion. So if you want another opinion, be my guest. But it's pretty simple: give up Giachetti or die. Your choice. I'll be back in tomorrow, and you can give me your answer. And remember, time is *not* on your side. Good day, Mr. Barboza. See you in the morning," Mitchell said as he got up and walked toward the door.

Barboza shook his head, pontificating if he should go with Carmen's lawyer. No way anybody could get him out on bail now, even if they did want to off him. But if they could intimidate jurors, maybe he'd stand a chance.

At Sing Sing, Giachetti was scheduled to meet with his lawyer that afternoon. Barry Mitchell, meanwhile, called the federal prosecutors and informed them of his meeting with his client earlier today and said he wouldn't know until tomorrow morning if Barboza would finger Giachetti for a plea. He'd wait to get the outcome of the meeting with Giachetti and his defense counsel before revisiting Barboza in the morning.

Giachetti was brought into the interrogation room to meet with his lawyer, Cecil Anthony, who was already seated at the table reviewing his notes. He stood up, and they shook hands.

"Hey, Frank. I'm Cecil Anthony. Nice to meet you." Anthony was an ex-con who had gone to law school after being released from prison. He was sent up for a bank heist and made parole after serving eight years for being a model prisoner. He educated himself in prison, taking college correspondence courses, and when he was released, he completed his undergraduate studies and enrolled in New England Law's night program. Four years later he passed the bar exam and had been defending criminals now for five years. Although older, he still had an ex-con's rough edges. He was short, overweight, and almost entirely gray. He had thick, bushy eyebrows, a white moustache and long gray sideburns. He didn't look anything like a typical attorney, and being well groomed was certainly not one of his attributes.

"Nice to meet you, Cecil. I hear you're the man to have represent me since you've been on the inside yourself."

"I guess that's the word going around. Yeah, I'm no fancy-pants lawyer, that's for sure."

Giachetti laughed. "Yeah, I've had my fill of 'em."

Anthony nodded. "So I've heard." He paused to clear the air. "Frank, you need to tell me everything so that I'll be able to give you the best legal advice possible. If you're not up front with me, then that makes my job almost impossible. The other side has built quite a case against you, so I need you to be straight with me—as I will be with you. You understand what I'm saying?"

Giachetti gave the man a long hard stare. "I get it."

"Okay, since we've laid the ground rules, let's move on. I met with the federal prosecutors yesterday, and they're prepared to offer you a deal. If you give up your hit man, Barboza, and reveal where you stashed the money, they'll take the death penalty off the table. You'll get life with no chance of parole, but at least you'll live."

"No deal. I ain't squealing on nobody. You know what they do to rats in this place? I can't take the chance. And as far as the money goes, I've already given it away, so there's nothing left."

Anthony leaned forward in his chair, closer to Giachetti, and, looking him straight in the eye, said, "Frank, that's bullshit. You were prepared to pay Barboza a hundred Gs. Nobody's buying that, Frank. And you didn't give three mil to the Sisters of Charity."

Giachetti had to laugh. "Okay, what if I give up the money but don't rat out?"

Anthony sat back in his chair. This, at least, was progress. "Don't think it'll work. You either give them what they want or buy the farm." Giachetti thought about this proposal for a moment. "Just let me tell you," Anthony continued, "Barboza's lawyer is putting this same deal before him, as we speak. And the first one who agrees is the one who gets the deal. The other one will face a trial and death row. The feds want you bad, Frank, and this deal is only viable today. They want to put you into isolation until you tell them where you hid the money. They still feel that you're a threat to the girl, since you still have access to the money to pay for another attack."

"Let's say I give them what they want. Can you get them to transfer me to another federal prison in another state?"

Anthony smiled. "Great idea. I don't see why not." He paused. "So I go back to them with this offer?" Giachetti nodded. "I can get the papers drawn up today. We need to do it before Barboza signs his deal."

"Okay. If they agree, you can tell them the money is in a safe deposit box at First Federal Bank, and my sister, Mary, has the key. She lives alone, getting up in years, and has been living on the money. She's the only one in the world I can trust. Got a piece of paper? I'll write down her address and phone number. Also, part of the deal is that she's left alone. She had no involvement in this at all and doesn't know where the money came from."

"How much is in there, Frank?"

"Well, it started off with three million, but she's been taking it out to live on. She's not the spending type, very simple and frugal. Most of it's probably still there."

"And are you willing to sign a statement stating that you hired Barboza to murder Michael Hudson and beat up Beth Scott?"

"Don't have much of a choice, huh?" Giachetti responded in an agitated voice.

"No you don't, Frank. And it's not up for negotiations. One more thing. What if they won't go for the relocation part?" Cecil asked.

"Get what you can get. I can take care of myself."

"I'll get everything drawn up and have it back first thing in the morning for your signature. I think you've made the right decision, Frank. I've never had a client get to death row yet. Pretty good record, I must admit."

"Whatever you say, counselor. I can do the normal time, but years in isolation while I'm waiting to die is tough to swallow."

"Oh, one more thing," Anthony said. "We'll need to settle up before you turn over the money to the feds. So call your aunt and tell her she'll need to bring me fifty thousand dollars for saving your life. I'll expect it tomorrow by five. Understood?"

Cecil Anthony hurried out of the prison and drove back to the city. Walking into his office, he told his secretary, Sharon, "Get Dale Wallace on the phone."

No sooner did Anthony sit down at his desk than the intercom buzzed. "Wallace is on line two," Sharon announced.

"Hello, Mr. Wallace, this is Cecil Anthony and I'm calling on the Giachetti case. Just wanted to inform you that my client has agreed to all of your terms. However, there is one caveat. He would like to be transferred to a federal prison in another state for his life term."

"He'll give up the money and Barboza?" Wallace asked.

"Yes."

"Okay, I can live with that. Draw up the paperwork immediately and send it over to my office."

"I'll have it to you within two hours."

"That's great news, Cecil. You've saved the federal government a lot of money. I'll meet you at Sing Sing tomorrow morning. Does ten o'clock work for you?"

"Perfect. See you then."

Anthony buzzed his secretary. "Sharon, bring in your pad. I need to dictate terms of the agreement with the federal prosecutors."

Cecil Anthony took a deep breath and was pleased to have another notch under his belt. He was getting quite the reputation now for defending these scumbags in prison. But he wasn't complaining, for it was providing him with a very comfortable living. And after all, it wasn't long ago that he was walking in their shoes. He was much happier on the other side of the bars, that's for sure. In his case crime *did* pay.

Chapter
Twenty-Two

Over the next three months, Beth and Brandon's relationship deepened. They enjoyed as much time with each other as their work schedules would allow. He spent nights at her apartment, and when he had to be at the hospital early she stayed at his place. Rarely did they sleep alone at their respective apartments. They were in love and grateful to have finally connected under such trying circumstances. Beth had been back to Boston to meet Brandon's family, who were as taken with her as their son was and could see how well suited the two were for each other. They were also excited about the prospect of having a daughter, since Brandon was their only child, and in their minds he couldn't have picked a better person than Beth. They fully supported Brandon's decision to stay in New York to build his career, especially since Beth had only a few more years to be appointed a partner in her law firm.

Beth greatly admired Dr. and Mrs. Burton, both of whom were well respected in their professions. Mark was one of the country's leading heart surgeons, which could have been overshadowing for Brandon, but instead he never competed with his father and sought to establish his own identity. And Mark never faulted Brandon for making his own career choices in medicine. Beth could detect a very sensitive side to Brandon's dad, even though he projected a strong, in-control personality. Brandon's mom, Barbara, was not only very accomplished in pediatric medicine but also a published author. She and Beth got along well, and she already treated Beth as one of the family. They spoke about Beth's career and how she wanted to continue working after she and Brandon started a family.

"I think it's wonderful that you plan to follow your career and still manage a family," she told Beth. "It won't be easy—I know from experience. But if anyone can do it well, it's you. If I may give you some advice that I wish I had followed: take time off when your children are born, always be there in the mornings to see them off to school, and try to be home for dinner as often as possible. That way they will know they come first. There were many days I couldn't be there for my son, and to this day I cannot forgive myself for it."

"I understand, and I think your son does, too. He's told me that despite all the missed meals and bedtime tuck-ins he never doubted your love for him. You did your best, and I know he doesn't fault you in any way whatsoever."

Barbara's eyes teared up. "Thank you, Beth. That was so kind of you to say. I can see that my son's a very lucky man to have you in his life."

Their future was set, and by mid-December, although they were not yet engaged, they were talking about marriage. Beth wanted a fall wedding, but Brandon, not wanting to wait, preferred to be married in the spring. Beth talked to her parents, and they agreed this was enough notice to plan for the wedding of her dreams. She didn't want anything elaborate or over the top, just a classy yet simple event. Beth had a hunch that Brandon would propose on her birthday, January 14; but he had something different in mind. Brandon had already chosen the ring, one she had pointed out when they visited jewelry stores together. He wasn't the least bit surprised with her selection, for it was small and elegant, with the most dazzling sparkle—one that matched the sparkle in Beth's eyes.

New Year's Eve was approaching rather quickly. Beth and Brandon were going out to dinner with Lisa and her new boyfriend, Henry Stone. A few months after her divorce, Lisa had been introduced to Henry by a mutual friend at a party. They had had an instant connection and had started seeing each other immediately. Beth liked him a lot, but it was still much too early to tell if the relationship had staying power. Henry was also a doctor, and so he and Brandon had a lot in common, as well as similar tastes. Beth found it ironic that she and her best friend, whom she had grown up with and who had chosen the same career, might even have husbands in the same profession. She wondered if close childhood friends had bonds like twins.

For New Year's Eve, Brandon had reserved a window table for four at The View, the only revolving rooftop restaurant in New York. He was sure this would be the perfect setting to bring in the New Year and make his proposal. It was romantic, elegantly designed, and there was no better view of the skyline. It had started snowing in the afternoon, and by the time they arrived at the restaurant, the city was covered in a blanket of white. What venue could be more exquisite for a wedding proposal? Beth loved the cityscape views, the night lights, and the lightly falling snow. She had often told Brandon that nothing was more magical than New York during its first snowfall of the season. That night the city looked and smelled clean and fresh.

Beth and Brandon and Lisa and Henry were having a spectacular evening. The food was phenomenal, the band exceptional, and just being together with good friends made for a perfect celebration. While they were enjoying their wine, Brandon stood and took Beth's hand. As she stood up beside him, he thought how spectacular she looked in her fitted short black dress, with its V neck edged in small seed pearls and the thin pearl belt that cinched her tiny waist.

"It's almost midnight, Beth. Would you come with me, please? I have something I want to show you." Brandon had alerted the maître d', who had cleared a spot for them along the window for the appointed time. The snowfall was heavy by now, and the city looked like a painting, with its twinkling lights from the skyscrapers reflecting off the Hudson River. Christmastime in New York was wonderland. It was one minute to midnight and the band was counting down the clock. At the stroke of midnight, Brandon reached into his pocket and took out a small black velvet box.

He got on one knee and said, "Beth, you are the love of my life, and I love you in a way that I never knew I could. Will you make me the happiest man on earth and marry me?"

Beth immediately began to cry tears of joy. He placed the ring on her finger, and it sparkled as brightly as if it were the most radiant diamond in existence.

"Yes, of course I'll marry you, my dear Brandon." He stood and took her hands.

"I'm in shock! I thought it would be on my birthday. Oh my God, I can't believe this is really happening to me. I feel like I'm in a dream and I'm going to wake up and none of it will be real. Brandon, I'm so unbelievably happy right now."

"Baby, this is true, and it is real. You can bet your life on it!"

Brandon kissed her for the longest time, never wanting to release their embrace. He, too, had never known such happiness. Now it was official, and they'd be married shortly.

After another long kiss and warm embrace, they walked back into the main dining room, where everybody was celebrating the new year, and shared the good news with Lisa and Henry.

"Oh, Beth, I'm so happy for you both. We had no idea where you two had run off to." Taking her hand, Lisa added, "This ring is so you, Beth. It's just gorgeous. Great taste, Brandon...and Beth." She knew that they had picked it out together.

The evening only got better from there. Beth called her parents to share the good news. They already knew, however, for Brandon had visited a few nights earlier to tell them when and where he was going to give Beth the ring. Brandon had also told his family when the engagement was to take place, and he and Beth planned to call them in the morning. They danced and sipped champagne until two in the morning, laying the foundation for one of the most memorable nights of their lives. No one wanted the night to end, and their exhilaration permeated throughout the room. Needless to say, they didn't get to sleep until hours later.

The better part of New Year's Day was spent calling their friends to share the news. They talked about the wedding, and Beth finally agreed to a late spring date. She, too, didn't want to wait any longer now. They looked at the calendar and chose the Saturday night of Memorial Day weekend, pending workplace commitments. She called her parents and told them what they had decided and wanted to know if the date worked for them.

"Honey, whatever date you two choose is fine with us. You now need to think about your venue, for there isn't much time."

"Okay, Mom, we will. But we need to catch our breath for a moment."

"I understand, honey."

They talked about places and decided to call a wedding planner to recommend the perfect venue. Beth would ask around at her office for the name of someone since a few of her colleagues had gotten married in the past year.

The next day at the office Beth was given the names of two wedding planners and placed calls to them right away. She knew many venues would already be booked at this late date so she hoped to speak with someone as soon as possible. After interviewing them, she hired the one who best understood her vision. Otherwise, her day was filled with clients, and she had two new ones coming in today who sounded desperate.

"Beth, Mrs. Hillary Harris has arrived. Would you like me to show her in?"

"Yes, Maria, that would be great. Thanks."

Beth came from behind her desk and greeted Mrs. Harris as Maria showed her to a chair.

"Nice to meet you, Hillary. I'm Beth Scott. Please tell me how I can be of assistance."

"Ms. Scott, I've heard so many wonderful things about you, and I know you'll do a great job for me."

"Thank you so much. I appreciate your confidence in me. Please tell me about your situation, and I'll take some notes as we go."

Beth spent over two hours with Mrs. Harris, inputting the notes onto her computer with the monitor off to the side so as to keep her client in view. Hillary's case was going to be challenging. Her husband had been abusive to her throughout the five years of their marriage, and she had had enough.

"I've threatened to leave him many times, and he said that if I did he'd kill me. I've been living in fear for so long, but I can't do this anymore. Can you please help me, Miss Scott?"

"Of course, I can. You've come to the right place. And please call me Beth."

"I'd be so grateful. I don't work, and I have no way of supporting myself. I guess that's why I've stayed for so long. But I don't love him anymore. In fact, I loathe him and can't wait to get away from him. I'd rather be penniless than stay."

"Well, Hillary, you're not alone. Most abused women stay in the marriage for the very same reasons—fear and money just about sums it up. But don't worry about money, Hillary. We'll be suing him for enough to take care of you the rest of your life. Let me handle that part. Do you have any money at all in your own account? Or do you have any jewelry that you can sell to raise some cash? You'll need to pay my retainer of twenty-five thousand dollars up front. If you don't have it, I understand, and can have it taken out of your settlement. But my firm would prefer to be paid up front."

"No problem. I've saved about a hundred thousand dollars in a separate account that the bastard doesn't know about. I also have credit cards, but as soon as I leave I know he'll cancel them."

"Have you tried to leave before?"

"I've threatened many times, but never followed through due to his threats. I was too frightened of him to do anything."

Hillary showed Beth the bruises on her arms and legs from the times he'd thrown her down the past week alone. She was fearful that one day he'd act on his threats and get away with it, using his political connections and monetary resources.

"Have you ever gone to the police?"

"Yes, I did once, and when I got home he beat me so badly I couldn't get out of bed for two days. He's worn me down, Beth, and just about shattered my spirit, but I do not want to give up. I may have no choice but to go into a shelter or change my identity, but I'm ready to do whatever it takes to get out of this marriage for good. I've finally reached my breaking point and can no longer go on like this."

"There are shelters where he'll never find you. Once we get you relocated into one of them, I'll start the filings for divorce. First, what is your husband's name and financial status?"

"His name is Anthony Harris, and he owns one of the largest meat packing companies in the tri-state area. It's called Harris Meat Packing, Inc. I have no idea what his worth is, but we live in a three-million-dollar apartment overlooking Central Park, which he let me decorate to my liking without a budget. He gives me an allowance of two thousand dollars a week, and I have credit cards with large limits. He's always been very generous with me, and I guess that's why I stayed as long as I did. It was a trade-off—put up with his controlling, abusive behavior and be rewarded lavishly—but it turned out to be too high a price to pay. It was fine in the beginning, for I liked having someone take charge and take care of me, and I actually loved the brute, until the rough stuff escalated. Now I'm at the point where no amount of money or material things could keep me with that sick animal. I want out. I'm done."

"Mrs. Harris, I want you to listen to me very carefully. I can help you, but you must do everything that I'm about to tell you. Do you understand?"

"Yes, I do."

"Okay, the first thing we'll do is put a plan of action on the table. You must wait a few more weeks so I can do some investigating into his business holdings and other assets before he starts hiding things. You were smart to have stashed away some cash. So first thing I'll do is call some shelters and find one that is suitable for you. You'll need to stay there until you're legally divorced. I'll also let the police know that your husband is an abuser. They might have a record on him from previous women he's abused as well. They'll definitely want to speak to you and get it all down for the record. This will happen once you're in the shelter. I'll send over a hairdresser and a makeup artist, and we'll select some different clothes for you to wear. Anytime you go out in public wear a hat and sunglasses, day or night, because he'll hire a private investigator to find you. You'll be registered under an alias, and you'll go by that name as long as you're in the shelter. Understood?"

"Of course, I'll do whatever you say."

"I'll make all the arrangements and call you with the details by the end of the week. Does your husband ever come home during the day? Is there a place he goes every week when you know where he is on that particular day, besides the office?"

"Yes, he plays golf every Wednesday at the country club, and he never misses a week. If the weather is too bad for golf, then he plays cards with the guys."

"Okay, let's plan for all this to happen in two weeks from Wednesday. That'll give me the time that I need to check out his finances. This is a community property state, so that's in your favor. Although you haven't been married long enough to be entitled to half his assets, I assure you that you won't ever have to worry about money again once this is done. During the next two weeks be thinking about what you'd like to take with you. Plan on taking all your jewelry, but don't start your preparations ahead of time or he might get suspicious. These types of men are almost always paranoid, so you must be very careful. That also means not overcompensating by being too nice to him. Everything just stays as it is between you." Hillary nodded. "What time does he usually return from the club on Wednesdays?"

"Around six o'clock."

"Okay, in two weeks from Wednesday, as soon as your husband leaves for the club start packing your things and I'll come pick you up. What time do you think you'll be ready?"

"Well, if he leaves at nine o'clock, I'll probably be ready by one. I'm only taking some clothes, jewelry, cosmetics, and pictures of my family. I don't care about anything else. I'm sure the place isn't that big, and I can't take that much with me, anyway."

"I want you out of there early just in case he decides to leave the club early that day. I'll pick you up at three o'clock. Only take as many suitcases as you and I can carry ourselves. I'll park in the basement, and we'll take the elevator straight down. I don't want the doorman to be alerted." Beth paused for a moment as she had another thought pop into her head. "One more thing. If you have help in the house, please give them the day off."

"Good thinking. They're all friends with my husband. He's a big Christmas tipper."

"Do you have any family out of state?"

"Yes, I have a sister in Virginia, but that'll be the first place he'll look, so if I go there he'll come after me."

"That's why we have shelters," Beth said, shaking her head. "Most abusers' victims have tried to flee to their families, but they're always found." Hillary nodded. "However, I want you to call your sister and let her know what you're planning to do. You must not tell her where you're going—don't even mention the word *shelter* to her. Then on the night that you arrive in the shelter call your sister and tell her to call the house looking for you; that way he'll realize that she knows nothing. Trust me, Mrs. Harris. I've done this many times before. The plan works well, and he'll never find you, as long as you do what I tell you."

"I'm so grateful to have found you, Ms. Scott. You're going to save my life. I can't thank you enough."

"Oh, one more thing: I'll give you a new cell phone so he can't trace you. Nothing will be in your name. Cut up all your credit cards the day you leave. You'll have to go on an all-cash basis—for he could trace your purchases if you use a credit card. There are safes at the shelter for your jewelry until you need to sell it. Your husband's P.I. will be checking pawn shops, so to keep you from being identified I'll be the one doing the selling. Any questions?"

"No. I'll be ready two weeks from Wednesday, and I'll have your retainer at that time."

"Okay, Hillary, I think we have a plan. Do you have any reason to believe that he could be following you now?"

"No, I've said nothing about leaving him, and I've been acting like everything is fine. He has no clue what I'm about to do. I've told no one."

"Okay, great. Then we shouldn't have a problem."

"The only reason we'll speak again before Wednesday is if there's no room at the right shelter, and then you might have to wait a little longer until space opens up. But let's hope for the best. If you don't hear from me, then we follow the original plan. And if you need to call me, please do so, but don't use your home phone or cell phone. We don't want him to know who I am at this point. That'll come later."

"I'll absolutely do as you say. Thanks so much for helping me start a new life, Beth."

"I'll do all I can to get you out and set you up with everything you need. You must be very careful not to tell anyone where you are once you get settled in the shelter, and always use your new cell phone, which will have an unlisted number and will be in my firm's name. Just be very cautious about the people you speak with, and don't tell anyone about the plan." Beth gave Hillary a big hug then escorted her to the elevator and advised her to remain focused and unwavering until their Wednesday getaway.

Beth spent the next hour on the phone trying to get Hillary placed in the shelter that she thought was best suited for her—one outside of the city, in New Jersey, that catered to women of means. It was a private shelter with no state funding and was run strictly on contributions from corporations and wealthy donors. Giving up one's freedom and going into hiding was as bad as being imprisoned. To afford these women some comforts of home while going through this terrible ordeal, each occupant was given her own apartment with a kitchen, living area, and bedroom and bath. The rooms were beautifully furnished and had many of the amenities the women had been accustomed to at home.

"Hello, may I please speak to Valerie Johnson? Tell her Beth Scott is calling from Cavanaugh, Lewis and Strong."

"Yes, Miss Scott, please hold one moment and I'll get the administrator for you."

"Thank you so much."

"Well, hi, Beth. I hope you're well," Valerie said with concern.

"I'm doing better, Valerie, but it's been a struggle." She paused. "Unfortunately, I have a client who I need to place in your facility very soon. Please tell me that you'll have a room available two weeks from this Wednesday."

"Give me a second while I check the schedule." A moment later, she continued, "Yes, you're in luck, Beth. I will have an apartment available next Tuesday, and that'll give us a week to get it ready for your client. It happens to be one of our nicer ones."

"Oh, that's great, Valerie. Can you hold it for my client?"

"Be happy to. Who should we register it under?"

"Let's call her Dorothy Patrick. She's a lovely lady. I think you'll like her, and I know she'll end up being a huge benefactor after she receives her settlement."

"Glad to help, and, of course, we'd welcome her donation."

"I can't thank you enough, Valerie. We should arrive by four-thirty at the latest if we don't get caught in traffic coming out of the city."

"Yes, the George Washington Bridge can be a challenge that time of day."

"Thanks for helping me save another life, Valerie."

"Beth, I'm always happy to receive your clients, and they've always proven to be wonderful supporters of our mission. I look forward to seeing you in two weeks. Good luck!"

Chapter Twenty-Three

*M*uch needed to be done in a short time for the wedding, and fortunately Beth performed at her best when she had deadlines to meet, leaving no time for procrastination. She tried to remain focused on the wedding, but still had lingering fears when alone. The attack had left her restless, with flashes of that night sometimes reappearing in her head.

She and Brandon met the wedding planner, who had the perfect place in mind: a hundred-year-old stately mansion in the countryside of Connecticut. She showed them pictures of the home; it was surrounded by large, mature trees and dozens of flower gardens. And there was a serene lake at the back of the property that could serve as a backdrop for the ceremony. The venue was exactly what Beth had imagined. The date of May 29 was available, and they would drive there the next day with Beth's parents to check it out.

When they arrived at the mansion, everything looked as it had in the pictures. While walking the grounds and viewing the lake, they fell in love with the setting. And upon exploring the smaller of the two ballrooms inside, they were taken by its elegant beauty.

"Wow," Beth said, "look at the crystal chandeliers and the padded walls of silk in my favorite cream and gold tones. The warmth just draws you in." The boxed-in design of the ceiling in a rich, dark wood gave the room a homey ambience. Beth took Brandon's hand. "I think we've found our dream spot for the wedding, even if it is the first place we looked at."

"I couldn't agree more. Let's sign the contract and wrap it up," Brandon said. Pulling Beth closer to kiss her, he whispered, "This is it, baby! This is where we'll blend our hearts together and become one."

"Just thinking about it gives me butterflies, Brandon."

The whole family was upbeat on the drive back to the city. With the venue under contract, Beth felt as if a weight had been lifted off her shoulders. Now she and her mom could begin planning the wedding with the staff at the mansion.

Work was getting increasingly busy for Beth. Every few days a new client was coming to her with complaints about their marriage. Rather than fight for their relationships, couples were giving up and moving on. Where is the commitment to the vows they made to each other on their wedding day? Beth wondered, knowing it would be very different for her and Brandon. From what she'd seen in her profession, most marriages failed due to finances or infidelity. She and Brandon would never have financial issues, for they were both good earners. As for infidelity, she was sure this would never happen in their marriage, due to the complete trust they had in each other. From the start, she would insist they never lie to each other, even white lies, which is where she saw things unraveling for many marriages.

Beth's intercom buzzed. It was Detective Stevens on line one. "Hi, detective. What's up?"

"I've got some good news for you, Beth. Barboza confessed and turned state's evidence on the DiNunzio crime family and will testify against them when they are brought to trial. He'll avoid the death penalty but will spend the rest of his life in prison with no chance of parole. And, of course, Giachetti had already made his deal by giving up Barboza and the bank money. So, Beth, it looks as if we can finally close the file on this one and put it behind us."

"Walter, you've made my day. I was dreading having to testify at a trial. I can't thank you enough for everything you've done in this case."

"Well, you nailed it with your ID of Barboza in the lineup. That took real courage."

"Thank you. And I've got some good news, too. Brandon and I will be married on Memorial Day weekend in Connecticut, and we'd love you and Rob Matthews to come to the wedding."

"We'd be honored, Beth. I think I'll put in today to have that weekend off so there won't be any work conflicts. I wouldn't miss this for the world. Thanks so much for the invite, and I know Rob feels the same. I look forward to it."

"Thank you, detective. It wouldn't be the same without you both."

Hillary was now settled in the shelter and doing well. Beth had filed the divorce papers and served Hillary's husband. He didn't take it lightly. His attorney had called twice saying that his client wanted to speak directly to Hillary to work things out. Beth told him that Hillary never wanted to speak with him again. And if he didn't agree to the divorce, she was prepared to file criminal charges against him for assault and battery, and drag his name and reputation through the mud with a court trial. She told him that the police had phone tapes on four different occasions where Hillary had called them asking for help but had never filed charges. So if Mr. Harris wanted to save himself the embarrassment and bad publicity, he'd better not contest the divorce. Beth really wanted Hillary to come out on top for all the pain and suffering she had endured through the years. She was certain she could negotiate a substantial settlement for her, given that her husband was a very wealthy man, and she would never have to worry about money again.

Beth was just finishing up with her last client of the day when Maria buzzed her to say that Mr. Harris was on line one.

"Oh, this isn't going to be pretty. Put him through."

"Hello, Mr. Harris, this is Beth Scott. What can I do for you?"

"Where's my wife?"

"Mr. Harris, please know that I cannot speak with you about the case. You must communicate with me only through your attorney. I must advise you that this conversation is being recorded."

"I don't give a shit! Who the fuck do you think you are? Some fat-cat lawyer sitting behind a big desk admiring the view out her window. You've taken my wife from me, and I want to know where you put her." He paused, but instead of calming down, he got more agitated. "Look, lady, you better not mess with me or you'll regret it. You hear what I'm saying to you? I've got lots of resources, and I'll use them. I want her back, or you'll both be sorry."

"I'm sorry, Mr. Harris, but I must end this conversation. Any further communication will have to be through your attorney. Have a good day," Beth said and hung up.

Beth was greatly disturbed by Mr. Harris's threats, so she now walked down the hall to the senior partner's office and arrived visibly shaken.

"What's wrong, Beth? You look disturbed," Jeff said. "Please, take a seat."

Beth sat across from him and proceeded to tell Jeff about her conversation with Mr. Harris.

"What should I do, Jeff?"

"Let me handle it. Have Maria send me a copy of the recording. I'm going to make a police report immediately, and I'll call his attorney as well. Have Maria give Molly his name and number." He took Beth's hand. "Please don't worry about him. We'll stop this right now. I'm so glad you told me. As I've said, we'll not tolerate such threats against our attorneys."

"Thanks, Jeff. I guess I'm just not ready to deal with something like this so soon after Michael's death. I could resign from the case and turn it over to another attorney. But Hillary trusts me, and I don't want to abandon her. I need your advice, Jeff."

"Beth, whatever you decide to do, I'll support you one hundred percent." He paused. "Another option would be to co-counsel with someone since you're so familiar with the case. And the co-counsel could deal directly with Mr. Harris and his lawyer. That way it takes you out of the forefront and lets you focus on your client's well-being."

"I like that idea, Jeff. I'll think about who I'd like to work with and bring that person in on the case. I'm just not up to dealing with someone threatening me again. Not so soon!"

"I agree, Beth. Wise decision. Think about Tom Casey. He's a damn good lawyer and can be tough and intimidating. It sounds like that he's who you need to go up against this guy."

"Perfect. I'll call him and see if he's up for it."

"Good. And, Beth, don't worry."

When Beth got back to her office, Maria informed her that Brandon had called. "Okay, thanks, I'll call him right back. But before I do, I need to tell Hillary about her husband's call."

Beth called Hillary on her new cell phone. "How's my favorite client?"

"Beth, I just love it here. Everyone is so nice and caring. I've never met such wonderful people. And I've already bonded with a few of the women. My friend Suzi has gone through the same thing: an abusive husband, the beatings, the threats. Others here have been through much worse. I feel like I have friends who've got my back, and I've never felt like that before with anyone. You chose the perfect place for me. I don't know how to thank you."

"I'm so happy for you, Hillary. I knew you would find friends there, and that's what you need now, more than anything. But

I need to tell you that your husband called me this morning demanding to know where you are, and threatening me and you if I refused to tell him. I informed my senior partner, and he's going to file charges against him. Also, I plan to engage another lawyer, a partner from my firm, to take the lead on this case. I'll be right beside him the whole way, but I'll be out of the line of fire, as it were. I'm sure you understand my reasoning, given what I've just been through."

"Yes, of course, Beth. Whatever you think is best. I'm so sorry to have put you in this position. But I'm happy you'll still be on the case, and I thank you for hanging in there with me."

"I'm glad you understand. But don't worry—now you'll have two attorneys for the price of one, and I'm sure you'll be pleased with the outcome."

"Thanks again, Beth. And my apologies for my husband's bad behavior."

"Hillary, I'd like you to remain in the facility for as long as necessary and not go out right now. I'm sure he's going to press his P.I.s to turn over every stone to find you."

"Whatever you say. I feel safe and secure here, and I'm happy to stay inside, especially in this weather. Don't worry, Beth, I'll stay put."

"Good. I'll be in touch and keep you posted. Take care and enjoy your new friends."

Beth felt a little down after speaking with Hillary, and needed to call Brandon back. He always brightened her day.

"Hi, sweetie, it's me. How's your day going?" she asked.

"Hi, baby. You sound down," he said.

"It's been a tough day. How about you?"

"Well, I've got some great news."

"Good. I could use some great news about now."

"I was offered the position with Dr. Tracey's surgical group on the Upper West Side. Remember this is the group with the best reputation in town, and they were interviewing three other surgeons for the position? They just called to offer me the slot. Beth, I'm so excited."

"Oh, honey, that's just wonderful. I'm so proud of you. You've worked so hard, and now it's finally paying off. We have to celebrate tonight. Where would you like to go?"

"You pick. I'm on call, so I really should be near the hospital."

"I'll come up with a place and send you a text. What time?"

"I can make it about seven forty-five."

"Okay, that works for me. Love you."

"Love you back, baby."

Beth hung up the phone and started to think about Jeff's suggestion again. She had thought about choosing another woman attorney, but taking into consideration how Harris treated women, she dismissed that idea. She needed somebody to back down Harris and his equally difficult attorney, and Tom Casey seemed perfect.

"Hi, Tom, Beth Scott calling. Do you have some time to discuss a case?"

"Of course, Beth, Jeff clued me in. Sounds right up my alley. If you handle the property breakdowns, I'll be point man at the settlement meeting and face off with them."

"Exactly what I was thinking. Let me fill you in."

Beth and Tom discussed the case for over an hour, then they engaged in a conference call with Harris's attorney, Richard Parker, so Beth could introduce Tom. She told him about the call from Mr. Harris and how he had threatened her and Hillary.

"I know," Parker said. "Jeff Greene has already informed me." Then Parker apologized, and Tom told him that the firm would be pressing charges. He tried to dissuade them, but Tom was firm and told him to expect a police inquiry.

"I understand," Richard finally said. "I'll have a meeting with him and will let him know that he could go to prison for those threats. I assure you it won't happen again."

"Thanks, Richard," Beth said, "and I appreciate your being on the same page with us on this matter. Please get back to us after you've spoken to Mr. Harris."

"I certainly will, Beth. Nice to meet you, Tom, and I look forward to working with both of you. Good afternoon."

While celebrating Brandon's job offer, he and Beth talked about where they wanted to go on their honeymoon. June was a beautiful time of year in the Caribbean, and they talked about a small island called Nevis with a Ritz Carlton that was supposed to be magnificent. It was only a little over two hours by plane. They wanted to soak up some sun since the winter had recently turned so bitter. This would also give Brandon a nice break before starting his new position. They'd still check out other places, but for now Nevis was at the top of their list.

A couple of months had passed since their New Year's Eve engagement, and everything was working out well with the wedding plans. Brandon's parents were coming to New York to meet Beth's mom and dad in a few weeks. They thought it best for their families to meet before the wedding. They were two well-educated, career-minded families with many of the same values. Beth's mom was planning a dinner at their home, which would provide a more personal and quiet atmosphere for the first meeting. Joseph and Miriam loved Brandon, and couldn't be happier that they'd soon have a son. They'd already gone through so much together during Beth's coma and recovery and after Michael's murder. They'd never forget the empathy Brandon showed them throughout Beth's battle for her life, and how he had cared for their daughter during her grieving period. They felt that his parents had to be quite special to have raised such a compassionate son.

The evening with Brandon's parents went extremely well, and everyone easily engaged in conversation as if they'd known each other for years. Brandon's father was a very handsome man, tall and well built, with salt-and-pepper hair and brown eyes. You could tell that Mark took good care of himself by exercising and eating right. There was no denying that he and Brandon were father and son. And Barbara Burton was as lovely as Miriam had expected. Very classy, well spoken, and kind. She was beautifully dressed in a tailored Chanel suit and wore it well with her slim figure. Her hair was styled in a short bob, which moved fluidly as she walked. She projected a confidant exuberant demeanor.

Miriam took a seat next to Barbara and began a conversation. "We're so glad you're here and able to spend an evening in our home."

"Believe me, Miriam, the pleasure is all ours. We adore your daughter and are so pleased that she and Brandon have chosen each other. She's an extraordinary young woman, and now after meeting you, I can see why."

Taking Barbara's hand and smiling, Miriam said, "Thank you, Barbara. I appreciate your kindness. Beth speaks very highly of you and Mark, and told us how you both made her feel at home when she and Brandon visited."

Joseph, appearing with a bottle of fine champagne, said, "This calls for a celebration." He popped the cork and poured everyone a glass. "I'd like to make a toast to the merging of two wonderful families and to our future son-in-law."

Everyone nodded and sipped the champagne. The time was passing quickly, and after a delicious dinner Miriam served her homemade apple cake from her grandmother's recipe that had been in the family for over a hundred years.

Barbara took a bite and said, "This is a special treat, Miriam; I never have time to cook or bake, and it's always wonderful to have a home-cooked meal. I thank you so much."

"Please enjoy, and if you decide to take up cooking I'd be very happy to share my family recipes."

"I'd like that," Barbara said. "As would my husband," she added, and Mark smiled in agreement.

Mark then raised his glass and said, "I'd like to make a toast. To Miriam and Joseph, for having us tonight in their lovely home, and spoiling us with such a delicious dinner. We thank you for your hospitality, and we thank you for the opportunity to share in your wonderful daughter's life, and feel blessed to have her join our family. Barbara and I couldn't be happier with this union, and salute you, Miriam and Joseph, for making it all possible by raising such an amazing daughter. And hopefully we won't have to wait too long for our first grandchild."

Beth looked at Brandon before responding to his dad's remark. "Well, let's not rush this. We'd like a few years together before we start a family. To be honest, I'd like to make partner first because I can't see working all those hours when I have a child."

Miriam turned to Beth and said, "We all know that you and Brandon must choose when the time is right. We're just excited since it'll be the first for us, as well."

Brandon's dad spoke up. "Now, if I may give my opinion: I don't think waiting too long would be prudent, for you'll both get so wrapped up in your careers and keep putting it off, and before you know it you'll have lost your window of opportunity."

"Dad, aren't you jumping the gun a bit? We're not even married yet, and you're talking about a grandchild."

"Well, son, I just want to make sure I'll be around to see my grandchild arrive."

"What are you saying, Dad? Of course you'll be around."

Barbara looked at her husband in a strange way, feeling uncomfortable about this lead-in as he replied, "Well, son, I'm sorry to put a damper on the evening, but since we're all family, I'm going in for a biopsy next week for a couple nodules on my lung."

"Oh, Dad, why didn't you tell me sooner?"

"It's really nothing, son. But the Scotts and us aren't getting any younger. That's all I wanted to say."

Miriam and Joseph looked distressed and didn't know what to say.

Beth spoke up. "Don't worry, Mark. You're going to be fine. You're very strong, and for sure you'll do whatever's necessary."

Beth poured another glass of champagne for everyone. "Here's to grandchildren."

All four would-be grandparents teared up and joined in the toast.

After dinner, Brandon hailed a taxi to take his parents back to the Waldorf, then he and Beth went back to Beth's apartment. "Wow, this was quite the evening! It's hard for me to grasp that my image of my father as strong is now going to be tested. I've never seen my dad ill, not so much as a cold. I'll step up to the plate, Beth, and do whatever I have to do. I know he'll get through this. He's one tough man with prodigious stamina."

"We'll step up together. And don't you worry, sweetheart. He's going to be fine. We'll get through this rough patch and only become stronger because of it. I'm grateful that we have each other and that I can be here to support and comfort you. But let's not rush to conclusions and assume it's cancer. Let's wait for the biopsy results. We'll have plenty time for worry."

"I agree. That's a good point. Now I want to talk about your toast to grandchildren! What was that about Beth?" he asked, then paused. "It was amazing; you're amazing."

"I meant it, Brandon. We can't think only about ourselves and our careers; our parents both had their children when they were older, and they regretted it. Let's just be open."

"Have I told you today how much I love you?" They kissed and headed back to the bedroom.

Chapter

Twenty-Four

As the wedding day approached, Beth still had much work to do at the office. She wanted Hillary's case settled before leaving on her honeymoon. Jeff, as promised, had filed charges against Hillary's husband for threatening Beth and Hillary. Tom Casey, who was now working with Beth on the case, would be addressing these charges with Harris's attorney.

Maria buzzed Beth to let her know that Tom Casey was on line one. "Thanks, Maria."

"Hi, Tom, what's up?"

"Beth, just wanted to let you know that I've scheduled a meeting next Monday at one o'clock with Richard Parker concerning Harris's threats against you and Hillary. Would you like to be present?"

"Absolutely, as long as Harris isn't going to be there."

"He won't be. This is just between the lawyers."

"Okay, then count me in, but I'd like to meet with you first to go over the game plan."

"Definitely, Beth. Let's get together Friday and strategize. I have a slot open at two, if that works for you."

"Perfect. I'll come to your office. See you then."

Hillary had been at the shelter for four months and had adjusted very well to her new environment. This was much better than Beth would have thought. Hillary was relieved to be removed from the stressful life with her husband, and realized that money couldn't buy her happiness. In the past it had provided a lucrative lifestyle, but what good were material things if you couldn't enjoy them with someone you loved?

Hillary was much happier now than she had been for a long time. The days passed by quickly, and she enjoyed spending time with her new friends playing bridge, reading, and having stimulating conversations. Her husband had hired a P.I. who was trying to locate her by visiting every shelter in the area and attempted to enter this facility. He was denied access at the front gate and was unable to obtain a list of the occupants. The shelter, used to dealing with such investigations, had armed guards stationed at the front gate 24–7.

Hillary had taken on a new identity: she had colored her hair black instead of its natural light auburn, and it was styled much shorter. She wore very plain, nondesigner clothes, and no one would ever suspect that she was a woman of means. She looked like a plain Jane, compared to how she was accustomed to presenting herself. No one would recognize her with this makeover, and especially with the dark sunglasses and hats she wore when she occasionally left the shelter to take a short walk. She was still getting used to her new look and sometimes didn't even recognize herself. When the divorce was final, she would relocate to Virginia to be near her family, and she would put this portion of her life behind her forever.

Beth and Tom Casey had a very successful meeting with Harris's attorney. Tom told Richard that he intended to use the charges filed against Harris for leverage in the negotiations of the divorce settlement. "Look Richard," Tom said, "we'll be willing to drop these charges if we get what we want for our client. I also understand that there are several police reports on file from when Mrs. Harris called 911 to report the spousal abuse. Seems like Hillary got knocked around quite often. She has digital photos of her beaten, swollen face. Richard, I don't think your client would like to have his ass hauled off to prison and have his face all over the news about how he used his wife for a punching bag. No longer will housewives buy steaks from stores carrying his brand once they discover how he regards women."

"My client fully apologizes for his behavior and doesn't want any bad publicity. So tell me what you want, Tom."

Beth interceded. "We want five million dollars up front and her car. He can have the West Side apartment and the beach house in the Hamptons. My client just wants to make a clean break— no alimony—and to go back to her family unharmed. Mr. Harris will have to agree to a restraining order to never contact his wife again; if he does, he'll be held in contempt, and we'll prosecute him for the spousal abuse. It's that simple, Richard."

"Well, let me talk to my client, and then we can set up a final meeting and have everything signed. I think that's a fair offer, and I'll advise my client to take it."

Tom said, "I don't want this dragged out for weeks. Our client wants to get on with her life. Talk to Harris, and let me know when we can all meet next week. Five million should be chump change from a person like your client, who has a net worth of thirty million. Wouldn't you agree, Mr. Parker?"

"Sure do. You got it," Parker said. "I'll set it up and get back to you by the end of this week."

Beth and Tom discussed the case on the cab ride back to the office. Beth said, "I didn't push for alimony because I want Mr. Harris to feel as if he'll come out the winner. With this type of hothead, it's always best to let him think he made the better deal, for then he'll leave his victim alone and not seek revenge."

"I like your strategy, Beth. Well done," Tom said. "I'll meet with Parker and Harris alone next week. In the meantime, let me know if there's anything else I need to negotiate."

"Of course. I've spoken to Hillary, and she knows what we're asking for and agrees to this strategy."

When Beth got back to the office, she called Hillary and informed her of the meeting. She asked her if there was anything else she wanted. "Just my freedom," she said.

"Beth, do you think he'll agree to all that money? I would think that he'd try to get away with giving me as little as possible. And to be honest, I don't care. I just want to be free of him and leave the state knowing I'm safe."

"Hillary, you deserve this settlement for what you've endured with him. He's a very wealthy man, and this amount of money won't make so much as a dent in his financial statement or his lifestyle."

"Okay, if you say so. Of course, I'm happy to receive it for it'll relieve a lot of pressure, and I won't have to find a job to support myself. Thank you so much, Beth, for taking care of me. You're all I have right now to help me get through this." She choked up.

This was the first time Beth had heard her so upset. "Hillary, if you're crying, I hope they're tears of joy and relief, for we're in the home stretch now, and it's almost over."

"They are, Beth. I'm relieved to finally be done with him and move on."

Anthony Harris, a well-respected, wealthy man in the community, wanted to avoid any scandal regarding his surreptitious life as a wife beater. Beth therefore felt pretty sure that when Tom presented him with his options he would quickly agree to the five million dollars and the other stipulations as well. It was highly unlikely that he'd try to contact Hillary again, given the consequences he'd have to face. Most of the violence in domestic abuse cases is swept under the rug and never gets into a courtroom or newspaper. That's the sad thing about it: deals are made, money is exchanged, and life goes on as usual for the perpetrator, who is rarely held accountable for his crime. Once the decree was signed by the judge, then Harris's attorney would release the check to Beth to give to her client. Hopefully, this would take no longer than two weeks. Casey would see to it that the decree was funneled to a judge who was known for acting expeditiously.

Beth, tiring by the end of the day, was eager to get home. As she exited the taxi and approached her apartment, she felt vulnerable not seeing her surveillance men outside the building, especially now that she had received threats from Hillary's husband. She quickly unlocked her apartment door and stepped inside, then shut and bolted it. Her cell phone rang as she was taking off her coat. "Hello, Beth Scott speaking." There was silence at the other end. She said, "Hello, who is this please?" No response. Beth hung up, assuming that it was a wrong number. About an hour passed and the phone rang again. Still no answer. This went on every hour for most of the evening. Now she knew that this was not a wrong number. Someone was trying to scare her.

She called Brandon and explained what was happening. He told her to call the police. She did, but Detective Stevens was unavailable, working on another case. And there was nothing at this point that the police could do. There had been no threats and no verbal exchange. Suddenly there was a knock at the door. She eyed the peephole and found no one there. She knew better than to open the door and search the hallway. Ten minutes later, another knock. She could see nothing from the peephole. She called Brandon to tell him to be careful when coming to her place tonight. The calls started coming more frequently, so Beth turned off her phone and alerted Brandon in case he tried to call her. Detective Stevens had received the message of Beth's call and tried to call her back but of course got no answer. Since it was now nine o'clock, he thought he'd try again in the morning.

Brandon arrived at Beth's apartment around nine thirty, and Beth told him she felt certain that Hillary's husband was using scare tactics against her and it was working. She was envisioning an attack. Would he break the door down? Would he grab her on the street? Would he just shoot her when she least expected it? Whatever he did, it would be quick, for he wasn't interested in rape or money—just bodily harm. She'd call the detective once again early tomorrow and advise him of what was occurring. She'd try to remain emotionally unscathed until this stalker could be identified. Easier said than done!

Beth didn't sleep well that night and leaned on Brandon for comfort. The first thing she did after brushing her teeth was call Detective Stevens. "Beth, I was just calling you. What's going on? My colleague told me this morning that you called last night. Something about phone calls from a stranger and hanging up? Want to fill me in?"

"Well, it started when I got home last evening from work. The phone rang every hour, and when I answered there was no one on the other end. Then the knocks at the door began. I never opened the door but checked the peephole, and no one was outside my door. I think I know who's doing this, but I can't prove it. I'm working on a divorce with a very angry husband. Is it possible I can get my surveillance back, detective?"

"I'm afraid not, Beth, since he really hasn't done anything to harm you. A series of silent calls and knocks at the door wouldn't warrant this type of expense by the department. I could never get it approved by the higher-ups. I'm so sorry, Beth. But I think it best that you hire your own coverage, at least for a few weeks until we can prove who's doing this."

"So I need to get hurt again, or maybe even killed, before I can get help?"

"Try to get me more information, and I'll see what I can do. Have you ever seen this man before?"

"Not in person, but I've seen recent pictures from my client. He's Italian-looking. Short, stocky, dark hair, and has a temper shorter than his nose. He's been beating my client up for years. Poor woman—she looked like she'd been in a war. So he's capable of some pretty bad stuff, detective. And the worst part is that he thinks I'm hiding her, which I am, so I know if he makes up his mind to get back at me, nothing will stop him. You know Italians. Stubborn and more stubborn."

"Okay, Beth, get your bodyguard today, and I'll see what I can do on my end. If the phone calls continue, then maybe we can put a chip in your phone and trace it. That'll be the best way to get 'em."

"Thanks, detective. I'll stay in touch. I need to call my bodyguard ASAP."

A week had passed, and today was the final settlement meeting on Hillary's case. The phone calls continued through the week, but less frequently. Beth felt safe with her bodyguard, and if Harris was planning anything, she was almost impossible to get to under airtight surveillance. She would have Tom question Mr. Harris at the meeting, but not before she spoke to his attorney. She called Parker to advise him that she thought Harris was stalking her and she wanted to meet with him before the settlement meeting started. Beth went to Parker's office thirty minutes early and told him what his client was up to. She told Parker that she intended to face Harris and question him about it. Parker suggested that she not confront his client and let him handle the confrontation after a settlement had been signed. "One issue at a time," Parker said to Beth.

"Okay, you're right. I'll wait in your office until it's done. I've also informed my partner Tom, FYI."

Tom Casey was led into a conference room, where he waited for Parker and his client. About five minutes later, Parker and Anthony Harris stepped into the room and took seats across the table from him.

"Good afternoon, Tom. I'd like you to meet Anthony Harris."

Tom stretched his arm out to shake hands, but Harris hesitated before extending his. "Sorry, I can't say it's a pleasure, Mr. Casey. After all, we are on opposing sides."

Tom took the agreement out of his briefcase and handed Mr. Harris and Richard Parker each a copy. "It's all there, Richard. Everything we discussed. Mrs. Harris is awarded five million dollars and her automobile. That's all; nothing else. And the second part is that you, Mr. Harris, will have no further contact with your wife," he said, as he stared directly into Harris's eyes. "If you make any attempt whatsoever to contact her, you'll be arrested and prosecuted for spousal abuse to the letter of the law. And believe me, sir, you will go to prison. So read this over, and if you have any questions, I'm happy to answer them."

Harris turned to Parker in extreme agitation. "Richard, you're just going to sit there and let this motherfucker come in here and walk all over me? You're my Goddamn lawyer, for Christ's sake. Do something!"

"We already talked about this, Tony. You agreed to the deal over the phone, so what's this all about? I told you that you have nothing to contest. You threatened your wife and her lawyer, and that's against the law. You'll go to jail for that and the abuse if you fight this. I was able to get them to wipe the slate clean by dropping all the charges against you, and no alimony, and you get to keep both homes. If she wanted, she could get the West Side apartment hands down. Trust me, Tony, you're getting away with much more than you should. Just let her go, and give her what they're asking. Feel lucky that your ass isn't getting locked up for what you've done, Tony."

"She's a fucking liar, and you think I'm going to let that bitch get away with what she's doing to me?"

"Mr. Harris, the cops have tapes of your wife's calls after you beat her up on three different occasions. She also has digital photos. I think you've got this backwards. She did nothing to you. This is all about what you did to her," Casey said adamantly.

"She was drunk, fell down the stairs, and made it all up. I didn't touch the whore."

"She fell down the stairs three times? I doubt if the police, or a jury for that matter, would accept your version of what happened."

Parker now leaned over to his client and said, "Tony, sign this or do the time. It's as simple as that. There's nothing more to discuss. Do you understand me?"

Before Mr. Harris could respond, Tom said, "Mr. Harris, you'll have more than prison time to worry about; you'll be reading about this in every newspaper in the tri-state area, and I assure you it'll make the local TV stations as well. 'Local Businessman Arrested for Spousal Abuse.' You've created a business brand that will suffer by association, not to mention your reputation in the community."

Harris did a slow burn but turned to his lawyer. "So I got no other options—is that what you're telling me, Richard?"

"I already gave you your options, but I'll repeat them for you one more time. Sign the agreement or face a trial and go to prison, where your reputation will be ruined and your business will suffer. What'll it be, Tony?"

"Give me the fucking paper. Where do I sign? One day that bitch will regret this."

Parker quickly admonished his client. "Tony, don't start with the threats again. Just move on. Hillary wants this over. Do you understand? There's no chance for reconciliation. Just sign under your name," Parker said and slid the agreement over to him.

He hurriedly scratched out his name. "Yeah, I get it. But I promise you, one day . . ." He then paused and looked up. His lawyer was shaking his head. Harris finished signing with a flourish, jumped up, knocked over his chair, and headed for the door.

"Just a minute, Tony. Please take your seat. We've got another matter that has been brought to my attention."

"Now what the fuck are you talking about? I've got a business to run, Parker. You want your big fat bill paid, right?"

"Just sit down Tony. Tom just informed me before the meeting that he thinks you are stalking your wife's lawyer. Any truth to this, Tony? Calling her every hour and hanging up, and knocking at her door at strange hours then skipping out of sight. You know where these tactics are going to land you, don't you?"

"Are you kidding me? I don't have time for that shit! Are you crazy, or what? Now what would I gain from that?"

"Well, do you remember that we had a little situation not too long ago when you called Ms. Scott and threatened her to tell you where your wife was? Remember that, Tony? Have I jogged your memory a little? No, I'm not crazy, Tony." Parker noticed that Tony was moving around in his chair as if extremely uncomfortable and, maybe, had himself cornered in a box.

Parker leaned across the table and said to Tony in an angry tone, "Stop this shit, Tony. Strong-arming doesn't get anyone very far. If you keep this up, the cops will put a tail on you and watch every move you make. And you will be done! Do you hear me, done!"

Tom spoke up and said that he was getting a restraining order on him and if he came within three feet of Ms. Scott, he would be arrested. "Do you understand, Tony?" Tony remained silent. "I don't believe I heard your answer, Tony."

"Okay. I heard you. I wasn't going to hurt Ms. Scott. I only wanted to scare her. She fucked up my life."

"Tony, the only one who fucked up your life was you. Now go back to work and do what you do best, and stop beating up and harassing women." Harris stormed out of the office and slammed the door behind him.

Tom gathered up the agreement and placed it in his brief-case. He stood up and shook hands with Parker. "I'm formally requesting that you put your client in an anger management program. If he doesn't go, and he lays a hand on my client or my partner, Ms. Scott, you'll find yourself in front of the judge too."

"I'll do what I can, Tom. But Tony doesn't listen to anybody."

Tom and Mr. Parker walked back into Parker's office, where Beth was waiting. Tom dropped the signed settlement agreement in her hands. "It's done, Beth. Congratulations. I also told the prick that we're getting a restraining order against him if he comes within three feet of you. He said he only wanted to scare you since you fucked up his marriage."

"Yeah, yeah, yeah! They always blame the attorney, and they're the good guy. Holy crap, sometimes I don't know why I do this. I guess I'm a masochist. What can I say?"

Tom replied, "I say let's go home. Job well done. Mission accomplished."

Hillary was elated to hear the settlement news from Beth and started to cry on the phone. "Oh my God, my nightmare is over." She couldn't stop thanking Beth. "And five million dollars! Wow! I never expected that much. I thought he'd agree to give me the divorce and throw in a couple hundred thousand. I'm so grateful to you, Beth. You did an unbelievable job representing me."

"Thank you, Hillary. I'm truly happy for you, and I know that you'll meet someone in the near future and have a wonderful life together. At least, you'll never have to worry about supporting yourself, and you can enjoy a comfortable lifestyle. You certainly deserve every penny of it."

The next afternoon, Beth drove to the shelter to get Hillary's final signature on the agreement. This was one of the happiest days of Hillary's life. "Just sign right here above your name," Beth said as she put the agreement in front of Hillary on the table.

"Does this mean I'm now divorced?"

"Not yet," Beth said. "The judge has to sign off on it, and that could take a few weeks, depending how much is on his docket. So you'll have to stay here until that happens, and then you'll be issued the check and you'll be free to leave the state. But Hillary, I'm hiring a bodyguard to escort you to Virginia, just to play it safe. Once you're home, you might still consider some security for six months."

"Oh, my brother-in-law is a tough guy. He'll watch over me."

Beth and Hillary embraced and they both shed a few tears. "Hillary, one final thing—you should make all of your travel arrangements for three weeks from now. We can be sure that everything will be finalized by then, and this will give you time to organize yourself, talk with your banker or investment people, and make your travel plans."

They talked about the divorce and how quickly everything had been resolved. Hillary had told herself that she would probably be at the shelter for at least six months, but it had taken only a little over four months. In the next few days she would start making all the arrangements to leave the city, and be ready when she got the word from Beth that the judge had signed her decree. Then she would get her check and set off for Virginia to be with her family. They were so happy that she was coming home. The first call she'd make tomorrow would be to her family to let them know it wouldn't be long now before they'd all be together again after so many years.

Beth went back to her apartment after her meeting with Hillary and called Brandon. He had a late emergency surgery and wouldn't be able to leave the hospital tonight. He told her that he'd call her in the morning. Beth needed to speak to Vivian, the wedding planner, to go over some final details, so it was best that Brandon wasn't coming over. The wedding was only four weeks away, and she had to have her final fitting on her dress and figure out the seating arrangement for the reception. Most all of the responses were back, and it looked as if they'd be right at seventy-five people, just as they had planned. Everything was moving along in accordance with their timeline—important for two professionals who were used to tight schedules.

Beth was a little less stressed out now that she'd closed the file on Hillary's case. Her other cases would take much more time, but weren't as pressing and didn't involve clients facing physical threats and requiring expeditious resolutions. It didn't matter if they waited until after the wedding and honeymoon. She loved her job and couldn't think of anything else she'd rather be doing than practicing family law. And she was damn good at it. The partners in the firm were very pleased with her performance and respected her capabilities, and it wouldn't be too long before she would be joining the partnership.

After she spoke to Vivian, her wedding planner, Beth began to feel slightly dizzy and realized that she hadn't eaten since early morning. This was probably due to having a glass of wine with Hillary earlier on an empty stomach. She warmed up a bowl of soup, which made her queasy. She didn't need a stomach virus now; she was much too busy at work and with her wedding plans to be ill. She decided to go to bed early and was hopeful she'd feel better in the morning.

The next morning when she awoke, she felt a little better but very tired. She was able to keep down some oatmeal and left for the office. Planning a wedding was time-consuming, and between that and her job, she was exhausted. But it was a good exhaustion, and she thanked God for Vivian, who was handling all the last-minute details, giving Beth time to concentrate on more pressing matters at work. She drank hot tea and munched on crackers most of the day. She was finished by six o'clock and then had to go to Vera Wang for her last dress fitting. Her mom was meeting her there so together they could make sure that everything was perfect with the dress.

As soon as Beth returned to her apartment, Brandon called to find out about the final fitting.

"Hi, sweetheart. How'd the fitting go?"

"Great, Brandon. And on your end, how about the surgery?"

"It took almost four hours, and while we saved the guy's life, I'm pretty wiped out. I had a little dinner, and now I'm going to bed. Wish I could be with you, baby. I miss you."

"I miss you, too. But, I think I have a stomach virus, so better that you're not around me. My stomach has been acting weird lately, and I have some dizziness."

"Oh, sweetheart, it's probably just pre-wedding jitters. Can you believe we only have four weeks to go, and then we'll be married and sunning ourselves in the Bahamas?"

"Yeah, I could use a little of that right now."

"Well, let's get away to the beach this weekend. It's supposed to be sunny and clear."

"That's a date. I love you."

Beth hung up the phone and got ready for bed. She had another dizzy spell while bending over the sink and brushing her teeth. Feeling like she was going to faint, she slipped into bed, and as soon as her head hit the pillow she fell asleep.

The next morning she was just waking up when the phone rang. "Hi, Brandon. Good morning."

"How're you feeling, sunshine? I've been worried about you, and I'm on my way over to check you out before you leave for the office. I should be there in twenty minutes. Wait for me. I just want to make sure this isn't an issue related to the assault."

"I'm fine, honey. No need to stop by, even though I can't wait to see you."

"Let's not take any chances. Don't leave." Brandon knew there was a very strong possibility that this dizziness could most definitely be related to Beth's recovery, and it was worrisome to him. Sometimes even a year later there could be some small blood vessels in the brain that eventually rupture and cause bleeding, which would be causing Beth's dizziness. Of course he wouldn't alarm Beth until he observed her and was more certain of a diagnosis.

"Okay, doctor. I'll hop in the shower, and I'll have breakfast ready when you get here."

"Great! My stomach is rumbling from hunger. Love you and see you soon."

Brandon arrived at Beth's apartment in the pouring rain. His coat was soaking wet, so he left it in the hallway and slipped off his shoes. He could smell bacon and eggs cooking as he walked inside the apartment.

"Sure smells good in here, and I'm starving."

"Hi, honey, so good to see you."

Brandon put his arms around Beth and kissed her passionately. He didn't like going even one day without seeing his future bride.

"Now let me look at you and try and figure out what's going on with my sweetie."

"Let's wait until after breakfast. It's ready."

Brandon sat down, and Beth served breakfast. They ate and talked about things in general—he didn't want her stressing out over wedding plans.

After helping her clear the breakfast plates, Brandon walked over to the sofa with Beth. "How long has this stomach upset and dizziness been going on?"

"Just since yesterday. But I feel much better."

Brandon performed a neurological exam on her, and everything appeared normal. He wanted to be sure the dizziness was not related to her concussion from the attack, and he concluded it was just a virus.

"It's most likely a viral infection, so you won't need an antibiotic. Let's see how long this continues, and if you don't shake it in a few days I'll run blood tests. Beth, maybe you should stay home today and rest."

"I can't, Brandon. With only four weeks until the wedding, I have too much work to do. I can't afford to miss one day. I'll be fine, I promise." Still, Beth couldn't help but wonder if something else was going on in her body stemming from her attack. She wanted to trust Brandon's diagnosis, but she knew her body, and something wasn't quite right. She immediately dismissed her concerns, determined to carry on with her day.

"Okay, but if you feel dizzy at work, I want you to go right home. That's doctor's orders."

"Yes, I promise."

Beth kissed and hugged Brandon and thanked him for coming over to look after her. She knew this was the type of husband he was always going to be—someone having her best interests at heart and forever putting her first. And this is how she felt about him as well. She would do anything for him.

After breakfast, Brandon called a cab to take Beth to work and then drop him off at the hospital for another twelve-hour shift. He was so happy that in two months these long grueling workdays would be over. Once he joined his new medical group, he'd be working regular eight- to ten-hour days and would be on call only every fifth night. He could have a normal life again. But most importantly, this life would be with his new wife. Just the thought of that excited him, put a smile on his face, and would get him through the day.

Beth arrived at her office, and there was already a client waiting to see her. After spending about an hour with the client, she made herself a cup of tea. Her stomach seemed to be settling down a bit, and she no longer felt dizzy. Brandon was right, it was probably just a twenty-four-hour bug. To be safe, she would have only hot tea and toast today. Despite the low-calorie intake, she was able to log a full, productive day without a problem. She spoke to Lisa about the wedding, since she was her only attendant. She'd be bringing Henry, as they were an item now. Things were going extremely well in their relationship, and Lisa's feelings for him were growing stronger by the day. She and Beth had much to be happy about and couldn't wait until the wedding. It appeared that Lisa had moved on with her life and put her divorce behind her due, in no small part, to Beth's hard work and perseverance. Beth was a loyal friend, and they had much history together. Lisa was happy that Beth had found such a terrific man to share her life with.

Maria buzzed Beth to let her know that Victoria was on the phone.

"Hi there. How've you been, girlfriend?"

"I'm great, but the question is, how's the bride? Are you getting nervous? I can't believe how close it is."

"I'm doing sensationally, and no, I'm not the slightest bit nervous. A better word would be excited to marry the love of my life."

"Beth, I'm so happy for you. It's going to be a wonderful affair, and I'm so looking forward to sharing it with you. Is there anything I can do to help you in these last few weeks?"

"You're so sweet, Victoria, but between my wedding planner and my mom, it's all under control. It really hasn't been that stressful; Brandon and I knew exactly what we wanted and that helped us make the tough decisions."

"Would you like to get together for a drink after work?" Victoria tentatively asked.

"I'd love to, but I've been fighting off this stomach flu, and I really can't drink. But I can meet you for a cup of tea if you'd like."

"I don't care what we drink; I just want to see you and catch up."

"Okay, perfect. I'll be ready about six. Will that work for you?"

"Sure," Victoria, said. "Let's meet at the Starbucks at 48th and Lex."

"Looking forward to it. See you at six. I'll text you if I'm running late."

Beth and Victoria had a great time talking about their careers and what had been going on in their lives since the last time they got together. They really hadn't spoken in depth about the attack, and Beth had never told her how sorry she was that Victoria had been the one to find her that night.

"I just can't imagine how awful it must've been for you. I'm so sorry that you had to experience that terrible nightmare."

"Please don't apologize for anything. It wasn't your fault. I was just glad that I found you when I did, and you could get to the hospital right away. Let's not dwell on it, Beth, for you are fine, thank God."

"I agree, but there's one more thing I wanted to tell you: my assailant—and Michael's murderer—was caught, pleaded out, and is now serving a double life term. No trial."

"That's wonderful news, Beth, and the timing couldn't have been better. You can now put this behind you and get on with your new life with Brandon, knowing that that animal Barboza will spend the rest of his life in prison."

"Yeah, it's getting close, but I still have to tie a lot of loose ends before the wedding. I'm trying not to take on any more new clients until I get back from my honeymoon."

"And where, may I ask, are you going?"

"To a small island in the Caribbean called Nevis. It's known for its clear blue water and white sandy beaches. It's only a little over two hours by plane and is a serene and beautiful spot. We didn't want to spend a lot of time traveling since we'll be so eager to get there after the wedding."

"Sounds like the perfect place. I know you two will have an awesome time."

"Thank you, Victoria."

"Beth, I need to speak to you about something that I've been putting off for a long time now. I wanted to wait until the right moment, and didn't want to bring it up while you were recovering."

"What is it, Victoria?"

"Remember the last time we spoke, you suggested that I try a dating service to meet someone. Well, I did."

"Oh, Victoria, that's fabulous! So, tell me all about it."

"I signed up, and had about five different dates, all of whom were very nice men. But to be perfectly honest, I had no interest in any of them, and not because of them but because of me. I think I've finally realized, Beth, that I can't stuff my feelings for women any longer. I know now that I prefer women to men. And not just for girlfriends."

Beth could see that Victoria was struggling to articulate her feelings and was very uncomfortable. "Beth, what I'm trying to tell you is that I'm gay. I've known for a long time, but I had to finally prove it, so I put myself to the test with the dating service to be sure. Well, I'm sure! I'm so sorry to disappoint you, Beth."

"Victoria, please don't apologize for being who you are. I'm happy that you decided to come out, and I think this will relieve a lot of stress in your life. You'll never be completely happy without being true to your feelings. I'm very proud of you, and I wish you all the happiness in the world. I so admire you for being honest with me, and you can be sure that it'll change nothing regarding our friendship."

"Thanks, so much, Beth. I knew you'd understand. But there is something else that I must get off my chest. You've always been a good friend to me, and at times I had wished that it could've been more. I never wanted to make overt advances toward you knowing you were straight, but I tried to show you in so many discreet ways how I felt. You never caught on. I guess I've always been in love with you, but could never tell you. I didn't want to lose you as a friend, so I remained silent."

"Victoria, I don't know what to say. You have shocked the hell out of me, for I never suspected that you felt anything other than friendship. I don't understand these feelings for me, so I can't begin to wrap myself around this. If you felt rejected in any way, then I apologize. I had no clue."

"No, Beth, you didn't reject me; you were still my friend. You just didn't respond to me like I had wished."

"I'm so sorry, Victoria, but I need time to absorb this. I'll call you in few days, after I've had a chance to sort things out. I have to figure out how our friendship can continue without me feeling really weird about . . . us. I hope you understand."

"I do, Beth, and I'm so sorry. I know I've made you feel very uncomfortable."

Beth was digesting Victoria's revelation on the cab ride home from the coffee shop. She had always wondered if Vic might possibly be gay, for she had never showed any interest in men. Now, thinking back, it all made sense. She was secretive about her social life, and was always distant when it came to personal issues. She was obviously tormented about her sexuality and was trying to figure it all out. When Victoria dropped the bombshell about being in love with her, Beth didn't know how to react or what to say. She needed to discuss this with Brandon, to help her sort it all out.

Beth got back to her apartment about eight thirty. Brandon was coming over later that night. While waiting for him, she took a shower, put on her PJs, and sat on the couch watching television. She was eager to tell him about Victoria's secret.

She made herself a cup of tea. Brandon walked in about ten and embraced her.

"I missed you, sweetheart. Are you feeling better?"

"Yes, I'm fine, and even better now that you're here. I missed you, too."

"So, how did your visit go with Victoria? Did you get caught up?"

"Oh boy, did I ever."

"What do you mean?" Brandon asked curiously.

"Well, I was kind of shocked, yet somehow I wasn't, when she told me that she was gay."

"Boy, that's surprising."

"She said she's known for a long time but never let on. I guess she finally realized that her life will be much easier by owning up to it. So she wanted to tell me that she'd decided to come out."

"Wow, I must say. I never would've guessed it of her."

"But, wait . . . there's more. She then proceeded to tell me that after we'd been friends for a while her feelings for me grew into love. Brandon, she told me that she was in love with me but too afraid to tell me because she knew I was straight and she didn't want it to end our friendship. I didn't know how to respond. She told me that she tried to give me signals but I didn't pick up on them. I'm still in shock, and don't know what to do."

"Beth, there's nothing you can do. Just continue to be her friend and be supportive. Let her be her and you be you. She'll understand and eventually move past it. She just needs time. There's no reason for you to feel awkward. She's the one who'll have to come to terms with it."

"I know. I'd like to try to help her, but I don't know how."

"Just be there for her. That's all she wants. Since she feared that telling you would destroy your friendship, prove to her that her coming out will change nothing."

"I totally agree with you, and I like your advice. Thanks so much, honey. You're the best, and I love you."

"Just curious—regarding this conversation with Victoria that ended up to be confessional, how did it begin?"

"Well, she called and wanted to meet for a drink. We'd never discussed the night that she found me, so I wanted to apologize for putting her through all of that. I told her I felt awful that she had to be the one who found me almost dead. I couldn't imagine what it was like for her. Then I told her that my attacker and Michael's murderer was behind bars serving life sentences."

Suddenly Beth gasped. "Oh my God!" Then she put her hands up to her head as if in shock. "I can't believe this!"

Brandon said, "Beth, what's going on? Tell me." He put his hands on her shoulders and pulled her around to face him.

"She then proceeded to tell me that the timing couldn't be better with the capture of Barboza, so we could get married and get on with our lives. Brandon, how would she know the name of my attacker? It wasn't in the newspaper because that was part of the deal with the D.A. Barboza became the informant for the FBI on everything Mob-related in order to escape the death penalty. Honey, I have to call Detective Stevens and let him know this. He had a suspicion about her all along. I remember him telling me it was too much of a coincidence that she arrived immediately after my attack. I think she agreed to help set it up, but only if I wasn't killed and she could call 911 right away to save me. Now it all makes sense. She had a love-hate relationship with me, and when I ignored her advances she couldn't handle it. You know, Brandon, I never knew much about her background or her family. And I also found it very strange that she had no friends. This is unbelievable. She informed Barboza when she was coming over so he'd know when I'd be home. Stevens was right all along. What a smart man. He knows his detective work—that's for sure."

Beth called Stevens and told him the story. He agreed that there was no way she could've known Barboza's name. He speculated that Barboza discovered who her friends were and did a background on them. Victoria must have needed the money and also been the most tenuous. Of course, this would all be verified when they brought her in for questioning. "Well, Beth, this is quite a revelation. It seems as if this case just keeps picking up new legs. I'll keep you abreast. Right now I need to hang up and make an arrest. Get some rest. You've earned it, my friend."

After a late snack, Beth and Brandon snuggled together on the couch. Even though Beth was not feeling her optimal best, she wanted to cuddle and be close to the man she loved. She realized that love between two human beings had no boundaries; she could understand how men can be too sexually oriented and women more sensitive, and how someone like Victoria could choose a woman over a man for a partner. But for Beth it was different: she liked having a male sexual creature in her life.

And right now she and Brandon wanted to make love. Brandon kept kissing her and telling her how much he loved her. He buried his head in her neck and moved his mouth up to her ear, kissing it gently while blowing soft breaths of air around it, giving Beth chills. He was sensual, and the scent of his body was pleasing to her. She also felt protected and warm, wrapped in his arms. She could hear the rain pitter-patter against the window and loved being close to Brandon when it was so cold, dark, and wet outside. There was something about making love in the rain that excited her. To think that she was going to have this man making love to her for the rest of her life sparked excitement.

As they lay side by side, she felt Brandon's erection pushing against her lower body. He gently squeezed her nipples until they became fully erect, all the while nipping at her earlobe and blowing softly around it. The sensation was startling when he used his tongue to circle her breast from the areola up to her neck and back down to the middle of her breast. Brandon's finger then entered her wetness. His eyes were fixated on her, as he felt her breath accelerate. Beth started to pant, and with a rigid body was completely ready to submit. Within a few seconds she climaxed, while still holding him firmly in her hand. She was now lusting for him. She mounted him guiding him inside her. She glided her body back and forth, hoping to savor the feeling as long as she could. Both their bodies were warm and moist to the touch. His tongue on her nipples sent shivers down her spine and a rousing sensation to all of her erogenous zones. While inside her, he wedged his hand down in between their bodies and began gently massaging where she yearned for him to be. She was panting from wanting him so much, while at the same time rejecting submission. She wanted to feel this inexpressible pleasure for as long as possible. They were both heavy with breath and sighing softly. Neither of them could wait any longer. Their release came simultaneously, hers for the second time. They lay in silence, not moving. They both felt an innate sense of contentment. They owned each other's passion. One thing they knew for sure was that they had already achieved sexual compatibility in their relationship.

After lovemaking, Beth and Brandon took a hot bath together and relaxed in the tub. It was nearly eleven o'clock before they went to bed, wrapped in each other's arms. While the rain continued to pour onto the windowpanes, they drifted off to sleep to the pleasant-sounding tapping rhythm that was almost hypnotic, feeling completely happy, content, and grateful to have found true love.

Chapter

Twenty-Five

The taxi pulled up to the front of the Ritz Carlton on one of the most glorious days Beth and Brandon had ever experienced. The sun was shining brightly, and there was a balmy breeze amidst temperatures in the high seventies with little humidity. They could see a view of the ocean as they exited the cab. After check-in, the bellman drove them in a golf cart to their villa, which was situated on the sands of Pinney Beach, only steps from the crystal-clear Caribbean. It was a private villa that stood away from the others, with a living room, kitchen, huge bedroom and bath, and private swimming pool. They had a personal butler who, in response to the push of a button, would be at their disposal throughout their stay. Brandon had spared no expense when booking their honeymoon. After all, a person only does this once, he had told himself.

When Beth stepped inside the villa, she was at a loss for words. The place was light and airy, with comfortable yet stylish beach decor throughout. Her eyes immediately focused on the alluring furnishings—the blue-and-white striped cotton sofa, the complementary blue-and-white floral print chairs, the basket-weave bamboo rug in the center of the room, and the wicker tables at each end of the sofa. The butler opened the windows, and immediately a cool breeze flowed inside.

"Do you like it, Mrs. Burton?" Brandon asked, smiling at his bride.

"It's the most beautiful place I've ever seen, honey." As she watched the butler slide back the doors from the middle to the end of the wall, leaving nothing but wide open space between the villa, the patio, and the sandy, pure white beach and ocean. "Wow, look at that view. It's breathtaking," she said as she sat in one of the chairs staring at the ocean. "I think I've just found Shangri-la. This is it. I'm never leaving."

"I'm right with you, baby. This is paradise. Without a doubt," Brandon said.

He tipped the butler, who refused to take it. "Sir, the gratuity is included in your honeymoon package, and I'm here for whatever you need." He showed Brandon where the buzzer was located when they required service. "Sir, is there anything else I can get you now?"

"Yes," Brandon replied. "I'd like a bottle of your finest champagne."

"Yes, sir. Coming right up."

"Thank you, Alfred," Brandon said, glancing at the butler's name tag.

Beth and Brandon unpacked and changed into bathing suits. Deciding to start off their vacation with a swim in the Caribbean, they walked down to the transparent aquamarine-colored water holding hands. When they later returned to the villa, the champagne was chilling. They wrapped themselves in large beach towels, and Beth sank into one of overstuffed lounge chairs on the patio while Brandon popped open the bubbly.

Raising his glass, he said, "To my beautiful wife. My love for you is as deep as that ocean."

"And to my amazing husband, who completes me. You've made me the happiest woman in the world," said Beth.

They kissed, then clinked their glasses and sipped the champagne. Tired from the weekend's events, they immersed themselves in the serenity and beauty of their surroundings while reflecting on their wedding.

The wedding had turned out to be everything they had hoped for and more than they had anticipated. Brandon teared up when he first saw Beth step through the double doors to begin her walk to the altar. She looked like an angel coming out of the clouds. He'd never seen anything more beautiful in his life. Joseph Scott was tearing up the entire walk down the aisle, in awe of this day yet recalling the events of just a year prior. The ceremony was personal, intimate, and very romantic in the elegant candlelit room.

They had written their own vows and read them out loud. Beth's had brought tears to nearly everyone's eyes.

Brandon, our love story was definitely unorthodox from the beginning. You saved my life more than once, and for that I'll be eternally grateful. But as I got to know you during my long recovery, I believed there was something very special about you that I wanted to explore further, for I recognized that you went much deeper than just being a great physician. After a while, I realized that you were the person I wanted to be with. You make me feel so loved and so needed. You bring out the best in me in every situation. You make me laugh, and you have shown me the meaning of real happiness. But most importantly, you've shown me what it is to love someone more than yourself. To me, this is the meaning of true love. I thank God every day that I've found my soul mate, and I pledge to you on this, our wedding day, that my love is forever. I give you my heart and will be there for you through the good and the bad. My ring will always be symbolic of my love for you, and I

*promise to never let it leave my finger, representing, as it
does, the circle that has no end. It will serve as a constant
reminder of our unity until the end of our natural lives.*

The reception had been elegant and stylish. The room was
dimly lit with crystal chandeliers, beautiful ivory tablecloths
with gold threads, and centerpieces of white roses, orchids, and
hydrangeas. Tapered candles at the top of the flower arrangements
provided subdued lighting and a romantic ambience.

Beth and Brandon's first dance was magical. They both loved
to dance, and every guest in the room was mesmerized by their
ability to be in sync with the music. Miriam and Joseph shed
tears of joy as they saw Beth's face radiate with happiness and
joy. It was a night they hoped never to forget. For the bride and
groom, their special occasion was about to become a memory
that would remain embedded in their hearts forever.

While lingering over glasses of champagne at their private
villa, Brandon looked deeply into Beth's eyes, then proposed,
"When we get back, we should look for a new place to live. My
apartment is too small for us, and I don't want us to live in your
apartment, where the attack occurred. The bad memories may
cast a dark shadow over us, and this isn't how I want us to start
off our marriage."

"I agree," Beth said.

"We can pick a place between your office and mine so neither
of us will have a long commute."

"Sounds like a plan, honey. Shall we look for a three-bedroom
so we can have an office?"

"Yes, it would be nice to have an office and a guest room.
Then one day, when we have a child, we won't have to move
right away. I think this is a good plan, don't you? Oh, and one
more thing, Mrs. Burton. We'll be purchasing our apartment, not
leasing it."

"What do you mean, Brandon? I don't think we'll have

enough for the down payment."

"Well, I have a surprise for you. My parents are buying us an apartment for a wedding gift. I told them that it's much too generous and I couldn't accept such a gift, but they wouldn't take no for an answer. They'll be giving us a certain amount, and if we choose to spend more or less, then that's our option."

"I can hardly believe it. Your parents' generosity is overwhelming. What a wonderful thing to do for us, honey. I'm so happy, Brandon. I don't know how to thank your parents enough. To have a place to call our own so early in our marriage is very special."

"They feel strongly about it, so I can't argue with them. It gives them great joy to see us enjoy this money now and not have us wait until they have passed on. I guess they feel that their entire estate will be bequeathed to me anyway since I am an only child, so why not start now. I think my dad's diagnosis of lung cancer played a role in their decision—that at least this way he'll be able to see us enjoy our own home while he's alive."

"I don't know what to say, Brandon. Your parents are amazingly bighearted, and I love them so much for that," Beth said, then kissed him. "You're the best, and I'll always love you."

"Why aren't you drinking your champagne? If you don't like it, I can get you something else."

"No, no. I love it. I'm just drinking slowly and savoring the moment."

Over the next week, they enjoyed everything the island had to offer and indulged in many activities they'd never engaged in before. They especially loved learning to water ski and scuba dive. One day they chartered a boat and did both, admiring the exotic fish and plant life in the crystal-clear water, and photographing many different varieties with an underwater camera.

They also slept late, had breakfast in bed, took long walks on the beach, dined in intimate waterfront restaurants, and watched magical sunsets that looked like David Miller seascape paintings with a clear blue ocean and tall palm trees in the background, bordering the beach. Every day was sunny and beautiful, without a cloud in the sky. The sand, of a very fine consistency, was as white as snow and soft as silk, free of shells and debris. The balmy air that blew off the ocean bathed the beach in a comfortable breeze and cool temperatures. It couldn't have been a more perfect honeymoon.

Although Beth's health was superb most of the time, every now and then she felt a little unsettled in her stomach and slightly dizzy. She didn't tell Brandon since she didn't want him to make a big deal of it. After nearly two weeks of symptoms she began to think it was more than a simple virus—more likely, a latent emotional effect from the trauma, playing out through her gastrointestinal tract. Remembering that the psychiatrist in the hospital had told her some symptoms of post-traumatic stress disorder could occur up to three years after the incident, she decided to make a doctor's appointment after returning home. For now, with only one day left on her honeymoon, she was determined to enjoy every last moment of it.

Beth and Brandon spent most of their last day on the beach. They took a long walk admiring one of the island's most scenic spots, enjoying the water, the landscape, and the magnificent blue sky. They made love in the morning, after lunch, and before bed. They did some shopping in the small village and bought souvenirs for their family and friends. They tried on silly hats and floral shirts and had a good laugh about how funny they would look wearing this attire back home. Beth bought her dad a floral shirt and her mom a wide-brimmed straw hat with plastic fruits around the brim. She knew her mom would have a good laugh. They talked about when to start a family and how many children they wanted. Since they were both their family's sole child, they wanted their children to grow up with siblings. Beth had always wanted a career, but it had also been her hope to have a family of four—and she was convinced this was right for her and Brandon. They discussed possible names for their children, and talked about the family spending weekends and holidays at their country home. And they vowed to return to this island on special anniversaries.

Their flight home was uneventful, and Beth's parents picked them up at the airport and took them back to her apartment. They both looked so rested and boasted of beautiful bronze hues to their faces.

"Tell us all about your trip," Miriam said. "You're both glowing."

During the ride home Beth and Brandon went on about two of the best weeks of their lives. They both were aware, given their careers, that it would be a few more years before they'd be able to take another long vacation, but were grateful to have their honeymoon pictures to enjoy every time they felt nostalgic.

The next morning, Beth booked an appointment with her doctor and then left for work. Her desk was stacked with files that needed her attention. But first she spent more than three hours with Maria, who brought her up to date on her various cases. She later went through her mail, where she found a beautiful letter from Hillary, telling her how happy she was to be back in Virginia with her family and that she had heard nothing from her ex-husband, for which she was not only pleased but surprised. I must write her a note this week, Beth thought to herself. She asked one of her colleagues for the name of a good estate agent to help her and Brandon look for a new apartment. She then called the agent and made an appointment to see some properties on Sunday, while giving her parameters for their search. The mere thought of Sunday's viewings made her smile. She wanted an apartment with a doorman, for instance, to ensure her safety when Brandon had to stay late at the hospital.

On her fourth day back, Beth was buried in work, had meetings with several clients, and the appointment with her doctor at four o'clock. Brandon would be home around six, so she would pick up dinner on her way home from the doctor's office, she figured.

Her intercom buzzed. "Beth, you have a call from Detective Stevens on line one."

She thanked Maria then picked up the phone. "How are you, detective?"

"I'm good, Beth. How're you doing now that you're an old married lady?"

"I'm wonderful, and very happy. But I do think I might be suffering from a little PTSD. I read that typically symptoms can manifest up to three years later. I'm seeing my doctor about it."

"Beth, it's not unusual, and hopefully it won't last too long. You're a strong person, and if anyone can move past this, it's you. It's important that you've identified it for what it is and are getting help."

"Thank you, detective. Enough about me. So how can I help you?"

"Well, Beth, I must regrettably inform you that I received a call from a Detective Benson in Charlottesville, Virginia, about a woman you represented by the name of Hillary Harris."

"Yes, detective, I settled her divorce, and I just received a letter from her thanking me and telling me about how happy she is in her new life."

The detective's voice softened as he told Beth about the call from the investigator on Hillary's case. "It seems that your client was attacked in a parking lot walking back to her car two nights ago, not far from her sister's home. The assailant beat her pretty badly, left her on the ground beside her car, and luckily a Good Samaritan called 911. She's in the hospital in critical condition. They wanted me to call you for any information that can help solve the case. They interviewed her sister, and she gave them Hillary's ex-husband's name. Nobody saw anything, and they have no suspects at this point, which is common in cases like this since any witness knows they'd be asked to make an ID and would never choose to get involved. Her sister is certain this attack has her ex-husband's hands all over it. They're all waiting for Hillary to regain consciousness to see if she can identify her attacker. If you have an address or phone number for this guy, we'll pick him up."

Beth's face turned white. " The poor woman! Everything she went through, and now this! That bastard!"

"Beth, so you think he's the assailant?" Beth started to choke up and couldn't speak. After a minute of silence, Stevens asked, "Beth, are you all right? I know this was a terrible shock for you. But the doctors do think she's going to pull through."

"Detective, he was a wife beater, and the NYPD has the 911 calls and photos of her injuries. As part of the divorce decree that he signed, there was a permanent restraining order against him, and if he breeched it, then he can be arrested and prosecuted for the abuse. His attorney is Richard Parker, and I'll have Maria send over his contact information. I truly believe this sick son-of-a-bitch is your man, detective. His name is Anthony Harris, and he owns Harris Meat Packing. He's a total control freak with a violent temper. I hope you get him, detective, and lock him up and throw away the key."

"Thanks so much for your help, Beth. I'm going to take care of this right away. I'll keep you posted. But don't let it get to you. It's not your fault. You freed her from the bastard, and if he's the assailant we'll nail him but good. I know it opens up old wounds for you. Take care of yourself."

After Beth hung up the phone, she stepped over to her refrigerator for a bottle of water. She buzzed Maria and asked her to send Richard Parker's contact information to Detective Stevens. "And, Maria, please hold all my calls for thirty minutes." She needed time to compose herself and decide what to do. She wanted to fly to Virginia and visit Hillary, but this weekend she and Brandon were scheduled to look at apartments. The showings would have to wait. She knew Brandon would understand and support her decision to go. She booked a flight out for Friday night after work and a return flight for Sunday afternoon.

Beth left the office early and arrived home before Brandon. She opened up a bottle of Sauvignon Blanc and poured herself a glass. She then realized that it wouldn't be wise for her to drink it, so she heated up the Chinese dinner she had picked up for her and Brandon and set the table. Brandon walked in about thirty minutes later and immediately noticed that Beth was upset.

"Hi, sweetheart. Bad day?" he asked, stepping over to her and giving her a hug.

"Well, it started off pretty well but ended up terrible."

Brandon gave her a puzzled look. "I'm all ears, honey."

Beth tried to keep her composure but sighed deeply before she began to speak. "I received a call from Detective Stevens. My client Hillary Harris was attacked in a parking lot and beaten pretty badly. She's in the ICU but should pull through," she said and paused for a moment. "I just can't believe this! Her ex-husband apparently went down to Virginia, ignoring the restraining order, and almost beat her to death."

"They know it's him for sure?" Brandon asked.

"No witnesses, and she's still unconscious, but who else could it be?" Beth shook her head in dismay. "That poor woman. She was so happy to be free of him, and now this had to happen. Sometimes life just isn't fair, is it?"

Brandon gave his wife another big hug and patted her on the back. "So you're planning to visit her, right?" Beth nodded. "Do you want me to go with you? I wouldn't mind. I'm off on Sunday anyway.

"No, sweetheart, I'll be fine. The firm's sending me; this is business, and personal. We're going to put the guy away. I want you to still do the viewings with the real estate lady on Sunday."

Brandon nodded. "Okay, but I won't make any decisions without you."

Beth smiled. "You'd better not. Anything you see that you think I'll like, we'll visit next weekend. Okay?"

Brandon smiled at Beth and said, "Or maybe I'll have a surprise waiting for you when you come back. That would be one way to cheer you up."

Beth grinned and replied, "I'd be fine with that but would prefer that we choose together."

"I know, honey. No need to worry. This is something I'd never do without you."

Brandon and Beth sat down for dinner, and he saw the open wine bottle sitting on the table. "I see you started without me."

"Actually I didn't," Beth replied slyly.

"Oh, okay. I'll pour you a glass then."

"No, sweetie. I was tempted, but won't now." Beth retreated to the living room and retrieved her purse from the coffee table. "I have something to show you."

"What's wrong? Are you okay?" Brandon's face expressed concern.

"I went to the doctor, and he said I was fine."

"That's great, but what did he say about the stomach upset and dizziness? Is it related to the attack?"

Beth reached inside her purse and pulled out a white plastic cylinder displaying the color blue in the square box. She held it up in front of Brandon with a smile from ear to ear. "This is what he said."

Brandon's eyes lit up. "Baby, does this mean what I think it means?"

Beth nodded and started to cry.

Brandon stood up and hugged her. "Why are you crying, sweetheart? Aren't you happy? I'm thrilled, Beth. We're going to be parents. I'm going to be a father! I know our timing isn't as planned. But so what? This is wonderful news."

"I *am* happy, and I guess I was relieved that something else wasn't wrong with me related to the trauma. I mean, I never even gave *this* a thought. We'd been so careful." She paused and sighed again. "But I wanted to enjoy our being married for a while before a child came along. Am I being selfish?"

"No, Beth, you're not at all. And I understand how you feel. But we'll have the rest of our lives to be together. This is a blessing; it wasn't a mistake. This baby was conceived out of love, Beth, and I couldn't be happier." Brandon poured Beth a glass of water in a wine glass. "I want to toast our baby, and you, my amazing baby-making mamma. I love you both."

Beth held up her wine glass. "So do you want a girl or a boy?"

"It makes no difference. I just want a healthy baby. And I want you to start taking care of yourself by not working so hard."

"I'll be fine, honey. I'll just try to get home earlier so I can rest before dinner. I know the first trimester is when fatigue sets in. I'm glad we decided to get a three- bedroom."

"So when do you want to tell our parents?" Beth asked.

"Well, I think it would be difficult to withhold this from them for very long, given our excitement. Beth, I'm so thrilled that it happened now. I keep thinking about my dad's tenuous condition, and I hope and pray he'll be here to meet his first grandchild. That's huge, honey."

Beth nodded. "But I'd feel better if I were further along before we tell them. It's still very early. I guess I just want to make sure everything is okay before we get everybody's hopes up and we're all filled with excitement."

"Whatever you want to do, baby. It's your call."

"Let's just wait until they hear the heartbeat."

"Yes, but it's going to be hard to hide mine."

Beth smiled at her husband. She couldn't have chosen a better husband and father, and she suddenly realized that she was getting closer to her dream of that family of four.

Epilogue

A year had passed, and Abbey Isabella was now three months old and the center of Brandon and Beth's universe. She looked very much like Beth, with the biggest and brightest blue eyes and skin as soft as velvet. She had curly blonde hair and rounded cheeks. She looked like a porcelain doll, and sometimes she seemed too perfect to be real.

Life could not be better for Beth and Brandon. They had relocated to a three-bedroom apartment on the Upper East Side, across the street from a park—a doorman building with security comparable to that of Fort Knox. They routinely strolled in the park with Abbey on weekends, and had hired a nanny who took her there during the week. Brandon loved his new practice; and Beth was promised admittance into her firm partnership in only three more years instead of five.

Her best friend, Lisa, had become engaged to her boyfriend, Henry, and was planning a spring wedding the following year. She and Brandon loved Henry, who had decided to remain in New York to practice orthopedic medicine. Lisa and Beth were looking forward to raising their children together in the city.

An article had recently appeared in the paper announcing that Justen Bennett was arrested for stalking a woman for over a year and was sentenced to a year-long probation plus one year of weekly outpatient therapy.

Brian Paul, Lisa's ex-husband, had married his dental assistant, with whom he was cheating while married to Lisa. They deserved each other since once a cheater, always a cheater, Lisa figured.

Victoria had admitted to informing Barboza about where Beth would be on that fateful night by setting up a dinner with her. In return, she received one hundred thousand dollars, which she used to pay off her school loans and credit card debt. She had entered Beth's apartment as soon as she saw the assailant climb into the getaway car that was waiting out front. She is now serving five years for accessory to attempted murder, with the possibility of parole after two. Beth hasn't seen her since.

Valerie, from the shelter where Hillary had remained during her divorce, called to tell Beth that Hillary had made a one hundred-thousand-dollar donation and wanted a room in the shelter to be named for Beth.

Hillary's husband, with his with a long history of spousal abuse, was now serving three years for assault and battery. His willingness to make a handsome donation to the Women's Shelter had helped his lawyer make a deal with the D.A. He is eligible for parole in two years if he demonstrates exemplary behavior.

Detective Stevens had called Beth to inform her that Barboza wouldn't be serving his life sentence without parole after all. He explained, "It looks like the Mob, knowing that Barboza turned state's evidence to avoid the death penalty, had him killed in prison. No surprise."

Beth's parents were on cloud nine with their first grandchild. They could not stay away, and at least three days a week would go over and help the nanny with Abbey. She was the shining star of their lives.

Brandon's dad had completed his treatment for lung cancer and was doing well. He was very grateful to have lived to meet Abbey.

Brandon and Beth's relationship had taken on a whole new meaning with Abbey in it. Their world now revolved around their child, a beautiful gift from God, who had awakened within them a new type of love, one with depths that were impossible to fathom. It was unconditional love to the fullest degree, created out of their great love for each other. Abbey was their miracle of life, and Beth and Brandon were justifiably overprotective of her—until one day while at the park, the nanny looked the other way for a split second, and suddenly Abbey Isabella was gone.

Author Bio

Diane Lynn grew up in Virginia and pursued her nursing career in Baltimore, Maryland, where she specialized in surgery and emergency medicine. After marrying her husband, an attorney, she relocated with him to Phoenix, Arizona, where they raised their two children. Having successfully raised a family and managed a career, Diane is now able to follow her long-time passion for writing. This is her first book, and she is currently at work on a sequel.

AC   6-30-16
ET   9-8-16
OM   11-10-16
PL   1-12-17
ST   3-16-17
TC   5-18-17
WH   7-20-17
OS   9-21-17

OS   9-21-17   KP